PASSAGE FROM INNOCENCE

Book One of "THE FINAL FAREWELL"

A Trilogy of the Vietnam War and its Aftermath

STREATER FENTON

1st WORLD
PUBLISHING

PASSAGE FROM INNOCENCE

STREATER FENTON

© Streater Fenton 2007

Published by 1stWorld Publishing
1100 North 4th St. Fairfield, Iowa 52556
tel: 641-209-5000 • fax: 641-209-3001
web: www.1stworldpublishing.com

First Edition

LCCN: 2007931206
SoftCover ISBN: 978-1-4218-9993-0
HardCover ISBN: 978-1-4218-9994-7
eBook ISBN: 978-1-4218-9995-4

This material has been written and published solely for educational purposes. The author and the publisher shall have neither liability or responsibility to any person or entity with respect to any loss, damage or injury caused or alleged to be caused directly or indirectly by the information contained in this book.

This is a work of fiction. Any and all characters that may have a resemblance to real people are purely coincidental on the author's part. Names, places and events also fall into this category.

PRAISE FOR "PASSAGE FROM INNOCENCE"

Streater Fenton has written a sprawling saga of the Vietnam War and the era in which it was fought...a must read for those who experienced it first hand and for those who have forgotten the many sacrifices of our men and women in uniform. The combat passages in this novel are so authentic you can feel the heat of battle and the anguish of lost comrades.

Henry S. Bullock
Lt. Colonel U. S. Army (Ret.)

The Final Farewell is an authentic action novel of the Vietnam War that will appeal to all walks of life. It is an in-your-face look from the American soldiers' side and that of the enemies. Politics' aside the novel will make you weep, laugh, and. feel a deep seeded pride in US servicemen the world over.

H. G. Hutchinson
Colonel U. S. Army (Ret.)

Follow the saga of two young boys who become men in the mountains and valleys of Vietnam. The combat scenes are so realistic you'll swear that you can smell the cordite and hear the sounds of battle. The Final Farewell is one of the first War novels that actually put you on a personal level with the troops. Experience their fears, loneliness, and the tight-knit bond they share that only can be acquired in combat.

Major Joseph A. Russum
USMC (Ret.)

DEDICATION

To my wife, Judy, who put up with my pestering requests until her passing. I would also like to offer my gratitude and appreciation to Beatriz Weiss who believes in me and helped in so many unselfish ways to facilitate the completion of The Final Farewell: Book One "PASSAGE FROM INNOCENCE" Above all, let us not forget the brave men and women who sacrifice so much and serve our country so gallantly.

ABOUT THIS BOOK

The Final Farewell: Book One, "PASSAGE FROM INNONCE" is a fictional account about Green Berets who operated from obscure camps in the Central and Northern Highlands of Vietnam. Their primary mission was to force-multiply and gather intelligence on the elusive enemy who used the Ho Chi Minh Trail as a major cross-border infiltration route into South Vietnam. Their war was played underneath double and triple canopied mountains so deadly that only the strong could survive...if they were lucky.

It was a deadly cat and mouse game against an enemy who vehemently believed in their cause, and they were as determined to kill the hated American Imperialist as they were to reunify their war torn country. The goals of the Green Berets were far more simplistic: they were driven with fierce pride and professional determination to continue their missions in the manner in which they were trained, and hopefully survive another day.

CAST OF CHARACTERS

CLEAT DAVIS

Twenty-one-year-old Cleatwood Alexander Davis was born into an influential family and raised in the small southern town of Lakewood, Florida. He was a high school All-American and a consummate leader of men who dreaded the responsibilities of leadership. He had been the go-to guy since playing Little League sports, but soon his decisions would hold a much greater consequence than winning or losing on the field of athletics. In the jungles of Vietnam it would mean life, and the alternative was unacceptable.

MANDY HENSON

Cleat's high school sweetheart had worshiped him since the seventh grade, but he had hurt her so many times in the past she feared their relationship could not survive another heartbreak. A catastrophic event in high school will change her life forever.

JOHN TRUMAN

He had been Cleat's best friend since they first met in grammar school. His early years were spent in a broken home living with an abusive, alcoholic father, by the age of ten he had moved in with the Davis's and considered them his adopted family. He was Cleat's shadow, and would follow him to the gates of hell and back.

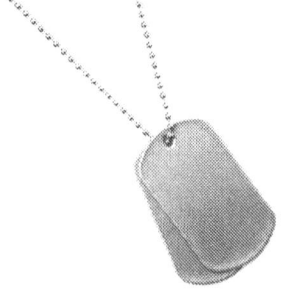

PROLOGUE

The wonderful innocence of pre-puberty in the mid-fifties and experiencing teenage adulthood during the early sixties was a period of time when joy and excitement flourished. With the birth of *'rock and roll'* and its controversial music, parents feared the loss of their children's innocence. The glitter of Hollywood added to parental concerns by portraying rebellious teenagers driving hot rods, and expressing little respect for conventional society. Fortunately, John Wayne was still a guiding force on the silver screen, helping to influence the youth of America in understanding right from wrong. It was a time when parents primarily worried over their children becoming involved in underage drinking, premarital sex, and automobile accidents.

These were times when neighborhood children played without worry and when the streetlights came on they knew it was time to say goodbye to their friends and go home. Times of laughter and shouts from sandlot games and young girls playing hopscotch filling the afternoon air with cheerful glee would soon be lost forever. No longer would doors be left unlocked and trust in humanity would be put to the test.

Unfortunately, the jungle-infested mountains of Vietnam and its watery patchwork of rice paddies brought the peaceful tranquility in the United States to an abrupt end. The harsh reality of our nation's treasured youth being killed and maimed in a far and distant land almost destroyed a nation.

In November of 1964, Lakewood, Florida was no different than the rest of the nation. When they turned on their television sets to watch the national news they were more apt to see an expose on the Beatles than the fledgling war developing in Vietnam. Occasionally a local newspaper editor might consider running a byline on the subject and if it was deemed worthy enough for print, more often than not you would find the article buried in the back pages next to the classifieds.

Throughout small town America and its larger metropolitan cities the major topic of interest after the thanksgiving holidays *was* football. November and early December was when championships were won and lost, be it Pee Wee, high school, college, or the pros.

Lakewood was a smallish town nestled in the center of the Sunshine State, but compared to communities within a thirty-mile radius it was a metropolis, a Mecca for young and old alike to shop and seek "city" entertainment. The quaint southern town had four grammar schools, one junior high school, one senior high school, three drive-in movies, two indoor theaters, one bowling alley, and a city park, which included a public swimming pool. To a nonresident there was very little that distinguished the town from any other throughout the state, but to those proud citizens of Lakewood it was home to the Lakewood Senior High ***Fighting Spartans***.

The week after Thanksgiving Lakewood was still unbearably hot, and like clockwork the afternoon sun continued to drive the temperature into the high eighties by 2:00 PM. To the local residents it was atypical of how the weather could change from one extreme to the other. At 7:00 AM you had to dress conducive to the early morning, forty-degree chill before leaving for school, and by noon student lockers were full of discarded clothes.

The shedding usually began by mid-morning, and when the final bell rang at 2:45 the majority of students were dressed in little more than summer attire. Of course, by early evening the temperature would dip again and the cycle would begin anew. The weekend weather forecast was calling for something much different in Lakewood; an early storm had raced across the Great lakes a few days earlier, and by Wednesday evening five inches of snow was dumped on the city of Atlanta, paralyzing the commercial hub to a virtual standstill. In Central Florida they weren't worried about snow, but they *would* be experiencing lows in the twenties and highs in the mid-fifties, perfect weather for football.

CHAPTER 1

Cleatwood Alexander Davis whipped his black '57' Chevy convertible into one of the few remaining parking spots at Pip's Drive-in restaurant. His car was five-years-old when his father bought it as a present for his sixteenth birthday. Mister Davis got a deal from a hot-rod enthusiast in Orlando whose son had acquired one too many speeding tickets. It was two years older now, but it still looked almost brand new. Before shutting the engine down, Cleat punched the accelerator, shooting a little extra gas into the four-barrel charged 327cc V-8 Corvette motor sitting underneath the hood, its throaty roar was loudly accentuated though a duel exhaust system featuring a pair of Glass Pack mufflers.

"Cleat, do you think we'll win Friday night?" Mandy, asked from the passenger seat. "It's the only thing the town's been talking about all week. We've just gotta win Cleat, everybody's counting on it."

"I said we would," Cleat sighed, tired of the same old refrain. "What more do you want?"

The year before Cleat had been an All State quarterback, and an All Conference outside linebacker; talk was he was destined to repeat the feat until he was switched to wide receiver his senior year. The coaches installed a new offence designed around speed and at six-foot three, one hundred and ninety eight pounds of bone and muscle Cleat was the second fastest man on the team, behind his best friend John 'Coon' Truman. Actually he was faster than Coon in the 100-yard dash, but he *was* a split second slower in the forty.

The football team went 10 and 1 their junior year, losing in the first round of the playoffs to Miami Senior, their archrival. Miami Senior went on to beat Edgewood in the championship game. Colleges throughout the nation had been salivating over the prospect of signing Cleat and Coon to their athletic program, but the two stars signed letters of intent to play college football together at Auburn, which was in keeping with the proud Davis family tradition.

Cleat fleetingly considered playing professional baseball, as several teams were interested in drafting him as a pitcher, or converting him to play outfield —he was that fast and had an arm like a rocket, plus his batting average of .579 broke every record in the sate. Cleat was a definite first round draft pick, but his father wanted him to play college ball and get a college education first. After all, three generations of the male Davis's had graduated from institutions of higher learning and he wasn't going to permit his youngest son to break family tradition.

Mandy shifted her position so she could look at Cleat straight away. She was always enchanted by the clear color of blue in his eyes. "Well," she said, "I'm worried, because most of the papers seem to think we'll lose, except the *Lakewood Ledger*. The out of town papers say Lakewood's too small, and all the talk is how big Edgewood is. I know we're both undefeated, but their school has more than twice the enrollment of LHS. During breakfast dad read the *Tribune* and he said their sports writer predicted we'd lose by two touchdowns."

"Look Mandy," Cleat unintentionally snapped, "do you want to believe the papers or me?" He had been feeling extreme pressure from his Dad and everyone else in town, for him tomorrow night couldn't arrive fast enough.

Mandy sat staring out the front window; her feelings were hurt, but she was determined not to pout. She brushed a golden curl off her forehead before turning to face Cleat. "It must be nice to be so confident in everything you do. Can't you for *once* be apprehensive or uncertain how things are going to turn out?"

"Christ, Mandy, what's the matter with you? You act like you *want* me to say we're going to lose! Well, I can't allow myself to think that way, too many people are counting on us to win, and that's what we're going to do."

He looked at Mandy's inquiring face. She was beautiful, her long blond hair sparkled like spun gold in the late afternoon sun. Though it was ruffled from the drive in his convertible, she still looked fabulous. There was a twinkle in her deep blue eyes as she defiantly returned his gaze. The cold stare was intense enough to count the pores on his face. She was tall and slender, and the warm Florida sun had tanned her skin the color of old copper.

He had to admit, Mandy Henson was by far the prettiest girl in school, and sometimes when he was near her he felt weak, as if his body was going to melt. It was an emotion he wasn't particularly fond of, and he couldn't afford the luxury. Everybody thought he was somebody special, and he would like to be that person, but he wasn't the outstanding individual everybody perceived him to be, especially Mandy.

They'd been going steady off and on since the seventh grade, and he'd cheated on her more times than he could count. Luckily he'd only been caught three times, most recently last summer when she and some of her friends paid a surprise visit to his parents' beach house at Daytona Beach. That was a scene best forgotten.

"No, I *don't* want you to say that…it's just…oh, I don't know *what* I'm saying, let's just forget it, and talk about something else. I love you, Cleat, and I so want to understand you better…the *real* you, not who you portray."

It grew uncomfortably quiet as she watched Cleat drumming his fingers on the steering wheel staring into nothingness. She waited patiently for him to say something; the steady tapping was beginning to fray on her nerves. Surely he wasn't going to just sit there without saying a word.

A tall, heavy-set youth walked up to Cleat's side of the car. "Hey Cleat, Friday night's the big one…we're gonna maul those Edgewood Panthers. Right, Cleat? Jesus, I can hardly wait. I'm gonna break some bones and kick some ass."

"That's right Bo, we're gonna stick it to 'em buddy. Lakewood's gonna be the next state champs."

"Yeah man, we're going to beat the shit out of 'em," Bo answered as he squeezed his large frame into the back seat. "Hey Mandy, you keeping super stud here real loose, aren't cha?"

"Oh sure Bo," Mandy sneered, her voice dripping with sarcasm, "don't you worry about a thing. Cleat has assured me we're going to win tomorrow night." Mandy leaned against the dash trying to force Cleat into recognizing her presence, but he held the same far away look in his eyes. His hands were gripping the steering wheel so tight his knuckles were turning white.

"Mandy, let's don't fight."

He said it so softly she wasn't sure he'd said anything at all. "We're not, Cleat, I just wish you'd open up a little and tell me what you really feel. If just for once you would…"

"All right, dammit," Cleat yelled. "I'm not sure…hell, I'm not sure of *anything*. I'm so nervous I can hardly sleep or eat, and when I do manage a little sleep, I wake up in the morning throwing up. I've lost ten pounds this week, because of this damn game. It's all anybody wants to talks about. Christ, if it's not my dad, it's the town, the *Ledger*, the school, the coaches, the players, the student body, and now it's *you!*"

Cleat exited the car abruptly, slamming the door behind him. He uttered an oath as he ran his fingers through the light shaggy brown hair he wore longer than most. Taking a deep breath, he walked over to one of the large oak trees bordering the local drive-in restaurant and sat on the curb.

"Jesus Mandy," Bo whispered bewilderedly, "did I cause all of that?"

Mandy smiled at Bo, he was such a big, lovable oaf. She reassuringly placed her hand on his, and squeezed it gently. "No, it has nothing to do with you silly, it's been building up since we beat Plant last week in the semis."

"Do you want me to go over and talk to him? I'll do it if you think it'll help."

"Thanks, but I can handle it, Bo, just don't mention his outburst to the other players or anybody else, there's no since in getting everybody worried. I appreciate your offer Bo…you're sweet." She patted his hand before leaving him alone in the car.

Mandy walked quietly over to where Cleat was sitting, she stood for a while looking down at his long, muscular body. His handsome, bronze face was knitted in a rigid frown. Sighing, she sat next to him leaning her head against his broad shoulders. After sitting in silence for several seconds she placed her fingertips on his cheek and began stroking his face ever so lightly just the way she knew he liked.

"Cleat, I love you. I love you more than anyone could ever know or understand. I think of you constantly." Mandy tilted her head and kissed his brow lightly, then whispered softly in his ear, "Oh, Cleat, if only you knew how I truly feel." Closing her eyes, she leaned against his body, drawing comfort from his warmth. "Darling, when I go to my room and crawl in bed at night, I lie there thinking of nothing but you. Before I fall asleep my prayers are for you to be in my dreams."

Lifting her chin, Cleat sweetly kissed her on the lips. "I dream of you every night, too."

"Hey, there'll be none of that out here," a voice rudely interrupted the moment. A tall, thin middle-aged waitress scolded them good-naturedly; her dyed red hair missed looking natural by several shades. She was carrying an aluminum tray of hamburgers, French fries, and cokes to a car parked several spaces down from where they were sitting. "If you're not careful it'll sap your strength honey. You gotta be in tip-top shape for Friday's big game. You know the whole town's counting on you boys."

Mandy gave Cleat a guarded look, wondering if he was going to explode again. Slowly, a faint, crooked smile began to creep across his youthful face, and then suddenly the two of them broke into a hysterical laughter that brought tears streaming down their faces.

The waitress turned at the sudden outburst and shook her head, mumbling to herself about "crazy kids" and how she'd "never understand them." Still shaking her head and muttering, she hooked the tray to the waiting car and made her way back inside.

Cleat stood up, drying his eyes before reaching down to clasp Mandy's outstretched hand. She was beautiful, sitting there in the shade of the old oak as shafts of sunlight filtered through the branches highlighting her upturned face. The tears on her cheeks sparkled like diamonds.

When they returned to the car, they found Bo sitting in the same spot as where they left him. Climbing inside, they discussed what they were going to order. By the time they placed their order his car was filled with friends and teammates. A larger crowd had gathered outside, some were perched on his hood and trunk like so much ornamentation. Several conversations were going on at the same time, but eventually all the talk drifted to the big game Friday night.

A buxom brunette approached the car on Cleat's side with a leering smile. "Hi Cleat, we'll be cheering for y'all on Friday, just like we always do."

"Thanks Audrey, we really appreciate what you cheerleaders do."

"Anything for the team, you know that," she smiled wantonly. "Hey Mandy, if we're going to practice those new cheers at your house, we'd better leave now. After all, you're the team captain and it's your responsible for everything going smoothly tomorrow night. Oh, I almost forgot, my dad said they were going to film the game and televise it Saturday morning. Isn't it all so exciting?"

"No shit?" John Truman walked up to Cleat and rubbed the top of his head. "We're going to be on TV, stud. How 'bout that pretty-boy?"

Cleat slapped his hand away. "Knock it off Coon, before I get out of the car and kick your skinny ass."

"Yeah, you better bring your lunch, brother!" Coon began dancing around the asphalt parking lot shadow boxing an imaginary opponent.

Coon was the star running back on the team and, more than that, he was like a brother to Cleat. He'd been living with the Davis's since he was a kid and shared a bedroom with Cleat. Coon's dad was an *incurable* drunk, all but incapable of caring for a small child growing up. He and Cleat were inseparable during the early years of grammar school, and since he'd moved in with the Davis's they were closer than ever.

When Cleat's older brother Randy left for Auburn on a football scholarship three years ago, they'd contemplated having their very own bedrooms during Randy's absence, but chose otherwise. In reality, he'd become part of the family since they were in third grade. Cleat's parents treated him like one of their own. Mister Davis was even going to buy him a car for his sixteenth birthday, but Coon refused the offer, stating that being his surrogate parents was more than enough.

Before turning six years old his mother deserted him and his father. His dad never got over her abandonment and apparently held his son responsible. Mister Truman was drunk more often than sober and barely held onto his job with the railroad. It was common gossip the only reason he had not been fired was because he had saved his boss's life during the Korean War and happened to win the Distinguish Service Cross in doing so. As for now, he was just a mean spirited drunk with a hateful, nasty disposition.

Coon acquired his nickname from Cleat's dad during hunting season when the boys were ten-years-old. His father laughingly teased that John got so excited about going hunting he acted like his old coon dogs, and there the legend of Coon Dog began; later on, his name was shortened to "Coon."

Over the years, Coon had become Cleat's shadow and best friend. He was as devoted to athletics as Cleat, if not more so. At eighteen-years-old he stood five-foot-nine and a hundred and eighty pounds. Sure, he was six inches shorter than Cleat, but he had speed to burn, and he reveled being one of the premier running backs in the state of Florida, if not the entire south. His features were rough, but handsomely Slavic and his soft brown eyes were soulful enough to touch the devil's heart. On top of his head unruly dark brown hair curled and frizzed in every direction.

Coon laughed. "Can you believe it! TV...holy crap if that don't beat all.

We're going to rip those Edgewood punks a new asshole, and it's all going to be on TV."

"All right everybody out. I've got to get Mandy home." Cleat started his Chevy with a roar, indicating to everyone it was time to get out of the car. "Do you need a ride Coon?"

"Don't you two love birds worry about me; I'll catch a ride later." Coon hopped over the backseat

"Are you sure?" Mandy smiled lovingly.

Coon's heart melted several degrees. "Yeah, y'all go on."

Gene Reese, the starting junior quarterback hollered from his two-year-old red 1962 Thunderbird convertible: "Hey Cleat, you wanna catch a few balls this afternoon? I want my number one receiver ready for Friday."

"Naw, not right now. I got some things to do around the house, but I'll see you at the field house tonight."

"Okay Cleat, stay loose…see ya tonight."

Audrey skipped over to Gene and asked provocatively, "How about giving me a ride over to Mandy's, *Mister* Quarterback?" As she bent over the passenger door of the sports car, her white pleated skirt rose high, exposing a great deal of her shapely legs. Her breasts were showcased under a tight-fitting navy blue V-neck sweater.

"Ouch!" Cleat yelped, as Mandy's elbow struck him sharply in the ribs. "What was that for?"

"You know full well what it was for."

"Aw, come on Mandy…you know I only have eyes for you."

"Let's not go there."

"That's not fair, Mandy, that was way last summer, and besides, it wasn't like I was with the girl, they just happened to drop by. She's a local I've known for years, her older brother and I have been good friends since we were ten-years-old."

Mandy stared at Cleat, raising an eyebrow. Just as she was about to say something, Audrey leaned her head out as Gene was pulling away.

"See you in homeroom tomorrow, Cleat."

"Bitch!" Mandy whispered between her teeth. "A real bitch in heat, that's just what she acts like." Mandy's face was a dark crimson, creating a sharp contrast with her flaxen hair. "God, I just can't stand her. She's so brazenly sexual, it just makes me sick."

"Now Mandy, that's very unbecoming. What would your parents say if they heard you talking like a sailor on shore leave?" Cleat bit his lower lip to keep from laughing.

"Oh shut up! Dammit Cleat, you know she's been after you ever since the eighth grade. I'm thankful for the times we've broken up you haven't gone out with her. I just don't think I could live with the thought of you ever being with her. Promise me you'll never date her no matter what…please, please promise me Cleat?"

"Why do you dislike her so much?"

"Promise, please promise?"

"Okay-okay, but tell me why? What is it between you two, why is it you hate her so much? For Christ's sake Mandy, we all run in the same crowd."

"It's everything about her. She's so boy crazy…it's all she ever talks about. Audrey's had the hots for you since that MYF hayride y'all went on when I had the mumps in the eighth grade. And that body of hers, she's always flaunting it in the way she dresses, her jeans look like she's been poured into them. Every time you're near her she starts to drool."

"Well, at least she has *excellent* taste."

Mandy punched him in the left shoulder. "Cleat, sometimes you make me sick."

Laughing, he pulled out of the parking lot and turned on the radio. The Platters were in the middle of singing "My Prayer." It was several years old, but it was still one of their favorites. They both loved to dance and they danced well together, of course they had a lot of practice over the years.

They rode through downtown Lakewood in reverent silence, amazed at the transformation that had taken place over the past few days. The stores were decorated with Lakewood's colors of orange and black. Some of the storefronts even had mannequins dressed up as football players in authentic school uniforms. Large banners hung overhead from one side of the street to the other with big, bold letters that shouted, "BEAT EDGEWOOD." Orange and black crepe streamers were wound around lampposts, telephone poles, and parking meters. Cleat mentally chuckled…the town didn't decorate this much during Christmas! Yep, Lakewood had gone all out for the *big game* on Friday. They were ready to crown the new state champs.

A short trip around Lake Holly and up Cambridge Drive brought them in front of Mandy's beautiful antebellum home with its large gothic columns. The stately house stood fifty yards from the street, carpeted with an immaculately manicured lawn heavily landscaped by professionals. Truth be told, it was the envy of half the town. Several of the cheerleaders had already arrived and were waiting on the veranda sitting in white, ornate rockers.

Cleat leaned over for an innocent kiss and surprised Mandy by cupping his left hand under her breast. Mandy pulled away and struck him as hard as she could on the shoulder as some of her friends were walking across the lawn.

"Cleat," she slugged him again. "Why do you like embarrassing me so much? You know how private I am." Her face was red as a beet; frustrated, she hit him again.

Cleat yelled, holding his shoulder and pretending he was in pain.

Audrey approached the car from the passenger side. "What are you trying to do, put our star player out of action before the big game? Don't damage the merchandise Mandy, he's hot stuff."

"It's not any of your concern, Audrey."

"Oh but you're wrong, without Cleat catching touchdown passes we haven't got a chance."

Mandy fought to keep her composure as best she could while she opened the car door and stepped onto the lawn, forcibly producing a smile. "I'll see you tomorrow, Cleat...call me after the game films tonight."

"Okay sugar."

Five minutes later Cleat was pulling into his own driveway in the same posh neighborhood. His parents' home was a walled-enclosed two-story sprawling Spanish style hacienda that easily took up two of the four lots the property sat on. A northern industrialist who made his fortune during WW II had built the house back in 1947. Cleat's family bought the house in 1954 when the owner was killed in South America racing sports cars. His father's law firm handled the estate sale, and Mister Davis jumped at the opportunity to buy the hacienda.

The purchase came with all of the furnishings, which included wonderful antiques, lamps, oriental carpets, authentic oil paintings, expensive silver. It even had pots and pans, plus lavish bed linens and bath towels. There were

5,800-square feet under roof housing five bedrooms, six bathrooms, a private study, a fully stocked library containing vintage books bound in leather and gold of unknown value. In the rear of the house was a large game room with a pool table, wet bar, and gaming table.

The dinning room was large enough to seat twelve people without dwarfing the room, and the kitchen had a separate breakfast room large enough to handle the entire family plus several guests. There were five fireplaces in all, one in the library, one in the game room, one in the formal living room, one in the master bedroom. Lastly there was a huge stone fireplace in the massive den with a thick slab of teak serving as a mantle where at Christmas time they hung their stockings.

The den was everybody's favorite room in the house; it also served as the TV room. It was located in the rear of the house next to the kitchen overlooking the swimming pool and cabaña that backed up to the country club's golf course. The famous eighth fairway was almost in their backyard. Cleat, Coon, and Randy used to get the biggest thrill gathering errant golf balls that occasionally flew over the five-foot wall surrounding the property. Each fought over who could accumulate the most to earn their dad's praise, to the youngster's chagrin they were never able to defeat Randy.

When the family first moved in they were surprised at how new the house looked. In reality they shouldn't have been astonished since the previous owner only lived in the home three months out of the year. At first his mother was worried about the cost, but his dad had assured her that he'd gotten a good deal and the law firm was doing quite well, thank you very much.

"Cleat honey," his mom called from the front door, "supper will be ready in twenty minutes and your dad wants to speak with you before then."

"All right mom, I'll be there in just a sec." Despite the invitation, Cleat stood looking at his pride and joy. Frowning, he took the tail of his shirt and wiped some handprints off of the hood. Taking a step backwards he admired the fender skirts and spinners he added last summer. They really added a touch of class to his ride.

"Come on in, son, and let's talk." His dad was standing in the den doorway.

"Yes sir, I'm on my way." Cleat took one last look before going inside. He found his dad sitting in his favorite brown leather chair with a dry martini in one hand and a folded newspaper in the other. Mister Davis was an inch shorter than he, and 30 pounds heavier. Although there was evidence of middle-aged thickening around the waist, he was still solid as a rock. His dark brown hair wasn't showing any hint of thinning, and except for a sprinkling of salt and pepper around his temples he looked five years younger than his forty-two years. He still looked like he could suit up and play any sport he so desired. Between father and son, the only thing that showed any inkling of family resemblance, excluding their frame, were their bright blue eyes laden with heavy lashes.

Auburn had become the family school ever since his dad and his twin brothers Slade and Wade won athletic scholarships to the prestigious southern university. Because his father was held back in the second grade for contracting scarlet fever, the brothers entered college at the same time. They graduated from just after the Japanese bombed Pearl Harbor.

The three brothers rushed down to the Federal Building in downtown Lakewood to join the Army, but his father failed the physical and was classified 4-F because he destroyed his left knee playing against Georgia Tech in the final game of their senior year. His brother Slade ended up flying fighters in North Africa and was killed in a dogfight high over the desert sands of the Sahara in 1943.

Wade served as an officer in the 101st Airborne and participated in the Normandy Invasion and the Battle of the Bulge. He was wounded three times and won the Bronze and Silver Star for bravery. Wade now owned a twenty thousand acre cattle ranch and grew citrus just outside Yeehaw Junction.

In 1946, Wade entered a high stakes poker game with the money he saved during the war and every dime he could scrounge. After cleaning out the high rollers, he bought the acreage for cash at $2.50 an acre. People thought he'd lost his mind buying what they considered "worthless land" in the middle of nowhere. With the leftover money he purchased fruit trees and cattle, since then he bought land whenever he got the urge. Now, he was the biggest cattleman in the south and owned more acres of citrus than anyone in the United States.

Cleat still heard stories about "The Big Game" at the barbershop and other places where the longtime residents gathered. Uncle Wade was almost larger than life, but if you saw him downtown you would've never guessed him to be anything other than an out-of-work cowboy dressed in a kaki shirt and pants with a wide belt and big silver buckle. On his feet were scuffed cowboy boots, and on his head was the ever-present cowboy hat he never took off outdoors unless it was to greet a lady.

His wife and eight-year-old son were killed on Highway 60 coming back from Lake Wales where they'd gone to buy school clothes. He never remarried, but half the eligible women from around the world chased him relentlessly. He was the most exciting, fun loving man Cleat had ever known and he was proud to call him uncle. His Uncle Wade and dad were as different as oil and vinegar, but they got along great because they both loved to hunt and fish.

In 1942 Cleat's dad married his high school sweetheart and, after a brief stint at teaching and coaching high school football, he entered the University Of Florida School Of Law. By the time the war was over he'd already started his own practice, bought their first house, and in 1950 built their vacation home on the south end of Daytona Beach near Inlet Harbor. This was where they spent their summers and warm weathered weekends during the year.

"Look at this write-up in the *Ledger*, son." His dad shook the local newspaper for emphasis. "They say you're the best athlete from these parts in thirty years, and they go on to say Lakewood will win Friday night by six points. Now, that's the kind of reporting I like…not like the damn *Tribune* where they're predicting us to lose by twelve. They must be out of their minds, or jealous because we beat every school they threw at us two years in a row. Lordy but it's a big game tomorrow night. I hope you boys are ready. You *are* ready, aren't you?"

"Sure dad, no sweat." Cleat had never seen his dad so excited over something he was involved in. In the past it had always been Randy this, or Randy that. He rarely went to any of *his* games.

"The stands are going to be full of scouts. I know one's going to be here from Auburn, and another two from Florida and Georgia, but those are just the ones I know about. You give it everything you've got tomorrow night and you'll be on your way."

"Dad, please, I've heard enough about this game to last me a lifetime. It's going to be all right, I'll have a good game, and my timing will be fine."

"Okay, okay. Did you catch any balls this afternoon?"

"No sir, Gene asked, but I didn't feel like it."

His father lumbered out of his chair, "What the hell do you mean you didn't feel like it? Son, you've got to live, eat, and breathe football until we win this game. Christ on a crutch, I can't believe you. Your brother would be out there doing what it takes to win. All you seem to think about is when's the next party and going to the beach."

"Dad, lets don't start, I'm not in the mood."

"I just wish you had the same kind of drive as your brother. There's no telling what you could accomplish. Randy would've…"

"He never made it to the playoffs, not once, and he was never All-State."

"What! You think that somehow makes you better? Christ, I thought you had more sense than that, but that's the way you kids think nowadays. Fun and games, right? Well, let me tell you smart-ass, there's more to life than what you've experienced. Hell, when I was growing up I had one pair of shoes and I had to put cardboard inside them because the soles were worn through. My two pair of pants had patches, same as my white dress shirt and a blue work shirt. It was hard times. You kids today have no idea what it was like growing up during the Depression. You've had it too damn easy. Just look at you, you're a prime example of what's wrong with the youth of today. You have your own car and that pretty little Henson girl who's never had to want for anything in her entire life. If only…"

"Hold it right there, dad." Both of their voices had raised several octaves since the beginning of their conversation. "I didn't ask for the car, you gave it to me as a gift. If you don't want me to have it, then take the damn thing and sell it."

"You watch your mouth, Cleat. You're not going to use that kind of language in my house. By God I'll not stand for it, not for one second…"

"That's enough!" Cleat's mother shouted from the doorway leading to the kitchen. "Please don't you two start again?" She stood on the verge of tears, staring at two men in her life that were driving her crazy. It had been hard on both her husband and son since Randy left for Auburn, but it had been much worse on Cleat.

Cleat and his father were never close, there always seemed to be an inner conflict between the two, and it was never more evident with the absence of Randy. Without his presence there was no longer a buffer between the two, and it was sorely missed. Coon, bless his heart, and Sissy tried to take his place, but the rift between father and son had widened.

Although she was only five-foot-two, Cleat's mother was an imposing figure in the doorway, and she was well aware of where she stood in the pecking order of her brood. When she put her foot down, which was on rare occasions...she ruled. The men of the house were unaware of this phenomenal creature's power, but when she chose to use her dominance in keeping the harmony it was absolute—without her all hell would break loose—she knew it and reluctantly shouldered the heavy burden.

"Can't you two sit and talk like two normal, intelligent human beings instead of screaming and shouting at one another? You are father and son and it's about time you start acting like it. Both of you know how much it upsets me when you go on this way. I'll not stand for it."

"Its okay mom, dad and I are just a little excited about the game tomorrow."

"Sweetheart, it's just a game. There are so many things more important in life. I think this game has been completely blown out of importance, the whole community has turned Friday night into something more than it is."

"Just a game!" Mister Davis threw his arms up. "My Lord June, I can't believe you said that...you must be living in a different world. This game's for the state championship, something this town has never had, nor have they ever had a shot at it before. No, it's not just a game...it's THE GAME, and by all that's holy our son's playing in it, furthermore he's the main reason Lakewood's there in the first place. This game is important to this town, it's important to the school, and to this family. Cleat's got to..."

"That's enough! I don't want to hear anymore about it." Mrs. Davis stomped her foot for emphasis.

Randle Davis was so surprised by his wife's outburst he stood, mouth agape, unable to utter a word. He retreated from her stare and returned to his leather chair. Only *after* he was sure his wife was no longer standing in the doorway did he mutter under his breath, "It's still more than *just* a game."

Cleat sat on the sofa next to where his grandmother Marie usually sat. Stretching his long legs in front of him, he peered around the room, stopping at the Davis's trophy case full of memorabilia from as far back as his dad's own glory days.

In the rear on the third shelf was an 8 x 10 glossy his mother had framed of him in his Little League uniform holding a bat in a batter's stance. It was the year he won the league's batting title and led his team to the city championship. It was the same year Coon virtually moved in with his family.

The thought of Little League brought back painful memories to Cleat, all the times he looked for his dad in the stands and never found him. His mom always made excuses as to why he was unable to make the game, most often it was because he was either at the office late, or he was just too tired. None of those reasons were needed when it came to Randy's varsity games; his father *never* missed a home game, *or* a road game, for that matter. It made Cleat try harder to be the best he could be so he might attract some of his father's adoration, but it all went for naught. All the talk around the house was about Randy, even though Cleat made every all-star team in baseball, basketball, *and* football.

He reflected on those lonely, terrible nights when he and Coon would hitchhike home from the games after sitting in the stands, or hiding under the bleachers until the lights went out. They did this so no one would know there wasn't anyone who cared enough to come to their games and take them home afterwards. There were many nights when they were the last ones at the park, surrounded by darkness with broken spirited tears streaming down their faces as one tried to console the other.

Cleat didn't like to think of those times; it made him feel empty inside and he fought hard to keep them in the past where they belonged. He shook his head to clear his thoughts, keeping painful memories buried deep was becoming a specialty of his. It was his way of protecting himself when he knew there was nothing he could do, or change.

"Hey tiger." Christina, Cleat's sister, bounced into the room unannounced. Everyone called her "Sissy." She was four years his junior, but she was going on twenty-one trying to assume the buffer role between her closest brother and father. As for now, dealing with puberty was secondary in the scheme of things.

Sissy was wearing one of Cleat's blue oxford dress shirts with the sleeves rolled to her elbows, and the tails hanging well below her knees. It hung loosely around her youthful body, hiding an adolescent figure in bloom. The tight-fitting Levis were form-fitted from the first day she bought them. After slipping them on at the store she went swimming in the pool and wore them all day until they air-dried. Now you couldn't grab enough material between your fingers without pinching her skin.

The bottoms of the jeans were folded several times until they reached mid-calf, showing the navy blue inseam. Below the raised cuffs were black and white saddle oxfords freshly polished, and accented with a pair of fluffy white angora socks that were neatly arranged around her ankles just so. Sissy's golden hair was tied in a flowing ponytail held in place with a bright red ribbon; a slight trace of freckles ran across the bridge of her nose, fading girlishly onto her cherub cheeks. Her dark blue eyes reflected the adoration she held for her brother. At five-foot-eight it was apparent she inherited her genes from the men.

"Where's Coon, I thought he'd be with you?" Sissy had a painful crush on Coon that was plainly visible to all but her father.

"Mandy and I were together this afternoon, but I'm sure he'll be along in a few minutes...I've never known him to miss a meal."

"Mom wants to know how hungry y'all are before she starts cooking the cube steaks."

"Tell her we're starved, as always."

"Okay," she replied, spinning on her heels whipping her ponytail from one shoulder to the other.

"Hey sis?" Cleat queried.

Sissy stopped in mid-stride, turning to face her brother. "Yeah?"

"How old are you?"

"I'm fourteen...you know how old I am. Why'd you ask?"

"Well little sister; you're really starting to look good. It won't be long before you're going to be a real knockout."

Sissy went running back to where Cleat was sprawled on the sofa and gushed, "Gee Cleat, honest...you really mean it? You're not just saying that are you?"

"Of course I mean it. Don't you look in the mirror every morning and see how beautiful you are? By the time you're a sophomore you'll be the prettiest girl in school."

Sissy brought a trembling hand to her face, lightly brushing her fingertips across her blushing cheeks. "Thank you, Cleat, that's the nicest thing you've ever said to me." Suppressing a tear, she quickly turned on her heels to leave the room before she started crying.

"Hey Sissy," Cleat called.

Sissy spun around smiling. "Yeah, Cleat?"

"How about polishing my loafers after dinner?"

"Doggone you Cleat…I knew you were teasing." Sissy grabbed a cushion off her mother's nearby chaise lounge and threw it at Cleat. "You jerk, I should've known better."

Cleat caught the projectile just before it slammed into his face. "Aw come on Sissy, I meant every word I said."

"Honest? Cross your heart and hope to die?"

Cleat crossed his heart, flashing a crooked grin in the process. "I promise."

"Oh Cleat, sometimes I don't know when to laugh or cry around you. Slip them off and I'll polish them after supper for seventy-five cents…that's a quarter cheaper than downtown."

"Fifty cents and you got a deal."

"Nope, seventy-five cents or you can do them yourself." Sissy folded her arms across her chest, tapping her foot on the Mexican tiled floor.

"Okay, but you better do a good job."

"Satisfaction guaranteed, brother." Sissy left the room to help her mother in the kitchen.

"Son, you shouldn't tease your sister like that. She's becoming a young woman and her sensitivity level is becoming high-strung."

"Yes sir, I know she is," Cleat looked hopelessly at his father, "but I meant what I said. Sissy is going to be a real knockout. In a couple of years every boy in town will be knocking on the door dying to take her out. What upsets me is I'm not going to be here to look after her, it's all going to be up to you and mom."

Mister Davis leaned over the armrest, shaking his paper at his son. "By God, I'll tell you what. There's not going to be any parade of pimply face boys coming to my front door. I'll tell…"

"For goodness sakes, what's all the shouting about in here?" Sissy rushed into the room with a look of concern.

"It's just dad worrying about how all the boys are going to be knocking down the door wanting to take you out on dates before too long."

"Oh dad, don't be silly, it'll be at least two years before you'll even allow me to date, and besides I'll be able to handle myself like a lady, just like you and mom raised me to be." Turning to her brother she smiled. "Cleat, I went into the bathroom and looked into the mirror and I must say you are right…I *am* going to be a knockout." Winking at her brother, she whirled around and left the room with an exaggerated swishing of her hips.

"You're still just a little kid with freckles and a ponytail...don't you forget it Miss Prissy." Cleat threw the cushion at his sister's retreating form, but he missed as it sailed high and to the right.

"Son, look at me, promise me you're taking this game seriously."

"Dad, I promise I am. Don't you think I realize how important this game is to everybody?"

"I know how you are son, and what you're like...everything comes too easy for you. You have more natural ability than anybody I've ever seen, and because it takes less energy for you to excel you tend to be lackadaisical in your approach to athletics. It even shows in your academics. Instead of being an average student you should be making straight A's.

"Come on, dad. I wouldn't classify A's and B's as *average*."

"That's not the point, Cleat. I know what you're capable of, and because of your lack of desire, and your lousy work ethic, it's a going to cripple you and that'll be a crying shame to see such potential go to waste."

"Dad, you think you know me, but you don't, you've never taken the time. You don't know what I feel, or what I think. Whatever you think about me is your own volition. When have we ever talked about what I want, or expect out of life? You don't have a clue as to who I am." Cleat lifted himself from the sofa and faced his father. "No, dad, you don't know me at all." Cleat departed to the kitchen, but not before his father noticed the tears welling in his son's eyes.

"That's not true son. I know you better than you know yourself." Mister Davis rankled having to speak to his son's back. "June, if supper isn't ready soon we'll have to call it breakfast," Randle hollered to lighten the mood and take his mind off of Cleat's piercing words.

When Coon arrived he found his family sitting at the dinning room table. Out of breath he said, "Sorry I'm late."

"Have a seat, son...we've just sat down."

"Thanks." Coon took his place between Sissy and Cleat.

"What's with the huffing and puffing?" Cleat inquired.

"I ended up running home from Pips."

"You could've called and I would've picked you up."

"Naw...I needed to burn off some energy, besides, it's only three or four miles."

Mister Davis smiled, "That's the spirit, son. How's the team looking …they're ready aren't they?"

"Please, Randle, not at the table. I think we've heard enough talk about the game." Mrs. Davis forced a smile in her husband's direction.

"Football, what a silly game," Grandmother Cleatwood chided her son-in-law. "Young men should have better things to do."

Cleat's father bristled over Mama Marie's statement. He felt she was one of the main reasons Cleat wasn't tough like Randy. His mother-in-law and wife pampered Cleat as a young child, and his mother-in-law teaching Cleat and Coon her native tongue irritated even him more. He had no use for the meekly French, or their faggot language, besides everyone *knew* they hated Americans.

"Come on Coon, eat up buddy. We've got fifteen minutes to get to the field house, and I plan to be on time for once. The last time you made us late we ended up running wind sprints until we almost passed out."

"Two more minutes and I'm done."

"Don't speak with your mouthful, Coon," Mrs. Davis frowned.

Coon gulped his food down. "Yes ma'am, Mama June, I'm sorry."

It was dark outside when the two of them stepped out the den door into the cool night air. Cleat inhaled deeply, standing on the porch enjoying the chilling breeze gently caressing his flesh. He knew it would be much colder in the morning. The gardeners had already covered the plants prone to freezing. Looking toward the heavens through the branches of a large oak tree over-hanging the drive he could literally see thousands of stars twinkling above; there didn't seem to be a cloud in the sky.

This winter had been unusually warm, even by Florida standards. Just last weekend he and Mandy, along with some of their friends, went water skiing on Lake Holly. The sight of her sitting on the dock in a light green, two-piece bathing suit was enough to slow traffic around the lake. The special way she threw her head back when she laughed was almost spiritual as the sound of its carefree innocence carried across the water.

He could close his eyes and visually see her sitting in the early afternoon sun, soaking up its warmth as it graced her beautiful body deepening the tan she held year round. She was so gorgeous, with her long blonde hair sweeping off her forehead with waves of golden curls flowing down her back. There was nothing sexier to Cleat than seeing a beautiful girl cloaked in sweat, whether it was from exertion or just lying in the hot sun.

Cleat's mental picture of Mandy with trickles of perspiration mixed with coconut based sun tan lotion rolling in rivulets down her firm, glistening stomach was exciting. He could see her navel filling to capacity and overflowing past the little brown mole just above her waistband. He smiled thinking how she always tried to hide it without much success. Cleat professed a thousand times how much he loved her mole, but she still insisted it was grotesque and continued to make every attempt to conceal it. It was the same with the hair on her arms, she thought they were grossly hairy and would wet them down with hair spray before leaving the house in hopes it wouldn't be as noticeable.

Cleat's mind flashed back to the summer of 1962 when they had gone to the drive-in theater to see a second showing of Troy Donahue and Sandra Dee in *A Summer Place*. That particular night became a warm, humid inferno as they sat in the car making out. The front window was steamed, and the green coil burning on the dash acting as mosquito repellant wasn't doing a very good job of keeping them away.

Their sophomore summer was when going steady took on a different meaning between the two. It was when love bloomed and flourished to proportions neither of them had ever dreamed possible. He could remember their first night of love making as if it were yesterday.

"Cleat, I just loved the movie," she gushed. "They seemed so innocent and frightened."

Cleat kissed her lightly on the cheek before replacing the speaker on its stand. Starting the car he smiled over at Mandy. "I still think it's the best picture we've seen together in a long time. Do you think in real life Troy and Sandra ever dated? They make a great looking couple."

"It would be nice to think so, because they kind of reminded me of … us." Mandy leaned her head on Cleat's shoulder.

The two young lovers rode in silence as Mandy snuggled close to Cleat. It wasn't until they drove into Pip's that the silence was broken when Coon walked over to join them. The three ordered cherry cokes and sat talking for a while until Coon began to feel like he was the third wheel. After politely excusing himself, Mandy and Cleat sat staring at one another with expressions only young lovers seem to possess.

"Mandy," his voice was hoarse with a yearning passion, "let's go parking. I found a spot just right for us."

She reached over, touching him lovingly on the cheek. "All right, but you've got to promise just for a little while. My parents are still upset from last week when you got me home past curfew. I know it was only twenty minutes late, but you know how they are."

"I promise we won't be late."

CHAPTER 2

O n the south side of town Cleat turned onto a rutty dirt road that led deep into an orange grove heavily laden with fruit. All the while he carefully navigated between rows of trees, hoping to avoid the outcroppings from scratching his car. When they were far enough for the privacy he desired, Cleat shut the engine off and cut the headlights. Darkness enveloped them immediately; only a small sliver of moonlight dappling through the overhead branches kept it from being pitch black.

"Gosh, it's kind of spooky out here," Mandy said, suppressing a rigor.

"No it's isn't," Cleat soothed, inching closer, "just quiet and secluded. Look, you can see part of the moon through the trees."

"Oh yes…I see it. It's really beautiful."

"Just like you," Cleat said as he slid from under the steering wheel, slipping his arm over Mandy's shoulder.

"You're so sweet." Mandy nestled her head into the nape of his neck. "I love you more than life itself."

"I love you too Mandy," he whispered, leaning over kissing her full on the lips. Mandy moaned as she opened her mouth to accept his probing tongue. They held their kiss until both of them were breathless. Cleat slowly began easing her down onto the seat, brushing their heads lightly on the door panel. He lay softly on top of her, supporting most of his weight on his elbows.

Cradled between her legs, he fumbled briefly with the buttons of her blouse until the last one broke free, exposing her stark white brassiere. Mandy cooed with a sharp intake of breath when Cleat slipped his hand inside her bra and cupped her breast. Her nipples were hard and he could feel the pulsating heat from her body. Pushing the bra above her young, tender breast he bent over and began kissing them with his tongue flickering back and forth from one to the other.

Mandy was beside herself, filled with excitement at the forbidden desires she'd always tried so hard to control. They'd never been this far before, and yet what she was experiencing tonight seemed so natural. She was afraid, but yet she wasn't. She loved him so much. Grasping his head in her trembling hands, she started kissing his ear, darting her tongue in and out while softly whispering her love over and over.

Cleat was crazed with his desire for Mandy. Pulling her skirt up, he lay between the shadows of her virtue, placing his erection firmly against her. Cleat found Mandy's mouth once again and kissed her excitedly, pressing his lips against hers and nibbling playfully at her tongue. He began to move methodically back and forth, pushing his maleness against Mandy's virginity.

Slowly she began responding to the hardness pressing next to her...she was only guessing how she was to respond. It embarrassed her somewhat, but she didn't care, because she had never felt this close to Cleat. He was her love...she could never love another.

"Mandy," he moaned, "Oh God Mandy, I want you so bad. I love you...please Mandy?"

"Oh my darling, we can't...what if I got pregnant?"

Cleat slid his hand down her bare stomach, feeling her body tremble as he slipped his hand under the elastic of her panties. Eagerly, deftly, his hand continued until he held her purity. The feel of her wet heat and pubic hair almost made him ejaculate prematurely.

Mandy trembled and closed her eyes. She arched her back to the suddenness of his touch, and when she felt his finger enter she quivered. "Oh, ohhh Cleat!" She groaned, clutching his face while searching desperately for his lips. Thrusting her tongue deep inside his mouth she clawed savagely at his back.

"Oh, Cleat, I love you," Mandy whimpered, holding back sobs of pleasure.

Cleat turned sideways to unfasten his Levis...struggling with fingers that felt like all thumbs he finally managed to disrobe without ever lingering from Mandy's lips. Gripping Mandy's panties from the waistband he pulled them downward until they slipped off her feet...he dropped them to the floorboard and snuggled between the warmth of her quivering thighs.

The fiery heat from Cleat's naked body lying on top of hers was almost suffocating; her breath became quick and rapid. Suddenly she was afraid of what might happen if this went any further, but she wasn't sure if she could stop him, or even if she wanted to.

Cleat gently pushed her outside leg off of the seat as he scooted between her thighs, and put the head of his penis inside the outer lips of her vagina. He could hardly control the emotions running through his mind. My God, it was like a dream. He thought of the hundreds of times he'd dreamed of making love to Mandy…tonight it was happening for real.

"Cleat…no we can't. Please, don't do this." Mandy pushed with all her might trying to force Cleat away.

"Mandy, please…I love you so much. I want to love all of you." Cleat moaned as his lips sought hers. Kissing her wantonly, he moved his penis out of the way and eased his finger inside the lips of her vagina. Cleat gently massaged Mandy with slow, rhythmic strokes, rotating his finger in and out until she began to react with each movement. Her body shook beneath him.

"Oh Cleat, what are we doing…I love you…I love you…oh my darling, I love you."

Cleat laid his cheek next to hers…the scent of her hair smelled like jasmine. "I love you too Mandy…I want to show you my love." He gave her a long, lasting kiss as he continued his massage.

Mandy broke away from his kiss crying in a raspy voice, "Oh Cleat…love me. Put him inside…Oh God, do it Cleat…love me, pleeeease…hurry Cleat…hurry…I love you my darling."

Cleat knew Mandy was a virgin, because he was the only one she had gone steady with since the seventh grade. Unlike Mandy, his own prelude to sexual education began at fourteen and was instigated by Randy when he took him over to an older girl's house that was more than willing to initiate Cleat into a world he had only heard stories about.

Over the past couple of years he was one of the fortunate few of his friends who had plenty of sexual experiences with girls, but only Lisa Stephens from Daytona Beach had been a virgin. Cleat knew he had to be slow and easy with Mandy, not only because of her virginity, but also because of his size. He knew this from showering with his teammates in the locker room and the constant ribbing he endured since puberty. One day when Lisa's parents were gone for the afternoon they slipped into her bedroom and made love. During his penetration she let out a blood-curdling scream that scared him silly, and would haunt him for months on end.

With more tenderness and control than his years warranted, Cleat slowly invaded the inner depths of Mandy's coveted chastity. He sensed her body initially draw back and become rigid before she relaxed, finally surrendering herself to the historical moment of entering into womanhood.

She tried as best she could to emulate Cleat's movements, but try as she may the fear of becoming pregnant was prevalent in her thoughts. Her mind was saying yes, but the pain of Cleat being inside her was too much for her to completely relax. She had no idea the act of making love could be so painful… she wondered if it would always be like this, or was it because it was her first time. She hoped it was the latter as she stifled a squeal when Cleat pushed ever deeper. She held on tightly as his movements increased to a crescendo of wild throws…she kept her eyes shut, wishing it would be over soon before she began screaming from the torture.

"Mandy, oh my God, I'm coming. Oh Jesus, I love you Mandy." Suddenly his body stopped pounding hers, and she heard him grunt her name. His body became contorted and he started making animalistic sounds that frightened her. Finally he collapsed on top of her and was still.

She felt smothered with all of his weight pressed against her, gasping for breath she tried to shift his weight to one side.

"Mandy, please, don't move…I can't take anymore."

Take what? She thought. If she weren't so terrified of suffocating to death, she would've laughed out loud. Somehow she had to get out from underneath him, it was sweltering hot, and their bodies were clammy from perspiration. The air was thick with the scent of their love making, and it was extremely difficult to breathe. Just when she was about to scream he finally lifted his body from hers, leaving a damp coolness in its wake.

"Are you okay Mandy?" Cleat sat up, and reached under the front seat for a clean towel he always carried for just such an occasion. Handing the towel to Mandy he smiled. "I love you."

Timidly, Mandy accepted the towel, assuming she was to use it to clean up with. Briefly she wondered what it was doing under his seat, but only fleetingly, because she felt so exposed sitting there half-naked. Slipping her bra into place, she used the towel to wipe the sweat off of her body. The wetness between her legs was another matter. How could she wipe down there with Cleat sitting next to her?

"Cleat, would you step outside…I uh…I need some privacy?"

"Uh…sure Mandy…no problem. I love you." Cleat kissed her sweetly on the forehead, tasting her salt before he exited his car. The interior lights on the door lighted the inside, but out of respect for Mandy he refused to look, knowing she was modest almost to a fault.

That was two summers ago, and since then there'd been many wonderful moments to remember, except for the two months they were separated when Mandy and Patty Dubose showed up unannounced at the beach house catching he and Coon with a couple of locals they picked up earlier in the week. That took some getting over, and some tall explaining, but now they were inseparable, and were teased constantly by their friends. They laughingly shrugged it off, content with living in their own private world filled with inculpable love of pretend and make believe.

"Hey 'hot dog,' I don't know where you are right now, but you'd better get your mind back to basics if you know what's good for you." Laughing, Coon rapped his knuckles on top of Cleat's head.

"Yeah you're right." Cleat laughed.

Pulling out of the driveway, Bobby Darrin was singing his 1958 hit "Splish Splash" on the radio. He remembered it as being the first song to which he let Mandy try and teach him how to bop, and only then because it was in the privacy of her Florida room where there was no one around to laugh at him or make jokes. At the time most girls danced with each other if it wasn't a slow song. Cleat could only think of a couple of guys besides him and Coon that could bop. In the tenth grade he secretly took a few lessons with Coon at Arthur Murray's Studio, but when the fear of being caught by his friends became too great he quit.

"You'd better step on it if we're gonna make it on time."

Cleat took Coon's advice and pressed on the accelerator. The Chevy responded immediately by chirping its tires and surging forward. With the top down, the night chill blew in their faces, causing them to shiver from the cold. Suddenly, flashing red lights bounced off the interior. Cleat looked in the rearview mirror and his heart skipped a beat when he saw a police car following close behind. His eyes darted to the speedometer, the needle indicated he was going over fifty miles per hour!

"Shit!" he spat. The speed limit around Lake Holly was thirty. Easing off the gas pedal, he flipped his right turn signal on and slow-cruised his car to the curb. Catching Coon's shit-eating grin he frowned, "Dammit, you know this is *your* fault."

"Hey, I was just sitting here minding my own business. You're the one that's behind the wheel, not me."

Cleat sat gripping the black leather custom steering wheel with all his might. He could envision his father's preaching once again about maturity and responsibility. Last summer he'd gotten a ticket on the way back from Daytona driving ninety-five miles an hour and his father had an absolute conniption. Cleat suffered his dad's decree of being grounded for two weeks.

"Would you please step out of the car?" Even though the officer was kind enough to use the word "please," it was definitely a command.

Cleat reluctantly obeyed. When he saw who the officer was, he felt like throwing up; it was "Ball Buster" Lassiter himself. Nobody ever got a break from the man. Sergeant Lassiter didn't care, or listen to reasons; he simply enforced the law to the letter whether you were a great grandmother or a beautiful blonde. Rumor had it he gave his wife a ticket for running a stop sign. Most of all he especially liked busting teenagers full of mischief.

"Well...where's the fire, son?"

"Nowhere sergeant." Cleat hadn't felt this low in a long time.

"Do you know how fast you were driving, Cleat?"

"No sir, not until I saw your lights flashing."

"You boys are on the way to the field house to watch some game films, aren't cha? You were too busy thinking about the big game tomorrow night instead of driving safely, huh hotshot?"

"Yes sir, I suppose so." Cleat looked at the citation book and pen the sergeant held in his hand. The ax was about to fall. His father had already warned him that if he got another excessive speeding ticket he would sell his car. He wondered if twenty-five miles over the speed limit was considered excessive. Either way, in his father's eyes it would be, the man wasn't exactly known for his tolerance.

"I sure hope you boys pull it off tomorrow night. The town's really counting on y'all winning. We've never had a state championship in anything before...I'm telling ya, it'll be the biggest thing to hit here since Elvis came to town. We're sure proud of y'all. Win, or lose, you're one fine bunch of boys."

"Yes sir, thank you sir."

"Cleat, I'm gonna do something I've only done once before in my thirteen years of service, and that was with my wife. I know what people say, but there's no truth to it. I gave her a verbal warning, and that's what I'm going to give you, but don't let me catch you speeding again or I'll throw you under the jail —*with* your dad's full approval."

Cleat's head snapped up so fast it startled the sergeant, causing him to take a step backward. "Thank you Sergeant Lassiter. I can't tell you how much this means to me." He reached out, clasping the officer's hand, which still held his citation book. "Thanks, thanks a lot Sergeant."

"I'm doing this for the team, and you'd better not tell a soul about this, or I'll come down on you like stink on shit." The burly sergeant growled, pointing a stubby finger at Cleat.

"Yes sir, I promise."

Sergeant Lassiter gave Coon the evil eye in the front passenger seat.

"Yes sir, me too…I promise." Coon shifted lower in the seat as the sergeant went back to his patrol car.

Cleat stood off to the side of the road as the squad car rolled past. He waved at the sergeant, but Lassiter never acknowledged his presence.

"Coon, can you believe what just happened?"

"Hell no, and I sat right here as a witness."

"God, I can't believe "Ole Ball Buster" let me go."

"I'll tell you what I don't believe: I don't believe coach is gonna be happy with us being later than hell."

Pulling into the school parking lot a few minutes later, Cleat skidded to a screeching stop, filling the air with dirt, dust, and the smell of burnt rubber. They were both out of the car, running neck and neck racing toward the varsity room. They were the two fastest runners in school, but no one could determine who was the fastest. One day Cleat would outrace Coon, and the next time he would lose to Coon. One thing the two could agree on: Coon was the quickest. He seemed to be at full speed after his first two steps…for Cleat it took at least three or four. At least they kept their claim to fame in the family.

The field house was in sight when they rounded the corner stride for stride. Most of their teammates were standing outside all bunched up clowning around, a few stood off to the side throwing a football under the floodlights.

"Hey look, here come the celebrities!" Gene Reese's shout brought on hoots and hollers from the rest of the guys.

Cleat and Coon gradually slowed to a gait, as they halfheartedly waved at their friends. They were just thankful the coach wasn't in sight.

"I don't know, it looks like the 'Hardy Boys' to me," Bo called out.

"Hell no, they look more like the 'Bobbsey Twins,' except they ain't twins." An unrecognizable voice brought more laughter.

"How about Mutt and Jeff?" Another yelled.

That's when Butch Werner, the teams' six-foot-four two hundred and sixty five pound star defensive tackle sauntered over to Cleat and Coon. He stood close enough to be considered invading their space. A sinister sneer spread across his ruddy face, showing a wide gap where two of his upper front teeth should've been.

"Naw, its Tarzan and his little monkey friend Cheetah." Before he could laugh over his witticism, something struck him in his gut that felt like a sledge-hammer.

Cleat hit Werner with a hard right fist, burying it deep into the middle of his overly large stomach. Werner had always been a bully as far back as Cleat could remember. When Butch bent over gasping for breath, Cleat hit him with a wicked right cross, splitting his left cheekbone open; blood came gushing out, spilling onto the concrete. Butch let out a tortured yell as he dropped to the ground screaming. After the initial shock, some team members grabbed Cleat just as he was about to jump on top of the downed Butch.

"Hey Cleat, cool off man…that's enough." It was Coon standing in front of him, holding his arms in a vice-like grip. "It's okay Cleat, forget it. Let it be," Coon pleaded.

"Okay…okay. I'm all right dammit. Everybody let go," he yelled, pulling away from everyone's grip.

Just then the metal door of the field house flew open, slamming against the outside structure as Coach Dunn rushed through the doorway followed closely by his coaching staff.

"What in the hell's going on out here?" he barked. "Get your asses' outta the way. Make room dammit." Dunn bore his way into the middle of the crowd, shoving players aside until he was in the eye of the storm. He observed several of his players helping Werner to his feet. His face was a mess; half of it was covered in blood. "Werner, what in the hell happened to you?"

"He hit me coach…he hit me in the face," Butch cried out, pressing his hand firmly against the wound trying to staunch the flow of blood.

"*Who* hit you?"

Butch pointed a bloody finger straight at Cleat. "*He* did coach! Cleat sucker punched me for no damn reason." A thick scarlet oozed from the gash in his cheek, and ran freely down his neck staining his white T-shirt a deep crimson. "Damn coach, I'm bleeding like a stuck pig."

"Here, let me take a look." Dunn tilted the boy's head to one side, allowing the floodlights stationed on the corners of the field house to cast a better light on the wound. The gash was at least two inches long, high on the cheekbone, just under his left eye. Already, the swelling around the cut was stretching the skin so tight it gave the appearance of being worse than it actually was, but still the laceration would definitely require stitches.

"It doesn't look too bad," came the verdict, "but you're gonna need some sewing up. Coach Herndon, how about driving Butch over to the emergency room and let the doctors fix him up? Get back here as quick as you can." He gestured for the offensive line coach to assist Butch.

"Cleat, is what Butch says true?"

"Kind'a, sort'a coach," Cleat confessed. He still couldn't believe he let his temper get the best of him; something inside just snapped and before he knew it Butch was on the ground. The thing that scared him the most was that he couldn't even remember hitting him. He hadn't been in a fight since he and Coon participated in the Boy's Club Golden Gloves program.

"Get your butt inside," Coach Dunn growled through clenched teeth. "I want to get to the bottom of this."

Cleat meekly followed the fearless head coach into the empty room, wondering what was going to happen. Once inside the coach slammed the heavy reinforced steel door with such force that rust sprang from the hinges forming little clouds of orange powder that floated silently in the air. As the echo of the explosion subsided, loose plumes of dust from the overhead rafters filtered down on the two as they stared silently at one another. The brief silence that followed seemed an eternity to Cleat. A cold chill ran up his spine as he waited for Coach Dunn to say something.

"All right, let's hear it!" The coach's voice was surly, leaving no doubt he was highly agitated over the scuffle between two of his star players right before the biggest game of his coaching career.

Leaving nothing out while meeting Dunn's glaring stare, Cleat explained as best he could how it all went down. After finishing the tale, he stood there bracing himself for the stinging retort that was sure to follow. Refusing to blink…his eyes began to burn and glaze with tears as he held Dunn's fiery stare.

His nose started inching, but he was determined not to move or bat an eye, for he had his say and now it was up to the coach to hand out any disciplinary actions he deemed necessary. As he knew from past experience, the coach demanded absolute adherence to his authority…even more so than his dad.

Coach Dunn shook his head from side to side, finally breaking the deadlock. "Goddammit son, for the life of me I can't believe you'd pull something like this when the biggest game in this school's history is just on the horizon. Shit-fire son, you go out and injure the best two-way lineman that's ever played for Lakewood. You better pray to all that's holy he'll be able to suit-up for tomorrow's night's game, because if he can't, we ain't got a chance in hell of defeating Edgewood. Tell me, who are we going to put in his place? Willis? Hell, he couldn't block or tackle one of the cheerleaders." Dunn yanked the ball cap off his head and slammed it on one of the training tables in disgust. "What in the hell were you thinking, son?"

"I don't know coach…it just happened, that's all."

"It just happened that's all," Dunn mimicked. "Get the hell out of my sight before I say or do something I'll regret."

Cleat hurried out the door, but not fast enough to avoid a swift kick in the ass that sent him sailing into the night.

Coach Dunn stood in the doorway with a scowl on his face, vainly rubbing his hand over Wednesday morning's haircut. He purposely kept it short to hide the fact that he was prematurely going bald, not only going bald, but also turning gray. Just this morning he'd decided if that happened he would forego haircuts and just start shaving the damn thing like Yul Brenner.

His boys were the finest he'd ever had the privilege to coach. They had the heart of lions, and the desire of champions. Overall they weren't the biggest, or the fastest, except for a few of the players like Cleat, Coon, and Werner. The senior leadership was what made the team great, and their genuine love for each other. What he had was what every coach dreamed off...the very definition of *team*...the same one that Webster saw fit to define in the dictionary.

The team was half-assed assembled out front and not many of them had the fortitude to meet Coach Dunn's glare. After all, his black eyes had caused many a knee to tremble under their steely scrutiny. Most of them valiantly tried to avoid the chilling effect; in fact, some players had to be coerced into not quitting the team once they were singled out as not being tough enough to play varsity for the Lakewood Spartans.

"Get your butts inside...on the double!" A mad stampede toward the doorway ensued. Coach Dunn was intelligent enough to quickly step out of the way.

"Knock off the chatter!" Coach James Tensely, the defensive coach, hollered above the noise. Coach Dunn walked to the head of the room examining the faces of key individuals along the way. A stoic expression was etched on his hardened face. Grabbing a ruler, he rapped it sharply against the blackboard, instantly bringing silence to the crowded chambers.

He stood facing his players, rocking back and forth from heel to toe with his hands clasped behind his back looking very military. Staring at the sea of faces, he was reminded of those heady World War II days when he served as a captain with the 101st Airborne Division during the invasion of France.

"Men," Coach Dunn usually always referred to his boys as men during his speeches because he was raising them to be just that. "We're going to pass out notebooks and pencils; make sure you use them. Do not, I repeat, do *not* rely on your memory. After the film we're going to breakup into our designated groups...there will be questions and answers." A few were brave enough to let out some audible groans, but Dunn chose to ignore them. "The assistants and I spent all week highlighting Edgewood's bread and butter plays on defense and offense. We also paid special attention to their key players. So without further ado roll the film."

Coach Bailey Richardson, his young offensive coordinator and a recent graduate from "Ole Miss" turned off the lights while one of the trainers started the projector. Over the whirring of the machine one could hear metal chairs scrapping on the rough concrete floor as players jockeyed to get a better view of the silvery screen.

Suddenly Lakewood's scoreboard appeared on the screen: Home 24,

Visitor 0. As the camera panned the field, a man on a white horse dressed as a Spartan Warrior raced across the goal line. The mighty stallion rose on its haunches as the warrior saluted by crashing a sharpened spear against his shield.

The locker room exploded in a thunderous roar. More than a few of the stalwarts witnessing the theatrical scene had goose bumps racing up and down their arms. Until this year the school mascot had never been anything more than a silly little dweeb running up and down the sidelines dressed in an awful looking costume. The mascot was the brunt of jokes coming from the opposition, and more often than not, the hometown fans as well. Here on the screen was a true warrior on a magnificent white stallion. It brought chills of pride to everyone in the room…subtle movements amongst the players went unnoticed as they wiped away prideful tears.

It was a full five minutes before the yelling and backslapping subsided. A smile eased across Coach Dunn's rough-honed features as he stood listening to his men's jubilation. Electricity was in the air, and you could feel the pride among the players and coaches alike. It had the type of response Dunn had hoped for.

"All right, everybody settle down…eyes to the front. The first plays we're going to study are their belly series. I want you defensive linemen to pay particular attention to their blocking schemes…you'll notice every time the guard double teams with the center on the nose guard *that* will be the side they run to…the offside tackle will brush block the defensive lineman and release to the inside linebacker, allowing the fullback to clear whoever's still in the hole. Notice that both ends release downfield and lead interference. You defensive backs be careful…don't commit to the run too quickly or they'll burn you with a play action pass that has the same look." The coach nodded for the film to continue.

The team sat in awe as they witnessed a huge hole open against Boone, allowing Edgewood's halfback to bust loose in the secondary creating havoc by breaking tackles and running over people…he didn't stop until he crossed the goal some 67 yards downfield. Opposing bodies littered the field.

"Hold it right there, and back it up Coach Ewell," Dunn called out to the offensive back coach, ignoring the "oohs" and "aahs" coming from his football team as the film went into reverse. "I'd like to introduce y'all to number 31…Harvey Blake, Edgewood's All Conference-All State senior halfback. He will be heading to Notre Dame this summer on a full scholarship. He's five-foot-eleven and weighs two hundred and twenty pounds of pure dynamite. Not only is Blake the schools all time rusher; he's also the leading rusher in the entire state, with over twenty-two hundred rushing yards this year alone. Number 31 is hell on wheels, and if he gets into the secondary he's a tough man to stop. You men didn't get the chance to play against him last year, because he sat out with a sprained ankle, but tomorrow night you're going to have to put him down, and I'm *mean* put him down hard. If you don't wrap him up he'll run over you, or through you."

Cleat watched intently as the film ran backward, some of the guys laughed seeing number 31 run in reverse, but he didn't see a damn thing funny. Blake was a brute, and he seemed to enjoy inflicting pain by running over smaller defensive backs. Cleat noticed toward the end of his run he had a clean shot at the end zone, but he veered off course to annihilate an undersized defender just to show who the better man was. Any player who was unfortunate enough to warrant such attention lay crumpled on the ground in the wake of Blake's grueling challenge.

Cleat remembered the hit he took from a defensive back when they played Boone earlier in the year; he also remembered lying spread-eagle on the ground when he ran a slant over the middle, as a matter of fact his neck was *still* sore. The following week when the same guy challenged Blake, he was knocked out of the game. It was going to be his responsibility when he switched to line-backer on defense to stop this human wrecking machine.

"This film is from the Edgewood-Boone game, who they beat 42-19. Edgewood had 429 yards rushing, and Blake had three hundred and twelve of them by the third quarter when he was pulled from the game. If you men recall, we barely squeaked by Boone with an 18-13 win. We gained less than seventy yards in that one, and were damn lucky we walked away with a win. I realize we played Boone in a torrential downpour, but it'll give you some idea of what we'll be up against."

The meeting went on for another hour and a half. It was midway through the film when Coach Herndon returned with Butch in tow. All heads turned briefly to see who was entering their private domain, when they saw it was only Butch wrapped in his red badge of courage their interest quickly returned to the screen.

Suddenly the film came to an end, making a clicking sound as the reel continued to spin. Someone flicked on the lights, and illuminated the room with such brilliance it was painful to the eyes. Players began talking loudly amongst themselves, each voice trying to drown out the other in order to be heard. Naturally, all conversation was about "The Game." The talk ended as quickly as it had begun when Coach Dunn cleared his throat.

"Knock it off you bunch of deviants." The smile crossing his face was broad enough to crease his leathery skin. "Men, there are some things I'd like to say before dismissing you tonight." His eyes sparkled as he faced his men; slowly he reached up and ran his hand over his short GI haircut.

"I want you to know how proud the coaching staff and I are. You're the best damn team this school's ever fielded, and you're the best men I've ever had the pleasure to coach." This last statement brought on cheers and enthusiastic applause from his players. "We worked hard all summer in the weight room preparing for this season, and we worked our butts off to get where we are today. We played injured and sick, but we accepted the pain and the challenge like true warriors. I hope you feel the same as me...it was damn well worth it."

Coach Dunn was interrupted again, but he didn't mind the interlude. "I can remember when we began this heroic journey. We were young, unknown, and untested. Most of the papers had us picked near the bottom of the confer-ence, even as low as the cellar." Catcalls were shouted, and a few cuss words were mixed in. Cussing wasn't usually tolerated, but this was on the eve of a very special night for them all and so passed unpunished, though not unno-ticed.

"I recall a sports writer for the *Tribune* who wrote in his column that Lakewood should forfeit their first game of the season against Miami Senior, being they were last season's champions, and were favorites to win again this year." Hoots of laughter and several raspberries halted his speech...Dunn noticed wryly that his coaches were enjoying the proceedings as much as the players.

"Of course, we went down to Miami and kicked their butts 42-06, but everybody claimed that as a 'fluke.'" He waited patiently for the screaming to die down. "The following week we played our first home game against the mighty powerhouse Coral Gables, if I remember correctly we blanked those guys 44-0."

He continued over the noise: "The Hillsborough game came next, and we took them on their home field and beat 'em 62-0. The following week we found ourselves on the road again with a 35-0 win over Grant, who we could've beaten worse than the score indicated if we had chosen to leave our starters in after half time. The papers claimed we were riding a bubble that was about to burst when undefeated Jacksonville came to town. They were wrong again: we put a 28-0 whipping on them, and sent their ass packing."

He paused briefly, staring intently at his men wanting to permanently engrave in his mind the faces of the young warriors sitting before him. An enormous feeling of pride swept over him; one day when they became grown men with families of their own, he hoped some of them would consider him to be a coach, mentor, and lastly a friend.

"Well, now here we were halfway through our season still undefeated. Our defense has allowed only one touchdown through five games and our explosive offense has scored 211 points...not bad for a team that was supposed to finish last in the conference."

By now the noise in the room was deafening. Every time a victory was announced the players screamed and hollered, coupled with backslapping and foot stomping, it soon grew cacophonous. Led by Coon, they were all standing with balled fists raised yelling, "LHS, LHS, LHS." Coon stood on a chair and began a new chant, "WE'RE NUMBER ONE! WE'RE NUMBER ONE!"

Coach Dunn knew one of the main reasons for their outstanding season was Coach Richardson; he convinced him to throw out the Winged 'T' offense he'd been running ever since he'd arrived at Lakewood twelve years ago. The young enthusiastic coach installed the NFL's pro-set offense, and in practice it became an instant success. And why shouldn't it? It was more suited for a smaller team that relied on quickness and deception.

Lakewood became the first high school team in the state to vary from the old school of running the football out of various formations from the archaic "T," and winged "T" that most of the high schools ran. It required some major changes in personnel, mainly moving Cleat from quarterback to wide receiver because of his size and speed.

This move took some major convincing, because Cleat had played quarterback his whole athletic career starting at age six, and was an All-State quarterback the year before. Gene Reece moved up from an undefeated junior varsity squad to become the starting quarterback. He was tall and lanky at 6' 4" and 188 pounds, but on the negative side he was slow of foot. Still, he made up for his lack of speed with quick feet, plus he was as intelligent in the classroom as he was on the field, and the boy had a magnificent arm with great timing.

Before the season began there were lingering doubts telling him the new offense could collapse into chaos once the whistle blew. There was so much motion with different sets to contend with, and that wasn't even considering the fact of learning a whole new language. Another new concept was the quarterback had the option to check off at the line of scrimmage to a different play by using a hot color if he didn't like the way the opposing defense was set up. This was almost unheard of in high school football. On more than one occasion he thought of reverting back to the old offense he was so familiar with, after all he had been coaching successfully for more than a dozen years. One of the contributing factors convincing him to stay the course was how the players readily adapted to new offense. The biggest surprise of all was Coon. Last year he played strictly defensive back, and it never entered Dunn's mind that the team prankster would have the capabilities to excel at running back. Boy, what an oversight *that* was.

Talk about being nervous as a cat on a hot tin roof, but all of the jitters disappeared after their first game, the players loved the new offense, and the coaches did too. It made their lack of size and depth the most dangerous offensive team in the state. By attendance, they were the smallest school in the conference, but they were feared as no other because of their explosive offense. No one had figured out how to stop their pro-set formations, and the motion kept the other teams off balanced and confused. The constant shifting was enough to draw an average of four offside penalties a game.

The Spartans defense was smallish, and more than half of them played both ways, but they were quick and tenacious as any team playing the game. Every yard that was gained against them was a personal affront. They led the conference in turnovers and scoring defense. There was as much pride on the defensive side of the ball as there was on offense side.

Coach Dunn held up his hands, motioning for the players to settle down. After all, he wasn't finished yet; there were still glorious battles to tell. "The Lincoln High Cougars, another arch rival, came to town during Homecoming weekend." A low groan in the foreground mixed with cuss words built to a crescendo with vehement shouts as the players were reminded of the game that almost made them mere mortals, but in retrospect, it actuality made them a better team, though they wouldn't realize it until they became much older.

"At the half we were down 13-0. We couldn't do anything right and they could do no wrong. There was an upset in the making. We were missing tackles, blocks, fumbling, missing assignments, throwing interceptions, dropping passes, jumping offside…you name something bad happening and we were doing it. I remember it as if it were yesterday when Cleat blocked the coaches from entering the dressing room at half time. He asked us to stay out so the team could have a *private meeting*. To this day I don't know what was said, or what went on, but I can tell you men one thing, whatever took place I'd like to have a patent on it. The final score was 27-13. It's the victory I'm most proud of, because you men took a gut check and showed the kind of fiber you're *really* made of."

Cleat scooted further down in his seat, feeling his teammates' eyes staring holes in his back; his face was flushed, remembering the halftime confrontation. He busied himself tracing some initials carved in one of the student desks scattered around the room. He involuntarily flashed back to the Lincoln High game, and the locker room scene that ensued.

After Coach Dunn agreed to his request, Cleat walked into the turmoil erupting in the team's dressing room. There was pandemonium inside. They were still arguing and bickering back-and-forth when he climbed on top of one of the old wooden tables. He listened to his teammates whining and complaining with utter contempt. It was disgusting to hear them lay the blame on everybody but themselves. A wave of nausea boiled in the pit of his stomach, unable to stand the quibbling any longer, with all the force he could muster he hurled his helmet across the room. It struck a metal wall locker creating a thunderous explosion. The helmet fell to the floor splintered down the center.

The startled players turned to see Cleat standing above them with his feet spread wide apart, his fists were on his hips looking like a Viking God of war straight out of mythology. The fire in his eyes was enough to intimidate the strongest as he glared at them unwaveringly. Silently they waited for their lofted leader to speak. A deadly quiet settled across the room with only an occasional cough breaking the ensuing stillness. The only intrusion was the muffled sound of the band playing their school fight song. The music filtered down through the Gothic concrete structure into their chamber of despair and futility.

The young faces of battle-tested veterans were dirt smeared and streaked with sweat. They were battered and bruised, blood could be seen everywhere you looked…it was on their clothes and skin. Their uniforms were ragged and torn, they resembled extras in a WW II movie, but worst of all their pride and manhood had taken a devastating blow during the first half.

To Cleat they already looked defeated, it was registered in their eyes; they were lifeless and filled with the acceptance of defeat, and that was something he could not accept. There was a second half to play, and that meant there was still a chance for redemption if they pulled together and executed as a team.

He didn't know what the hell he was doing standing in front of everybody, but he had to do something. There was no way he was going to give up, and he sure as hell wasn't about to let the team give up. Being the team captain it was up to him to make them believe in themselves again. Lakewood was a far better team than Lincoln, shit their opponents had lost four games in a row.

Out of desperation, Cleat reached up and grabbed the open neck of his jersey with both hands, and gave it a downward jerk ripping the garment from his body. Parts of it hung from his pads dangling in shreds. Grasping the remains he yanked them free and rolled them into a wad before flinging it to the floor.

"I quit!" he spat. Bending over, he pulled his shoulder pads off and threw them across the room, causing several of his teammates to duck. His upper body glistened with sweat, and with every heave of his chest muscles rippled.

"Hey Cleat, what'cha doing?" Bo challenged, stepping forward with a puzzled expression. "You can't quit."

"The hell I can't, you quit on me when they scored first. I've been playing my guts out while most of y'all have been pissing and moaning and pointing fingers at everybody but your own damn selves. Y'all are fighting more with each other than you are against Lincoln. Well, by damn, I've had enough embarrassment for one night! I'm not going back out there with a bunch of cry babies and losers."

"What's the matter Cleat?" a voice from the disgruntled throng rang out. "You chicken?"

Cleat flinched, "Yeah, I'm chicken enough to kick anybody's ass in this room, and I mean right-by-god now…just step up and get in line!" It had gotten way out of hand; he hadn't meant for it to go this far, and now he was at a loss. He'd wanted to give them hope and courage, to inspire them, but instead he'd done just the opposite and alienated himself.

Just when it looked as if there was going to be a free for all, Coon jumped on the table beside Cleat. "Hold it right there, dammit! What Cleat's trying to tell you bunch of dumb asses is you've already quit, and you're too damn stupid to realize it. There's not much sense in any of us going back out there to make fools out of ourselves in front of our coaches, school, friends, family, and the town folks. Dammit, we're supposed to be a team, but we're acting as individuals. As a team we've shared blood, sweat, and tears through two-a-days and worked our asses off in the weight room with one common theme: to believe in each other and function as a team. I'm not willing to lie down and give up, but if y'all aren't going to pull together and play to win, then I'm with Cleat. I'm tired of making those jerk-offs look like the goddamn Florida Gators."

"Come on Coon…those guys are better than we thought," Bo whined.

Butch angrily shoved Bo out of the way."Bullshit, Bo, you're a wimp. Those guys ain't shit, and they're over there laughing at us. We're playing like a bunch of whores, and making them look invincible. Goddammit, this is my senior year same as Cleat and Coon. Most of y'all are juniors, you guys have another crack at this, we don't, and I ain't planning on going out a damn loser."

Big Oak lunged from the training bench, "Butch is right; this is our chance to be part of something special, something we may never have a chance to experience again. I ain't throwing in the towel." Big Oak put his helmet on and snapped his chinstrap with resolve. "I've never been a quitter, and I sure as hell ain't starting now."

"Me neither, dammit," Coon yelled. "Hell boys, it's our Homecoming for Christ sake, we're letting a team that ain't worth a shit kick our ass. I don't know about y'all, but I'd hate like hell to go to the dance with my ass dragging." Coon inhaled deeply as he gazed over the crowded room. The upturned faces meeting his defiant stance were now full of guilt and embarrassment. "Dammit, we're a team, it's what's made us who we are. We've fought hard all year as a unit, so let's pull together and go out there and kick some Lincoln ass. Let's show them what happens when you mess with the Fighting Spartans."

"Hell yeah, Coon," Butch hollered above the cheers. A bandage across the bridge of his nose was stained dark red. "I'm gonna rip some heads off."

Cleat held his hands up, effectively quieting the room. "Listen up, we're only down 13 points, and that's not enough to keep a championship team from blowing their asses off the field. This is Spartan turf so let's show 'em Spartans ain't gonna give up a blade of grass without a fight."

"Who's number one?" Coon screamed over the cheers.

"*We're* number one!" the players screamed. "We're number one" resounded over and over while the players revitalized their enthusiasm. Self-confidence abounded as they pounded helmets and threw their bodies into wall lockers in a frenzy of zest and zeal. Bo and Butch grabbed each other by the shoulder pads and crashed violently into one another. A bench sailed across the room, careening off of a wall and landing harmlessly beside a urinal. The room shook from the players' hyper reaction as they continued their antics and hollering their chant while virtually destroying the locker room.

Coon opened a box full of miscellaneous equipment and found several cans of black grease paint used to prevent the glare of sunlight or bright stadium lights. It was something they'd never used before, but Coon felt it was time to put it to use. Smearing the grease on as if it were war paint, he caught Butch's attention.

"No shit, Coon, that's freaking cool…hey put some of that shit on me, but make it look more Halloween like. I want to scare the shit out of 'em."

"Damn, Butch you're scary enough as is, any scarier you'll give somebody a heart attack."

"Shut the hell up runt, and just do it," Butch smiled at his smaller teammate.

The fad caught on quickly, and before long the whole team was painted with a variety of horrific faces. They ended up looking like the scariest monsters from every child's nightmare.

Coach Dunn flung the door aside and stuck his head inside. "It's time to go men." The players burst through the doorway like a thundering heard of banshees, rudely knocking him off balance and unintentionally sending him butt first to the hard concrete floor. As he skidded several feet he questioned his vision: Had his players really turned into black goblins? Getting up slowly he noticed a hole in his brand new black pants. Cursing silently he turned in time to see Coon helping Cleat slip on a new game jersey…the last tug brought it cleanly over his head. He was shocked at what he saw.

"What the hell have you done to your faces?" he asked.

"We decided to put on some war paint before we go to war!" Coon yelled as he and Cleat ran up the tunnel leading to the field. "Come watch us kick their ass, Coach."

CHAPTER 3

The second half turned out to be a complete reversal. Fighting and scratching with clawed fist, Lakewood pulled together, working like a well-oiled machine. The defense shut Lincoln down, allowing only twenty-four yards of total offense during the second half, while Lakewood's offense exploded for twenty-seven unanswered points.

Cleat gave one of the finest performances of his football career, snatching eleven passes in the second half alone and running three of them in for touchdowns. When the final seconds ticked off the stadium clock, Cleat had caught fourteen passes for a total of two hundred and ninety three yards, setting a school record that newspapers claimed would never be broken.

Their first score came 2 minutes and 37 seconds into the third quarter when Coon intercepted a pass by stepping in front of Lincoln's halfback swinging out of the backfield for a flare pass. He read it perfectly and caught the ball running full speed. Fifty-three yards later he was crossing Lincoln's goal line. That explosive turnaround set the tone for the rest of the game.

After the third quarter there was an official time out called due to the complaints of Lincoln's coaching staff over Lakewood's painted faces. The officials held a mid-field conference that exceeded five minutes discussing the rules, but they couldn't find any covering "excessive face painting." Two weeks later the Florida High School Athletic Association convened, banning the procedure by inserting a special clause covering the subject. It was a game the local fans would discuss at the workplace for years to come. With each telling of the game's devastating tackles, catches, runs, and blocks, the story grew to superhuman proportions, but no one cared because it was one of the greatest come-from-behind victories in school history.

That evening Lakewood's Homecoming dance at Lakewood's Teen Center was full of jubilation, more so because Bo succeeded in spiking the gallons of punch provided for the annual event. Cleat and Mandy had been pronounced Homecoming King and Queen during the halftime ceremonies, but there was little fanfare since Cleat was in the locker-room with his teammates and missed the event.

At the dance, Harris Weinberg, president of the senior class and captain of the heralded debate team, took center stage by announcing it was time to honor the king and queen of the dance. When he called Cleat and Mandy's names as the honored couple, they were ushered on stage to be officially crowned. After the crowning and applause died down, Cleat took the microphone from Harris's hand. Uncomfortable over all the adulation, he took a deep breath before addressing the crowded floor.

"It was a great victory for our school and football team," he was quickly interrupted by another round of applause. "We fought long and hard to win this game for our Homecoming, and Mandy and I are honored that you have chosen us to represent our class as Homecoming King and Queen."

More applause allowed him to clear the frog out of his throat. "At this time I'd like to have John Truman join us on stage." The students looked around with puzzled expressions, whispering among themselves and all the while wondering what was going on. Even Mandy hadn't a clue.

Coon slowly climbed the steps leading to the stage; his eyes never left the floor as he reluctantly made his way to where Mandy and Cleat were waiting. He stood paralyzed from an acute state of shyness. He had no idea why Cleat called him to the stage. Sweat trickled down his brow, making its way into his eyes causing them to burn insufferably, but he remained immobile, frozen in place.

Cleat motioned for the crowd to silence. "I want to thank everybody once again for voting me your King, I'm deeply honored, but I'd like to relinquish my crown tonight to John Truman, who truly deserves the crown more than anybody I know. Without his leadership, our victorious Homecoming game wouldn't have been possible." Cleat then placed the jeweled crown on top of Coon's fuzzy head.

During the thunderous applause and accompanying cheers, Mandy sweetly placed a kiss on Coon's lips and gave him an affectionate hug. Tears were streaming down his face as he listened to the crowd's response. The emotional scene touched everyone and if there were a concession selling Kleenex it would've sold out in the first five minutes.

The band had selected the theme from *A Summer Place* as the spotlight dance, and when the music began Mandy reached out for Coon's hand and led him to the dance floor. The spotlight centered on the couple as their friends' gathered, misty-eyed, to view the symbolic ritual.

Coon held Mandy in his arms ever so lightly as they danced under the circle of light following their every movement. Its brilliance shimmered off of Coon's tear-streaked face and highlighted Mandy's hair of glittering gold. Coon was pleased that he'd learned to dance as well as any instructor. He whirled Mandy gracefully across the dance floor in grandiose style. It was a moment in time he would cherish for the rest of his life.

Saturday's papers lavished Cleat with laurels befitting a superstar. Headlines throughout the state read "Cleat Davis-Friday's Hero," "Cleatwood Davis-Super Hero," "Lakewood's Davis Annihilates Lincoln," and his personal favorite, though he would scarcely admit it: "King Davis Still Reigns."

While every other line saw Cleat's name in print, very little was mentioned about anybody else on the team. Cleat was embarrassed over all of the attention given to him. Only one or two lines were devoted to Butch's fumble recovery, with not one word printed about the jarring hits he created on both sides of the ball. There was even less said about Gene Reece's stellar performance of completing 15 of 21 passes in the second half, and throwing for three touchdowns.

Out of the four and a half columns the *Ledger* devoted to the game, only one small paragraph contained Friday night's real hero: John Truman. Without Coon taking on the responsibility of regrouping the team at halftime, the *Ledger's* article would've been reduced to a mere paragraph or two. His interception for a touchdown was barely mentioned, and his 127 yards rushing weren't even noted except in the game stats.

Coach Dunn's voice abruptly brought him back to the present. Sitting up straight, his eyes darted around the room to see if anyone had noticed him daydreaming.

"Plant High came to town boasting they were going to be David who felled the mighty Goliath. We whipped 'em 38-0 and sent them home in fine fashion. Apollo Beach was a personal embarrassment to me because I let you men go to sleep in the second half. We didn't score one dang point, but the 20 points we scored in the first half were enough since our stellar defense held them scoreless."

Coach Dunn leaned heavily on the podium and looked into a sea of young faces he had grown to love and respect. "That worried me some, because we were facing a good team in Chamberlain. The week before we played them they'd only lost one game by a total of 3 points. They were going to be tough, especially playing them on their home field. If you recall, the coaching staff worked your butts off that week."

He continued over the moans and groans: "We went down there and found out pretty damn quick we were going to be in for one hell of a fight. It was dog-eat-dog until we blew it open in the forth quarter when Truman gave us some breathing room by busting a seventy-seven yard touchdown off left tackle. It was tooth and nail, but we managed a 34-22 win. That contest made a few more believers out of both our fans, and *our* detractors. People began to realize that Lakewood had one hell of a football team. Bradenton was no match for us, hell we had them down 28-0 at the half. In the second half I pulled most of the starters and played our younger players so they'll be primed and ready for next year. I didn't want to run up the score on a good friend of mine who happens to be Bradenton's head coach. Hell, we still won 42-13."

The field house roared with chants of, "We're number one, we're number one." It was some time before the coaches were able to settle them down for the final roll call.

"We all knew the last game of the regular season was going to be tough, for some reason Boone always played their best game of the year against us. It was a do-or-die must win for us…a win would springboard us into the state playoffs with a 10 and 0 record. That night we played in the pouring rain on a sloppy field, and we executed even sloppier. We were fortunate to walk away with an 18-13 victory. You know it, and so do the coaches, but nonetheless it put us into the playoffs undefeated.

"In the playoffs the following week, we met Ft. Lauderdale, who we dominated like we're capable of doing. We played an almost perfect game—no fumbles, no interceptions, no missed assignments, no missed tackles, and only two penalties—and beat them 24-03. You men play like that every game and it'll add up to a win every time. Surprisingly, last week Clearwater was flat and we were damn lucky, because we didn't play our best game, either."

Hissing and booing interrupted him. Dunn laughed for the first time. "Yeah, I know the score was 34-07, but we didn't execute with authority, and there wasn't much team play that I could see. Tomorrow night you men *better* play as a team, eliminate mistakes, and capitalize on Edgewood's weaknesses, what few they have. They are bigger and stronger than any team you've played all year. We're 12 and 0, and so is Edgewood. Friday night the two best teams in the state are playing for the title. To win, we're going to have to dig in and play harder than ever before. They have a hard-nose team that likes to run the ball right down your throat, but they'll have to do it against the stingiest defense in the whole damn state."

Coach Dunn held his hands up for quiet. "They are a great team, but so are we. We are opposites...we rely on quickness and finesse while they rely on brute strength. Edgewood averages over 300 rushing yards a game, while we've only allowed 67 a game. Edgewood has scored 180 total points this year, 24 on defense and 156 on the ground; we've scored 370 in rushing and passing, the other 30 we acquired on defense and specialty teams.

"It's going to be one hell of a match up, men. Don't leave anything on the field but your blood and sweat. All I ask if for y'all to play up to your capabilities. A championship is something special, not many people ever have the opportunity to play for one, but as long you give it your all, you'll always be champions in my heart. Go on home now and get a good night's sleep. I'll see you men at the pep rally tomorrow." Coach Dunn left in a hurry before he made an emotional ass of himself.

"All right, men, you heard what the coach said," Coach Herndon bellowed from the rear of the room, "the meetings over, go on home and get some rest."

Once outside, the boys gathered in groups under a starlit night talking excitedly about Friday's game. Cleat spotted Butch with some of the linemen only a few steps away. He needed to apologize to Werner, and now was the time.

"Butch," Cleat called out, getting his attention. Placing his left hand on Butch's shoulder, he held out his right. "I'm sorry. I didn't mean to hit you. It happened before I could think." Butch stared at him for what seemed like an eternity. The original white bandage was now a dark brown where blood had seeped through the gauze.

"Hey, don't sweat it Cleat. I shouldn't have said what I said, but I was only kidding. I didn't mean nothin' by it, hell I ain't got nothin' against y'all. We've been friends forever, I just tried to say something funny and it didn't come out right…that's all."

"Hell, I know that Butch, we've known each other since first grade. Shit, the game's got me uptight I guess. Well, anyway, I just wanted to apologize."

Butch grabbed Cleat's hand, giving it a firm shake. "Shit, don't worry about it buddy…its over and forgotten, besides the scar will remind me of our championship year."

"Thanks. I really appreciate it, Butch."

"No sweat Cleat, see ya at the rally."

Cleat turned to leave and slammed into an immovable object in the form of a human. It was Harold Trim, also known as "Big Oak," or just plain ole "Oak." He was Lakewood's weak-side tackle on offense and played right tackle on the other side of the ball. Harold stood six-foot-five and weighed three hundred and twenty five pounds. By far the biggest guy on the team, he was also the biggest football player in the state.

"Whoa there, buddy, you might hurt yourself." Harold lifted Cleat off his feet effortlessly and set him down a few paces away. "What'cha think about Edgewood after the film tonight?"

"They're good," admitted Cleat, "but we're better. They haven't got the speed to keep up with us, and with you and Butch on the field I don't think they're any bigger than we are."

Coon joined the twosome. "Hell yeah, we're gonna kick their ass."

"You said it, Coon." Cleat threw his arm over his friend's shoulder.

Harold smiled at his two closest friends, feeling a tinge of jealously over their special relationship. Cleat and Coon were the only ones that never teased him for being different than everybody else. They'd always treated him like he was normal and not some kind of freak. An overactive pituitary gland had caused him to grow rapidly in height and weight at a very early age, which in turn created adverse side effects; one among many were his large, protruding eyes.

Behind his back he'd heard classmates call him "bug-eyes" and other hurtful names. All of them were derogatory and cut deep. He knew he was ugly, but he didn't have to be reminded of it every day. The only time he felt comfortable was when he was at home with his family, or around Cleat and Coon. Of course, that was discounting the fact that when he put on his football uniform he became and integral part of a team and easily transformed him into a holy terror.

"Hey, 'Big Oak,' you gonna open up some holes for me aren't cha?"

"Shit, Coon, ask me something tough to do, just a little crack is all I need for your skinny ass to get through." Harold loved the nickname Coon christened him with back in the fifth grade. It was a hell of a lot better than "bug eyes" and it gave him a sense of power and strength.

Coon's shrill laughter rang out. "Shit, if anybody can it's you. All you have to do is fall forward like a big oak tree."

Gene joined the small group with a constrained look on his face. The junior quarterback wanted more than anything to have a good game on Friday night. He wanted to win, but even more important was his individual performance. He knew the stands would be full of college scouts, and the only way he was going to be able to attend college was by playing football. His parents always tried to give him more than they could afford, but college was out of the question without a scholarship. "I saw some weaknesses in their secondary. Did you see 'em too, Cleat?"

"Yeah, it looks to me like their backs are playing up *too* close to the line of scrimmage, if they try that against us we'll blow right by them."

"Yeah, I saw the same thing, and their linebackers are playing too tight…that should open up our flare pass to Coon."

Cleat punched him lightly on the arm; he could tell Gene was a little nervous. "Hell, Gene, don't worry about a thing, they can't stop the best passing attack in the whole damn state. Besides, if they try, Coon will run right by 'em."

A nervous laugh escaped from his mouth. "Yeah, I was thinking the same thing."

"Well fellows, Coon and I will see y'all tomorrow…we're heading home."

After their goodbyes the two long-time friends walked silently to the parking lot. When they reached the car, Coon was the first to speak.

"Cleat, you mind running me by my dad's house to check on him?" Coon had quit calling it "home" years ago.

"Sure, no problem buddy." It was a strange request from his friend. As far as he knew Coon hadn't spoken, or seen his father in over a year. The drive wasn't five minutes from where they sat.

"Cleat, another thing: I can fight my own battles."

"I know you can."

"Well, I just wanted you to know."

"I do."

"Cleat?"

"Yeah."

"Thanks."

"You bet, buddy."

A few minutes later they were pulling in front of Coon's ill-fated house. He watched his friend run across the overgrown lawn, side-stepping all of the strewn litter. When Coon bounded up the steps Cleat saw him lift a figure off of the front porch floor. Cleat's heart went out to his friend.

Five minutes later Coon jumped over the passenger door and settled in the shotgun seat. His gaze bore straight ahead.

"Everything okay?"

"Yeah...drunk as usual, but he's breathing. I put him to bed...before I left I asked if he would go to the game Friday night. He said, and I quote, 'Screw the game, and screw you.' What an asshole."

"I'm sorry, Coon. He loves you...he's just forgotten how to show it."

"Who're you trying to kid? That man has no conception of what the word love means. He's just a mean old man that doesn't give a shit about anybody, including himself. I don't care if I ever see his sorry, drunk-ass again. Fuck him."

The den lights were on when they pulled into the driveway. Cleat hoped his father had retired early. He'd had enough game talk for the night.

When the door opened Mrs. Davis was relieved to see her boys were home. She'd been worried they might stay out too late on a school night because of all the excitement over the game. She always made it a point to stay up until they were home safely. "I'm glad y'all are home at a reasonable hour. Are y'all hungry? In the kitchen you'll find a fresh apple pie straight out of the oven."

"Thanks mom that sounds great." Cleat leaned over and kissed her forehead.

Coon rubbed his stomach. "Yes ma'am Mama June, apple pie sure sounds good to me."

Mrs. Davis followed the boys into the kitchen to slice the desert; she'd seen first hand how they could butcher a pie or cake. "Y'all get a glass of milk and have a seat while I cut the pie."

"Have a piece and sit with us, mom."

"You know what. I think I'll do that very thing."

As she settled in a chair she placed her hands on theirs. "Sweethearts, you know how much I love y'all, but this old game is being ballyhooed way beyond its importance."

Cleat laughed. "Don't let dad hear you say that."

"Phooey. I'm not afraid of that old bear. It's a football game, that's all. No matter how it turns out, it's still, and always will be, young men playing nothing more than a game. Win or lose, you shouldn't make more of it than what it is. Just go out and have fun. Yes, I *know* how your father feels, but it's you boys I worry about. Y'all are barely eighteen for goodness sakes, your whole adult lives are ahead of you. Don't get caught up in all of the hoopla, and frenetic extravaganza going on in Lakewood. It's absolutely insane the amount of importance everyone has placed on this game. Y'all just go out and do your best, and remember nobody's life depends on the outcome."

Placing a fork on her empty plate Mrs. Davis sighed deeply and kissed them both on the cheek. "Now, y'all finish up and get some sleep. I'll have a big breakfast waiting for you in the morning." As she began to ascend the stairs she turned to face her boys. "Don't forget to rinse your glasses and brush your teeth."

In the master suite she disrobed in the bathroom so the light wouldn't disturb her husband. Before applying her nightly face cream she inspected her reflection in the lighted mirror for any new wrinkles. Satisfied there were none, she smiled, admiring the youthful face staring back at her. As yet she hadn't started showing her age. How many years she had left before it began she wasn't sure, but for now she was pleased.

Sitting on the edge of her bed listening to her husband snore, she had a fleeting vision of snatching her pillow and pounding him with it. She was still upset over his recent behavior with Cleat. The whole confrontation was so uncalled for. Cleat and his father seemed to be at odds with one another for as long as she could remember. If there was any humor to glean from the friction between the two it was because, in many ways, they were so much alike. Except for Cleat being demonstrative an unafraid to show his sensitivity, in fact, they were almost identical. Much more so than Randy, who was full of mischief and always happy-go-lucky, failing to take anything seriously.

Cleat was the only one in the family that never forgot her birthday. He always remembered every special occasion in the family. She recalled the time when he was seven-years-old, and took odd jobs all over the neighborhood to make enough money to buy her a new watch. He had overheard she lost hers at the country club while playing golf. His gift fell apart years ago, but she wore it with more pride than any expensive trinket she owned. In fact, it was still one of the most treasured possessions she kept in her jewelry box. His loving, caring sensitivity had created discontent with his father more than once.

The most crucial of times was when her husband took Cleat hunting with the new 410-gauged shotgun he'd bought him for his upcoming ninth birthday. When Randle spotted a squirrel crawling up a branch he handed the gun to Cleat, telling him to shoot the animal. Cleat took one look at the small, furry creature and refused.

His father insisted on Cleat shooting the squirrel by calling him hurtful names. Cleat threw the gun down yelling, "No," and started to cry. Disgusted, her husband brought him home and whipped him with a belt, calling him a "sissy," and screaming that no son of his was going to be a crybaby.

When she came onto the scene, the look in her son's eyes was heartbreaking. It was a moment in time she would never forget, nor would she ever totally forgive her husbands brutish behavior. Stepping between them, she pulled Cleat away from her husband. The words she spoke would be remembered forever, but never mentioned again. Angrily pointing her finger at Randle she shouted, "If you ever lay an angry hand on one of my children again I'll pack up and leave you, and you'll never see us again." It was the first and last time she'd threatened her husband in any capacity, it was also the last time any of the children were spanked. Sadly, she knew the whole ugly scene was still vividly imprinted in her son's mind as if it happened yesterday.

Cleat lay in his bed waiting patiently for Coon to return from the bathroom; once again, his friend had beaten him to the punch. The wait wouldn't be so bad if Coon didn't take the longest showers known to mankind. Thinking of Mandy a warmness spread through his body recalling how, after the homecoming dance, they'd gone parking on Lake Holly. Overhead the night sky was blanketed with thousands of glittering stars, while a full moon pierced the black water. The lakeside rendezvous started out innocently enough until their first kiss, soon after it became more intense. Closing his eyes, he thought of that special night; gradually he could feel her in his arms.

Cleat's tongue probed deep inside Mandy's mouth searching, exploring her cavity…his left hand trembled when he embraced her breast. He heard her murmur softly from his tender caresses as he slid his hand beneath her bra finding her flesh warm to his touch, while the pounding of her heart rushed to his ears.

When Mandy shifted her body to a more comfortable position her fore-arm accidentally came to rest on his hardened maleness. She moved her arm back and forth, pressing ever so lightly against his firmness. It excited her when she felt Cleat respond. Reaching down, she fumbled with his belt and the hook of his dress pants; fidgeting with the zipper, she drew it down to where she could slide the trousers to his knees.

Grappling with his underwear, Mandy was finally able to free him from the cramped confines. Mandy gently seized his member, fascinated by both its size and shape. Holding it softly in her grasp, she began to gently stroke his heated desire and slowly rub her thumb over its sensitive head. She knew mas-saging it this way would drive him crazy. Mandy laid her head on his chest, and watched through half-closed eyes as her hand tenderly fondled Cleat. It was like an out of body experience. Her hand seemed foreign, but yet she was aware that it was hers, and she was excited over the sheer pleasure her touch could generate. Absently, she listened to Cleat calling her name over and over as she increased her tempo.

Cleat squirmed in the seat experiencing soaring heights of passion. Placing his hand on the back of her head, he gently pressured her downward whisper-ing passionately, "Kiss me Mandy…oh God, please kiss me, I love you so much."

Only inches from Cleat's erection she knew what he wanted, and she was afraid of what he was asking. Frankly, she had never thought of doing such a thing, but she loved him so much the fear she held within was nothing com-pared to her desire of wanting to please him. Closing her eyes, she leaned forward, brushing her lips over the tip. It jumped from her initial touch, and she found it wet and sticky.

"Oh God, Mandy...I love you. Please kiss me my darling?"

Listening to his passionate pleas, her forbearance quickly vanished and was replaced with the fervor of her undying love and complete devotion to his desires. She ran her tongue lightly over the tip, tasting his secreted love. Wildly intoxicated over the zaniness of the moment, she opened her mouth fully, accepting the head of Cleat's penis. She felt him physically rise in the seat with a sharp intake of breath as she rolled her tongue around the hardness in her mouth.

"Sweet Jesus, I love you Mandy."

She felt his hand gently apply more pressure until she suddenly widened her mouth, receiving his full erection. Moving her head up and down, she held his sack in the palm of her hand and with her thumb and forefinger she firmly gripped the base of his shaft, pulling him to her. At first her movements were erratic, but soon she fell into a rhythm of drawing her lips from bottom to top as if trying to suck Cleat's whole body into hers. She was delirious with primal lust...she couldn't believe what she was doing, it was surreal, but she loved it because she was giving him so much pleasure, and giving him pleasure made their love that much stronger. She felt his fingers digging into the nape of her neck as she rapidly increased her tempo. She was lost in the throws of wantonness and desire so powerful she thought she might lose her sanity.

"Oh God...I'm going to come! Mandy I'm going to come!" he yelled, pulling her up to his chest. He squeezed her tightly as he ejaculated. His body convulsed with each spurt of his sperm. Cleat trembled from the erotic experience. Never had he been driven to the extent of losing complete control.

"Oh Mandy, I love you so much." He held her in his arms listening to her sniffles.

"Hold me tight, Cleat...please hold me tight...never let me go?"

"Don't cry, Mandy, please don't cry." Cleat brushed the locks of gold from her face, and kissed her sweetly on the cheek.

"I love you, Cleat...I love you more than life itself, but I feel so ashamed. I'm afraid you won't love me as much anymore."

"That's crazy talk Mandy, if there was any way I could love you more after tonight I would, but I already love you with all of my heart and soul. One day we'll marry and remember this night forever, and always."

"Oh Cleat, kiss me...kiss me my love."

Cleat tilted her chin and kissed her passionately, but she didn't respond in the way he'd expected. Breaking the kiss, he looked into her eyes. "What's the matter? Why are you acting so cold?"

"I...uh, I feel so cheap and ugly," Mandy whispered, holding a tissue to staunch her flow of tears.

"Mandy, you love me, and I love you. What happened tonight was something special, and I want to love you in the same way. There is nothing I wouldn't do to prove my love for you. I love you and I always will. We were meant to be together forever and ever."

"Oh Cleat," she whimpered between sobs, "I'm so in love with you I simply lose my breath just thinking of you. You are my life...my everything."

Cleat held her close. "Mandy, I'll always be yours. Nothing in this world will ever come between us."

"Would you do me a favor, Cleat?" she cooed.

"Sure sweetheart, just name it."

"Take me home now, but before you do, would you please pull your pants up? I think my parents would take offense if they saw you like that."

He'd completely forgotten he was sitting exposed. Cleat's face burned as he quickly squared himself away. Partially raising his fanny, he slipped his underwear on and followed with his pants. There was a sticky mess on his jockey shorts, and he also felt something wet on his shirt. Reaching under his seat, he retrieved the love towel and cleaned up as best he could...he still couldn't believe the magic moment.

"Wake up slowpoke...it's your turn." Coon grinned at his best friend.

"It's about time. You stayed in the water longer than Ester Williams, for God's sake."

"If she were in there, I wouldn't be standing here."

"Yeah, only in your dreams asshole." Cleat laughed just before Coon popped him on the butt with his wet towel. "Owww...you little shit. I'll get you for that, just when you least expect it."

Cleat stood in the tiled shower, letting the hot water pelt his face as the room filled with a steamy mist. The steady drumming was mesmerizing as he slipped into an almost unconscious state. Grabbing a bar of soap, he lathered his body feeling the previous tiredness being replaced with a calmness so relaxing it was difficult to move. Slowly his body responded to the therapeutic heat, he became so invigorated he started singing his rendition of "Don't Be Cruel." Grabbing a washcloth from the rack he put it under his nose to smell if it was fresh...it wasn't even *close*. Wrinkling his nose over the unpleasant aroma, he decided what the hell and began scrubbing his face vigorously.

He was freezing when he stepped out of the shower. Not caring whether the towel was fresh or not, he snatched it off the holder and began drying in earnest. When he left the bathroom a long column of steam followed him down the hallway. Stepping naked into the center of their bedroom, he roughly began drying his hair.

"Hey, do you know if we have company?"

"I don't think so. Why?"

"Good, because I thought somebody upstairs was killing the shit out of Elvis."

"Hell with you, Coon," Cleat laughed as he finished drying his hair.

"Christ Almighty, do you have to stand butt-ass naked with that 'dong' of yours hanging out. Shit, Cleat, I find that cruel and unusual punishment."

"Screw you, you're just jealous."

"Shit, I wouldn't want that monstrosity hanging between *my* legs."

"Like I said, you're just jealous." Grinning, Cleat pulled out a pair of yellow-stripped pajama bottoms and smiled at Coon lying in bed with a World History book in his lap. "Is this any better asshole?"

"Shit, Cleat, you couldn't pay me enough to put something like that on. You look like a damn queer."

"It's better than sleeping in that tight-ass underwear." Cleat scowled, crawling underneath a set of cool, crisp sheets.

"It ain't so tight, not everybody's hung like a donkey."

"Goodnight asshole."

"Goodnight, freak."

Mandy sat at her vanity combing through a thick lock of silky hair. With her free hand she held the final strand high overhead and wound it tightly around a pink roller. Holding the band close to her head, she picked up one of the bobby pins scattered over the marbled vanity top and pried it open with her teeth. She held her forefinger between the prongs and slipped the pin in place with the skill of an expert acquired through tedious years of ritualistic repetition.

Finally the chore was complete. With a sigh, Mandy dropped her hands in her lap and relaxed. Her arms ached, and her lower back felt as if it were on fire. Looking into her mirror she frowned at the sight of her protruding ears. They seemed to be sticking out more than usual. She absolutely hated her stupid ears, and she religiously stuck to her grandmother's tip of applying the use of scotch tape to hold them close to her head while she slept. Before turning off the makeup mirror she leaned forward, inspecting her skin for any sign of a blackhead or pimple. Although she never actually had one, still she held to the horror of *getting* one. Satisfied, she glanced at her bedroom windows to make sure the blinds were closed, seeing they were she methodically disrobed, and folded her clothes into a neat pile before discarding them into the laundry chute. She never gave it a thought as to why she folded her dirty clothes; unknowingly, their maid was dying to ask, but she never garnished enough courage to do so. She just wrote it off to the fact that white people were strange folks.

On the way to her closet, she stopped briefly in front of the beveled floor length mirror and stared at her nakedness. Her firm, shapely breasts and youthful pink nipples were highlighted by the milky whiteness of her skin that had been hidden from the Florida sun. The patch of golden triangle between her legs glimmered in the soft light.

"Oh Cleat," she purred. "I'm yours forever and always."

Mandy stepped into her closet in search of a gown, but as she reached for one she stopped midway; on second thought, she decided to sleep in the nude. Turning off the lights she made her way across the room by the glow of a nightlight. Sliding underneath the satin sheets, she laid there quietly thinking of Cleat and the true love they shared for each other. She felt her vagina twitch with the thought of him touching her. The sudden heat rushing through her body made her realize she was blushing, but she couldn't escape the vision of Cleat kissing her down there.

Her whole body shuddered thinking of that night and all the nights afterward, especially the weekend they pretended they were married and snuck off to the beach house when her parents were away for the weekend. Cleat told his parents he and Coon were going up to do some yard work and patch the old roof over the garage. The three of them drove to the Daytona, but where Coon disappeared afterward she never knew. Frankly, she really never gave it a thought until he showed up two days later when it was time to drive back to Lakewood.

It was the most wonderful, exhilarating weekend of her life. They'd done things together she'd never dreamed she had the courage to do, like skinny dipping, sun bathing in the nude between the sand dunes, and walking around the house completely naked...not a stitch on.

Their first night alone in the sanctity of the front bedroom they lay in bed listening to the surf crashing ashore. Truly, it was heaven on earth, for more reasons than one: it was the first time he kissed her down there. Never before had she felt such monumental emotions; they were so explosive and over-whelmingly uncontrollable it frightened her, yet at the same time she never wanted him to stop, not until she became so sensitive she couldn't stand it any-more. She remembered screaming, yelling, whimpering, begging, cursing unmentionables, and then crying. When and where she'd lost her modesty she hadn't a clue.

She had such mixed emotions over their lovemaking, at first she felt guilty, but then it was replaced with a love so deeply committed that nothing else mattered. So total was her love she wanted to shout it to the world for all to hear. She wanted everyone to know of the joy and happiness she and Cleat had given each other, but on the other hand she would die if her mother and father got wind of what she was doing.

Her father would be emotionally destroyed if he knew his little girl had gone all the way. She had reasons to believe her mother might be suspicious because of some of the uncomfortable conversations they'd had lately. Even so, no fingers were pointed and there were no accusations. Since then, Mandy had become overly cautious; as far as she knew Coon was the only one who knew and he wouldn't dare say a word...not from fear, but from his love and respect for them.

Mandy didn't know, but there was someone else that knew: the maid who did her laundry knew beyond a shadow of doubt, but it wasn't her place to say anything. Live and let live was her motto, and she was going to adhere to that philosophy as long as she lived and breathed. She just hoped Miss Mandy would be careful, but from the looks of her panties the girl sure didn't know what a rubber was for.

CHAPTER 4

Gene Reese tossed and turned, desperately trying to find elusive sleep, but everything he tried failed. Sleep just wouldn't come to the junior quarterback. He'd already fluffed his pillows several times to no avail. Nothing worked and the pressure mounted with every tick of his Big Ben alarm clock, which by now sounded like a bass drum pounding in his head.

Throwing back the covers he grabbed the antagonist off the nightstand; its illuminated dial indicated it was 1:15 a.m. He opened his bedroom door and placed it in the dimly lit hall. Leaving it there might make him late for school, but that would be better than being mentally and physically drained before the biggest game of his life. Closing the door quietly, he crawled between the covers hoping he'd found the answer for some blessed sleep, but he wasn't so lucky. Never had he spent a more restless night. When he got up the following morning and retrieved his clock, he saw that he was running thirty minutes late, he also calculated that he had only three hours sleep.

Audrey lay in bed thinking how Cleat and Mandy always seemed so happy when they were together. She couldn't prove it, but she had the sneakiest suspicion they were going *all the way*. There was a certain way they looked at each other when they thought no one else was around. She'd first noticed it at the end of last summer, but everybody she'd queried said she was crazy. Deep down she knew she was right, that's all that mattered; the rest of them could go to hell with their goody-two-shoes mentality.

She admitted to herself she was sick with envy, but she'd die a thousand deaths before letting anyone else know how she felt. Fact was, there wasn't one single person at school she had the slightest bit of interest in other than Cleat. Well, except for when she had a slight crush on her chemistry teacher, the young and horny Mr. Thompson.

She smiled, thinking about the time he dropped by her lab table to observe her work. Her lab partner was Bo, who was about as bright as the drab green paint on the wall. When *Horny Tom* saddled up beside her stool, she made sure that he would become astutely aware of her sexuality by nestling her elbow into his crotch ever so slightly. His body flinched, but didn't move away, and she knew he was hers when she felt his dick get as hard as a broomstick handle. The not so subtle flirtation progressed at a snail's pace for several weeks, just a little touchy-feely going on, sometimes with her butt, sometimes a slight brush of her hand, or pressing her boobs against him.

He was sort'a cute and he was always nice enough to her give her extra credit when she needed it. Toward the end of the first six weeks he called her in after class for a special assignment. When she walked in he had her go to the blackboard where some of the problems were written for the upcoming exam on Friday. As she studied them, he moved in close behind her and pressed against her rear end. She could feel him starting to get hard, and a couple of times she pushed firmly into the hardness with a wiggle or two. His hot breath was stale and smelled of cigarettes and coffee. Suddenly he moved away, saying she should continue with her work. She would never forget what happened next, and the sound of his lustful voice would remain in her nightmares for a long time to come.

"Audrey, come over here a minute."

As she was turning to face him, she somehow knew all wasn't well. What she saw scared her so badly she almost peed in her pants. *Horny Tom* was sitting in his chair with his pants dropped around his ankles masturbating. The color of his pubic hair was startling black and his legs were covered with so much hair they didn't look real. There was a large purple birthmark close to his crotch on his right leg. She stood in horrific shock; no words were forthcoming as she stared speechless with eyes wide-open and her mouth agape.

"Come over here and suck my dick, Audrey…suck it hard. You know you want to…I won't tell anybody."

Without uttering a sound Audrey ran from the room and she didn't stop running until she reached her car located in the far south parking lot. The next morning she caught Mr. Thompson in the hall and pulled him aside before he darted off. She informed him in a very low whisper that she expected an "A" in his classes for the rest of the year, or she'd go to the principal and tell him everything he'd done. He stuttered before gaining composure, then proclaimed he would deny her allegations, but she countered by describing his birthmark with an artist's eye for detail. Suddenly, Mr. *Horny Tom* reconsidered his denunciation. Chemistry, biology, and zoology became her favorite classes, because she rarely needed to attend them to maintain an impressive 4.0 grade point average.

Audrey's only thoughts about tomorrow's game were about herself, she wanted to look her best in front of the thousands of people crammed into the stadium. She didn't care one way or the other who won the game, or of her date with Gene afterward. If he thought she was going to let him into her panties, brother was *he* going to be disappointed. She might let him feel her boobs a little, no harm there, but anything else was completely out of the question. The only reason she was going out with a junior in the first place was because she liked his car.

On the plush southeast side of town not far from Cleat's house the Collier mansion sat alone atop several landscaped acres. Unless you knew where to look it could easily be overlooked from the road. Massive oaks surrounded the acreage, and if you followed the spiraling brick road leading to their house you would be impressed with the ancient southern spruce lining either side of the driveway. They were posted like sentinels guarding against intruders. If one stood quietly just below the second floor landing, you could hear Bo's throaty snore coming from his open window. Its sound blended well amidst the rustling of leaves as a cool autumn breeze whispered through the trees.

Bo lay in a peaceful slumber oblivious to the stressful emotions others were experiencing on the eve of gridiron combat. His monumental concern before he turned out the lights and fell asleep was if the maid was going to make the huge stack of blueberry pancakes for breakfast like she'd promised.

"Cleat...Coon, it's time to rise and shine boys. Today's the big day." Mr. Davis stood in the doorway clapping his hands. He smiled as Coon popped out of bed fully awake while Cleat slowly uncurled from a fetal position, pulling the covers over his head. He could remember from year's gone bye a towheaded, barefoot boy wearing a pair of old Levis rolled up to his knees carrying a cane pole over his shoulder raring to go fishing. He felt a twinge of guilt, realizing how little time he'd actually spent with Cleat during his younger years, but dammit, there hadn't been enough time to do so, not if he was going to build the firm to where it would provide financial security for the family.

There had been too many seventy and eighty-hour weeks that added up to months, and even years, away from his youngest son. Now that they were secure, and he finally had freedom to be with his family it seemed no one cared, especially Cleat. He was actually closer to Coon than his own flesh and blood. How it came to be he wasn't sure, and the more he tried to become domestically involved the more everyone became estranged. Maybe he'd paid too high a price for success.

Mr. Davis resisted the impulse of reaching down with loving hands to roust his son out of bed. He wanted to express his love for him, but he couldn't force himself to do so. For him to outwardly reveal emotions of love and compassion were completely foreign to him. He desperately wanted a closer relationship with his son, but he just didn't know how to achieve the father-son companionship he desired. In his heart he felt it was too late; there just didn't seem to be a strong enough foundation between the two of them like he had with Randy. He wished now he would've made it a top priority to sit with his younger son and explain the circumstances that circumvented him from being around more often, but something always interfered with the one-on-one he needed with Cleat.

Cleat and Coon walked into the breakfast area chattering about the forthcoming game; the whole family was present, minus Randy. After a round of pleasantries they sat down to feast upon a meal fit for a king. His mother and grandmother spared no effort in preparing the food. There were buttermilk pancakes, eggs, bacon, biscuits, orange juice, and an assortment of fruit.

Sissy smiled at her two heroes. "Are y'all nervous about the game tonight?"

Coon placed an affectionate hand on top of her head and gave it a tussle. "Naw, we got everything under control, so don't worry your pretty little head. Those boys ain't got a chance."

Mrs. Davis flinched. "John, please don't use improper grammar. We've raised you better. You know how I hate slang."

"For goodness sakes, June, leave the boy alone. I hear 'ain't' at the firm and in the courthouse by some of the most influential people in town."

"No sir, she's right, and I'm sorry Mama June. I'll try not to slip again." Coon smiled at Mrs. Davis.

"Thank you son, you know I only correct you for your own good."

"Yes ma'am, I know."

Cleat laughed. "Mother, Coon's been bringing home straight A's in English since the first grade, I think he's going to be just fine without any tutoring."

"I know he has, and that's just the point Mr. smarty pants. If he didn't know better I wouldn't correct him. It's just not a good habit to fall into, not everybody you meet will know whether you're using it as a way to express your-self, or if you're just plain ignorant."

Putting the last bite of pancake away Cleat looked at Coon. "Hey little brother, I've done ate, and I ain't gonna wait on you to finish."

Mrs. Davis slapped her son on the arm. "You rascal, you said that just to rile me. What am I to do with you two?"

When they pulled into the student section of the parking lot it was only a third full. Most kids didn't have an automobile of their own to drive. Sometimes their parents let them borrow the family car to drive to school, but most times not. Cleat eased into the first available spot near the gymnasium. The two friends hopped out of the convertible, and once they reached the cov-ered walkway they headed to separate classes.

Much of that morning was spent watching for the clock to strike twelve o'clock, signaling lunchtime for the whole school. Normally it was broken into two shifts, but because the pep rally was scheduled for one o'clock they changed the schedule so the entire student body would be able to attend. After the pep rally school was officially out.

When the clock struck high noon football mania exploded into the halls in the form of screaming teenagers rushing straight to the cafeteria. By the time the unruly mob reached the double doors the football team was almost through with their early lunch.

Cleat sat toying with his unfinished meal. A frown was etched across his forehead as a thousand thoughts raced through his mind. His left hand uncon-sciously clutched the knot in the pit of his stomach.

"Hey Cleat!" Bo called out. Failing to get a response, he roughly nudged Cleat's shoulder. "You gonna finish that steak, because if you ain't I'd like to have it?"

Cleat looked into Bo's chubby face, a clump of mashed potatoes was stuck in the corner of his mouth and a stream of steak juice was dripping down his chin.

"Jesus Christ, Bo, you're a human garbage disposal."

"I can't help it, Cleat. They don't feed me enough around here."

"Shit, nobody can feed your fat ass enough."

"Aw come on, I ain't that bad, besides I'm a growing boy." Bo's eyes never left Cleat's plate. "Well, what do ya say, are you gonna play with it or eat the damn thing?"

"Go ahead you big ox, you can have it. Be my guest." Cleat shoved his chair from the table and went to find Mandy. Unfortunately, the hallways were so crowded the only way he would've been able to spot her was to accidentally bump into her. Seeing some of his fellow teammates heading toward the gym, he joined their pilgrimage of horsing around, thankful for the chance to release some of his pent up tension.

Entering the air-conditioned gym, they took their seats in the roped off section of the bleachers. Cleat found Coon sitting halfway up reserving a space for him. Within minutes of their arrival the place was filled to capacity. A constant roar of excited students rumbled through the confines of the enclosed gymnasium. He looked across the way where the Booster Club was seated in hopes of seeing his father among the overzealous adults waving pom-poms and banners. Cleat wasn't surprised by his absence. His father was a major contributor monetarily, but subsequent to that he was a member by name only. The three years Randy played varsity his dad was the president of the boosters and the family attended every gala event.

Coach Dunn walked over to the podium center court and picked up the microphone, an electronic screech quieted the crowd. After a brief synopsis glorifying their undefeated season, he began introducing the coaches and players. One by one the players were invited to join him on the floor until there was only one solitary soul seated in the cordon-off area.

Cleat wondered how was it possible his name was overlooked. Hell, their names were in alphabetical order, and he should've been the fifth or sixth senior to be announced. He felt the heat of embarrassment from all the stares directed his way, but he sat quietly as a gradual murmur rolled through the bleachers. He sat squirming in his seat perspiring profusely; his palms were wet and the sweat on his upper lip was a continuing annoyance. Staring at his teammates gathered below, he had to quell the overwhelming desire to run down the steps and join them. He was reminded of the painful memories when he hid under the darkened stands clutching his best friend while they cried seeking solace from one another.

"Students, as you can see we have a player yet to be introduced, and that is Cleat Davis. If not for him, we wouldn't be gathered here today. He's been our leader, our captain, and without him all of this wouldn't have been possible. Cleat is the most superb athlete I've ever had the pleasure to coach, and I will forever be indebted to him for allowing me the privilege of being called his coach. This young man has given his all to this school, and his leadership has carried this team to our championship game tonight. Along the way he has shattered state receiving records with twenty-seven touchdowns and ninety-three receptions. In doing so he gained two thousand one hundred and seventeen yards...an incredible accomplishment. I wanted this opportunity to announce to one and all that Cleat Davis is the first ever from our school to be selected as a member of the National High School All-American Football Team." Coach Dunn had to scream above the applause for Cleat to come on down.

Thrilled over the honor, Cleat walked up to Coach Dunn and shook his outstretched hand. He couldn't help but wonder how proud his dad would have been if he had accepted his invitation to attend. When Coach Dunn handed him the mike, he was surprised.

"Go ahead, son...it's your day."

Cleat could hear the crowd yelling, "Speech, speech," as he held the mike by his side. He was really nervous standing in front of the student body...even his teammates had joined the madness. With the hesitancy of a small child meeting Santa Claus for the first time, he raised the microphone and with a stutter amplified through the sound system he began:"I...I...uh, would like to give all of the credit to my teammates and the best damn...uh, I mean best coaching staff ever assembled."

Classmates and teammates alike laughed over his slip of words, even the faculty and coaches joined in. Embarrassed, he continued, "Without them this would not have been possible. I'm thankful to have teammates I can call friends, and coaches that I admire and respect. We've been blessed to have coaches who believe in us and who taught us to believe in ourselves *and* the meaning of teamwork. Their teachings will follow us for life, and wherever that might take us I will be a better person for having known them. Last, but not least is the faculty, the school, our classmates, and our town. Without your support we would've never been able to achieve goals far beyond our dreams.

In doing so you made us a better team and more importantly, better individuals. These young men who stand before you are honored by your accolades." He turned to face his teammates, "We thank you. We thank you all." With a raised fist he hollered, "Spartans rule."

The student body rushed from the stands screaming and hollering. Like a massive tidal wave they poured onto the court and lifted Cleat to their shoulders and rode him out of the gym. Frantically looking for help, he noticed Coach Dunn and several other players in the same predicament. While riding their shoulders through the hallways he could hear hundreds of voices chanting over and over: "We're number one! We're number one." It was one of the most exhilarating experiences of his life.

Mandy didn't follow the crowd; once the gymnasium was emptied she stood with tears flowing freely down her cheeks. Wiping them with the palms of her hand, she reached in her purse for a tissue and staunched the flow of mucus dribbling from her nose. *My god,* she thought, *I love him so much. He is my life...he is the breath I take. Without Cleat in my life I fear I shall die.*

At the conclusion of the pep rally everybody that was anybody met early that afternoon at Pip's. This particular drive-in restaurant was the gathering place of the chosen ones; although there were exceptions to the rule, which in most cases were the school athletes. The majority of the clientele were from the Southside of town. Of course, there were no written laws to this edict, but for years it was understood and observed by the outsiders that this was where the so-called elite came to roost.

Today was special. It was THE DAY, and all observances were flagrantly cast aside, everyone was welcome. Pip's parking lot was overflowing, even the entrances were blocked and there wasn't a parking spot to be found for blocks. Inside the teen hangout was no different; there wasn't a chair, booth, or stool that wasn't occupied. Only standing room was available, and there was very little of that.

Cleat and Mandy were sitting with Coon and several others in a crowded booth sipping on cherry cokes enjoying an afternoon of freedom when Bo Collier decided to join them. Bo's dad, Doctor Clayton Collier, was a prestigious surgeon and one of the founders of the medical clinic in town. The whole family was snobbish, except for Bo. He was a constant embarrassment to his family, but he really didn't give a shit. One couldn't help but like Bo's easy manner. Playing center, he was one of the biggest in the conference standing six-foot-two and weighing two hundred and sixty pounds. (Albeit depended on *when* he weighed in.) On top of this mountain of flesh sat a small baby face looking as much out of place as a moustache on the Mona Lisa. This little giant with chubby cheeks and childlike whims seemed incapable of hurting a fly. He was like a cuddly teddy bear yearning for love and attention.

When he slipped on a uniform the transformation became nothing short of scary. In afternoon practices second and third stringers tried to avoid his wrath, but the watchful eyes of the coaches were aware of the maneuvering, and made sure they all had their turn with Bo.

"Six hours to go and counting! Man, I can hardly wait to take the field." He stood rubbing his meaty hands together spraying a mouthful of cheeseburger as he spoke.

"Yeah, Bo, all of us feel the same way. It's been a long week."

"If ya ask me it's more agonizing than waiting on spring-break. Hey, that reminds me, are we all going to Daytona again?"

"You bet we are."

"All right...see y'all later, I'm gonna get another cheeseburger."

Audrey sidestepped Bo's girth, barely avoiding being squashed. "Hey gang, how's everybody doing? Cleat, scoot over and let me squeeze in. There's not a seat left anywhere."

"Sure Audrey, come on and sit with us." Cleat was able to move just a few inches on the red vinyl seat, but it seemed enough for Audrey as she plopped herself in Cleat's lap, pretending not to notice the fire in Mandy's eyes. Slipping an arm around his neck, she smiled at Mandy. "I hope you don't mind me borrowing your boyfriend for a few minutes. Don't worry I'll be real careful with him." She laughingly tossed her hair.

"Oh, I don't mind Audrey. Cleat's big enough to take care of himself, and besides, he has impeccable taste and knows what's best for him."

"Well, as far as one's palate is concerned, scramble eggs on toast is quite nice, but caviar is divine." Squirming further into Cleat's lap, she slyly winked with the intent of infuriating Mandy even more than she already had...mission accomplished.

"That's true, Audrey, but I also hear too much caviar tends to make one nauseous." Mandy was seething with explosive anger.

"Must be an old wives tale, because no one can ever have too much of a good thing…isn't that right, Cleat?"

Cleat sat speechless, not wanting to be any part of what was going on.

"Where's Gene, I thought the two of you were dating?" Mandy's smile was false and catty.

"We did for awhile, but I broke up with him on Monday. I found him to be boorishly juvenile. After all we'll be off to college in the fall and he'll still be in high school. I thought it best to hurt him now instead of later…don't you think?"

"Personally, I don't think breaking up with him before *the* game was the wise thing to do, but that's not any of my business."

"No…really its not, beside with Cleat playing there's nothing to worry about." Audrey rumpled the top of Cleats head, "Isn't that right handsome?" Audrey flung her hair seductively.

Brushing Audrey's hair out of his face, he decided it was time to leave before all hell broke loose. The constant rubbing of Audrey's hidden hand on his inner thigh was distracting to say the least, and it was making him uncomfortable in more ways than one. "Mandy, Coon and I've got to go. We have to look over some of the new offensive sets and a dozen other things. If you want me to give you a ride home, it's got to be now."

"Oh Cleat, so soon? And just when I was getting to know you better." Audrey grooved her butt into Cleat's crotch and slid from his lap. She intentionally let her hand fall between his legs as she stood up. No one saw the slight of hand, but Cleat sure felt it.

When the three of them were outside, Cleat put his arm around Mandy as they weaved their way through the crowded parking lot to his car. He felt her slender body trembling with rage. The touch of her skin was so hot it felt like she had a fever. At the car he opened the door, and held his hand out preventing her from entering. "Mandy, you shouldn't let her get to you like that. You…"

"Don't you dare tell me how to act, or feel, around that bitch in heat," Mandy screamed, pulling away from Cleat. Her face was aflame. A blood vessel high on her forehead, almost hidden beneath a soft yellow curl, was pulsating wildly. The tears she'd been fighting to restrain suddenly burst forth, rushing down her flushed cheeks. Her hands sprang to her face to control the sobs of doubt and frustration. She accepted Cleat's outstretched arms and threw herself into the safety of his protective chest, seeking warmth and security from the most important person in her life.

"It's all right, Mandy. I love only you and I always will… honey please don't cry." Cleat put a hand on the back of her head and patted tenderly.

"Oh, Cleat…I…I just can't stand her. She…she makes me feel so inadequate, almost as if I were a child. She's mean and hateful."

"Honey, I'm sorry, but you have nothing to worry about. I'm yours alone, to have and to hold."

Coon felt out of sorts, but there was no place for him to hide. Yearning for obscurity, he hopped into the backseat and tried to shrink into the fabric, but he couldn't shield himself from being privy to the love shared between Cleat and Mandy. He was starving for the kind of relationship they had. What they shared together was sacred. He wondered what it would be like to have someone as beautiful and compassionate as Mandy to love him the way she adored Cleat.

Coon shook his head at the thought of being so lucky. He had to arrest a chuckle of sadness rising in his throat. Hell, all he needed to do was look in a mirror to realize that would never come to be, not in a million years. But hopefully someday he'd find someone to love and cherish him…hopefully. Granted, she might not be as pretty as Mandy, but what the hell, he wasn't as handsome as Cleat…not by any stretch of imagination.

Mandy sat close to Cleat resting her head on his shoulders. A rock-in-roll song was blaring on the radio but she was lost in thought and oblivious to any outside interference. *Audrey, God-in-heaven I detest her very being. I'm so angry for letting her get to me. Why do I let her control my emotions? She's always playing mind-games, and dammit, she enjoys doing it. Was it the fear of Audrey's unbridled lust for Cleat? Audrey certainly didn't try to hide her desires. Am I'm being unfair to Cleat? Isn't true love supposed to be based on trust and virtuous commitment? God, do my thoughts continue to raise doubts? I know that Cleat loves me more than anything in this world. He's compassionate, loving, tender, sensitive, and caring. He's everything a girl could want and dream of, so why am I so insecure when it comes to Audrey?*

"A penny for your thoughts beautiful." Cleat asked, but when he didn't get a response he nudged her with an elbow and repeated, "A penny for your thoughts beautiful."

"Wh…What?"

"I said a penny for your thoughts."

"Oh…I was thinking how lovely the day is. I love this time of year. The days are warm and the nights are clean and crisp. Christmas is near and the holiday season with all of its pageantry is simply breathtaking."

"Not as breathtaking as you."

Mandy squeezed Cleat's arm, "Cleat, you are so sweet. Please don't ever change from who you are."

Puzzled, Cleat asked, "What in the world does that mean?"

"Nothing, I just love the way you are, and I don't want anything to ever change."

"My love for you is constant. You are in my thoughts daily, and without you I would be lost."

Coon sat in the backseat wishing he had a pencil and paper to take notes. If he could remember half the shit Cleat said over the years he would never have girl problems. Cleat had it all, good looks, charisma, intelligence, athleticism, and an endless line of bullshit. He was the proverbial "Big Man on Campus" and those of the female persuasion literally oozed over him. Coon never doubted Cleat's love for Mandy, but Cleat's biggest problem was: he couldn't keep his pecker in his pants. Coon wasn't jealous over Cleat's attributes, but he was honest enough to admit there was a tinge of envy. Most definitely there were fringe benefits in being Cleat's best friend and sidekick. Coon received the rejects that didn't meet Cleat's high standards. When Coon was able to keep morose thoughts of his drunken father *and* the drudgeries of his previous childhood from clouding his mind…life was damn good.

After dropping Mandy off Coon remained in the backseat wondering how many girls like Mandy walked the face of the earth…he concluded very few. When the car rumbled into the driveway Coon sprang out of the car and noticed the garbage cans out front. "I'll bring the cans in and see you inside."

"Okay, thanks, I'll be in the kitchen pouring us some juice."

Dragging the empty cans back to the side of the house, he heard a screeching sound from high above. A hawk was in a desperate flight from two attacking sparrows that were darting in and out, relentlessly chasing the much larger bird in a late afternoon sky. Their fierce onslaught was seemingly tireless against the mighty bird of prey. They banked left and right, alternating turns while swooping down onto the hawk's exposed flanks. The boldness of the smaller birds' constant harassment astounded Coon as he watched the tiny aggressors battle in the sky. He was unable to tear his eyes from the aerial dog-fight. Suddenly, without warning the hawk singled out one of its miniature tor-mentors and dove with talons exposed, striking the startled bird a deathblow. In the blink of an eye the sparrow that was once full of bravado and defiance was falling silently to earth. There was no attempt to regain altitude from the lifeless form as it spiraled downward on its final flight.

Following the forlorn descent of its life mate, the lone surviving sparrow cried out remorsefully. Several times it flew close with wings flapping, trying to revitalize its companion, but the small battle torn body continued its plummet until it ended abruptly. After circling overhead for one *final* farewell the sur-vivor swiftly returned to its chicks before other predators devoured the results of their union. Now there was only one left to protect the nest, but she was willing to sacrifice her life to do so.

A stabbing pang struck Coon in the heart as he witnessed the sparrow's lifeless body fall from the sky; he shuddered from a chill traveling down his spine. He could see and hear the hawk as it circled above its victory. The first shades of doubt entered his mind about tonight's game. Was there an analogy to be drawn from witnessing the encounter of the larger bird being victorious over its smaller adversary? Could this be an omen?

His father claimed there was Indian blood running through his veins from his mother's side. He was told his great grandmother was a full-blooded Sioux who was forced to relocate in Florida during the late 1800s. Was the story his father told him the truth? And, if it was, should he worry about the gloom that suddenly veiled his confidence. He'd quit believing in his father a longtime ago, so why should he start believing now? Besides, his father also claimed the fam-ily was a distant relative of Harry S. Truman. That ought to tell you something about the crazy old drunk.

When Coon stepped through the kitchen side door Cleat greeted him by throwing his arms around his shoulders. "Hey…what's come over you man? You look like you've seen a ghost. Christ, you look a million miles away. Snap out of it, little brother. I need you by my side tonight if we're gonna kick some ass."

"Don't worry your pretty self about me, hotdog. I'll be there watching your backside as usual." He already felt better just being near his friend.

With juice in hand they took the stairs two at a time, heading to their room for one last look at the new plays Coach Dunn inserted into the game plan. While Cleat was in the bathroom Coon laid in bed thinking how lucky he was that the Davis's had taken him in as one of the family. It was unimaginable how different his live would've been living with his father.

He was a little kid when his mother ran off with another man. That had been almost twelve years ago and, as far as he knew, they hadn't heard from her since. There was absolutely no image of his mother left behind, or any of her family for that matter. It was like she never existed, everything was either thrown away or destroyed that could prove she ever existed...except for him.

His father had been an engineer on the railroad for twenty years, eight before Korea, and nine afterward. It was surprising to everyone that he had lasted as long as he did. He barely made it to his twenty-year retirement; if they hadn't counted his time in the army toward his longevity he might not have.

For a brief period after his mom left it wasn't so bad, but within two years his father sank into the deepest of depressions and became a stranger. Life held no meaning and the only way his father could escape the pain was in the form of a bottle. Coon vaguely remembered the rail yard and locomotives, and he couldn't for the life of him remember his mother. It was just as well, because if she didn't care any more about him than to run off...then good riddance. Of course, he hadn't felt that way when he was younger, back then it hurt more than he would readily admit.

His dad's heavy drinking accelerated to a point that nothing mattered except where his next drink was coming from. There were times when his father disappeared for days at a time, leaving Coon without out food or supervision. City utilities were turned off for weeks on end. Occasionally his father's old boss would help out when times got worse than acceptable, but nothing compared to the day they were evicted from their split-level, middle class home.

Coon was eight-years-old when the sheriff arrived with the eviction notice, and the whole neighborhood turned out to watch and applaud their departure. It was a day he would remember forever. They moved five times in two years, each dwelling was of lesser stature until they ended up at the shack his father currently called home.

Coon had it rough as a child, but he never complained to anyone. Instead, he shouldered the responsibility like a trooper. He went about his business of taking on small jobs to earn enough money to survive, there wasn't a job he wouldn't do if he was offered the chance. It didn't take him long to learn if he turned over his meager earnings to his father there wasn't going to be any food to eat. Most often what they ate came straight from the can, and sometimes he afforded the luxury of heating it over a can of Sterno. He quit buying that when his father drank two cans and ended up in the hospital for two weeks. Strange, he didn't realize he would miss his father until the welfare workers came for him. In the end, he narrowly avoided them. He spent those days in hiding until his father's release.

Over the course of years his father made valiant attempts to overcome his affliction, but their brevity was sporadic. During those episodes when he was sober they had long wonderful talks full of dreams of being together as father and son. The brief periods of sobriety provided the love and affection Coon had been deprived of for so long. He absorbed those moments of normalcy as thoroughly as a dry sponge would take to water.

Unfortunately, the insanity always returned with more intensity than before. One particular night after a two-day binge his father came home crazed with alcohol. He found Coon in the kitchen eating a can of cold beans, and without warning he began beating his son with closed fists and throwing him around the room like a rag doll. At the time Coon was a frail, malnourished nine-year-old, but he was agile enough to grab a cast iron skillet from the counter and slam it upside his father's head. The kinetic force sent his father to the floor in an unconscious heap. Coon never called the shack home again. Shortly afterward his new residence became the Davis household, which he now lovingly called home.

"You boys come on down…supper's ready," Mama Marie called up the stairway in heavily French-accented English. She'd met Cleat's grandfather in Paris during WW I, and became a war bride. She started teaching Cleat her native language before he was able to speak in a sentence, and when Coon joined the family he was quickly indoctrinated into the curriculum as well.

Cleat and Coon could smell the aroma of steak as they were racing one another down the stairwell. It wasn't even five o'clock yet…a full two hours before the family normally ate, but tonight was special…they had to be at the stadium by six o'clock.

Mr. Davis greeted them at the bottom of the stairs. "Son, we heard the news, I want you to know how proud we are of you earning such an honor. It speaks for itself in volumes."

"Thanks dad."

"I would've been there, but I was due in court on a serious matter."

"I understand, dad. It's okay, really."

Sissy bounced into the room, beaming with pride. "Well everybody, isn't it wonderful to be related to Lakewood's living legend? I'm the envy of my junior high school. I've even had the privilege of signing autographs, and you can't imagine how many new girlfriends I have who want to come spend the night."

"Aw, come on Sissy don't start."

"Now-now big brother, humility doesn't suit you. You should be strutting around like your usual self. I mean, for goodness sakes, you're a celebrity."

"Well, I don't feel like one, and I wish you wouldn't tease me about it."

"You're wrong Cleat, I'm not teasing. It makes me proud to be your sister. Every girl should be so lucky to have a brother like you." Throwing her arms around her brother she planted a kiss on the cheek. "I love you, Cleat."

His arms flapped helplessly at his side. He was unsure of what to do with his sister hanging onto his neck. Awkwardly he folded his hands around her lower back, and lifted her off the floor. "I love you, too."

"Hey, who am I, nobody?"

"Oh Coon, you're every girl's dream…don't you know that by now?" Sissy wet her lips before throwing her arms around Coon and gave him *more* than a brotherly kiss. It landed on his cheek catching the corner of his mouth. Her heart fluttered when he let go of her.

CHAPTER 5

A udrey Wellington sat at her vanity thinking of Cleat as she applied the finishing touches of makeup. In her heart of hearts she knew she'd be better for Cleat than Mandy. The mere thought of him heated her body with passion. She could imagine his strong, powerful arms wrapped around her, feeling his hardened desire pressed against her pelvis. When he wasn't with Mandy she often caught him staring at her with a look that led her to believe there was more than a passing interest in what she had to offer.

She thoroughly enjoyed the reputation of being a big tease. Her voluptuous body drove the boys crazy and she maximized the affect every chance that presented itself. All the boys she dated at Lakewood were fraught full of desire with one thought in mind, but none of them got further than a little feel here and there. Pitiful attempts of less than artful adolescent seductions left them wholly unsatisfied. If only once she could be alone with Cleat, things would be different.

No one, not even her mother, would ever know what happened that summer of her fifteenth year. She was too afraid and humiliated to tell anyone. It started out as a wonderful vacation, two weeks at the beach was always planned for early August before school started. This trip to the shore turned out to be something all together tragic for a young girl in search of maturity.

She met Tommy on their second day at Anna Maria Island while sunbathing on the pool deck in front of their motel. He was vacationing with three friends from the University of Florida; they'd just finished their last summer session and were partying before fall classes. He was tall, athletic, and handsome. To her, he was the most gorgeous thing she'd ever seen, and he'd taken an interest in her. Two days later in his motel room Tommy seduced her. She made it easy for him, because she had mind made up the first day he was the one she wanted to go all the way with. He was so heavenly divine.

After their first sexual encounter she had gone to his room again and again, experiencing new delights each time. It was more wonderful than she ever dreamed it would be. She felt so grown up and Tommy was so sweet and gentle. The hours they spent together were full of laughter and happiness until one painful, horror-filled afternoon when it all came to an end.

Audrey shuddered at the memory of what happened to her on that dreadful afternoon three years ago. It started out uneventful; nothing really unusual except Tommy and his friends had been drinking beer most of the day. What took place later in the day created nightmares that would last a lifetime.

She and Tommy were in his motel room with the drapes drawn, making love for the second time that afternoon. She was on top of his naked body pressing her hands against his bare chest as she rose and plunged above him. Suddenly the door burst open and Tommy's three classmates entered the room, locking the door behind them. Leaping from bed, she wrapped the top sheet around her nakedness and stumbled against the far wall trembling with fear.

Their wet bathing suits were dripping on the carpet as they stood leering at the young girl trying to cover herself. They drooled over the image of her servicing Tommy with zestful enthusiasm.

"Hey, don't be so shy," one of the boys called out, snatching the sheet from Audrey's grasp.

"Holy shit, would you look at that body!" The largest of the three exclaimed as he watched Audrey back into the corner trying to conceal her privates with her arms and hands.

"Shit, you've been having it too good Tommy boy, it's time to share what you've been bragging about." The skinny one with acne smiled as he pulled his suit off, exposing a full erection.

"Tommy," Audrey whimpered, fighting back her tears. "Please make them go away!"

"Oh hell, they're not going to hurt you. All they want is to have a little fun."

"Please no...don't do this. Leave me alone...I want to go now...please," Audrey whined as she sunk to the carpeted floor and closed her eyes. She felt fingernails digging into the flesh of her arms as she was lifted from the floor and thrown roughly onto the bed. Someone was trying to pry her legs apart as she thrashed about attempting to break free. Her valiant effort was useless, there were too many hands forcing her down.

"Noooo...please let me go! I won't tell, honest. Tommy, make them stop." She turned her head to the side when the person above her tried to kiss her. A husky voice smelling of stale beer whispered in her ear, telling her it was going to be okay and not to fight. In one last, futile attempt she freed one of her hands and blindly lashed out striking the boy above her across the face with her sharp nails. Immediately blood bubbled to the surface from a long, ugly scratch that raked across festering pimples.

"You freaking slut!" Pimple-face hollered, backhanding her across the face. "Goddamn you!" he bellowed, slapping her again. This time he caught her in the mouth, causing her lips to swell. A trickle of blood seeped from the corners of her lips. "You try that again I'll bash your face in you fuckin' whore." He squeezed her battered face. "Be still or I'll scar you for life."

Audrey was more frightened than she had ever been in her life. The blows she suffered to her face were the first time she had ever been struck by anyone or anything. In a trance-like state of fear she laid perfectly still as each took his turn. She was oblivious to time and their grunting sounds as they lustfully spilled their seed into her soiled loins. Praying it would be over soon, she squinted through half-closed eyes to see who was using her now.

"Oh my God...Tommy!" He was on top of her, painfully gripping her breasts as he raced for sexual gratification. His face was frightfully contorted with crusty, saliva caked in the corners of his mouth. She closed her eyes to the ghoulishness and cried. She heard a muffled scream escape from his throat as a warm liquid splashed onto her face and breasts. Her eyes squinted tighter as she stifled a scream. The bed shifted slightly when Tommy left to join his friends laughing and waiting across the room.

"Shit man, you should've done it in her mouth."

"Yeah man, I'm about ready for a blowjob. I sure don't want to stick my dick in her now, not after we loaded the bitch up."

Searching by touch alone, she found a spread and covered herself like a cocoon. It was dark underneath the covers and the smell of sweat and sex was suffocating, but she hadn't the courage to uncoil from her fetal position to face the ugliness. She heard the door open and Tommy call out for her to be gone before they returned, and not to come back. The final sound she heard was their laughter as the door closed behind them. Afterwards, only her cries filled the silence.

Bo pushed his large frame inside the breakfast nook. On the table in front of him was a double-layered vanilla cake covered with chocolate icing still warm from the oven. He sat the carton of milk down and sliced the cake in half. Belaying a fork he tore off a huge piece and crammed it into his mouth. With chocolate covered fingers he lifted the carton of milk and washed it down with one huge gulp. Wiping his mouth with the back of his hand, he reached for the remaining piece of cake.

"Bolivar Nathan Collier, what on heavens earth have you done?" Mrs. Collier yelled over the louvered café doors separating the kitchen from the hallway leading to the den. "Jasmine made that cake for my Saturday afternoon bridge club, and now she's gone till Monday. If you weren't so big I'd blister your fanny."

Bo grinned, picturing his socially conscious mother wielding a belt chasing him around the house. Purposely smacking his lips, he stuck each chocolate covered digit in his mouth, licking them clean. Grabbing the chocolate-smeared milk carton, he raised it slowly to his lips and chug-a-lugged what was left. "Ohhh ma, and here I thought it was meant for me."

Eleanor Collier cringed over his reference to her as "ma." He was well aware that she hated to be called anything but "mother" by her children. How could she have raised this child to have such terrible table manners? They were a family of prominence and Bolivar was a disgrace to society. She hated to admit her son made her physically ill. She was so thankful her young daughter Sandra was prim and proper, and an image of herself. "Bolivar, your appetite will be ruined after consuming so much cake."

Bo's answer was a loud belch originating from deep within an enormous cavern. It rumbled upward with tremendous momentum until it burst forth in a loud, thunderous explosion that shook the windowpanes overlooking the Tuscan terrace. "Heck ma that little bit of cake ain't gonna put a dent in my hunger."

"Bolivar, your table manners are deplorable, but compounding them with the language of an illiterate is something I will simply not tolerate. Your behavior is degrading and embarrassing. You have been raised above such commonness. If your little sister takes after you, I'll just be beside myself. I would never survive the humiliation. I'm glad the "Doctor" isn't present to witness his son acting like a slovenly buffoon."

"Ma, I don't think you have to worry about Sandy. She's only thirteen and the spitting image of you. She's so prissy she cries when she has to wipe the shit off her ass."

"Bolivar...how dare you speak that way...I will not have such language spoken in my presence, *or* in my house."

Sliding out of the booth, stooping apish-like, swinging his arms low to the floor, he approached his mother. When he towered above her petite form he placed his meaty hands around her fragile arms and lifted her high into the air. Staring into her startled face he said, "Ma you're such a prude."

"Put me down this very instant, Bolivar. You just wait until your father comes home and hears of this."

"What! He's not here?"

"Of course not, your father left this morning for a weekend medical seminar in New York."

"Nobody told me he wasn't going to be here for the game."

"What game?"

"The football game tonight mother. We're playing for the state championship for Christ's sake."

"Hush your blasphemy!" Mrs. Collier pondered a moment, "Oh, I think I remember someone mentioning something about a game at the country club luncheon, but it didn't register that you were playing in it. I thought y'all were through playing weeks ago."

"We will be tonight, mother." He set his mother down and left the room.

Nancy Dunn sat at the dinning room table quietly watching her husband toy with his plate of lasagna. The only thing he had eaten was the bowl of fresh garden salad. "What's the matter Coach, has it gotten cold? I can reheat it if you like."

"No its fine honey, I'm just not very hungry tonight."

"You always eat lasagna before a game. It's like a family tradition."

"I've had a couple of bites, that'll have to do." Dunn shoved the plate away. "Its delicious honey, just like always. I just can't force another morsel down."

"Coach, in four days we'll have been married for eighteen years and I've never seen you like this. I know how important winning this game is to you, but you have to try and relax. You'll do your best, and so will your staff *and* your players"

He gazed across the table at his wife; she was as beautiful as the first day he laid eyes on her. He was a twenty year old freshman attending college on the GI Bill and playing football when she stopped him cold in the hallway. She was an upper classman and when she walked by him she never even acknowledged his existence. It was strange how she affected him that way. He'd dropped over Normandy during the invasion of France and fought across Europe and was almost killed during the Battle of the Bulge, but nothing could have prepared him for Nancy. After she graduated the following year they were married. His only regret was they never had any children. They tried and tried but it was not to be. The doctors told them it would happen when they least expected it, but it never did.

"It's not the game Nancy; it's the fear of letting my boys down. This group is special. All through my coaching career I've dreamed of having players like I have now. They're a treasure, a gift of outstanding individuals and athletes. They put nothing above the team concept. They've given me their all and then some. Even the non-starters have given me everything they had. They believe in me, they believe in the coaching staff, and they believe in themselves as a team. For the first time in my life I'm scared. There were a few times in Europe when I was frightened, but nothing compared to this."

"Honey," Nancy moved around the table and put her arm over his shoulder. "You're the coach; you made them into a team. I remember last summer when you said there was only a handful of athletes on the whole squad. Look at them now; they are undefeated and tonight your boys are playing for the state championship. Let me ask you this Coach: would you have predicted that in August?"

Dunn laughed, "No...not on your life."

"Then I rest my case. You are the best damn coach I've ever had the pleasure to bed, and I want you to go out there tonight and coach your heart out. That's all I ask and it's what your players expect."

"Come here you vixen." Dunn pulled her into his lap and planted a wet kiss on her voluptuous lips. "Now how about heating up that lasagna."

Cleat thought they had left early enough to be some of the first ones to arrive at the field house, but when they pulled into the parking lot it looked as if they were the only ones missing. Their teammates were gathered outside waiting for the coaches to give the final word to board the two school buses parked parallel to the building. It was gonna be the seniors' final ride to Spartan Field. You could feel the electricity in the air, and its intensity grew as they loaded up for the drive through downtown Lakewood. Inside the buses the noise was deafening as they rode the five miles chanting and screaming out the windows at hundreds of fanatical fans that had joined the caravan. There were four buses in all, leading the motorcade was the high school band. When the caravan drove into the stadium parking lot several thousand Spartan boosters greeted them with banners and bullhorns blaring. Police were everywhere trying to enforce crowd control as the players were quickly hustled into the locker room located underneath the east stadium.

An athletic musk lingered in the cold, dank interior of the dressing room. The rankness wasn't gestating from just one season, forty years of sweat and blood from thousands of Spartans before them had used this room to dress for battle. Cleat's dad, uncles, and brother had donned their uniforms in this same chamber of sparseness where victories were won and lost. The stadium was built in 1918 right after WW I, and it had valiantly stood the test of time; it was still considered to be one of the best high school stadiums in the state. Across the way was Henderson Field, the high school's baseball park. It was started and finished in conjuncture with Spartan Field. It was quite a complex for high school sports, and the town was proud to showcase their facilities at every opportunity.

Sissy opened the car door and leapt out before her father had come to a complete stop. "Hurry up, everybody. I don't want to miss anything."

Her mother laughed, "Now sweetheart, don't get in a tizzy, your father has season tickets and I assure you the seats will be there when we arrive."

"But mother I don't want to miss any of the pageantry, it's not *just* any other game you know."

"We won't miss a thing dear, I promise." Smiling at her daughter's spirited enthusiasm, she couldn't help but give her a hug. "Why, I don't believe I've ever seen you so excited."

"Oh mother, I haven't been…never in my life. It's so exciting that Cleat and Coon are playing for the state championship. I'm so thrilled for them."

Mr. Davis didn't want to admit he was as excited as his daughter, and was anxious to get seated and watch both teams warm up. Putting his arms around their waist, he hurried them along weaving through the crowd. At the ticket booth guarding the Romanesque entrance he handed the Booster Club member his season tickets and waited patiently for the stubs. Once they were granted entrance the smell of hot dogs, onions, roasted peanuts, popcorn, and cotton candy assailed their nostrils. It was a carnival like atmosphere with thousands of people young and old milling about. Both of the school bands were already seated and engaged in a musical duel trying to overpower one another in bombastic screeches of horns and trumpets. The steady beat of base drums reverberated in the pit of everyone's stomach as they made their way up the stadium steps. The steady rumble of thousands of fans increased in volume as every minute drew closer for the game to begin.

Several boosters and other familiar faces waved cheerfully as the trio ascended the concrete steps. Chase Stoddard, president of Florida National Bank stopped their progress, "Randle, good to see you and June. My goodness, this can't be Cristina. Sweetheart you are as beautiful as your mother."

"Thank you Mister Stoddard." Sissy blushed profusely.

"Chase its good to see you. Don't forget about our T-time tomorrow. Be sure and bring your wallet this time. It's never easy taking money from a banker."

Chase laughed, "From my experience lawyers are worse than bankers."

"How do the teams look?" Randle nodded toward the field.

"They've only been on the field for a couple of minutes, but I can tell you this: those Edgewood players are huge."

Randle turned his attention to the boys dressed in black with red numbers, they were huge, and they out numbered the Spartan players 2-1. "Big doesn't make them better nor does it indicate the size of their hearts. It's what's inside that makes the difference, that and speed, and we have plenty of that."

"I hope you're right Randle."

Me too, Randle thought. "We'll know in a couple of hours. I'll see you later Chase." Randle escorted his girls to their seats.

June leaned forward and whispered to her husband, "Honey, is it fair that they have more players than we do?"

"Yes honey, it's fair." Randle smiled at how little his wife knew about the game.

"Well it doesn't seem at all fair to me. They have twice as many as we do, *and* why are they so much bigger than our boys?"

"Edgewood has twice the student body as Lakewood; ergo they have twice as many players to choose from."

"There ought to be a rule that negates unfairness. Isn't there a ruling body that governs such an imbalance?"

"There is sweetheart, schools are placed into classifications by enrollment, and Lakewood just happens to be at the lower end of the higher classification."

"Oh, okay, at least I feel better that someone is trying to make the game fair, but I still don't see that it is."

Mandy stood transfixed, watching # 88 run through the team's warm-up drills. Her eyes never varied as Cleat took long, graceful strides down field snatching passes out of the air at just the right moment. To see him perform his acrobatics in an environment so conducive to his athletic skills was majestic. He reminded Mandy of a deer bounding gracefully through the forest gliding effortlessly over and around obstacles.

Back home Mama Marie sat in her son-in-law's brown leather chair, her liver spotted hands shook as she fumbled with arthritic fingers to increase the volume on the radio. Sissy had placed it on the antique washstand within easy reach. She was thankful her granddaughter made sure the dial was on the correct station broadcasting the game. After listening to several commercials, the announcer's voice broke in with a long, drawn out, "Heeeeere Cooooooome the Spartans!" Settling back into the comfort of Randle's private chair, she silently prayed for Cleat and Coon's safety, the thought of winning or loosing wasn't given much consideration.

"Okay sports fans, Ted Albright bringing you the action as the team captains and co-captains are on the field for the coin toss…it looks like Lakewood has won the toss and they've elected to receive. The referees indicate the Edgewood Panthers will be defending the north goal…we'll be back to cover the kickoff after a brief commercial break…stay tuned to WQLF, and your local broadcast of the Lakewood Senior High Spartans Championship season."

Not one solitary soul at the game was seated as they watched their teams take the field. The uproarious noise in the stadium amassed in volume as ten thousand fans stood, packed shoulder-to-shoulder waiting for the much-antic-ipated spectacle to begin. It had been the talk of both towns for the past several weeks and now, tonight, it was coming to fruition. This evening there would be a new state champion, and by 10:00 everybody would know which school owned the bragging rights.

"Back deep to receive for Lakewood is John Truman and Lakewood's first ever High School All-American, Cleat Davis. The state championship game is only seconds from being underway. Heeeeere's the kickoff…Truman's going to receive the ball on Lakewood's 15 yard line…there's blockers in front as Truman carries the ball straight up the middle…ohhh my goodness, Davis just wiped out two of Edgewood's defenders, what a devastating block. Truman's cutting toward Edgewood's sideline…he's at the 25…30…35…40…across midfield…he could go all the way."

Coon spun from a would be tackler, and while sidestepping another his momentum slowed, but in two steps he was at full speed again changing direction and slicing across field. There was only one defender to beat…he could see # 31 quickly closing in. The defender had the angle, there was no way he was going to be able to avoid the inevitable. Coon knew from years of playing football he wasn't going to be able to break the tackle of the much bigger opponent, his only chance was to try and leap over him when the linebacker was committed. Timing his jump almost perfectly, he sailed over Blake's lowered helmet, but on the way down his left foot clipped Blake's shoulder pads, sending him head over heels. He landed hard on the back of his neck. An array of colorful starbursts exploded inside his skull as he lay out of breath on Edgewood's 28-yard line.

"What a tackle by # 31…Truman's down inside Edgewood's 30-yard line…wow he went sailing like a rag doll. I swear I thought he was going to go all the way, until Blake came from out of nowhere and brought him down with a spectacular tackle…I hope Truman's alright…the trainers and coaches are running onto the field. We'll pause from the action for a commercial…don't go away, we'll be right back."

Cleat was first on the scene. "You okay, Coon?"

Coon opened his eyes; his right arm was numb, and his neck felt like someone had judo chopped him, but he was still holding tightly to the football "Yeah, I guess I'm okay for surviving a train wreck." He sat up, raising his left hand for Cleat's assistance.

"Hell of a run, Coon."

"Thanks, but I couldn't have done it without that block you threw."

In the huddle Gene squeezed his hands so nobody could see they were shaking like a leaf in a hurricane. "All right Spartans lets show 'em whose boss. Pro set…split left…Slot right motion…24-power on two, ready…break."

Before the snap of the ball Cleat went in motion down the line of scrimmage. When the ball was centered Coon counter-stepped left, and then broke right. The handoff from Gene was a little high, but Coon was able to control the ball and follow the fullback leading through the four hole. Cleat in turn drove off the tight-ends outside shoulder to drive the linebacker out of the lane. He caught Blake's blind pursuit to fill the gap squarely under the armpit, knocking him on his ass. Cleat felt Coon rush behind him.

The local announcers physically jumped out of their chairs screaming when they saw Cleat's block clear the way for Coon crashing through the line unencumbered. They couldn't control their jubilation…they knew beyond a shadow of doubt he was going to score. "Truman's busted through the line, he's in the open…he's going to score, he's going to score…TOUCHDOWN! TOUCHDOWN LAKEWOOD!"

The cheerleaders went running down the sidelines yelling, screaming, cart wheeling, to join the celebration at the north end of the field. Most of them missed Coon's run because it happened in the middle of one of their new cheers choreographed especially for the game. Watching the crowd's reaction, they quickly forgot about their cheer in time to see Coon racing across the goal.

After Lakewood's extra point was good the scoreboard lit up: HOME 07 VISITORS 0. Following the extra point Lakewood kicked off to Edgewood and their stingy defense held the Panthers to minus 3-yards on their initial series of downs, forcing them to punt from their own 31-yardline.

Coon was standing on his own 38-yardline itching for the ball…he'd never been so wired before…he felt invincible. It was a high kick, and when Coon was finally able to catch the ball he was hit simultaneously by two defenders, even so he still staggered forward to their own 42.

"Okay, listen up." Gene's nerves had calmed somewhat after their quick score. "Pro-set, X-tight, 24 Z-slant on first sound. Get that everybody? The count is first sound. Give me some protection. Okay, let's break!"

The team loudly yelled break and trotted to the line of scrimmage. Cleat was the Z receiver spread far right, the Z-slant 24 was a play action pass designed for him to slant over the middle. He shook his hands, limbering them as he waited for the line to charge forward…with all the noise around him there was no way for him to audibly hear the snap count…he had to visibly react to his offensive's line movement. This particular play had worked for them all year, more than a couple of times he'd broken it all the way for a touchdown. He was primed and ready. Suddenly the ball was snapped and with a burst of speed he slanted over the middle anticipating the ball when suddenly all forward momentum came to an abrupt halt. An excruciating pain electrified his whole body…his helmet went flying through the air. He landed on his back, expelling what few ounces of breath he had left in his lungs. Every joint in his body felt like they'd been fused together. He lay struggling in the grass, wheezing for oxygen. The ringing in his ears sounded like his grandmother's teakettle. His dazed senses made it difficult to draw air into his deprived lungs. He was afraid he was going to die. Looking up through glazed eyes he came face to face with a ginning stranger bending over him. The menacing face had two front teeth missing and at least three days growth of black whiskers.

"Payback's a bitch pretty-boy. That little love tap was to let you know I personally don't like 'Hot dogs' in my area. You best stay where you are before you really get hurt. This is a man's game, cheerleaders should stay on the sidelines" With an evil laugh #31 trotted off to join his teammates.

"Oh my Lord Randle, Cleat's hurt." June's left hand clawed into her husband's leg.

"He'll be alright sweetheart. He just probably has the wind knocked out of him." He hoped that was the case, because he'd never seen such a brutal hit. It looked as if it was intended to knock his son out of the game.

Several of Cleat's teammates rushed over to help him to his feet. Rubbery legs failed to support him. His mind was still groggy, his eyes were distant as he tried to put names to the faces surrounding him, but he was unable to recognize anybody…he wasn't even sure where he was. Everything looked so strange, and out of focus.

In the reserved section of the stadium June Davis let a sigh of relief escape her lips when she saw her son assisted to his feet. Had it been only two minutes? To her it felt like a lifetime. For a brief moment she'd thought her son was dead. When the boy who brutally hit him bent over and engaged Cleat in conversation she knew he was alive. She was pleased to see movement in his extremities. She had always dislike football, even when her husband played, and now, if it were possible, she hated the stupid game even more.

Jeff Hart, a senior defensive back, met Cleat and the coach halfway, and offered his shoulder to lean on. "Man, that #31 clobbered the shit out of you Cleat. That was the biggest hit I've ever seen."

"I never...saw it coming, Jeff. Hell, I don't even know...what happened. One second I was looking for the football, and the next thing there was nothing but pain."

"Hell, I saw the whole thing. When you went over the middle he clotheslined you. Shit, I've never seen anything like it. Y'all were both going full speed and then BLAM, you were up in the air doing a complete flip, and when you freaking came down you landed on your head. Hell, I thought he killed you. Goddamn Cleat, I'm not kidding man...he knocked the ever-living snot out of you. I can't believe you're up and walking around after something that brutal."

"You're telling me." Cleat rubbed the back of his neck, now he knew why he was so sore. Harvey Blake. Coach Dunn had warned them about #31. Cleat smiled, thinking how he would make it a point to properly reintroduce himself to Mr. Blake.

"Cleat, are you all right son?" Coach Dunn inquired, peering into his eyes. He held up two fingers in front of Cleat. "How many fingers am I holding up?"

"Thr...uh, two...yeah, two fingers Coach."

"Get your butt over to the sidelines and shake it off, son. It's early in the game and we ain't gonna take any chances on you getting hurt. Now move your butt, and don't give me any lip. Coach Ewell, help him over to the sidelines and have the doc take a look."

The Spartans failed to convert a first down and had to punt from their 45-yard line. Lakewood's punt coverage gang tackled the Panther's return man on the 27-yard line. Edgewood's first play from scrimmage was a quick handoff to Blake, diving over left guard for a couple of tough yards. Second and eight was a power play with Blake following the fullback through the three-hole picking up 5-yards. On third and three Edgewood set up in an unbalanced backfield, the quarterback used a long count trying to draw the defense offside, but the Spartans held fast, waiting for the snap.

On the previous play Cleat had reentered the game at strong side linebacker. His eyes never left Blake, peripherally he kept most of the field in his vision, but primarily he was honing in on number # 31. Blake was over ninety per-cent of Edgewood's offense, and if Lakewood was going to win they needed to curtail his performance.

When the ball was snapped Cleat saw the right guard pull to his side for what looked to be a power sweep. Rushing across the line of scrimmage he brushed the offensive end out of the way with a powerful throw of his left arm and arrived about the same time Blake caught the pitch-out. He zeroed in on # 31 full bore with his shoulders low and head up, and powered his body through Blake's with such violence you could've heard the collision of pads on pads outside the stadium. The ball squirted high in the air, and when the football hit the ground it bounced backward end over end until Bo hooked the fumble under his stomach at Edgewood's 17-yardline.

Not far from the action Cleat was laying on top of the stunned Harvey Blake, their faces were only inches apart. "Just to let you know, I have my own territory staked out smart-ass, and visitors aren't welcome." Cleat smiled before roughly shoving on Blake's chest before regaining his feet.

"What a break for Lakewood," the announcer blared over the airways. "It's Lakewood's ball on the Panthers 17-yardline. Bo Collier's recovery has put us in terrific position to score, Bill."

"How right you are Ted, but what about that bone jarring tackle by Davis? I don't believe I've ever seen anybody totally wiped out like that in a high school game…heck, you could hear leather pop clear up here in the booth."

"Yeah, me too Bill, I'm surprised either one of them got up unassisted. It's amazing how these kids can give, and dish out such punishing blows. We've got a real battle going on between Davis and Blake, and I believe it's going to be like this all night. They're the two best athletes on the field, and both of them realize how important a role they play in their teams' chances of winning."

"Okay Ted, back to the action…Lakewood's in a spread formation with Davis wide right. Reese is over the center…he takes the snap…oh no, there's a fumble on the play…from the pile-up I can't tell who's recovered the loose pigskin…the referees are un-stacking them one-by-one…its Edgewood's ball…# 77 has recovered for Edgewood. It'll be Edgewood's ball on their own 21-yardline."

"Bill, it looked to me like one of the offensive linemen stepped on Reese's foot as he was backing away from center."

"As a matter of fact, Ted, I believe it was the center, Bo Collier. Wow, Collier was almost knocked into the Spartans' backfield by the Panthers' nose guard."

Coach Dunn was furiously pacing the sidelines. "Damn it all to hell, Coach Ewell, get Bo out'a there, and send him to me."

Bo sheepishly ran over to where Coach Dunn was standing; he could tell by the coach's demeanor the man wasn't happy. "Yes sir, Coach. You wanted me?"

"What the heck happened out there, Bo? Can't you block that nose guard long enough for us to get a play off? Hell, at least don't let him knock you into your own backfield. You can't let # 77 push you around like that!"

"He outweighs me forty pounds coach, and he's playing dirty."

Coach Dunn grabbed Bo by the front of his jersey, "Dammit Bo, toughen up for Christ's sake…quit whining. He's eating your lunch out there. Get mean boy, show him whose boss."

"Yes sir…uh, can I go back in, Coach?"

"Not right now, go on over and see Coach Ewell." Dunn looked toward the bench and summoned Rafe Halliburton, his junior nose guard and backup center to go in for Collier. Rafe wasn't as big or experienced as Bo, but he was quicker and meaner than a junkyard dog with a sandspur up his ass. At five-foot-eleven and two hundred and thirty-five pounds he had the tenacity of a pit bull; if he couldn't beat you fair and square then he would get nasty-mean. "Rafe, I want you in there stirring things up. Create as much fear and havoc as you can…go a little crazy and scare the hell out of 'em."

"Yes sir Coach, you can count on me." Rafe slipped his helmet on and rushed onto the field, screaming as if his balls were on fire.

On first down Edgewood tried a power play through the two-hole, but Rafe plugged the hole stopping the lead fullback dead in his tracks. Blake was able to grind out two yards on sheer determination before Cleat barreled in, and threw his body into the fray taking the whole pile to the ground. On second down the quarterback ran a play action pass faking the ball to Blake and dropped back to pass. He saw his receiver streaking down the sidelines wide open, but before he was able to set his feet and throw, Lakewood's crazy nose guard was in his face howling. In a desperate attempt he let the ball fly downfield, and then he was hit harder than a quarterback should ever be hit. His mouthpiece popped out his mouth…his helmet crashed down onto the bridge of his nose and he felt something crunch inside. Blue, orange, and purple dancing polka dots filled his vision as he fell to the grass…tasting his own blood.

"The quarterback handed off to Blake up the middle…no wait, it's a fake…he's dropping back to pass, and he's got a man open down the sidelines. There's a Lakewood defender busting through the line…it looks like # 64, Rafe Halliburton. The ball's in the air, but it's poorly thrown…it must've been deflected. Truman's breaking for the ball INTERCEPTION…INTERCEPTION…Truman intercepted the ball and he's tearing across the field untouched…Davis takes out the only defender in pursuit…Truman's at the 50-yardline…the 40…35…20…he's going to score…TOUCHDOWN! I can't believe it, Ted, what a turn of events. There have been two turnovers in less than two minutes and we're up by two touchdowns…not only that, Edgewood's powerful running game doesn't look so powerful. They can't seem to get anything going."

"You are absolutely right. They certainly aren't living up to their reputation, but what's even more astonishing to me is: Truman has scored both touchdowns…one on offense and one on defense. Now that's not to say he's not a great player, but everyone thought Davis would be the one to watch."

Halliburton squatted beside the prone quarterback, situating his butt close to the signal caller's face and let out a horrid, foul smelling fart reminiscent of what he'd eaten for supper: raw oysters and pickled eggs. When he stood up to walk away he kind of accidentally stepped on the quarterback's hand with his size-fourteen shoe. The rubberized spikes would leave a painful reminder, but Rafe didn't feel too bad because he'd made sure it wasn't the guy's throwing hand.

It was some minutes before they were able to attempt the extra point because several dozen excited fans ran into the end zone celebrating. After the police politely helped them off the field, Lakewood lined up for the try. Gene Reese gave the signal to snap while Benji Ellis, the team's junior place kicker, stood ready. It was a perfect snap from Bo, but Gene wasn't able to handle the ball cleanly, which threw the timing off between him and Benji. The ball never got high enough to clear the cross member. Lakewood's score would be the only one to change: HOME 13 VISITORS 0. The mostly partisan crowd roared their approval.

For the second time in the waning minutes of the first quarter Lakewood kicked off and held the Panthers to virtually no gain. Coon was able to return their punt 17-yards to Edgewood's 48-yardline, two running plays later they were facing third and long with little less than 5-yards to go for a first down. Edgewood's defense had become more determined, they weren't in a panic mode as yet, but they knew they needed to start tackling and reading their keys better. They had to stop the Spartans' offense so their offensive team could get on the field and start scoring points.

"Okay, it's third and five on Edgewood's 41-yardline…LHS is in a pro set formation…Davis goes in motion…Reese drops back in the pocket and fires a pass to Davis on a deep corner…Ohhh, what a catch! Davis caught the ball one-handed and was driven out of bounds at the 19. To all of you out there listening to this broadcast I want to be the first to say it was one of the greatest catches I've ever seen. He had a defender draped all over him, yet somehow he managed to bring the ball in one-handed. It was absolutely utterly fantastic." The listening audience could hear the adulation in the announcer's voice.

"I second that, Bill. It was truly a thing of beauty. Davis is really living up to his credentials, but we still have a long way to go before this night's over. I don't want to sound like a worrywart, but the daunting question I've struggled with all week is: can we hold up physically against a bigger team like Edgewood, who has the luxury of playing two-platoon football? What I mean by that statement is our cross state rival has enough solid players to field a separate team for defense and one for offense. The only player I know for the Panthers who goes both ways is Blake. On the other hand, we have eight players who play first team defense, and offense. I firmly believe the Panthers are shell shocked right now. They haven't been outplayed like this all year, nor have they given up this many points in one game all year, and here we're threatening to score again, but the fourth quarter could be the determining factor in this game."

"I totally disagree with you, Ted. Lakewood's playing the way they have all year. They have a quick strike offense and a stingy defense that'll get after you as if you were attacking their mama's virtue. They're not intimidated by anybody, and they just go out and play their game no matter who they face. What our football team's doing tonight is proving to me that Edgewood's not all they've been hyped up to be. They're too one-dimensional for one thing…their entire offense is based on Harvey Blake having success running the ball. They have no passing attack whatsoever…you saw that flutter ball Truman intercepted. All we have to do is shut the running game down and LHS will be the new state champs."

Coon's number was called two plays in a row, but he was only able to gain four yards. In the huddle he listened to Reese call out the next play.

"Pro tight, twenty-four cross buck...X-drag...Y-out...Z-post, on one. Okay Spartans...let's put this game away." Reese repeated the play twice before breaking the huddle. He checked the defense; if they stayed in their six-man front with no middle safety he knew without a doubt Cleat would be open. Reese anxiously waited for his offense to get set. All he had to do was put the ball on target to get his first touchdown pass of the game. He wondered how many scouts were in the stadium watching.

Cleat stood relaxed, he should be able to score with ease if a safety didn't cover the middle. This was one of the new plays they inserted in their game plan. When the play was set in motion, Cleat's first few steps were deliberately slow as he peered down the line of scrimmage trying to lure the man covering him to play the run, When the defensive man took the bait Cleat burst down the field, cutting into the end zone uncovered. The throw was high, but Cleat leapt into the air and was able to get his fingertips around the ball and tuck it away. A smile crossed his face as he lay on the turf listening to the crowd screaming in the background.

The play had worked to perfection, but converting an extra point was becoming a serious problem, primarily due to Edgewood's # 77. This time he powered over Bo causing the snap to sail high over Gene's outstretched hands. HOME 19 VISITORS 0.

During the second quarter it settled into a hardnosed defensive contest with neither side allowing the other to cross midfield. Crunching blows and tackles caused minor injuries but no one was going to willingly leave the field. They would have to be dragged off, or ordered off. Everyone watching, or listening to the game knew there were two battles being fought, one between the opposing teams, and a personal battle between Davis and Blake, the two boys mirrored each other almost every play.

There was 4:21 left in the half when Edgewood finally began to mount a drive; it started on their 39-yardline with a misdirection play to Blake who careened off left tackle for 7-yards. The next play fooled almost everybody when Edgewood's fullback carried the ball on a quick opener. It was his very first carry of the game and he rambled for 8-yards and a first down before

Coon was able to bring him down. Blake's longest run of the night came when he took a handoff from a power "I" formation. He rushed to the three-hole, but when he saw Big Oak shooting through the gap he reversed field catching Lakewood's defense over-pursuing. If it hadn't been for Doug Lowenbrau, the Spartans' junior safety, making a desperate shoestring tackle he would've gone all the way for a touchdown. The game clock stopped at 2:16 while the officials moved the sticks.

It was the first time Lakewood's defense had allowed the Panthers to cross midfield into Spartan territory. Blake's 23-yard scamper was significant to the morale of the Edgewood players. They were rejuvenated and a new surge of energy was flowing through their veins. It was turning into their kind of game: smash-mouth football. It's what brought them to the dance, and they could tell the Lakewood players were gradually wearing down. They weren't quite as fast off the ball, and they were a step slower in pursuit. Power and strength was synonymous to Panther-ball. Their coaches had preached it all year, and now it was beginning to pay off. Nothing fancy, no finesse, just knock your opponents on their ass and run it down their throats. It wasn't pretty to watch, but they had been winning with that philosophy for years.

On Edgewood's next three plays Blake ran the ball for 6-yards, 9-yards, and 11-yards. The ball finally came to rest on Lakewood's 12-yard line when the Spartans called time out with 0:53 left in the half.

Lakewood stood in a loose defensive huddle huffing and puffing trying to catch their breath from Edgewood's sudden blitzkrieg. Several looked at the game clock, wishing the clocked read 00:00.

Cleat understood his teammates' fatigue, but he saw something else, something he thought he'd never see…fear. "Goddammit, to hell, we gotta stop these assholes. We're letting them run all over us. For Christ's sake, all we have to do is stop # 31. Let's pull together…we can't let these assholes score right before halftime. Let's key on that son-of-a-bitch and bust his balls…he's all they've got.

We're gonna go with our six-two goal line defense. I want the inside linebackers in tight and the line to submarine the gaps." Cleat finished just as the referee blew his whistle, signaling it was time to play ball.

Lakewood stopped the drive cold; Edgewood actually lost 2-yards on three plays and called their last remaining timeout with 0:05 seconds left on the game clock. First down meant nothing because there would be no time available to run another play. It was now or never for both teams.

When Edgewood broke the huddle and fell into a spread formation, there was mass confusion on the other side of the ball. Lakewood couldn't believe their eyes; all of them looked to Cleat for guidance. He was as confused as the rest of them, but held his composure. It was definitely a passing situation, but as far as he knew Edgewood had never gone to a pro set all year, the most they'd ever varied from a two tight end full backfield was occasionally sending out a flanker. Cleat hurriedly called for an eagle blitz, sending both inside linebackers shooting the gaps. He made sure the defensive backs were in front of the goal and every Edgewood receiver was covered. The only man in the backfield was Blake.

"Ted, are you surprised as I am with Edgewood's spread open formation?"

"I sure am Bill, but with fourth and long you got to hand it to them for trying something different." Like everyone else, the broadcasters were on there feet, waiting for the snap.

"Chadwick's under center calling the cadence…he's dropping back to pass…the receivers have released down field…no, wait a minute, it's a delayed draw to Blake…he's busted through the line of scrimmage, and shooting past the blitzing linebackers…our secondary has their backs turned covering their receivers…only one defender has a chance…ohhh he just got steamed rolled…Blake's going to score…he's going to score. Touchdown Edgewood…not a soul laid a hand on Blake except the lone defender unfortunate enough to get in his way. I couldn't make out the number…let's see he's getting up now, it's # 32, John Truman…he looks okay Ted, but what a gutsy call by the Panthers. They fooled everybody. It's a new ballgame come second half."

"Doggone'it Bill, it's a crying shame. Lakewood's defensive play was spectacular all night until the last series. Edgewood scoring just before halftime is a bitter pill to swallow."

"It certainly is Ted. The Spartan's defense has been superlative, but you have to admit none of us thought we could keep Edgewood scoreless. They are a great team and we're in for a great second half."

Coon lifted himself off the ground; his right shoe lay several feet away. Walking over to pick it up, he knew Edgewood scored…the groaning fans told the story. When he realized it was a draw play it was too late, by the time he dropped off his coverage Blake had already exploded into the secondary. The linebackers' were caught in no-mans-land and their outstretched arms were no match for Blake's brute strength. The all-state running back went through them like a tornado. He sprinted towards Coon full speed ahead with his helmet lowered and thick powerful legs pumping like pistons on a runaway locomotive. Blake's eyes were crazed, his determination and intent was obvious. Coon would swear later, he saw smoke coming out of Blake's ear holes and nostrils.

There wasn't enough time for Coon to protect himself, much less have a chance in hell bringing Blake down. The collision was imminent...he remembered the initial shock of contact and briefly flying backward...his next conscious thought was how humiliating it was to be run over in front of ten thousand screaming spectators.

The half was officially over, but the teams remained on the field for Edgewood's extra point. HOME 19 VISITORS 7, the scoreboard didn't tell the true story of what transpired. Two teams left the field at halftime...one walked off tired and dejected, while the other *ran* off celebrating their new-found confidence.

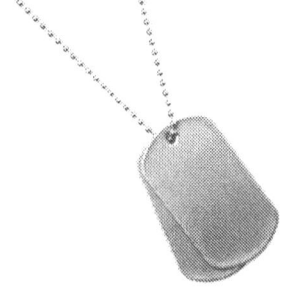

CHAPTER 6

Lakewood entered the dungeon-like corridor under the stadium and followed the ramp to their dressing room. Usually you would expect to see grab-assing and hear shouting inside a locker room where a team was leading by twelve points at halftime, but tonight the mood was somber. Players were sprawled on the floor, or resting their backs against clammy walls.

Cleat was the last player to enter the room and was greeted with an unfamiliar sight…his teammates looked defeated. In ten years of playing the game he could only remember losing four times. He stood for a moment, mentally calculating how many total games he'd played, a hundred at least, probably more than that.

"Hey…goddammit, why aren't y'all celebrating? Hell, we've pushed these guys around for two quarters. For Christ's sake we're ahead by 12 points, not behind …start acting like it. Come on, Butch, let's hear some damn noise, that goes for you too Bo, get off your ass and do a little dance. Dammit to hell we're winning not losing."

Most of the seniors got to their feet and began shouting obscenities at one another as they pulled underclassmen off the floor. Soon they were body-slamming and screaming LHS…LHS…LHS. A screeching voice everyone recognized as Coon began yelling above the rest: "WE'RE NUMBER ONE! WE'RE NUMBER ONE!" Soon the entire team took up the chant.

That was the scene Coach Dunn and his assistants were confronted with when they filed into the locker room. Calmness swept over the coaches, filling them with a deep sense of pride as they stoically listened to and watched their players screaming at the top of their lungs, and raising their helmets to the rafters.

Coach Dunn stepped on a bench and held his hands up for silence. "Men, we're all proud of you…you've played one hell of a first half." He was interrupted briefly, but he didn't mind because they deserved the right to be proud of themselves. The cheers quickly died down when he raised his hands again. "We have another half to play and if we play like we did in the first half we'll be the new state champions."

A standing ovation took place, applauding the seniors and their leadership. "Now with that said I'd like to point out the second half is going to be balls-to-the-wall. After that touchdown Edgewood went into their locker room high as a kite. It revitalized their spirits into believing they can whip us, but that ain't gonna happen, because we're a better team than they are." Once again the players exploded with chants and shouts. "Having a chance to be champions is a rare thing in any sport; most people go a lifetime without ever having the opportunity you have tonight. Your time has come, and you've earned that right by hard work. Remember the blood, sweat, and tears. Remember the hot sun during two-a-days, the pain, the cuts and bruises, the gut-wrenching thirst, *and* the sandspurs we laughingly called grass. Remember the grueling hours in the weight room when you busted your guts to lift that extra five pounds. Remember the long hours on the practice field with no cheerleaders, no fans, and no boosters, just coaches screaming at you when you were dog-tired. No one has ever worked harder than you men to become champions."

"You bet your ass coach" Coon hollered.

"Men, the second half will determine your fate. Now what I know is this, it's not always the better team that wins. Most often it's the team who's better prepared, and has the greatest desire. Those teams will always rise above themselves to sacrifice any, and everything toward a common goal. You men are like that. When you feel worn out and have nothing left to give…then by God suck it up and *dig* deeper. It's what you have in here," Coach Dunn pounded his chest with a closed fist, "that'll carry you to victory. Give me a team with heart and I'll field a winner every time. It all comes down to who wants to be state champions the most. You have to want it more than the other guy. You men have nothing to prove to me or anyone else. In my heart you'll always be winners and Champions."

Again he had to pause before continuing. "Before your position coaches meet with y'all I would like to say it has been an honor and a privilege to know, and coach you men. You have all done me proud."

The fans rose to their feet with a tumultuous ovation when the hometown heroes took the field. The stands came alive with orange and black pom-poms.

Lakewood's band was playing the school's fight song at a feverish pace and the cheerleaders were jumping with joy pushing their hands skyward encouraging everyone to stay on their feet for the ensuing kickoff.

Lakewood's kickoff vaulted high in the air and was caught on the 12-yard-line; Edgewood returned it to their own 28. Their first play from scrimmage was a quick pitch to Harvey Blake that picked up 7-yards, but there was a clip on the play and they were penalized 15 yards. The referee stepped the yardage off and placed the ball on the Panthers' 13-yardline, it was now first and twenty-five. Blake rambled for a quick 6 on a trap, and then for 8 more up the middle. On third and eleven Chadwick took the snap and rolled to his left, finding a wide open receiver for 13-yards and a first down. It was first and ten on Lakewood's 49-yardline.

Cleat held the defensive team in a loose huddle. "Alright, let's pull together. We gotta stop these guys. I want you linemen and inside-backers to key on Blake. I want anything up the middle stuffed…force the ball outside. I don't want any receivers getting off the line clean…jam 'em, or knock 'em on their ass…I don't care which…just don't let 'em break free. We're gonna stop them right here and now."

On the next three plays Edgewood gained a net of 2-yards and was forced to punt. It was a high, wobbly kick angling toward Cleat. He waited patiently as the ball tumbled through the air end over end. When the ball fell into his arms he spun left making the first defender grab nothing but thin air. Coon threw a wicked block, giving Cleat an opening down the sidelines; he violently stiff-armed a third defender before # 31 sent him crashing out of bounds on Edgewood's 41-yardline. Cleat's twenty-one yard return electrified the fans and his teammates alike. It was the spark they were looking for to ignite the offense.

After three prior attempts running the ball, Lakewood's offensive unit found itself looking at third and ten. Coach Dunn ran his junior wide receiver, Dean Palmer, in with a play calling for Cleat to run a deep post over the middle. Reese dropped back in the pocket and pumped-faked to the receiver in the flat. It was enough to make the defense bite. Reese waited for the right moment to throw the ball. He knew without looking where Cleat was going to be, it was one of their favorite patterns he and Cleat practiced for hours on end. One afternoon after practice he wanted to see if he could complete the pass with his eyes closed. Cleat willing obliged and was surprised that Reese completed three out of seven attempts.

A gut feeling told him it was time, stepping forward he released a perfect, spiral to the spot where Cleat would be after his final cut. The ball arrived a split-second after Cleat turned his shoulders. He snatched the ball out of the air and was able to take a few steps up field before a paralyzing blow hit him in the lower kidneys. He was driven face first into the grass. He didn't have to look for the guy's number that drilled him…there was only one guy on the field that could hit like a ton of bricks

"You ain't going nowhere, pretty boy…you ain't fast enough. Shit, my grandmother can outrun you."

Cleat smiled, "Hang around and watch the show hotshot," he could tell by looking into Blake's eyes the bone jarring tackle hurt Blake as much as it did him. They were both grimacing from the blow.

"Tears are the only thing you're going to show me when we take home the trophy." Blake sneered.

Cleat's only retort was a chuckle. He was still laughing when he tossed the football to the referee, and ran back to the huddle.

"Nice pass, Reese."

"Thanks, Cleat…let's keep it up. We're in the groove tonight." Gene smiled at his All-American receiver. "All right listen up…pro-set right…halfback motion…X delay…Z corner…Y-curl on one." Gene repeated the play before breaking the huddle.

This was one of Cleat's favorite plays. It called for him to run ten yards and fake an inside move to the post, then break toward the corner sidelines. He had a good feeling on this one. There was no way Edgewood's defensive back was going to be able to cover him without some help. Cleat took off with blinding speed, after approximately ten yards he planted his right foot and made a hard move to the center of the field pulling the defender with him. Once the defensive back took the fake, Cleat cut underneath and sprinted toward the sidelines. Looking over his right shoulder he caught sight of the football about twenty feet away, it was coming in high and over the wrong shoulder. Without breaking stride he reversed his shoulders and caught the errant pass at full speed. If Gene had put it on the money he would've scored easily, but his forward momentum carried him out of bounds on Edgewood's 16-yardline.

The next play was a power play to Coon, but Gene turned the wrong way and missed the handoff. When he tried to follow Coon through the hole # 77 was in his face and blasted him a mighty blow. The football shot one way and Gene went the other. Edgewood's # 31 caught the ball in mid-flight and returned it eighty-one yards for a touchdown. When they kicked the extra point the scoreboard lit up: HOME 19 VISTORS 14.

"Ohhh, what a turn of events sports fans...I just can't believe it." You could hear the sadness in the announcer's voice. "What a bad break for Lakewood...just when it looked like they were going to put the game away. The hometown fans are in a state of shock. You know, Ted...it looked to me as if it was a busted play."

"You're right, Bill...from my view point it looked as if Reese forgot what play he'd called, whatever happened, it fell apart pretty darn quick. Number 77, Olin Michaels, lowered the boom on Reese. That guy's been in Lakewood's backfield all night. Somebody's got to do something about that big fellow or he's going to cause more mischief than a barrel of monkeys."

"If I'm not mistaken, we'll be hearing more from Michaels in Gainesville next fall."

"You're right, Ted, he signed a letter of intent last week. I bet the coaches for the University of Florida are drooling over his outstanding play.

Coon received the kickoff on the eight-yard line and returned it to the twenty-four, before being sandwiched between two tacklers. Their next two plays from scrimmage netted them four-yards. On third and six Gene took the snap and quick-pitched to Coon who was running to the wide side of the field with two pulling guards leading interference.

At first glance it looked like a power sweep...the same one the Green Bay Packers made so famous, but suddenly the play transposed into something much different. Coon suddenly stopped and threw the football to Cleat who was running downfield wide-open. There wasn't a black jersey within ten-yards of him, and eight seconds later he was crossing Edgewater's goal line. It wasn't until he flipped the ball on the ground and faced his teammates that he realized there was something dreadfully wrong. The crowd was booing loudly, near the original line of scrimmage was a penalty flag lying on the ground. Bo Collier was called for holding #77 during the play. The fifteen-yard infraction placed the ball on their nine-yard line...it was now third and twenty-four. The subsequent play picked up little or no yardage and Lakewood was forced to punt.

The 3rd quarter was purely a defensive battle between two teams determined not to give an inch without the other paying the price. They'd change possessions several times, but neither team was able to advance the ball past the fifty-yard line; most of the scrimmages were taking place between the forties.

Surprisingly, very few flags had been thrown during the hard-hitting contest. Edgewood had three for a total of twenty-five, and Lakewood had three for thirty-five yards. The referees were letting them play hard-nosed football, and seemed to be enjoying the competition between two teams who were as diverse on the field as Yin and Yang. One relied on speed and finesse and the other unquestionably overshadowed Lakewood with brute strength and sheer numbers. Which team was going to come out on top was as much of a mystery to the officials as it was to everyone else.

With 3:34 remaining in the 3rd quarter Edgewood returned Lakewood's punt to the 15-yardline. They lined up in a power I formation. Chadwick took the snap and reversed pivoted, he stuck the football in the pit of Blake's stomach and watched the star running back blast through the line. His powerful legs drove him forward bowling people over and trampled one of Lakewood's linebackers. Before the defensive backs could react he rambled for 18-yards. Without calling a huddle Edgewood quickly lined up on the ball with a unbalanced line. Cleat was still calling out defensive adjustments when the ball was snapped. Chadwick spun from under center and pitched the ball to Blake on a power sweep.

Even the announcers were surprised. "It's a power sweep...Blake's got blockers in front... Davis shoots through the gap...ohhh, Blake shrugged it off...he's turning the corner...he could go all the way. He's at the 25...30...35...40...he's cutting across the grain...Wow what a hit...did you see that? Truman came from out'a nowhere and laid the lumber on Blake. He never saw it coming, and right now Blake's getting up very slowly wondering what kind of truck just ran into him. I'm sure Blake must've thought he was going to score right up until Truman rang his bell."

Cleat offered a hand to his friend. "Hell of a tackle, Coon."

"Thanks, big brother." Coon shook his head free of cobwebs. "You don't see any body parts missing do you?"

"Nope, you're all intact."

"If this keeps up somebody's gonna die out here."

Blake walked over to the two friends. "Was that you who hit me?"

"Yep."

"Christ, I thought it was a tractor-trailer. I felt my brain rattle inside my head."

Coon laughed, "Hell, it was probably mine you were hearing."

Blake slapped Coon on the shoulder pads, "Next time give a guy some kind'a warning."

"How about a whistle?"

"Yeah, that'll do." Blake started to walk off, but as an afterthought he turned back to Coon and Cleat. "If I don't get a chance after the game I'd like to say y'all are the best damn team we've played all year." Without waiting for a response he trotted to where his team was huddling.

"Shit, what do you make of that Cleat?"

"I don't know, but it sure as hell doesn't change a damn thing."

On Lakewood's sideline Coach Dunn was in a heated conference with his assistant coaches. "Coach Tensely come up with a scheme to stop this guy...Blake's killing us. I don't care what it is, we've got to do something pretty damn quick."

"We've tried about everything, Coach...we could get into our six-three-two goal line defense and run some stunts, that way we'd plug #31's running lanes. The downside is we'll be susceptible to the pass."

"Pass? Jesus Christ on a crutch, Jim, they've only *thrown* the damn ball twice, and one of those was intercepted. Run a six-three and see if we can't stop Blake. Christ, he's their whole damn offense." Coach Dunn knew his boys were tired, but they still had the lead, and they were the toughest, finest boys he had ever coached. If sheer will power alone could get the job done then they would win hands down.

Coach Tensely motioned for one of the reserve backs to send in the new defensive adjustments. He was hoping beyond hope this would be the answer.

Cleat was relieved to hear the change in strategy. With him playing left outside linebacker his main responsibility had been outside containment and cover the offensive end if he released downfield. Edgewood had been running Blake on power plays and quick openers between the tackles, thus keeping Cleat out of the action. That was going to change now. In this new set-up he would be positioned between the left defensive tackle, Butch Werner and Rafe Halliburton. Rafe was shifted from nose guard to play the gap between center and Edgewood's right offensive guard. Bo Collier reentered the game and was playing in the other gap between Edgewood's center and left offensive guard. Now the defensive ends' responsibilities were switched to outside containment. With Butch, Rafe, Bo, Big Oak and Brad Connors on the defensive line they had the biggest players on the team to stop the Panthers running attack. He looked over at Tommy Pritchard, the 6'0, 190lb. junior inside linebacker playing next to him and gave an encouraging wink. Cleat felt a wave of confidence, he was head-up in the trenches, and he could hardly wait for Edgewood to snap the ball.

Their first two plays were run to Cleat's opposite side and Blake picked up a tough 9-yards. Cleat was exasperated and began to verbally harass the Edgewood players to make sure they knew how he felt. His verbal attack was relentless and it got so bad the umpire had to caution Cleat for taunting.

The Edgewood team came to a set in their familiar power I formation they seemed to favor. The quarterback set-up underneath his center, and began calling the signals. Cleat watched the quarterback's eyes, trying to determine where the play was heading. He scrutinized the quarterback's body position to see if he was leaning in one direction or other, but he couldn't pick up any tells. Suddenly the ball was snapped and everything seemed to be happening at the speed of light. A huge hole opened before him when the offensive guard and tackle double-teamed Butch and drove him to the ground. The center fired off the ball and threw a cut block taking Rafe's legs out from under him. Cleat rushed to fill the gap and was brushed off balance by the fullback; he tried to recover in time, but came face to face with a snarling Harvey Blake running so low his punishing knees were almost touching his chin. When he bore through the opening he hit Cleat with the strength of an angry grizzly. The sound of the collision was like nothing anyone had heard at a football game. The force of the two bodies running head-on created a noise so devastating it raced across the field, reaching the spectators seated at the very top of the stadium. A grimacing moan rolled down to the playing field as the fans gasped in shock. To those who witnessed the blow it was frightful. Players and fans alike flinched when the two gridiron gladiators collided.

Cleat was totally unprepared for the strength of Blake's bull-like charge. He felt like an armored truck hit him square in the chest. The collision knocked him backward…he tried desperately to hold on, but his numbed fingers wouldn't respond and Blake steamrolled over him slamming his body to an unforgiving turf. His head bounced off of the hardened field with such momentum it felt like his eyes popped out of their sockets. The turf gruffly accepted his body without remorse or pity. Over the decades Spartan field never played favorites, not since the first blade of grass was planted and nurtured.

Air, he thought, *oh God I need air.* He tried to cry out for help, but no sound escaped from his lips. *Oh lord, please don't let me die.* The world around him grew gray and out of focus. Lying perfectly still he could feel the numbness in his neck creep down his arms and legs, soon his whole body felt like it had fallen asleep. He had never been so frightened. Unwillingly, he succumbed to the darkness.

When the abyss swallowed his consciousness his muscles began to relax and allow much needed oxygen to enter his lungs. At first they were shallow intakes, but gradually his breathing became normal. Slowly he returned to the world he'd briefly left behind. The numbness was ebbing, leaving in its place a tingling sensation. When he was able to open his eyes he saw Coon bending over him loosening his pants allowing him to breathe more freely.

"You okay, Cleat?"

"Yeah." Even the one word answer made him feel like he'd preformed an immeasurable task…he was physically drained.

During an official injury timeout his teammates escorted him to the sidelines. The fallen hero was welcomed with a standing ovation. As they sat him on the bench he shook his head, trying to clear the fuzz muddling his brain. Coach Dunn was hovering over him like a mother hen. He broke an ammonia capsule and swiped it under his nose.

"I'm okay, Coach, just give me a minute." Cleat pushed the coach's hand away. Looking downfield he saw Edgewood forming up on Lakewood's 32-yardline. "Shit," he muttered. That meant Blake not only ran over him but he picked up over thirty-yards in doing so. Cleat's pride was hurt, but that wasn't what concerned him…his stomach was killing him. Loosening his jersey for a visual inspection he noticed for the first time there was a considerable amount of blood on his jersey. Exposing his belly he stared in awe: there was a large imprint of Blake's cleats embedded on his tortured skin. It left raw strawberry-colored marks where they had dug into his flesh. Not only had Blake literally run him over, but he had branded him as well. Enough was enough. Cleat got off the bench and ran to where Coach Dunn was talking to Coach Herndon.

"Coach, I'm ready to go back in."

"Son, are you sure?" Dunn looked closely into Cleat's eyes.

"Goddammit…I said I'm ready!" Cleat yelled into the coach's face.

"You've got a busted nose son, but if you say you're ready then get your butt out there!" Dunn hollered back. He smiled as he watched Cleat run onto the field. "God, if I had a half dozen boys like Cleat I could whip Notre Dame."

Cleat rejoined his teammates with high hopes and newfound enthusiasm, but frustration quickly set in as Edgewood's sheer strength was proving to be overwhelming. Their constant pounding of the ball drove them down to Lakewood's 3-yardline. It took only one play for Blake to bully his way over for another score. The extra point was good: HOME 19 VISTORS 21.

Coon received Edgewood's kickoff and returned it to the 24. Lakewood ran a split right…fullback motion…24 trap. The play worked to perfection with Coon picking up 16-yards. Next, the fullback carried the ball on a quick pop up the middle for a gain of 6-yards. A toss sweep to Coon rambled for 12-yards with Cleat throwing a crucial block taking Blake out at the knees.

"You cocksucker…I got your number asshole." Blake pointed his finger at Cleat.

Cleat blew him a kiss.

"You faggot…you're dead meat."

Lakewood's drive stalled on Edgewood's 42-yardline; it was 3rd down and they needed a long 6-yards for a 1st down. Gene called for a timeout, and ran over to the sidelines…it was their second of the half, leaving only one remaining.

Cleat kept his team in a loose huddle, offering encouragement as the clock at the far end of field revealed there was only 6:21 left in the game; time was becoming their foe as much as Edgewood.

Gene rejoined the huddle. "Okay, here's what we got, pro-set…slot right…X-drag…Z-rocket…on one." The huddle broke to the line of scrimmage. The play called for the two wide receivers on the right to fly down the field and for the left end to drag across the middle. Gene completed the short pass to Billy Nauls, Lakewood's tight-end and gained the much-needed 1st down on Edgewood's 34-yardline. Cleat was glad to hear his number called on the next play…he was to run a deep slant and split the defensive backs. They had scored on this play seven times this year, and he was looking to do so again. At the snap of the ball he was off and running.

Gene dropped back in the pocket, but before he could set up # 77 was bearing down on him, trying to step out of the big nose guard's way, he was off-balance when he aired the pass downfield.

Cleat knew from the flight of the football it was going to be high and off-line, keeping his eye on the ball he followed it all the way until his hands clasped around the seams. Jake Adam's, Edgewood's senior all-state defensive back hit Cleat immediately, causing Cleat to loose his grip. Just as he was about to regain control of the football Blake arrived and threw a forearm to Cleat's jaw sending them both hurling through the air. The incomplete pass tumbled harmlessly out of bounds.

The cheap shot from Cleat's nemesis left him spread-eagle on the ground with the metallic taste of blood lingering in his mouth. Wiping it from his bruised lips he stuck a thumb and forefinger in his mouth to make sure his teeth were still intact. They were but one of them felt loose. Several feet away he spotted his mouthpiece lying next to Blake's outstretched body. Cleat groaned when he pushed himself upright to retrieve the molded rubber. He picked it up and brushed the dirt and grass free on his tattered jersey. Towering over Blake, he spit a mouthful of blood close to where his opponent lay, and flashed him a crooked grin outlined in crimson. Pointing a bloody finger at his bitter enemy, he cautioned, "If that's the way you want it asshole, that's fine by me."

"What's the matter cry baby...can't take it?" Blake laughed propping himself up on an elbow. "This ain't the powder puff league, pretty boy, if it's getting too tough for you why don't'cha run home to mama."

"Asshole!" Cleat lunged for Blake, only to be restrained by a referee who saw it coming. The man grabbed Cleat by the shoulder pads and forcibly shoved him toward his teammates.

"All right boys, that's enough...we're here to play football, not grab-ass."

Blake answered with a "yes sir" and trotted over to his teammates cackling all the way. His teammates gathered around their one-man demolition team slapping him on the back. He must've said something clever, because they all started laughing and pointing their fingers at Cleat.

Cleat was oblivious to his surroundings as he stood staring at the enemy.

He had been angry before, but never like this. His anger was fueled with hatred. His hands opened and closed into fists, as of this moment the game had become more personal than ever. He wouldn't be satisfied until he'd tasted revenge.

Standing in the huddle, Gene glanced at the clock...they still had plenty of time, but a little voice inside his head screamed the importance of this drive. "Okay, let's keep it together...we're moving the ball again, but dammit I have to have more time. Bo, you've got to stop # 77...the son-of-a- bitch is busting everything up. I don't have time to even handoff much less throw the damn ball."

"Shit, Gene, I'm doing all I can," Bo whined. "The guy just keeps coming...I need some help with that big bastard." Bo refused to face the stares of his teammates...he stood teary-eyed, feeling the blame for his team's failures.

"Goddammit, Bo, quit whining; just do your job, at least slow the son-of-a-bitch down long enough for me run a play."

"Fuck you Gene, he's doing the best he can," Big Oak yelled. "Run the damn ball to my side, I ain't letting nobody come through me."

Bo was humiliated; he'd never been dressed down in front of an audience before, and what hurt the most was everything Gene said was true. He wasn't doing his job, but it wasn't from lack of trying. The simple fact was...the bastard was too damn good. Bo was black and blue from the beating he'd been taking.

"Bo, come here." Coon pulled Bo off to the side and held him in a whispered conversation. When they returned to the huddle, the chastised center bent over and clandestinely scooped a handful of dirt and grass in his left hand. He listened to the next play and lined up on the line of scrimmage anxiously waiting for Gene to call the signals. On the snap-count he centered the ball with his right hand and threw dirt and grass into the nose guard's face with his left. Bo caught # 77 by surprise, and released his pent-up frustration with a vicious forearm blow under the big man's chin. It knocked #77 ass-over backwards. The play sprung Coon for 6-yards.

Walking back to the huddle Bo passed his man sitting on the ground rubbing his eyes and spitting debris from a bloody mouth. "Jesus, you need a bath asshole."

"You bastard...you son son-of-a-bitch, you're mine."

"You ain't nothin' but all mouth, fat boy."

"You're one dead son-of-a-bitch." Michaels ran a hand across his mouth and flung his blood on the ground. A sinister grin followed Bo's every move. His eyes were the color of onyx.

When the referee walked up to Lakewood's offensive huddle Bo complained about # 77's dirty tactics and asked if he would please watch the nose guard to ensure there would be no more unnecessary roughness. The referee nodded his head and told Bo to play ball, and leave the officiating to the referee's.

Breaking the huddle, Bo ran up to the ball anticipating what was going to happen. He couldn't keep the smile off of his face when he looked across the line of scrimmage at Michaels glaring face and flaring nostrils. Bo centered the ball on cue and braced himself for the pain he was about to receive for the team. Sure enough Michaels fired across the line catching Bo in the stomach with a balled fist. Bo grabbed his belly and let out an agonizing screamed before collapsing dramatically to the ground in a heap. Michaels laughed at Bo and intentionally stomped a size eighteen shoe into the small of Bo's back. Bo rolled on the ground squealing in pretentious agony until he heard the whistle blow. Out of the corner of his eye he saw the penalty flag flutter to the ground.

From start to finish the official had seen it all. Pointing an accusatory finger at Michaels he yelled, "Number seventy-seven you're out of the game. You are ejected for a flagrant personal foul with vicious intent to cause injury."

"Noooo! You can't do that...the son-of-a-bitch started it. He threw shit in my face first," Michaels yelled in defiance.

"Son, if you don't leave now you're going to penalize your team more than you already have."

Several of Edgewood's players had to forcibly drag the vocal nose guard to the sidelines, but Michaels wasn't through venting his anger. He stood on the sidelines angrily yelling insults at Bo, the officials, and the Lakewood players. Finally the umpire had enough of #77's tirades. He went to see Edgewood's head coach and told him the ejected player would have to leave the field or face another fifteen yard penalty, and quite possibly a forfeiture of the game.

The referee marked off the yardage and placed the ball just inside the Panthers' 13-yardline, signaling it was a Spartan first down.

The play called in the huddle was a pass designed for Cleat to run a corner fade in the end zone and Coon was to flare out of the backfield toward the sidelines. It was a perfect call. Cleat had beaten the defensive back by several steps and was in the clear. Gene rolled to his right, but failed to take the correct angle and ran headlong into Blake who was blitzing from the outside. They crashed violently helmet to helmet. It was no contest. Gene wasn't able to secure the ball before he was leveled. A defensive lineman recovered the loose pigskin on Edgewood's 17-yardline.

After the change of possession eight of the eleven Lakewood players remained on the field to play defense. Uncharacteristically the Spartans' were tired, sore, and emotionally deflated. The sudden shock of a turnover just when they thought they were going to score was like a dagger in the heart. Time was running out *and* the will to continue their quest for a state championship was slipping away and no longer seemed attainable.

Cleat stood in the middle of the defensive huddle glaring at his dejected teammates, surprisingly, even Coon looked down in the dumps. "Hey, come-on, there's still plenty of time...don't give up on me now. Damn it to hell, we can beat these guys. We're not quitters' dammit and we're not going to start quitting now. All we need to do is stop these assholes and get the ball back. Suck it up and play like Spartans'...we didn't bust our ass all year to lie down in the championship game. We're a team and we can still win this game."

"Dammit, Cleat's right." Coon stepped into the center of the huddle. "We know who's gonna be carrying the damn ball...all we got to do is stop the son-of-a-bitch. Hell, we can do it...let's pull together. This is our field and nobody's gonna push us around. Look at'em over there...those jerks think they have the game won." Coon reached over and grabbed Big Oak by the jersey and yanked him forward, "Big Oak and I say they ain't won shit, ain't that right Oak?"

"You bet your ass Coon." Big Oak gripped his massive hand around Butch Werner's face mask and pulled him into the inner circle. "What do 'ya say Butch, are you ready to kick some Panther ass?"

"Arrrugh...I'm ready to kick ass and forget about taking names. Bo get your ass in here. Are you ready to play some hardnosed football and rip some heads off?"

Bo closed his fists and raised his arms high overhead before yelling, "Somebody's going to die tonight!"

The outer circle of players became a tight-knit group as they formed around their senior leadership. Someone began shouting: "Kill...kill...kill." The rest of the team joined in the chant.

Cleat struggled quieting his teammates, "Alright, listen up. We've got one last stand…it's now or never, there ain't no second chances."

Edgewood fell into a tight T-formation with 4:19 remaining. Chadwick settled under the center and used a long count to drain the clock as much as possible. On the count of four he surprised everybody by faking to Blake and handed off to Simpson, who followed his lead blocker through the number five-hole. The misdirection play was executed flawlessly and gained 24-yards to their own 41-yardline before the defense could recover.

The next two plays were run from the Power-I formation and Blake grinded out another 8-yards putting the ball on Edgewood's 49-yardline. It was 3rd and two with 2:11 on the clock and counting. Blake carried again for five more yards…then for six and another for eight. The referee placed the ball on Lakewood's 32-yardline, the Panthers needed to reach the Spartans' 30-yardline for another 1st down. In the hometown end zone the game clock showed there was 1:28 seconds left before the buzzer. In the stands not a soul was seated when they witness the miracle they had all been praying for.

Cleat and Butch Werner gambled on a hunch, instead of Butch taking his normal inside responsibility he twisted to the outside. As planned the offensive guard tried to double team Werner with the offensive tackle. They had used the same blocking scheme most of the night and it was exactly what Cleat and Butch had hoped they would do. Cleat blitzed through the vacant hole untouched and arrived in Edgewood's backfield just as the quarterback was about to handoff to Blake. The ball was jarred loose and squirted to the ground taking crazy bounces. Werner was able to recover the ball just before it rolled out of bounds. It was Lakewood's ball on their own 37-yardline.

The crowd's roaring approval could be heard from blocks away as they rejoiced in their good fortune. Lakewood's Senior High Marching Band struck-up the Spartans' fight song as Gene Reese trotted onto the field. You could feel the excitement in the air as loyal fans from both sides remained standing. All eyes were on the scoreboard at the far end of the field…1:20 was frozen in time.

"Okay, let's move the ball…pro set…slot right-28…Z reverse on one." Gene repeated the play to make sure everyone was on the same page before breaking the huddle. It was one of the new plays inserted for tonight's game. Taking the snap, Gene tossed the ball to Coon who was sweeping right. Cleat was in the slot, and took a quick step forward as if he were going to release downfield. At the count of one he pivoted and reversed his direction. He took the hand-off from Coon and circled wide to turn the corner. Gene delayed a count to make sure there wasn't a fumble on the exchange and then followed Werner pulling from the right side. Big Oak also rolled left to lead interference. Edgewood was completely fooled into thinking it was a power sweep and were caught flowing to the wrong side of the field.

One of Edgewood's defenders slipped past the first block but Gene was able to get in the guy's way long enough for Cleat to get by without much difficulty. Making his cut up field he dipped back a few steps to avoid another tackler, after that he was in high gear following Werner and Big Oak's broad fat asses. Butch Werner trampled over the first assailant, and knocked another would-be tackler senseless when he lowered his shoulders and plowed through him. Unfortunately the big senior tackle was unable to maintain his footing and fell. Cleat had no choice but to run over his teammate. Big Oak was still in the mix until he left his feet and squashed a defensive back. When Cleat leapt over his childhood friend he couldn't even see there was a body underneath him.

Cleat saw several Panthers trying to head him off at the sidelines, so he planted his left foot and cut against the grain causing them to lose their angle of attack. Anything that was thrown in front of him he crushed, head-butted, or stiff-armed out of his way…including some of his teammates. Changing the ball from his right hand to his left he broke back to the sidelines. When he realized there was no way on God's green earth he was going to score he killed the clock by stepping out of bounds on Edgewood's 36-yardline. Tossing the ball to the referee he looked at the game clock…there was 1:07 left in the game.

On 1st and 10 Gene was sacked for a 7-yard loss…their next play was a quick slant to Cleat that managed only 4-yards to the Panthers' 39-yardline…on 3rd and thirteen Cleat ran a deep slant trying to split the defensive backs, but at the last minute Edgewood changed their coverage by dropping Blake into deep middle safety. The two of them arrived at the same time as the ball, but Cleat was able to tuck it away for a 14-yard gain and step out of bounds killing the clock. The play gained another 1st down just outside the 25-yardline.

The scoreboard clock was at 00:37 when Gene called two plays in the huddle. The first play was a post to Cleat, but Reese saw he was double-teamed and threw it to Pritchard on an out pattern…the ball went high and wide for an incomplete pass, stopping the clock at 00:32. The Spartans' quickly lined up for their second play, a deep corner to Cleat, but once again he was double-covered. Reese opted to throw the ball to Ryan Cheatham; Lakewood's split-end who was running a corner-post…it too went incomplete, landing far downfield. They were now facing a 3rd and 10. Thankfully the clock had stopped with the incomplete pass. With 00:14 remaining in the game Coach Dunn signaled for them to use their last time out and motioned for Reese.

Lakewood's faithful watched with heightened emotions praying for another miracle. The true believers were hoping beyond hope there was still some magic left in the night. Being witness to a game filled with such intensity and so many highs and lows, it was unthinkable to walk away without the coveted trophy. Both teams had showcased their talent on the field, demonstrating no one deserved to lose, but there would be only one winner, if justice prevailed Lakewood would capture their first state title in the next fourteen seconds.

"Gene…what are you thinking son? Dammit boy, throw the ball to Cleat."

"He was double-covered, Coach. I…I…"

"For Christ sakes son…he's an All American, I don't care if they put the whole damn team on him…just throw him the ball and he'll catch it. Are we clear on that?"

"Yes sir…what do you want me to ca…call next, Coach?"

"If we throw a down and out to Cleat, and he steps out of bounds for a first down we can win this thing with a field goal, at least it'll stop the clock and give us enough time to run another play. If we don't make a first down throw him a post corner on the next play. You got that, son?"

"Yes sir, throw an out to Cleat…if we don't pick up a 1st down throw him a post corner. Coach, if we make a 1st down do we go for a field goal?"

"I'll think about that when it happens…just go in there and do like you've done all year…be a winner and make us proud."

"Yes sir, Coach." Reese ran back to the huddle more nervous than he had ever been in his life. This was supposed to be fun, but right now it seemed as if the weight of the whole town was riding on his shoulders. His feet felt like he was wearing a pair of clown shoes three sizes too big.

"Okay, y'all listen-up…pro-right slot-right…double-cross with a roll. I want maximum protection…we're going for the 1st down…let's show these assholes that Spartans rule." Reese repeated the play and the snap-count before breaking the huddle with a loud clap of the hands.

Cleat was in a two-point stance one yard deep from the line of scrimmage eyeing the defense. The timing of the play was critical...when Pritchard made his cut to the middle of the field Cleat was to go underneath and run his pattern to the sidelines. It was almost a pick, but they'd gotten away with it all year. The thought of not being able to make the catch never entered his mind...his thoughts were all about scoring a touchdown, or getting out of bounds with time still remaining on the clock.

When Bo snapped the ball Cleat exploded off the line with a new burst of adrenalin. Eight yards up field he broke his fly pattern off and cut toward the sidelines. He turned his shoulders to receive the pass and was surprised to see the ball wasn't there, it wasn't even halfway. A split second before the ball arrived a sudden blur cut in front of him reaching for the late pass.

Harvey Blake read the play perfectly and timed his move with the skill of a surgeon, but just as he was bringing the ball in Cleat hacked his right arm. All #31 could do was watch helplessly as the ball bounced out of his hands and fall to the ground. Blake had been so close to ending the game right then and there, but as fate would have it the Spartans were left with one last gasp.

Blake was disgusted with himself; he turned to face Cleat lying on the ground. "You got lucky, pretty-boy...I should've had that one."

"You're one hell of a player, Blake...with one hell of a mouth."

"Hey, what can I say...it's the *only* fault I've got." Blake offered a helping hand to Cleat. "You're the best I've ever played against, Davis. At first I thought the write-ups were all bullshit, but now I know different. It's a shame we'll never have the chance to be friends. I think we would've made good ones."

Reluctantly, Cleat reached for Blake's extended hand and pulled himself upright. "Maybe...who knows? Right now I just want to take home the trophy and go soak in the whirlpool. My body aches all over."

"My thoughts exactly." Blake gave Cleat a friendly wave before trotting off to rejoin his teammates. They received their leader with applause and admiration. Cleat watched stoically with mixed feelings as Blake humbly accepted his teammates' gratitude.

When Cleat returned to the offensive huddle he was visibly shocked at their appearance. They looked like battle scared veterans assembled from a battlefield. Every one of them had been treated for some type of injury; gauze and tape were wrapped around arms, and legs. Their once proud uniforms of orange and black were now worn, tattered and covered with blood smears. Some of the blood was theirs, and some were from their opponents. Various parts of their equipment were sticking out here and there, but most startling were their eyes, they registered defeat and the pungent smell of fear filled the air."Hey, come on dammit, we've still got six seconds left. It's time to put up or shut up. We're going to win this game right here and now. Call the play, Gene, and throw me the damn ball."

"Pro-set...slot right...Z-corner...Y-slant on one. All right you linemen, protect me like I was your virgin sister...I don't want a hand laid on me. Tonight we're going home state champions."

Cleat was lined up in the slot poised and eager. A feeling of calm swept over him when Gene called the play. He never felt more relaxed in his life. When the ball was centered he glided up field selling an inside post route before cutting to the corner. Running full speed he looked over his right shoulder and saw Gene was in trouble. Breaking off his pattern he ran toward Gene waving for the ball. At the last second the junior quarterback spotted Cleat and threw a desperate pass before he was dragged to the turf.

As the ball drew nearer Cleat spread his fingers and physically watched them wrap around the seams. Tucking it close to his side he didn't hear the blare of the horn signaling time had expired. Edgewood's safety quickly closed the gap and threw his body low into Cleat's legs sending him airborne. Cleat somehow braced himself with his free hand and landed on both feet. He regained his balance and was off and running for the end zone. His body was leaning forward and his strong legs were churning up the yardage.

Coon went streaking by and threw a body block on a defender, both players vaulted out of bounds. Their momentum rolled them through the Edgewood cheerleaders like a bowling ball seeking pins. Several of the girls were flipped into the air with their arms and legs flailing wildly. Judy Pennington, the auburn-haired beauty, landed her attractive derrière on top of Coon's face mask. In her discombobulated descent her undergarment had worked its way into her crack. Coon couldn't help but smile at the two half-moons mere inches from his face. He thought, *thank you lord for this show of gratitude. I owe you one.*

A Panther slight of build came from out of nowhere making a desperate attempt to bring the ball carrier down, but there was little chance of that happening when Cleat lowered his head and shoulders and struck the assailant a devastating blow. The defender's helmet flew off and his body went reeling sideways. Cleat ran five more yards unencumbered until someone latched onto his arm, he could feel fingernails digging into his flesh. Thrusting his forearm and lunging forward the groper fell by the wayside. Cleat accidentally put his size 12-½ shoe in the boy's face.

The end zone was only 10-yards away when Cleat stiff-armed an Edgewood player, his stabbing fingers slid underneath the defender's facemask as he was violently shoved aside. Another player slammed into him from the rear, causing him to break stride, he stumbled forward, and received another hit on his left side. Cleat struggled valiantly towards the goal line fighting every step of the way. On his quest, two Edgewood players held death grips on each leg.

Unexplainably, Cleat reverted back to the nursery rhyme his mother used to read to him as a child, "The Little Engine That Could." He began screaming over and over again: "I think I can, I think I can, I think I can." A defender leapt on his back and wrapped a strangle hold around his neck, another attacked him from the front, but he dove his helmet into player and he disappeared under a tangle of feet.

The goal was within reach when *the* freight train plowed into his back, pounding him to the turf. Surely the sky had fallen, for he couldn't see or breathe underneath the weight that was pressing his face into the dirt. A human mound of flesh and football paraphernalia lay on top of Cleat at the goal line.

"He's over...TOUCHDOWN!" Ted yelled into the receiver announcing Lakewood's victory over the airwaves. "I can't believe it, Bill...Davis must've broken at least six or seven tackles before he crossed the goal."

"It was absolutely unbelievable, Ted. Wow...I've never in my life seen anything quite like it. It was pure determination...Davis was not to be denied. Desire and guts drove that boy into the end zone. He should've been down at the 10-yardline, but he just kept on going...it was an outstanding run by an outstanding young man. What a wonderful game that young man played tonight."

Bedlam broke out in the stands when the scoreboard lit up in bright lights on the far side of the field: HOME 25 VISITORS 21. Lakewood's entire football team rushed onto the playing field with helmets held high screaming, "We're number one…we're number one." Hundreds of joyous fans both young and old poured from the stadium bleachers to join the celebration.

On Edgewood's side of the field there were no shouts of jubilation or victorious cheers. Some of the players stood in silent anguish, while others threw their battered helmets to the ground in utter frustration over the loss. Many of them were guiltless in their tears of sadness, they had done their best, and they had left nothing on the field of battle. Even so, they had that hollow feeling in the pit of their stomachs that every athlete who has ever put on a uniform and tasted the ills of defeat are familiar with.

Mandy's flaxen hair bounced with every stride as she wove through the crowd trying to reach her Cleat, along the way she tripped over someone's foot and tumbled head-over-heels to the asphalt track circling the field. Bounding from the rough surface in one fluid motion, she noticed the abrasions on her knees seeping small droplets of blood. As yet there wasn't any pain, but she knew by tomorrow her knees would be sore. Tossing her light honey-colored hair over her shoulders, she resumed her pilgrimage without worrying about how she looked.

"Oh daddy we won, we won." Sissy was jumping up and down clutching her fathers arm. The Spartans are state champions!"

Mister Davis drew Sissy and June into a bear-hug. "Yes we are honey. Our boys did it. God bless them. It was the greatest game I've ever seen. June, did you see Cleat drag half of Edgewood's team over the goal?"

"Of course I did silly. I'm so proud of Cleat and Coon *and* I'm so thankful this game is over with. It's too violent and by the grace of God no one was seriously hurt."

Randle laughed and kissed his wife on the forehead, "You're never going to change are you sweetheart?"

"Would you want me too?"

"No…no I wouldn't." He suddenly lifted her into the air, "I love you Mrs. Davis."

"Dad, put her down. You are embarrassing me to death."

Down on the field several referees were frantically running around blowing their whistles. They were trying to separate the growing mass of humanity from the players lying on top of each other at the goal line. During the confusion no one noticed that the men in black and white stripes hadn't given the official signal for a touchdown. Everyone at the game, including the players from both teams thought Lakewood won the game on the final play. As they hovered around the prone bodies, a gradual stillness swept across the field until an eerie silence encompassed the stadium. Nervous tension began to build as each exhausted player was assisted from the pile. Finally, the stack of bodies dwindled until all that was left were two physically drained Panthers covering Cleat's body.

The Edgewood sidelines couldn't be contained from rushing back onto the field. A new kindle of hope had sparked their dampened spirits. The Edgewood players and coaches alike silently prayed for a miracle. When they reached the end zone the referees were disengaging the last of the entwined limbs from the pile. Finally there was but one solitary figure lying on the field, one lone soul dressed in tattered orange and black.

Cleat lay motionless with his head and shoulders over the goal, his helmet was askew and his jersey was ripped at the neck exposing his shoulder pads. There were flecks of grass and dirt stuck to his sweaty face as bruised lips fought for each breath. Bloody fingers held the nose of the football in a death grip…it was six inches short of the goal line.

Without a moment's hesitation the umpire quickly stood up waving his hands back and forth signaling no touchdown was scored. The game was over, along with Lakewood's hopes for a state championship.

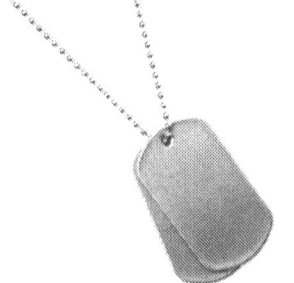

CHAPTER 7

Below the stadium the cramped quarters of Lakewood's dressing room was like a morgue. The only sounds to be heard were of lament and an occasional piece of equipment hitting the floor. Players were strewn across the room in various forms of disarray. No two were alike in their mode of dress; some were stripped to their jock straps while others still wore their complete uniforms, including their headgear. Cleat was among the latter, except for the helmet. Festering anger caused him to throw it across the room.

Lying spread-eagle on the cold concrete floor, he fought to suppress the frustration welling inside. His eyes were squeezed so tight little crows' feet puckered in the corners. He could shut out the sight of his teammates' bereavement, but nothing could extinguish the sound of their crying. He felt like crying himself, but he knew once he started he wouldn't be able to stop. The shock of losing the game would never wear off. The passage of time wouldn't mean squat. Not once had the thought of losing ever enter his mind, and now all he could think about was losing, and how they lost. His team-mates had entrusted him to win the game and he failed them miserably. Dammit, he'd been so close, how could he have not scored? He was sure of crossing the goal line before being tackled.

Coach Dunn straddled a green metal chair in the far corner of the room alienated from the rest of the world; *his* had collapsed a few minutes ago. Bloodshot eyes stared vacantly at the water-stained floor as he rested his head in the palm of his hands. There was a single tear traversing down his craggy cheek, stopping and starting between irregular cracks and crevasses. He could-n't help but wonder if there wasn't something he could've done differently. Had he made a mistake somewhere, or was it something as simple as not being the coach he thought he was?

Even though the emptiness gnawed his insides, he felt worse for his young men. They had fought Edgewood tooth and nail, and dammit to hell they should be proud of their valiant effort, but what was he to say to them? No matter what he said, there would still be the bitter taste of defeat and that was a hard thing to swallow, especially after going through an undefeated season. They'd been so close, but it wasn't meant to be *and* the saddest of all was his senior leadership would never have another chance at the state title. Who was he kidding; he would probably never see another opportunity either. This was to be *his* year with boys like Cleat, Coon, Werner, and Big Oak. He doubted there would ever be another group of seniors so dedicated and full of talent as those four. Every team needed a nucleus to build on, and he couldn't think of one junior that was capable of filling the vacancy next year, but maybe he was selling his juniors short…he'd have to wait and see. The problem at hand was: what to say to his boys…he had to get off of his ass and do something.

A knock at the dressing room door brought Coach Herndon to his feet. Shuffling to the door he raised a freckled hand and wiped away the tears. It was too early for the press, but they were going to have to face them sometime. Opening the metal door he was surprised to see a young solitary figure in the darkened hallway. He was properly dressed in a black blazer, gray slacks, white shirt, a red and black striped tie completed his attire. Cradled in the boy's arm was a scuffed football. At first the young man stood in awkward silence shuffling his black penny loafers back and forth avoiding the coach's stare.

"What can I do for you, son? Are you with the school newspaper?"

The youth looked into the older man's roughly honed face, and smiled sheepishly exposing two missing front teeth. "Uh…uh," the boy stammered. "Coach, my name is Harvey Blake."

Taken by surprise, the befuddled coach stumbled backward into the dressing room. Finding himself at a loss for words, he could only stare in disbelief at the Edgewood player who had caused his team such grief. If it hadn't been for him, Lakewood would have won easily.

"Uh…sir, I was wondering if I could…uhh…well sir, I would like to uh…" Blake cleared his throat, searching for the right words. "I would like to pay my respects, sir, if you'll allow me to do so."

Coach Herndon stood scratching his scalp wondering what the young athlete was up to. "Well son…uh, I…uh…guess its okay. Come on in."

As Blake stepped inside, the assistant went over and whispered into Coach Dunn's ear. The head coach took a handkerchief out of his rear pocket and loudly blew his nose, after rubbing it clean he meticulously refolded the linen before cramming it back in place. Without further delay he warmly greeted the visitor by holding out his hand.

"I'm proud to meet'cha son, mighty proud."

Blake swallowed hard and quickly dried a sweaty palm on his gray slacks before accepting the head coach's outstretched friendship.

"Thank you sir, the pleasure's all mine."

"It was one hell of a ball game wasn't it, son?"

"Yes sir, it sure was."

"You bet'cha it was. Now, what can I do for you Mr. Blake?"

A prelude of uncomfortable silence ensued before Harvey Blake summoned the courage to voice his request. "Uh…Coach Dunn, I'd like to say a few words to your team if it's all right with you."

"Sure son…that'd be fine with me, please be my guest." Coach Dunn turned to face his players. "All right, everybody listen up. We have a representative from Edgewood who'd like to say a few words to you men. I'd like to introduce y'all to one of the finest football players I've ever had the misfortune to coach against…I give you Edgewood's all-state, all conference halfback, and linebacker…Harvey Blake."

Following Dunn's announcement a general muttering erupted among the players as they maneuvered for a better position to see the infamous Harvey Blake. They were visibly surprised by how nice and friendly he appeared out of uniform. He actually looked like a guy you'd want to hang out with, instead of the destructive force he brought to the field.

"Uh…I asked my coaches and teammates for permission to come over here and pay our respect. I consider it an honor and a privilege to stand before y'all and sincerely express our admiration for your football program. We were lucky to win tonight and we'd be the first to admit it. Anybody that saw or listened to the game knows it could've gone either way. We feel very fortunate it happened to bounce in our favor. I'm sorry that someone had to lose, because you deserve the championship as much as we do, if not more. I know me standing here isn't going to make you feel any better, but all of us want you know how we feel as a team."

Blake took a deep breath and an audible whistling sound came from his mouth. "Oh shit…I forgot to put my teeth in." Blake joined in Lakewood's laughter as he reached in his side coat pocket and pulled out his retainer.

Grinning, he slipped it in place. Tapping the bridge with his forefinger he winked, "This is the trophy I took home after playing Miami Senior last year." More laughter filled the locker room; even the coaches had a good chuckle.

"Believe me I know how most of y'all feel, because I was in your shoes last year when Miami Senior beat the crap out of us." Raising a hand to his mouth he remembered the blow he'd taken from Pedro Suarez's forearm on the very last play of the game. "We cried the same tears you're shedding tonight. But the main reason I'm here is to let y'all know my teammates and I were proud to be on the same field with Lakewood tonight. I'm glad that I'm a senior, because I sure as hell don't want to face y'all again."

The Lakewood players were on their feet clapping and shouting. Someone started screaming "Blake...Blake," and most of the Lakewood players joined in. The noise they created from their underground sanctuary was so loud people who hadn't left the stadium would swear they heard rolling thunder on a clear night. Lakewood fans would later claim the heavens were protesting the outcome of *the* game.

Blake held up his hands, indicating he had more to say; he waited patiently for the players to settle down. Turning to Coach Dunn, he held up the football he brought with him. "Coach Dunn, my teammates and our coaching staff voted unanimously to give y'all one of the game balls, not to remind you of your loss, but for you to remember the night you fought so gallantly. All of us seniors, along with the coaches, signed it, and we would deem it an honor if you would accept this tribute of our respect."

Coach Dunn was momentarily speechless as he stood staring at the youth offering him the autographed football. After a pregnant pause his trembling hand accepted the gift. "Son," he began with a quavering voice full of emotion, "it's an honor and privilege, and on behalf of the players and coaches I want to tell you how much we appreciate this gesture of respect Edgewood has bestowed upon us." Choking back the tears, he continued with grave difficulty. "It makes us mighty proud to be honored by such an unprecedented act of chivalry. Tell your coaches and teammates we will display it proudly in remembrance of this contest waged by two of the best damn football teams I've ever seen."

The hush that followed was soon replaced with prideful sobs from the Lakewood Spartans. There wasn't a dry eye in the locker room, including Blake's. Even the most hardened of the disappointed warriors were caught in the emotional moment. Their heaving chests were filled with pride knowing they had done their best and were heralded by athletes who recognized their determined effort. Only those who had played the game would understand the camaraderie in the room.

Blake began stepping over discarded equipment and shaking hands with newfound friends who only a short while ago had been the enemy. Suddenly before him, blocking his way was an imposing figure towering above him in a tattered jersey with a number barely recognizable. His once white pants were stained with grass, dirt, sweat, and smatterings of blood. Huge hands scarred and bloody were resting on his lean, narrow hips; they were the largest hands he had ever seen. His light brown hair was now dark and plastered to his forehead. You could still see the red indentations where the helmet had been. Droplets of perspiration slowly trailed down his dirty, sweat-stained face and disappeared beneath his shoulder pads.

Blake wasn't intimidated by Cleat, even though he was at least four inches shorter; his single dad had raised him tough enough to handle most any situation. Rolling his broad shoulders he braced himself for the unexpected. He somewhat relaxed when he saw a crooked smile creep across the dirt-smeared face. When Cleat offered him an extended hand, Blake promptly ignored the gesture and roughly threw his arms around Cleat in a bear hug.

Cleat hesitated only briefly before putting his arms around Blake. Suddenly, and without warning all of the suppressed emotions he'd been holding inside burst forth in a torrent of sobs. He cried freely showing no fear or shame, he was beyond the point of caring what others might think. It wasn't long before Blake's tears joined Cleat's as they stood hanging onto each other.

A kinship was born that night between two opposing combatants, a bond built upon the sturdiest of all...that of respect and admiration, tempered on the battlefield of honor. Ending their embrace they felt a little foolish, but were confident enough in their masculinity that they didn't feel threatened. They shook hands gripping each other's firmly ensuring their manhood.

"It was one hell of a ballgame Davis." Blake winked at his new friend.

"Yeah, it sure as hell was. I don't think I ever quite got over that first lick you gave me."

Blake rubbed his neck laughing, "Me neither, I promise it hurt me as much as it did you. Hell, I think I had a stinger all through the first half."

Coon walked over to join the two of them. "So this is what the badass Harvey Blake looks like in street clothes, you don't look so tough to me."

Blake eyed the new guy closely, trying to read whether he was kidding or not.

"Harvey, this is my best friend John Truman, everybody calls him Coon...he's like a brother to me."

"So, you're that little scat-back everybody was chasing all over the field. Christ almighty how fast are you anyway? Nobody could catch your ass."

Coon stuck out his hand, "No hugs, please...the girls might get jealous."

Harvey laughed out loud, grabbing Coon's hand in a vise grip, "I'm taking it you're the smart-ass of the two."

"Give the man a cigar, Cleat. See, I told you he wasn't near as stupid as he looked. And to tell you the truth Blake, your IQ rose 10 points with those missing teeth. Shit, I'd leave that thing out when I was on a date. Hell I bet a girl's nipple would fit right in that gap. Man, you could drive them crazier than one of those French Ticklers."

"Is he always like this Davis, or is he just a little hyper tonight?"

"Every waking moment, Harvey. What you see is what you get."

"My friends call me Harv." Blake smiled shaking his head at Coon.

"Everybody calls me Coon...even my enemies."

"Okay, Cleat and Coon it is. Hey, I've got to go, but if you're ever in my neck of the woods be sure and give me a call. We're listed in the phone book under H. Blake. My dad's name is Harvey too, but I ain't no junior. We have different middle names." Harv winked at his friends and waved goodbye to the rest of the players as he left the locker room.

The throng of fans that once stood outside the stadiums east ramp had dissipated. Only a few parents and girlfriends remained in the semidarkness waiting ardently for their football players to exit their dressing room. The Davis's said their goodbyes to Mandy fifteen minutes ago and left her alone to stand vigil. After more than an hour of prolonged patience, and darting moths and other critters underneath the fading light, she was more than concerned Cleat hadn't emerged from the tunnel.

Coon's current flame, Anne Wilson, walked over to where Mandy stood leaning against the fender of Cleat's car. "Look, there's Coon."

Mandy quickly stood upright and was near hysteria when see didn't see Cleat walking by his side. *They were inseparable. Where could he be?* "Do you see Cleat?"

"No, but it shouldn't be too much longer…there can't be many left inside."

Mandy liked Anne, even though she was a junior, and not part of her circle of friends. She and Coon were going to ride with them to Pips before going home. She was really a sweet girl, her mother was a city clerk at the courthouse, and her father lived somewhere up north. Sadly, her parents had been divorced since she was a little girl.

Anne had beautiful features, but she was a little overweight and, being the daughter of a single mom she was unable to afford clothes that were considered fashionable. Oftentimes she wore ill-fitting and dated hand-me-downs from her older sister Rebecca. Her sibling was a junior at FSU attending school on a full academic scholarship. Rebecca was taller and much slimmer than her younger sister, henceforth Anne's slovenly, untailored appearance. Mandy's friends had christened her "Raggedy Ann" and Mandy was shameful that she didn't chastise them for their crassness.

"Hi girls, I'm sorry about the wait."

Anne rushed to Coon and threw her arms around his neck. "I'm so sorry y'all didn't win the game. Are you okay? Can I make it better? Is there *anything* I can do?"

"I have a few bumps and bruises here and there, but some well placed kisses in the right spots would definitely make my world more tolerable."

"Oh Coon, you're always trying to embarrass me."

Exasperated over their childish double entendres Mandy threw her hands up, "Where in the world is Cleat?"

"I don't know. Heck, I thought he was out here waiting on me. There's nobody in the locker room but Coach Herndon and a couple of trainers. Cleat left way before I did."

"Are you sure?" Mandy pleaded.

"I'm positive…he was gone when I stepped out of the shower."

Anne slipped her hand in Coon's and snuggled close, making sure her breast rubbed firmly against his shoulder. "Well, he didn't come out this way…we've been here the whole time."

Mandy started walking towards the tunnel leading inside the stadium, "I think maybe I know where he is." She was out of sight when she yelled over her shoulder that she'd be back in a few minutes. Darkness engulfed her as she made her way around the oval track surrounding the field. Her footfalls made crunching sounds on the loose gravel as she walked onto the asphalt track. The cold loneliness and the bleak emptiness surrounding her sent a chill down her spine.

The vacant concrete bleachers were barely distinguishable in the blackness. Absent from the arena were the beastly grunts and moans and the clashing of pads. The cries of pain and anguish had vanished with the wind. There were no screaming fans, cheerleaders, or marching bands blaring instruments. On this soulful night, at this very moment the loudest sound of all was that of silence, and it was deafening.

Moving to the fifty-yard line she slowly turned in circle taking in the panorama. She was disheartened when all that greeted her was a landscape littered with debris. A whimsical southern breeze magically danced the litter across the field in a ballet of the colors. Just when she was about to relinquish hope something caught her eye in the far end zone. As she drew nearer the object began to gradually take shape, it was someone lying on the ground. Being unsure of what to expect her pace slowed considerably. The excitement that she had originally experienced was replaced with trepidation. Had she found Cleat, if so, what was she to say or do? And what if it wasn't him? She was alone with no means of protection or any chance of being rescued if she were attacked. Frightful thoughts of danger raced through her mind. She scolded herself for being so foolish as to venture into the darkness unescorted. Coon would have gladly accompanied her if she had asked.

Mandy hesitated momentarily debating what action she should take. Would it be best to call Cleat's name to make sure it was he before venturing any further? *God, why in the world didn't he come out of the locker room with the rest of the players…he knew I would be waiting for him. Sometimes he makes me so angry and most of the time he's oblivious to the fact that he is responsible for my anger and that makes it even worse. Men can be so anal.*

Short of her journey's end she recognized the still form as Cleat, his feet were crossed at the ankles, and his hands were cradling the back of his head. Silently she lowered herself to the ground and settled beside him. An audible sigh escaped her lips to alert him of her presence. She clasped her hands and rested them in her lap hoping he would open his eyes. Seconds became agonizing minutes as she sat exhibiting patience far beyond her years. She knew he was suffering, and was reluctant to interrupt his private thoughts. If Cleat needed solace then she should've been the first person he came to. Cleat chose to be alone and that hurt deeply, if they were going to discuss his pain then it was up to him to begin the conversation.

Mandy plucked a blade of grass from the end zone and began nibbling on the tip. Her mind searched for ways to profess the wonder of *their* relationship without diminishing the outcome of tonight's game. The world hadn't come to an end, the sun would bring a new dawn, *and* most important of all: they had each other.

"Are you waiting for me to say something, Mandy?"

The intrusion startled Mandy. "I didn't want to bother you." He didn't answer so she continued: "I'm sorry, Cleat, so very sorry. I love you with all my heart." Mandy lay beside him, resting her head on his chest.

"And I love you." Cleat whispered.

Rising slightly, she propped herself on an elbow and methodically studied Cleat's features. As far as she could tell he hadn't moved a muscle since her arrival. "You were wonderful tonight, Cleat. I couldn't be more proud if we had won the game."

"Well, we didn't win…we lost because I let everybody down." Cleat sat up, resting his forearms on battered knees. "When I was needed the most I failed them, and because of *me* we lost. Dammit, I still can't believe we lost."

Running his fingers savagely through his hair, he looked at Mandy. "I was so sure we'd win. When Gene called the final play, I knew what it was before we huddled. I can't explain why or how, but I knew. I also knew that I was going to catch the pass and run it in for a touchdown. There's no explanation why I felt that way, except it was like it had already happened, and all I had to do was go through the motions. I know it sounds crazy, but that's how I felt. There was absolutely no doubt in my mind that I was going to score the winning touchdown."

Cleat's voice cracked, "God Mandy, what happened? It all went wrong; it wasn't supposed to end like this. I…I don't understand." Cleat lowered his head and sighed, "Ever since I was a kid I've had this strange belief that God put me on earth for a purpose greater than myself. I've never mentioned this to anyone *and* I realize what I'm saying must sound insane and self-absorbed, but I can't shake the premonition…I don't know what it is, nor can I explain it, but it's real. Call it destiny, preordained, or whatever, but its presence tonight was stronger than ever. It was like a protective shroud covering my body…it felt really weird. I don't know Mandy, it's hard to put into words, but I felt special…like I knew something no one else was privy to…then everything fell apart. God, I can't believe it happened. There must be a reason, but for the life of me I can't figure it out. Tell me it's all a bad dream, Mandy."

Mandy put an arm around Cleat's broad shoulders and snuggled closer. Her heart was aching for him and she didn't know what to say. She'd never seen him so distraught, he'd always been so strong and self-assured, but now he was vulnerable and it frightened her. She hadn't any answers and he was leaning on her for the kind of strength she wasn't sure she possessed. "Cleat, you can't feel guilty or blame yourself for the loss. It just wasn't meant to be. The whole team fought as hard as they could, including you."

"Mandy…you don't understand…I had the ball in my hand and the goal was within reach. I should've scored. It was *my* fault we lost the game. I let my teammates down and I've disappointed everyone who's ever believed in me.

"Your wrong Cleat, no matter how you feel at this moment, what you're saying is simply not the truth. Nobody blames you for the loss. Can you honestly say you could've done more?" Without waiting for an answer she continued, "I've heard Coach Dunn say, *if you've given your all, no matter what the outcome, you can always hold your head high knowing you had done your best.* I'm asking you now Cleat, and I want you to give me an honest answer…did you give it your all?"

Cleat avoided her question, along with her stare.

"Well, answer me dammit!"

"I don't know," Cleat mumbled.

"That's not acceptable. Could you have tried, or fought any harder?"

"No," he spoke softly. "I couldn't have done more…I did everything I could."

"I know you did and so does everybody else, including your teammates, coaches, and the fans. Everyone seems to know this, but you and now that you've admitted it to yourself, let's put the game behind us and think about more important things in life—like you and me." Smiling, she put her arms around his neck and kissed him on the cheek, tasting the saltiness of a tear.

Cleat placed his hands on either side of Mandy's cheeks and drew her to his lips. After a passionate kiss and lingering embrace he whispered in her ears, *I love you.*

"Anne, do you mind if I go inside and check on Mandy?"

"Of course not Coon, I'll be just fine."

"Are you sure?"

"Yes, but give a me a kiss before you leave."

"Absolutely!" Coon drew Anne into his arms and kissed her passionately, probing his tongue deep inside. He felt Anne's hot breath on his cheek as she responded in kind. Coon lowered his hands to her butt and gently squeezed her rounded cheeks. When she started to resist his grip tightened. The resistance subsided and she pressed her body firmly against his hardness. Coon's fingers gathered the folds of her skirt and slowly worked the garment up her ample thighs.

Anne gasped when she realized what was happening and abruptly disengaged from Coon's romantic endeavor. If she hadn't noticed her thighs were suddenly getting chilly the skirt would've hiked over her waist. "Coon, I'm not that kind of girl!"

"I'm sorry Anne. I know you're not. I just got carried away. You know how much I care about you."

"Coon, I love you too, but I'm just not willing to do what you want. I know other girls do, but that doesn't make it right." Anne smoothed her skirt and turned away.

Coon thought, God bless Catholics and all of their virtues. He placed a hand on her arm and stepped in front of her. "Come on Anne...don't be like this. I said that I was sorry. Let's not ruin the night."

"Ohhh all right, besides I can't stay angry at you when I look into those big beautiful brown eyes."

"That's my girl." He gave her an affectionate kiss on the cheek, "I won't be gone more that a few minutes

Coon left Anne outside the entrance and entered the stadium. He stood at the edge of the field and cupped his hands around his mouth: "Hey Cleat, are you and Mandy out there?"

"Yeah, we're over here." Cleat waved.

"How about let's get something to eat before I starve to death."

"We're on our way." Cleat pushed himself from the ground and offered Mandy his hand. "Let's go to Pips, I'm starved."

Arm in arm they laughingly walked towards the dimly lit exit speaking of better days to come.

CHAPTER 8

The remainder of Cleat's senior year should have been the best of times, but in reality it turned into something much worse. It all began with the end of basketball season; once again they found themselves playing for a state championship, only this time Clearwater was their opponent. In the semi final against Boone Cleat severely sprained his ankle and was saddled with a pair of crutches for the championship game. Lakewood won the state title by beating Clearwater 52-50. Coon hit the winning jump shot as the buzzer sounded. Even though Cleat led his team all year and played like a man possessed through the finals he felt alienated from the team. His only participation in *the* game was regulated to cheering his teammates to victory. Coon tried to lift his spirits, but it was to no avail. The sweet taste of victory never quite moistened Cleat's palate.

Lakewood's baseball team was a powerhouse too, every sportswriter and professional scout knew about Cleat. His athleticism was well known throughout Florida, *and* the entire nation. There was hardly a paper that didn't cover Lakewood's games, and that of its leader. When Cleat was pitching he concentrated on three pitches, a looping curve ball that broke off the face of the world, an off-speed pitch that made batters look comical, especially after seeing his awesome ninety three plus miles an hour fastball. When he wasn't on the mound he played shortstop like a pro even though he was considered too tall for that position. With Coon playing second base, they were the best defensive combination in the entire state. The two of them had broken last year's school record for double plays midway through the season, by the end of the season they shattered the national record.

Cleat was a phenomenal pitcher, his ERA was a ridiculous .097 and he pitched three no-hitters, one of them was a *perfect* game. He averaged two strikeouts an inning and had the lowest amount of walks per innings pitched by anyone in the country. To say he was an exceptional ballplayer would have been putting it mildly. He led his team in pitching, batting average, and power hitting, and was second to Coon in stolen bases.

The state championship was held in Fort Pierce, Florida between Lakewood Senior High and Jacksonville Senior high. Game time was at 7:00 PM. The eastern breeze coming from the ocean barely put a damper on the 98-degree temperature. It was still daylight when the game started, but by the fourth inning darkness would fall, and with it the insufferable heat. Other than the persistent mosquitoes, it was a perfect night for baseball.

Lakewood's baseball team was inundated with juniors. Cleat, Coon, Butch, and Pete Blair were the only senior starters. Cleat was playing short-stop, Coon was on second, Butch was catching, and Pete was playing left field. In the bottom of the 1st inning Rafe Halliburton led off with a zinger to short and was thrown out at first base, Bill Cassidy followed with a hot-shot to first base for the second out. Coon batted third and earned a walk on four straight pitches. Cleat was batting clean-up and hit a first pitch line drive that careened off of the left field wall and rolled into the corner for a triple. Coon scored easily from first. The next batter was Butch Werner batting fifth, he struck out on a 1-2 count and left Cleat stranded on third.

In the fourth inning Rafe hit a grounder past the second baseman's out-stretched glove for a single. Bill popped out to third and in turn Coon sacrificed a bunt to advance the runner to second. On Cleat's at bat he took the pitcher to a batters count of two balls and no strikes. Cleat stepped out of the batters box and scooped up a handful of loose red clay and rubbed his hands together. He owned the next pitch, he knew exactly where it was going to be *and* he absolutely knew where he was going to drive the ball. Sure enough it was a fastball coming down the pike belt buckle high…right in his wheelhouse. With perfect timing, and excellent hand to eye coordination Cleat took a mighty swing and hit the ball flush on the sweet part of the bat. The ball shot off of his bat like a rocket and screamed towards the deepest section of the park. Rafe was rounding third base when the ball bounded off of the center-field wall straight into the centerfielders hand. The Jacksonville player quickly turned and threw a strike to his cutoff man who pivoted and rifled a throw to second baseman. Cleat was held in check for a stand-up double.

Cleat stood on second base in a state of shock. He couldn't believe the ball didn't carry out of the park. He thought for sure the ball was over the wall and was mystified it fell short. The mystery was solved when a robust breeze blew in his face…the gods had spoken. When Butch stepped into the batters box hitless after two at the bat he was more determine than ever to reach base. He was a pure slugger and only Cleat led him in homeruns. His aggressive swings and go for broke mentality also caused him to lead the team in another category…strikeouts. Butch was well-known for his towering homeruns and the capability of striking a mortal blow every time he held a bat in his hand. Keeping that in mind pitchers had to be very careful when they faced the bruiser and hope they didn't make a mistake. Literally, it was either hit or miss for both batter and pitcher.

Butch flexed his muscles and gave the pitcher an evil grin. He stood crowding the plate with his eyes glaring towards the pitchers mound. He could see the pitchers Adams apple move after taking a nervous gulp. The first pitch was high and inside and it took everything he had to check his swing. He loved to swing at pitches shoulder high *if* they were anywhere near the strike zone. Those were the ones that usually got him into trouble because they looked so fat and juicy. Without a doubt he was a sucker for that particular pitch because he felt like he could blast every one of them out of the park. The next pitch was a tad lower and with a snap of his wrist he unleashed a BB down the third base line. It took a bad hop and blasted into the third baseman's chest. The defensive player kept the deflection in front of him and grabbed the baseball barehanded. He glanced towards second base to hold Cleat on the bag before whipping the ball to the first baseman's outstretched glove. Butch was a half-stride past the bag when he heard the slap of leather. With two outs and runners on first and second Chad Wilson entered the batters box. On a count of two and two he was handcuffed on the next pitch and hit a dribbler back to the pitchers mound for the third out.

In the bottom of the seventh inning the score was 3-2 in Jacksonville's favor and Lakewood's last turn at bat. Cleat stood in the batters box with the bases loaded and two outs. He gripped and re-gripped his Louisville Slugger relishing his chance for redemption. The ballgame rested on his shoulders, what he did in the next few minutes would determine the games outcome. Cleat held his right hand high signaling to the umpire he wasn't quite ready. His right foot dug a foothold into the red clay as he meticulously went through his pre-batting ritual. Not until he was squared away and ready to face the tall, angular lefthander did he lower his hand. Cleat thought about switch-hitting, he was only a few points lower in batting percentage from the left side of the plate, but that was before the lefty took the mound. The starting pitcher retired Lakewood's number eight and nine batters, but when the top of the order came to bat he ran into trouble. He walked Rafe, gave up a single to Bill Cassidy and hit Coon with a wild pitch to load the bases. That was enough for the pitching coach and manager. In came the lefty.

During the pitcher's warm-ups Cleat studied his release point and framed it in an imaginary window. He paid no attention to the string-bean's exaggerated wind-up; his entire focus was on the pitcher's release point. It was like being in a soundproof vacuum with no peripheral vision. From there he would have less than a second to determine what kind of pitch it was *and* if it was going to be in the strike zone.

Mrs. Davis and Sissy sat in the stands with several friends who made the ninety minute trip to watch the state championship game. She clasped her hands and leaned forward silently praying that Cleat would get a base hit. Peanut shells crackled under her feet, fans were screaming encouragement from both sides, but June was unmindful as the tension grew to unbearable heights,

Cleat swung at the first pitch, it was a fastball breaking sharply inside, his swing was a fraction off and the ball drifted foul over the left field wall missing a homerun by inches. The next two pitches were balls and the latter of the two was so wild Cleat had to dive out of the batters box to avoid being beaned in the head. After picking himself up he regretted not taking one for the team. It would've forced in the tying run, but his natural reflexes bailed him out of harm's way. The count was now 2 balls and 1 strike.

Jacksonville's manager hollered for an official timeout and indicated to the umpire that he wanted to visit the pitchers mound. The catcher stepped from behind home plate and trotted out to join the powwow. Cleat was unbothered by the interlude and used the delay to go through some stretching exercises outside the batters box. After a few minutes the home plate umpire hollered, "Play ball!" The impromptu conference officially ended when the barrel-shaped catcher gave the hurler an encouraging pat on the butt with his mitt.

When the umpire motioned for Cleat to step up to the plate, he was ready and willing. The confrontation between pitcher and batter began anew with an off speed pitch down in the dirt short of the plate. The count climbed to 3 balls and 1 strike, a hitter's count. Cleat salivated over the pitcher's lack of control, he told himself to swing at the next pitch *only* if it was fat *and* in the zone. A walk was as good as a hit; it would send the game into extra innings and if he got a hit it would more than likely drive in two runs and win the ballgame. Raising his hand for another timeout he stepped to the side and scooped up some dirt, rubbing his palms together he felt extremely confident, failing to produce was absent from his thoughts.

Back in the batter's box Cleat blocked out his surroundings and zeroed in on the pitcher, he would allow no distractions to interfere with their duel. Cleat swung at the next pitch grooving into the strike zone…it looked as big as a slow moving softball. The rotating curve ball caught him by surprise, but he still made enough contact to sizzle it into the opposing dugout scattering the Jacksonville players. The count became full *and* more tenuous, but he had faith in his physical attributes and for him to strikeout was a rarity. The following three pitches were all curve balls and Cleat foul-tipped them out of play over the ump's head. They struck the protective screen causing the front row fans to involuntarily duck. Once again Cleat signaled the ump for a timeout.

Looking toward his team bench he tried to quell his anger, the pitcher he was facing was a chump. During practice sessions he faced better pitching against Lakewood's junior varsity, hell he could name two underclassmen twice as good as the kid on the mound. All he had to do was be patient for the guy's ridiculous slow breaking curve. Loosening his shoulders, he took a deep breath and flexed his fingers around the smooth handle of the Louisville Slugger. He settled in, shifting his weight back and forth more determined than ever to make solid contact on the elusive curve. Glaring at the pitcher he became even more agitated when the idiot pantomimed drawing a pistol western style and pointing his finger at Cleat. Pausing briefly, he jerked his hand as if there were recoil. Afterwards he brought the imaginary gun to his lips and pretended to blow smoke from the barrel. After the theatrical pantomime, he continued the simulation by acting as if he replaced the revolver in a low-slung holster. The gangly boy pointed a bony finger at Cleat and smiled an unsightly, gap tooth grin.

The hell with you, Cleat thought, as he pointed the barrel of his bat at the tall, lanky redheaded pitcher and waited for the next pitch. He was prepared for anything but the ninety mile an hour fastball that dissected the plate just above his knees. Cleat stood frozen in place, oblivious to the umpire yelling, "Strike three…that's the ballgame."

Cleat was immobile as he watched through tear-filled eyes as Jacksonville players erupted from the bench. They raced to the pitchers mound to join their teammates in celebration He stood stoically as they piled on top of each other screaming and shouting in triumph. On the bottom of the pile he glimpsed a flash of red hair amidst the squirming humanity.

His coaches had always preached: *look for a fastball, but be ready for a curve.* He had done just the opposite. He chose to forgo the team concept by turning the confrontation into a personal duel and for this transgression he paid a heavy price. Self-service in organized sports often ended in disaster, and it was foreign to everything he had been taught playing team sports. The foundation of a team is based on rudimentary fundamentals, and it is essential for all participants to sacrifice for the greater good. Only then would you be able to attain cohesiveness and earn respect from your opponents *and* predecessors whether in victory or defeat. The cornerstones of teamwork are: dedication, unity, conviction, and selflessness. Achieving these would result in gratification. Cleat would remember the painful lessons of tonight's defeat *and* the tears he shed with his teammates after the loss.

The Saturday after Valentines Day was Cleat and Mandy's last official date. Cleat and Mandy had not been able to go out, or even talk on the phone. For a few weeks they met secretly, but somehow her parents got wind of what they were doing and restricted Mandy to the house. Over two months had gone by without any physical contact between the two, and Mandy's parents had given no indications they were entertaining any thoughts of lifting her restriction. Their lives were disrupted and their relationship had become estranged.

The fiasco began on a cool Saturday afternoon in mid-February when Cleat drove to Mandy's house. Her parents were out of town and weren't supposed to be home until late evening. With the house to their selves it wasn't long before their heavy petting on the divan escalated into unadulterated sex. Beforehand they had pulled the drapes in the sunroom in case someone happened to peer through the pane glass windows overlooking the patio gardens. In the heat of passion the two young lovers feverously disrobed each other, letting their clothes drop where they may. Cleat lay naked between Mandy's thighs, moving rhythmically inside her warmth. The couple was so engrossed in their loving caresses and mutterings of devotion they failed to hear the front door open and close. Moments later a hair-raising scream split the air above the two lovers, bringing their amorous endeavors to a shocking end.

Mrs. Henson stared down at her naked daughter in absolute disbelief as Cleat jumped from the divan, frightened out of his wits. Her ear piercing screams persisted and the noise increased in volume when Mandy hysterically joined in as she frantically tried to cover her nakedness.

Cleat's response during the maniacal shrieking was cowardly: he jumped into his Levis in record time, grabbed his T-shirt, and ran out the front door. Unceremoniously he left his underwear and tennis shoes on the floor as evidence to his culpability. Once outside he didn't bother to open the car door, he leaped over the passenger side, and nervously fumbled with the keys. When his trembling fingers finally inserted the key into the ignition he took off down the brick laid street with a roar of screeching tires. In a few blocks he was parked in the safety of his driveway shaking like a leaf. His bizarre first thought was the underwear he left behind. Mama Marie and his mother always told him to never leave the house without clean underwear, because one never knew what may happen in the course of the day. As far as he was concerned no truer words of wisdom had ever been spoken.

Only Coon knew what transgressed that fateful Saturday afternoon. The rest of the crowd could only speculate, except for the obvious fact they were no longer seeing each other. It was the common buzz around school, every one, including the teachers spent hours wondering what Mandy could have done so terrible. She was the most popular girl in school, a brilliant student, and never troublesome in or out of class. What warranted her parents to ground her so severely? She wasn't allowed to go out unless it was to a school function, and even then she was accompanied by one, or both, of her parents.

Cleat's weakness for the opposite sex was glaringly exposed during those torturous times. Try as he might he couldn't control his desires. It started out innocently enough with a simple phone call from sweet, mischievous Audrey. She asked him to come over and help with her calculus homework. There was no one to blame but himself for what transpired afterwards, but what virile eighteen-year-old male could possibly practice celibacy when a vivacious, sexy girl like Audrey threw herself at him. Cleat certainly couldn't.

Before long they were making love whenever they could meet clandestinely. Cleat knew he was treading on thin ice *and* it was important to him that their secret rendezvous remained hush-hush. Over the weeks he became fond of Audrey's precocious nature. She was a joy to be with *and* she weathered their shadowy covertness quite nicely. Through it all, he discovered she was a lot of fun. She amazed him with her zany antics, if they weren't making love, they were laughing, and if they weren't laughing they were discussing more serious things, like the Vietnam War half a world away. Unfortunately for Audrey, in the world of reality, Cleat still loved and missed his Mandy.

Coon was lying on his twin bed looking at Cleat with his big brown puppy dog eyes. Anger filled his thoughts. "Cleat, it's not fair what you're doing with Audrey. Christ, it'll break Mandy's heart if she ever finds out. Not only that, you'll devastate Audrey as well. Think about the consequences before it goes any further."

"Well, she's not going to find out, besides, what the hell am I supposed to do…join a monastery?"

"Shit, with your misdeeds and cold-ass heart they wouldn't let you inside for fear of desecrating a holy place."

Cleat rose from his bed and threw a pillow at Coon. It went whooshing over his friend head and hit the Venetian blinds covering the bedroom window. "Shit-fire, why'd her mother have to come home anyway? That's what fucked everything up."

"If I remember correctly, *that* was what y'all were doing."

"Are we going to discuss my problem, or semantics?"

"Hell, I know what your problem is; you can't keep your dick inside your pants. If you think seeing Audrey on the side isn't going to blowup in your face then you're crazy. Just like last Saturday when you took Audrey to Harv's party and invited Bo of all people. Hell, he couldn't keep a secret if his life depended on it."

Cleat laughed, "It does and I told him so."

"Oh yeah, how about when we stopped for gas and almost got busted by Cathy Smalls and her mother. Christ, when they pulled up on the other side of the pump I thought for sure your goose was cooked. If she hadn't been so busy primping in the rearview mirror she would've had you two dead-to-rights. Hell, she's the biggest gossip at school and she happens to be the editor of the school paper. Man I'm telling you straight-up; your bullshit luck ain't gonna last forever."

"Coon, you're gonna jinx my ass if you keep talking like that, and your wrong about Bo…he wont say anything…he's one of our best friends."

"Call him what you like, but in my book he's a bigmouth and a wimp. If he was a deaf, blind, and mute I wouldn't trust him. He is a fair-weather friend, but that's your affair. Speaking of affairs, in all honesty I wouldn't want to be in your shoes. The sad thing is, nothings gonna alleviate the situation unless you talk to Mandy's parents."

"Shit, are you out of your mind? There's no way in hell I'm gonna do that."

"Then picture this, her mother's last image of you was your nasty, hairy ass jumping off of her naked daughter. Is that what you…?"

"Hell yeah, that's just the point. How can I go over there and face them after something like that, no freaking way man."

"If you love her as much as you profess, you have no other choice." Coon sat up, never diverting his eyes from Cleat's. "Look, her parents grew up in Lakewood and they were high school sweethearts…you mean to tell me they didn't doodle a little before they got hitched. People have been doing the wild thing for a long time, brother. It's not something our generation invented. Hell, I bet Daddy 'D' and Mama June was getting it on before they ever got married."

"Now how in the hell is that piece of wisdom going to help me?"

"I don't know, but it's something to ponder."

"Shit, I don't even want to think about my parents lying naked and making love. Christ, it gives me the willies."

Coon laughed and flopped back on his pillow. "Well how in the hell do you think Mama June became pregnant with your sorry ass? I know you think you're God's gift, but I'd be willing to bet a lot of money you weren't immaculately conceived."

"Fuck you; I just don't want to think about it." Cleat lifted his keys off the dresser, "I'm going for a ride…do you want to come?"

"Naw, I'm going to take it easy and do some reading."

"Suit yourself."

When the door closed Coon thought about Harv's party. It was a close gathering of friends and Coon was captivated by a very pretty girl who happened to be unattached. Things were looking good, until #77, Olin Michaels walked through the door with a couple of his friends. The larger of the two was dressed in a Marine uniform.

"Hey Harv, I heard you were having a party." His words were menacing and slurred. Olin's legs were spread wide and his impressive body minimized the doorway. In each hand he held a quart of beer and the one he brought to his lips was half empty.

"Hey Michaels, come on in and join the party." Harvey didn't like Olin, and he wasn't alone, as far as he knew nobody else did either. Olin was an outstanding football player, but as an individual he was nasty-mean. In the tenth grade he and Olin got into a fist fight that ended in a bloody draw. After that encounter Olin pretty much left him alone, and sought easier prey to intimidate or beat to a pulp.

Olin swaggered over with his friends in tow. "These are my first cousins: Thomas is a junior over at Blaine, and this here Marine is his older brother, Jack."

Harv shook both of their hands and welcomed them to the party. The family resemblance between the three was uncanny.

"Jack is shipping out to Vietnam next month. That means the war will be over pretty damn quick." Olin laughed, "Ain't that right Jack."

Embarrassed, Jack shuffled his feet and muttered, "I'll do my best. It's what Marines do."

"Shit man, you're going to have fun killing those little fuckers. I wish the hell I was going with you, but my dad would kick my ass if I didn't play ball for the Gator's."

Harv didn't think "fun" and "killing" was to be considered synonymous. His father had fought in WW II and he was still a little messed up, and rarely spoke of the experience. "Good luck Jack, and keep your head down."

"Thanks, I will."

Bo physically cringed when he heard the name Olin Michaels. His hands started shaking and the greasy double-decker hamburger he was holding began falling apart. He never forgot the screaming threats of dismemberment when they drug Michaels off the field. Bo would never have come to the party if there was a remote possibility Michaels would be there. Fighting was never Bo's forte; as a matter of fact he had *never* been in a fight his entire life...not even a scuffle.

He was sixty miles from the sanctity of home and no place to run. Placing the demolished hamburger on the kitchen counter he scanned the surrounding area for Cleat. He saw him standing outside the sliding glass doors with a group of strangers.

"Hey you! Aren't you the Lakewood asshole who threw shit in my face and got me kicked out of the game?" Michaels yelled from across the room. All eyes followed his accusatory finger.

Bo felt his bowls rumble. "Huh?" was all he could muster through trembling lips.

"Yeah, you're the puke. I'd never forget that pudgy baby face." By now Olin was standing close enough to smell Bo's fear.

"Hey come on man, for Christ sakes y'all won the game." Bo couldn't keep the tremble out of his voice.

"You cheated asshole, and I'm gonna kick your fat ass." Olin roughly shoved him backwards against the countertop.

Harv tried to intervene on Bo's behalf, "Come on Michaels, don't start any trouble."

"Fuck you Blake, this is the jerk-off that got me thrown out of the game, and because of him I could've lost my scholarship."

"Yeah, but you didn't. You're going to the University of Florida and that's what counts. If you get into trouble they could take it away just like that." Harv snapped his fingers.

"Don't stand in my way Harv. This ain't about you."

"Then take it outside, my dad would kill me if we tore the house up." Someone in the crowd started yelling "Fight" and the throng wedged their way through the sliding glass doors.

Cleat was startled when the rush of humanity poured onto the patio. He had no idea what was going on, and when he saw the ghastly look on Bo's face he was even more perplexed.

Audrey squeezed his arm, "What's happening Cleat?"

"I don't know, but I'm sure as hell going to find out."

Cleat caught up with Harv and pulled him from the crowd. "Hey Harv, what's happening?"

"Your friend is about to get his ass kicked by Olin Michaels."

"Why?"

"Olin says it was your friend's fault that he was ejected from the game. I tried to talk him out of it, but he's made up his mind. Ain't nothing gonna stop him now."

Coon barreled past Cleat, "We'll see about that." Before Cleat could stop him he disappeared into the crowd of spectators. Wiggling his way into the circle surrounding Bo and Olin he pointed his finger and said loud enough for all to hear, "If you're going to kick anybody's ass then kick mine. I'm the one who told him to throw dirt in that ugly face of yours."

A hush swept over the spectators as they stared at the much smaller boy from Lakewood. They wanted to see an even match between the two big guys, not one so decidedly unfair.

"Shut your trap runt, or you're next." Michaels snarled.

"If ugly was bad then you'd be one mean son-of-a-bitch, but all I hear is a big mouth."

"Don't run off squirt, I'll be through with fat boy in no time. When he gets home his own mother ain't gonna recognize him."

"Put up or shut up retard. You can't take *me* much less him."

That was all it took for Michaels to forget about Bo and lunge after Coon.

Coon was ready for the wild charge and the haymaker that came with it. He easily ducked under the swing and laughed as Michaels lost his balance. "If that's all you got shit for brains then you're in a mess of trouble."

Michaels rolled his brutish shoulders and held his fist in a standard boxers pose. "You're a real smartass aren't'cha. I ain't even gonna break a sweat kicking your ass." His lips curled into an evil grin.

Harv tapped Cleat on the shoulder, "Cleat, I know Olin. He's gonna hurt Coon real bad if we don't try and stop this."

"Coon knows what he's doing, just step back and watch." A crooked grin spread across Cleat's face, "If it gets bad I'll intervene."

"Okay, but you can't say I didn't warn you. I've seen Olin in action, and those two behemoths with him are his first cousins."

"Okay, thanks. I'll keep an eye on them, but if they jump in it's going to turn into a free for all."

"I got your back."

"I know you do Harv."

Coon backed up several feet when Olin threw a lazy left jab trying to find the range. He circled to his left and bobbed under the next one. Coon noted the last jab had a little more snap and its intent was to knock his head off.

Olin grinned over his near miss, "What's the matter motor-mouth, did that one scare the shit out of you?"

Coon was through talking and paid little attention to what the bully had to say. He continued to stay on the balls of his feet and backpedal. His prior experience in the ring had taught him to focus on his opponent's chest and shoulders. By doing so it would telegraph his next blow. Pound for pound he was outclassed and it was paramount for him to avoid being grappled by the creature. To survive the fight he would have to anticipate Michaels every move. Coon was the mongoose waiting for the cobra to strike. He didn't have to wait long.

Olin faked a left hook and landed a solid right on the top of Coon's skull, the uppercut he threw in conjunction with the hook barely missed. Olin thought, *this is gonna be easy…real easy.*

Coon was fooled by the feint, but was able to lower his head just in the nick of time to deflect the Sunday punch. His brain registered a starburst of many colors when Olin's meaty fist rocked him backwards on his heels. The speed of Olin's hands caught him by surprise and the strength behind the blow was a real eye-opener. He paid the price for being overconfident, it wouldn't happen again. When the breeze from an overhand right whizzed by Coon's face he swiftly closed on the bigger man and punched him in the ribcage with a left-right combination. Olin grunted, but recovered quickly and threw a balled fist into Coon's lower shoulder causing his left arm to go numb. The next wild throw lifted him off of the ground. Coon landed on his backside and scooted on his hands and feet to gain separation.

"You bit off more than you can chew shithead." Olin growled as he pressed forward. It pissed him off that he allowed Coon to roll out the way and regained his footing. He should've stomped the little shit into the ground. "You should've stayed down asshole."

Coon knew that was a lie. If he'd stayed on the ground Olin would've either kicked him unconscious or jumped on top of him and pounded him senseless. The numbness in his left arm was dissipating and his anger was that of controlled rage. *Come on ass-wipe one step closer and you're mine.* He was granted his wish. Without a moments hesitation he threw his shoulder into a lightning left that connected soundly on Olin's cheekbone opening a two inch cut. Less than a millisecond separated the devastating right hook that exploded onto Olin's exposed jaw. The big man's knees buckled slightly as he tried to shake off the blows. He crowded Coon and made a desperate attempt to pin him with his massive arms.

Coon evaded the clinch by giving Olin a two fisted shove to create space between them. With the skill of a boxer he scored a thundering right to the brute's nose and felt the crunch of cartilage beneath his fist. Unrelenting, he followed with a left to the mouth and a right to the solar plexus. He heard the air whoosh out of Olin's lungs just before his uppercut caught the damaged fighter flush on the chin. Another straight right intended for Olin's cheekbone caught the bully high on the forehead as he was falling to the grass. The big nose tackle's eyes were white slits as he fell face first onto the dew covered ground; his body twitched twice and then lay still. Olin Michaels never had a chance to fully understand what happened. The hushing noise from the onlookers was that of shocked disbelief.

Audrey's mouth was agape."Oh my God…is he dead?" She stood in disbelief. Never had she thought Coon was capable of such brutality.

The cousins broke from the crowd and rushed to Olin's aid. Both of them had smiles on their faces.

Harv was stunned,"Holy shit Cleat. If I hadn't seen it with my own eyes I wouldn't have believe it. Nobody, but nobody has ever beaten Olin. He's a freaking legend around here."

Cleat laughed,"Whoever said: *the bigger they are the harder they fall,* sure as hell knew what they were talking about."

Coon rejoined his friends and tried to disguise the sly grin threatening to break out. He was barely out of breath."Just like I thought…all mouth."

"Holy crap Coon, where in the world did you learn to fight like that?" Harv asked in wonderment.

"Cleat and I boxed a little Golden Gloves when we were kids." Coon rubbed the top of his head and grimaced,"Shit, my noggin hurts like somebody hit me with a sledgehammer."

"I think he fused some of your vertebrates. You look two inches shorter," Cleat laughed.

"Oh Coon…you were wonderful." Audrey gave him a kiss on the cheek.

Bo walked over and held out his hand,"Thanks buddy."

Coon hesitated only slightly before accepting Bo's gesture of gratitude. "Like I said Bo, it was my fault. I'm the one that told you what to do."

"Yeah, well anyway, I appreciate you sticking up for me. You didn't have to."

"Yes I did, it was the right thing to do."

Cleat kept his eyes on the two cousins as they tried bringing Olin around. When they revived him to a semiconscious state the Marine lifted Olin into a fireman's carry and lumbered over to where they were standing.

"I could make excuses for Olin and say he's had a little too much to drink, but I'd be lying. He's always been an asshole and a loudmouth bully. He deserved what he got tonight." Jack shifted the deadweight drooping over his shoulders and offered his hand to Coon. "You're hell on wheels for a little guy." A hint of a respectful smile crossed his lips. "I hold no hard feelings."

"None taken." Coon shook the Marine's hand and grinned. "You look more like a football player than a Marine."

"I played freshman ball at LSU, but after my first year I couldn't hack the grades, so I decided to join the Marines. I'm shipping out to Vietnam in a few weeks."

"Good luck." Coon thought, *man you're gonna be one big ass target over there.*

"Thanks."

On the second of May, Cleat decided now was the time. He'd been without Mandy long enough. He hoped Coon was right about meeting with Mandy's parents. If not, he stood a good chance of never leaving her house alive, much less in one piece. Mr. Henson was a big man, he was six-foot-six and weighed at least two hundred and seventy five pounds, unfortunately for Cleat most of it was muscle. Back in the late forties after serving in the Marine Corps during WW II he played football for the University of Notre Dame. In the mid-fifties he became a successful financial advisor to big wigs and large corporations. His firm was known worldwide for its expertise in managing money, whether it was in the stock market or a multitude of other investments. He and Cleat's dad were close business associates as well as personal friends.

Standing at the Henson's front door he almost lost his nerve, if it wasn't for his love for Mandy he'd turn and run. His finger was shaking when he pushed the doorbell…it was too late to back out now. Just before the door opened a little voice in his subconscious was crying out for him to run like the wind. Mr. Henson's girth easily filled the doorway. Cleat suddenly wished to be anywhere in the world rather than where he stood at this moment.

"What are you doing here?" Mr. Henson growled.

"Uhh…I would like a few moments of your time, sir."

"I don't think that's a good idea." Mandy's father started to shut the door.

Cleat placed his hand on the door, "Please, Mr. Henson…it's taken me weeks to summon enough courage to come over here."

Mr. Henson paused, rethinking his decision. Opening the door wider, he stepped out of the way, "In the study if you will, and let's make this as brief as possible."

"Yes sir." Cleat was feeling a sense of relief and apprehension conjointly. He made a right past the formal living room and entered the confines of Mr. Henson's study. The sound of the door closing behind him sent a lump to his throat. The masculine décor left little doubt whose chamber he was in. Memorabilia lined the walls and mahogany bookcases displayed past accomplishments in sports and business. There were even photographs of Mr. Henson shaking hands with Presidents Eisenhower *and* Kennedy. Cleat politely waited for the man who became larger than life after viewing the pictures of such notoriety.

Mr. Henson sat behind his large uncluttered desk, a painted football with the logo and colors of Notre Dame proclaiming National Champions rested on a stand. "Well, what do you have to say for your transgressions young man?"

Cleat began his oratory by expressing how deeply he loved Mandy, and how she felt the same for him. He knew they were young, but at eighteen they were old enough to distinguish their love from infatuation. Soon they would be attending different colleges and would be separated by hundreds of miles, but even so their love would survive the separation.

After several minutes of the one-way conversation Cleat paused, wondering if he should venture into un-chartered waters, taking a deep breath he decided to continue. "Sir, I know you and Mrs. Henson were childhood sweethearts…if you could please put yourself in my situation and remember when y'all were in love. It was a different time and place, but love has been the same throughout the ages. That's not to suggest there were any improprieties during your relationship, but I'm sure you had the same devotion and love for each other as I do for your daughter. I will do anything you ask of me if you would reconsider letting us see each other again."

Mr. Henson rose from behind his desk and walked to the door. "You know the way out."

"Yes sir I do, and thank you for your time."

Three days later he answered the phone and was surprised to hear Mandy's excited voice on the other end.

"Oh my God Cleat, I don't what you said, but my parents have changed their minds...we can see each other again. I'm still in a state of shock...I can hardly believe it."

Although her parents were guarded and more demanding of their where-abouts, the following three weeks were unbelievable. Being reunited with Mandy were some of the happiest days he could ever remember, but on a lazy Saturday afternoon an unexpected phone call brought his world crashing down.

"Cleat, its Audrey...can you come over?"

"I'm sorry I can't Audrey."

"Please Cleat, you have to. I..."

"Cleat, this is Mrs. Wellington...I would like your presence within the next five minutes. Is that clear?"

"Yes ma'am." The cold aloofness in her voice sent a chill down his back. He wondered why Audrey's mother wanted to see him.

As soon as he rang the front doorbell Mrs. Wellington appeared. "Come in, and follow me to the Florida room."

Cleat tagged along until she motioned him to sit in a rattan chair next to the French doors leading to the pool deck. Audrey was sitting in a loveseat on the opposite wall with her hands clasped in her lap, her gaze never lifted from the terrazzo floor. She looked really nice, dressed in a pair of white shorts, pink blouse, and white tennis shoes. For some reason unbeknownst to Cleat he never felt so uncomfortable and he didn't even know why.

"Cleat," Mrs. Wellington stated, "I'm not going to beat around the bush, Audrey's pregnant and I want to know what your intentions are."

His first thought was how could this be possible, but that was absurd, he knew *how* it was possible. "Are you sure?"

"Of course we are. It's beyond deniability." Mrs. Wellington answered with more than a hint of indignation in her voice. "What we need to do is keep this quiet and get the two of you married before anyone realizes the pregnancy was prior to wedlock. This won't be difficult because Audrey's early into her first trimester."

The room began to sway as Cleat tried to digest what Audrey's mother was saying. When she mentioned the word "pregnant" everything afterwards was a blur. He looked over at Audrey, but she refused to meet his eyes. This had to be a dream...hell it was a nightmare. His stupor was interrupted when he realized Mrs. Wellington was standing in front of him.

"Do you want me to tell your parents, or do you cherish the tidings?"

"Uhh...I...uh, think it would be best if I did, Mrs. Wellington."

"Fine, then I'll wait to hear from your mom and dad this evening. That'll be all, Cleat."

"Yes ma'am...bye Audrey"

"Goodbye, Cleat." She whispered, "I love you" as Cleat was ushered from the room.

Cleat was so confused on the short drive back to his house he drove by it without even realizing he had done so. The hard truth of reality didn't set in until he walked into the den and sat down on the sofa. He was glad to have the house to himself. His dad was still at the office, his mother was attending the weekly Women's Club meeting, and Sissy was at cheerleading practice. Mama Marie was probably in her room, she rarely appeared until it was time to help with supper. Hell, even Coon was missing. He was over at Anne's house goofing off. A wave of relief swept over him, he wasn't in the state of mind to face anyone. Cleat climbed the stairway to his bedroom heavy-footed, once inside he sat on the bed wondering what he was going to say to his parents when they got home. He hated the thought of facing his father's discontent, he knew in his father's eyes he was the lesser son. *My God! What of Mandy, How am I going to explain my actions? This is monumental.*

How could he marry Audrey and have a baby when he loved Mandy more than life itself? He was trapped *and* saw no way out of the distorted web he had woven. The honorable thing was to marry Audrey and give her and the child his last name, but he knew when he pulled into his driveway that volition was beyond the realm of possibility. In a daze he moved to his dresser and opened his sock drawer. He withdrew a wad of money he had been saving for summer vacation. One hundred and seventeen bucks wouldn't last long, but it was all he had. Throwing some clothes into a carryall, he took one last look around the room before going downstairs, his eyes came to rest on Coon's twin bed...he was going to miss him.

Just before opening the den door Mama Marie called for him. Setting the bag in his father's chair he went to his grandmother's room to see what she wanted. She was sitting in her corner rocker with a light quilt covering her legs.

"Yes ma'am, you called?"

"Have a seat Cleatwood." She motioned towards a chaise lounge with an ancient bony hand covered with liver spots, "Where are you going my child?"

"Ma'am?"

"Will you be gone a long time? The reason I ask is because there are piti-fully few years left for me in this world."

"Don't talk like that, Mama Marie."

"Shush…don't change the subject. Grandson, what terrible forces compel you to leave your family and friends?"

"How in the world did you know I was leaving?"

"I know things beyond your imagination, my child. Now, tell me what is so wrong in your life to abscond like a thief in the night."

Cleat sat down and told her the whole story, beginning when Mrs. Henson walked in on him and Mandy. After he was through, he took a deep breath and let it out slowly. Considering public opinion, he knew by running away most people wouldn't accept his actions, nor would they believe it the manly thing to do. No matter, he just couldn't face marrying Audrey and raising a family. He was ashamed for what he was about to do, but he saw no other answer.

Mama Marie got up from her rocker and shuffled to her chest of drawers where she kept her jewelry box. She lifted the lid and withdrew two one hun-dred dollar bills folded into a tight square. Turning to Cleat she held them up, "I was saving this for a rainy day, *not* a hurricane, but it'll have to do."

"I can't take that, Mama Marie."

"Nonsense, I just wish there was more." She forced the money into Cleat's hand. "You be safe and come back to us when this is sorted out."

CHAPTER 9

The ride to Miami was long and uneventful. To fulfill his original plan of finding a job and earn enough money for an adventurous trip to South America now seemed juvenile. First and foremost he didn't have a passport, nor did he have enough money for passage. He spent the first five nights in the backseat using a carryall for a pillow. At first light he would walk to the corner filling station to use the bathroom, wash up, and brush his teeth. The rest of his time was spent looking for a job, except for spending thirty minutes eating the one meal a day allotted himself,.

His search for work was turning into futility until he wandered down a street that seemingly led to nowhere and ended up at the local docks. There were several fishing boats tethered at the pier, and there were dozens more arriving as the sun continued slipping below the horizon. After twenty emphatic no's and suffering the humility hobo's and vagabond's know to well, he approached the next boat with ebbing enthusiasm. It was nondescript from the rest of the trawlers and last to dock. Onboard there were two young men busy securing some large nets. They looked to be a little older than he was, both of them had jet-black hair and the sun had darkened their skin the color of burnt cinnamon. The one who appeared to be the oldest had long hair drawn into a ponytail in the same way a girl would wear hers. Cleat had never seen a man more handsome. The name *ATHENA* was painted in bold black letters on the hulls paint-peeling surface.

"Nicholas, we have someone interested in your beautiful hair."

"Hey, you down there…you no like my hair?" Nicholas jumped from the large wooden crate he had been standing on and landed lightly on the balls of his feet.

"Your hair's fine…I'm looking for work, not trouble."

"Hey, who wants trouble? My beautiful face she might get marred, and then pretty ladies would shun Nicholas." Ponytail held his hands palms up. "You get no trouble from me." Nicholas ran his fingers through his shiny-black hair, and flashed an exquisite row of the whitest teeth on the face of the earth. "Ohhh, but my little brother Tony he loves to fight, even more than he loves women. He is most not like me."

Cleat turned his gaze to Tony, who was also smiling. This wasn't what he wanted; it was foolish to think he could find a job on one of the boats. Cleat took a step backward when Tony jumped down to dock level. He wasn't afraid to take Tony on, although the big knife sheathed on a wider than normal belt might present a serious problem.

"Hey, hey, what kind of trouble are you two starting? You leave this boy alone or I will call Papa." A young girl with a red bandanna wrapped around her forehead stepped from behind a five foot stack of nets. Although the red sash prevented her thick, curly mane from running wild, raven ringlets spiraled past her shoulders, framing the most exotic creature Cleat had ever seen. He was staring at a goddess dressed in a pair of cut-off kaki shorts and a white T-shirt. Her scant attire left little for Cleat's imagination to wonder the promises hidden beneath. With pent-up hostility she threw a wet rag on target and splattered Nicholas soundly in the face.

"Athena, leave the men alone. This is man's business...you are my sister...go tend to your womanly chores."

The knife Athena pulled from her waistband was longer than Cleat's forearm. She stood waving the menacing blade back and forth. With each tilt of her hand it shimmered in the fading light. A language unfamiliar to Cleat burst from her mouth, and the venomous barbs she spewed must have held some humor, because Tony began laughing and pointing a finger at his older brother.

A short man of portly stature emerged from the wheelhouse dressed in black oil slick pants stuffed into calf-high, rubberized boots. Cleat assumed he was the captain of the waif. His upper body was engulfed in a white open-collared shirt showcasing a heavy gold necklace with a gold crucifix. His bloused sleeves failed miserably in hiding his huge, powerful arms. The elderly man's opening statements were directed at all three shipmates. The young girl stood alone, defiantly meeting the old sea-dog's gaze. Before he was finished she interrupted with a fiery response, directing an accusatory finger at Cleat.

Cleat had no idea what was going on, but he felt extremely uncomfortable being the subject of so much attention. "Excuse me," he interrupted. "I didn't mean to cause any trouble...all I wanted was a job."

Silence swept across the vessel as all eyes suddenly turned toward Cleat. The only pair remotely non-hostile was from the girl.

"You, come aboard," the stout man ordered in gruff, authoritarian English.

Cleat could tell by his inflection he was not used to disobedience. Without hesitating Cleat deftly leapt aboard. He ignored the icy stares from Tony and Nicolas and smiled at the girl named Athena as he followed the captain. Once inside the wheelhouse unfamiliar odors assailed his nasal passages and brought tears to his eyes. The assimilation of smells made the boy's locker room back home smell sweeter than a French whorehouse. Trying desperately not to gag, Cleat stood patiently watching the man fill his pipe. His eyes burned from the added scent of the captain's foul pipe smoke. All he wanted right now was a breath of fresh air. It was just his luck to be summoned to see the captain when they were battening down the ship.

The walls of the interior were covered with family photos and an assortment of religious paraphernalia. An 8x10 of Athena warranted particular attention. The glossy photograph captured her standing wide legged, clad in cutoff jeans and a flimsy halter-top several sizes too small. In one hand she was holding a spear gun, and in the other was a snorkel. Thick wet hair framed her high cheekbones as the sun shimmered off of her bronze skin. Droplets of water mixed with sweat and oil, glistened like pearls from the deep.

"Have you sailed before?"

Cleat almost jumped out of his skin when the captain spoke. "Uh...Yes sir, but only for pleasure. I've sailed my father's seventy-four foot schooner. We take it out during the summer."

"So, you are a seasoned sailor?"

"No sir, I wouldn't classify myself as such, but I do know my way around a vessel."

"You are a polite, good-looking young man...I like that. There's no one like you around the fleet. Are you lucky?"

"I beg your pardon?"

"Two of my deck hands quit three weeks ago because we have no luck with the shrimp. Now I ask again...do you think you are lucky?"

"Yes sir."

"You want work?"

"Yes sir."

"It is a hard life…can you do this? Me…I don't think you last one day. Take off your shirt."

Cleat pulled his T-shirt off and held it loosely by his side. The scene was bizarre and a drastic change from the life he was used to living. He saw the captain's eyes light up as he ogled his physique.

"But maybe I am wrong. You are strong young man. First…before I say yes you must tell me why you are here and not home."

In less than thirty minutes Cleat gave him a synopsis of his life and the circumstances that brought him to this moment.

"I do not approve of your decision, a pregnant girl must have husband, and a child must have a father. If you were Greek, the girl's family would have you hunted like an animal and killed, but it is your life to make. Now I say this, you were honest, and that is a good thing, something all Greeks admire. For that I bring you to work for two weeks, if we no find shrimp by then it make no difference because the bank she come take my sweet blessed *ATHENA*. If that happen, nobody have job anyway. I have no much pay, but you may sleep onboard *Athena* and bathe at the marina. Everyone use marina so not to worry." The Captain held out his hand, "I am Captain Zukos, but everyone calls me Papa Nick."

Their second trip out the Athena hit the mother lode. For the next couple of weeks it was haul-after-haul of the biggest, fattest shrimp the area had seen in years. By the third week, Cleat was sharing in the catch. He had become their lucky piece, and every shrimp boat in the fleet tried to bribe him aboard their boat. In fact, several promised he wouldn't even have to work…they just wanted him onboard for luck.

It was funny how much at home he felt with these people. They had taken him in on a whim and treated as one of their own. He had become close friends with the two brothers and he knew Athena wanted to become romantically involved. He was infatuated with Athena; it wasn't confined to her looks…it was all encompassing. Her willingness to work as hard as the men and the way her muscles rippled when she moved drove him crazy.

He tried to hide his lustful stares from her father and brothers by stealing hidden glances of her sweat-soaked body. It was sexually maddening to see her in sweat-stained clothes with her crotch and cute little rear end wet from the strenuous labor. Watching tiny rivulets of perspiration trickling down her bare midriff while she strained every muscle in her body to haul in the days catch was extremely tantalizing to say the least. Athena routinely worked closely with Cleat and came into physical contact with him on a daily basis. Sometime their bodies touched accidentally, but often times Athena purposely caused the encounter in a seductive manner. On more than one occasion she rubbed her hand over his butt, and several times she made it a point to press her boobs against him. There were nights he lay in his makeshift bed filled with fantasies of Athena's raving beauty and infectious sexuality.

Three weeks flew by before he knew it and as yet he hadn't called home. That Saturday night he made it a point to call his family. Outside the marina he used the payphone and waited for someone to answer. When it was Sissy who picked up on the first ring he was thankful. He told her all was well, and that it would be awhile before he came home. Through her cries of sadness he told her how sorry he was for not calling sooner, and he would call again soon. Before hanging up he asked her to please tell everyone he was safe and that he loved them.

When he returned the receiver to its cradle he paused a moment and listened to the melodic enchantment of Greek folk songs flowing through the open windows. He had made it a point to avoid going inside the Marina on Friday and Saturday nights. There was always a lot of drinking, and he didn't understand their language, nor was he familiar with their dances, but tonight was different. A taste of home created nostalgia and clouded his better judgment.

The Neptune Marina was a gathering place for the fleet. It served many purposes, first and foremost were delicious meals reasonable priced. During the week men and a few women would meet over drinks and tell wild stories of their exploits at sea. On the weekends it was a place to unwind, have a few drinks, dance and listen to music from the old country.

When Cleat entered the establishment he was met with incredible sounds and aromas so foreign to his previous environment he found them to be exhilarating. He could smell spices, perfume, alcohol, food, and some he couldn't begin identify. The band was playing loudly over the laughter and murmurings of a hundred conversations. Cleat made for an empty bar stool and ordered a carafe of wine. Glancing around the full house he spotted Athena across the room sitting at table having drinks with several girlfriends. He sat quietly sipping his wine stealing wanton glances at Athena's captivating beauty.

From out of nowhere a big brute of a man he had never seen before walked across the dance floor and bent over the table to whisper something in her ear. When she ignored him he forcibly pulled Athena out of her chair. She squealed as she tried to break away, but even for her he was too overpowering. He laughed maliciously at her feeble attempts to break free.

Cleat rushed to her aid without thinking, or considering he was an outsider in a room full of Greeks. "Hey…let her go."

"Who are you to say, my little friend?"

"I'll be your friend, and buy you a drink if you let the girl go." Cleat smiled at the stranger with long, greasy hair. They were about the same height, but the man's forearms were bigger than Cleat's thighs, and he outweighed Cleat by seventy or eighty pounds. He looked to be in his mid-thirties, and by the visible scars on his face he'd been in more than his fair share of barroom brawls, although Cleat didn't think the word "fair" was in the man's vocabulary. Athena struggled with all her might, but the big Greek held on effortlessly

"You go have a drink little man and leave me to dance with the girl. You stay here…I hurt you very bad. You not be so pretty anymore."

Cleat's eyes never wandered as he looked for a weakness. A large gold earring dangled from each earlobe, he wondered how much it would hurt if somebody yanked them out? The Greek certainly had a penchant for gold. He had two gold front teeth, a thick gold necklace, and a gold bracelet. Athena was on Cleat's left being held by the ruffian's right hand…that meant if the man swung at Cleat he'd be swinging with his free left arm.

"Please, I don't want any trouble, but you have to let the girl go because she doesn't want to dance with your ugly fat ass."

"What…*what* did you say?" The Greek had an incredulous look in his eyes.

"I said if you don't let her go I'm going to kick your ugly, fat *ass*."

Cleat was ready for the wild roundhouse the man threw with his left hand and easily ducked under the bully's swing. A short, powerful punch delivered by Cleat to the man's kidney was all it took to free Athena. The problem he faced now was the brute had two hands free and he was highly pissed. A large partisan crowd began forming around the dance floor. Several men shouted in Greek that sounded like encouragement…but for whom?

"I hurt you plenty now." The Greek rolled his shoulders and held his arms out.

"Shit, you can't beat your dick much less beat me. You're just a big tub of guts and ain't good for nothing except scaring girls." Cleat was trying to bait him into making another mistake. The one thing he had to avoid was letting the big man get hold of him. The man was too big and too strong.

The angry ruffian moved forward, but Cleat backed away with his hands held high. When the man was in range Cleat struck with two punishing left hooks to the side of the Greeks head and followed the combination with a solid bone-jarring right to the big mans jaw. Unfazed and, with the speed of a jaguar the man lunged at Cleat, grabbing him in a bear hug. The man's strength was awesome. Cleat heard things popping in his back that shouldn't be popping. He had to do something quick or he was going to lose consciousness. Cleat was extremely fortunate that his arms escaped the Greeks vice grip. Remembering the earrings, he grabbed one in each hand and snatched them out of his ear. The way he squealed and ranted you would've thought someone had stuck him in the ass with a red-hot poker, and the bone-crushing grip around Cleat's chest didn't loosen, as a matter of fact, it tightened.

Cleat slapped the man's ears with the palms of his hands like he'd seen in a movie once, and it worked, the vise around his chest loosened. He decided to do it again, and this time even harder. After his second painful blow the man let go and fell to his knees in excruciating pain. Cleat spun around and landed a jarring right to the man's jaw, and quickly followed the punch with a punishing left hook flush on the man's nose. Cleat felt the man's nose cartilage give beneath his knuckles, but still, the raging bull started to rise. Cleat picked up a heavy wooden chair and broke it on top of the crazed man's head. At last it was over, or so he thought.

Several men started to move toward Cleat. He didn't recognize them and figured they must be friends of the big guy. With these odds he would be lucky to escape with his life.

"Papa, Tony, Nicholas come quick. They are going to hurt our Cleat."

The arrival of the Zukos males was a blessing. When Athena told Papa Nick what transpired he spat on the floor next to the three men assisting their unconscious friend. He had to physically hold his sons from seeking vengeance. Papa Nick pointed a stubby finger at the four strangers and told them they were not welcome at the marina. He went on to say: if their shadows ever crossed a member of his family again all four of them would die. This was his solemn word, and not to be taken lightly.

They were extremely proud of Cleat for defending the honor of Athena and the Zukos family name. They realized Cleat had fought against all odds with total disregard for his own safety. After the confrontation in the marina bar he became part of the Zukos family and was never thought of as a hired deckhand again. The Greek fishermen followed suit and accepted him as one of their own, no one respected bravery, and honor, more than the Greeks.

Late that night Athena snuck onboard the ship to surprise Cleat. The illicit meeting began with sexual flirtations, but rapidly blossomed into amorous behavior. It came to an abrupt end when her hand ventured to the firmness between his legs. The voice of Papa Nick screamed in his consciousness, *if you were Greek you would be hunted down like and animal and killed!* That was enough for him to leap out of bed and whirl in a 360, searching for prying eyes. Looking into the startled, ink-black eyes of Athena he apologetically asked her to leave before it went any further.

Cleat thought of Mandy every day, but they were painful thoughts full of sadness, remorse, and guilt over how much pain and humiliation he must have caused her. He loved her, but how could he ever face her again, or the people back home. He was certain they had mentally burned him at the stake? Would he ever have the nerve to stand and be held accountable for his act of desertion in the face of controversy? God, teenage years were supposed to be carefree and innocent. What a mess he'd made of his life—and others.

In six weeks Cleat had used the payphone at the marina to call home three times, on his second call his mother answered the phone and he had great difficulty speaking to her amidst all of her crying. The best he could do was let her know he was fine, and that he would soon call again. Saturday night had been his most recent call and he was happy to hear Coon's voice. His friend filled him in on what was going on at home and how the school was surviving during his absence. The most shocking news of all was hearing that Audrey had left five weeks ago to live with her aunt in up-state New York. Coon's parting words to Cleat were for him to "come home."

Cleat spent all day Sunday thinking about going home and trying to put his life back together, but wasn't sure if he was ready. He looked at his watch…it was after mass so he decided to drive the few blocks to Papa Nick's and hope to find him at home. In less time than it takes to recite the Pledge of Allegiance he was pulling along the curb in front of a white two-story house with green shutters and a well-manicured lawn. It wasn't the type of house Cleat pictured Papa Nick living in, but he was beginning to realize life was full of surprises. Halfway up the short flight of stairs he was greeted by Papa Nick opening the screen door.

"Ahoy Capitan Zukos, request permission to come aboard, sir?"

Papa Nick laughed. "Please, have a seat my wayward son." Captain Zukos motioned to one of the twin white rockers. "And what brings me such pleasure?"

Cleat sat down and waited respectfully for the Captain to sit before he began explaining what was going on in his life since the last time they spoke of his past. Fifteen minutes later he was finished expressing his fears of returning to Lakewood and the unknown.

"You are a good man Cleat, this life you are living is an honest life, but there is so much better for you in this world than toiling as a fisherman. I've grown to love you like a son, and my sons have grown to love you as a brother. Athena, I worry about her for I fear she loves you in ways only a woman can love, but I have forbidden her to be alone with you. You were correct when you sent her away, even though I love you like a son you are not of our blood." Papa Zukos leaned forward, resting his massive forearms on his knees. "You must go back…I hate to see you leave for we have enjoyed the good fortune you brought to our family, but with my blessing you must do this."

Cleat shuddered at what might have happened if he hadn't listened to his inner voice that night. How did Papa Nick know? Was he being followed? He thought not, because he never went anywhere except to the marina. More than likely they were keeping an eye on Athena. He thanked God he didn't pursue her advances, not only because he'd probably be at the bottom of the ocean feeding the fish, his other reason was more personal: he'd grown to love and respect these people he now considered family.

When Papa Nick stood from his chair Cleat held out his hand, but the Greek patriarch roughly knocked it away and wrapped his big, hairy arms around Cleat in a fatherly embrace. "May you find happiness my son."

Resplendent in a father's warmth he'd never experienced before, Cleat laid his head on the captain's shoulder with great sadness. "I will miss you and your family, Papa Nick. Tell them I said goodbye and to go with God."

Papa Nick held Cleat at arm's length and slipped the gold chain and Greek orthodox crucifix from around his neck. Placing the heavy gold chain over

Cleat's head he smiled, "Bless you, my son. Wear this with God's blessing, it will keep you from harms way. My sons will miss you like the brother you have become, but I'm afraid Athena will be left brokenhearted. You must go…I will say goodbye in your place."

When Cleat arrived in town it didn't take him long in discerning everything was worse than expected. He was naïve in thinking that he would be anything other than the subject of attention once he retuned to school. On his first day midway through second period he was notified by intercom to report to the principal's office. All eyes were on him as he rose from his desk and walked to the classroom door. He could hear the murmuring whispers behind his back as he left the room. The long walk down the hallways was lonely and, one full of question he had no answers for. When he reached the front office he took a deep breath, opened the door and, stepped inside.

There was a noticeable chill in the air and it wasn't necessarily coming from the air conditioner. Everyone seemed to be extremely busy and no one was willing to make eye contact with him. He waited patiently until one of the secretaries came from around the counter and ushered him to the principal's office. She knocked politely and waited.

"Come in."

The secretary scurried off leaving Cleat to face the principal alone. Anxiously wanting answers to his summons he turned the doorknob and entered.

"Please, have a seat." The dower looking principal gestured toward one of the chairs facing his desk. The principal cleared his throat, "Eh…Cleat, I hate to be the barrier of bad news but it's my duty to inform you that you will not be able to graduate with your class this year. I know you must be disappointed but you've missed over eight weeks of classes and exams. There are but a few days left of this school year and there is simply not enough time for you to makeup the work."

"But sir…" Cleat was stopped short when the principal raised his hand.

"My first suggestion is to attend summer school, or if you'd rather, take the Florida State GED test."

"Yes sir."

The principal cleared his throat again and shifted in his chair. "Uh…one other matter son. Since you cannot graduate there is really no reason for you to continue going to classes. What the faculty would… "

"But…"

"Please hear me out. To put it bluntly, the administration and the faculty feel your presence on campus will disrupt classes and interfere with the curriculum. I know you want what's best for your school and your classmates."

"Yes sir."

Boys and girls who he once thought would be lifelong friends willingly turned their backs on him, and worst of all Mandy wouldn't acknowledge his existence. She wouldn't even speak to him when he ran into her at Pips, nor would she return his phone calls. Coon and a few others remained loyal, but he was blatantly ostracized from what his world used to be. It was like he had the plague.

Two weeks passed and the afternoon mail brought another disappointment, there was a letter from Auburn's athletic department notifying him that their offer of an athletic scholarship was being withdrawn due to his failure in meeting "standard admissions requirements." His life was turning into pure shit, and hanging around the house was a sentence in hell, especially when his father was home.

If life could get much worse he was absolutely sure that he was first in line for whatever was handed out. In the past two weeks he'd read four books, all of them had one common theme: ocean adventures. He rarely went downstairs except for meals, and even then, he arrived late and chose to eat on a TV tray in the den. Avoiding his family *and* especially his father were primary considerations. Cleat spiraled into a deep, lonely depression so dark that Coon could barely get a word out of him, much less a full sentence.

It all changed one afternoon when he received a call from Coach Dunn asking him to come over to his office. Cleat couldn't imagine what his coach wanted, but he missed him and the smells associated with the athletic department. It would be like old home week.

His hand trembled as he knocked on the coach's door. A familiar voice answered with a loud "Enter."

"Sit down, son…lord it's good to see you again. I don't need to tell you how worried we all were."

"*All* is a pretty broad term, Coach. I can name more than a few who would've been glad if they never laid eyes on me again."

"Screw them for being the assholes they are." Coach Dunn smiled, adding conspiratorially, "I can talk like that since you're no longer enrolled as a student."

"You're right, Coach. Screw them and the damn horse they rode in on."

Coach Dunn roared with laughter. "Damn that felt good didn't it?" He paused briefly before continuing: "Cleat, I know you received a letter from Auburn rescinding your scholarship, but don't let that get you down, because there are plenty of schools…"

"Hell Coach, I don't even have a high school diploma. How in the world am I going to go…?"

"Let me finish, Cleat. All you have to do is attend summer school, or take the GED. Once you do that I can get you into a junior college in North Carolina. The head coach is a friend of mine, and I've told him all about you. We served together in the 101st Airborne during WW II. He wants your ass up there after you get squared away. He's offering you a full scholarship and a job with the athletic department to earn spending money. Coach Danielson runs a good program and a lot of Division I scouts follow his players real close. When you finish at Wingate you'll be eligible to attend any college that'll have you, and believe me there'll be plenty of them drooling to get their hands on you…even Auburn."

Cleat let the coach's words sink in. Hell yeah, it would be good to get out of town and escape the gossip and cold stares. He would rather be somewhere else as a stranger than be treated like one in his hometown. "When could I leave?"

"As soon as you get a diploma, the GED would be the fastest way. He hopes you can make it up there by July so you can settle in before practice starts."

When Cleat left Coach Dunn's office he felt like he was floating on air. He held the brochures from Wingate Junior College tightly in his left hand, he was afraid if he lost them his good fortune would go with them. Folding them in half he shoved them in his jeans pocket before climbing into his car. School had let out twenty minutes ago and the parking lot was almost empty when he saw Gene Reese less than a stones throw away. He was walking arm in arm with a girl he didn't recognize.

"Hey Gene," Cleat waved. "I've got some great news."

Gene turned his way flashing a smile that quickly disappeared when he recognized who called his name. He turned his back and opened the door of the red T-Bird convertible his parents couldn't afford and waited for the girl to slide in. Without a backward glance he drove off.

Cleat was more hurt than stunned by Gene's reaction. Hell, even Gene wouldn't acknowledge he existed. *Fuck him,* Cleat thought. He wished now he hadn't made Gene look so good with all of the bad passes the asshole threw. He might have everybody else fooled into thinking he was a great quarterback, but Cleat knew Gene's weaknesses. If he didn't acquire better timing, more speed, better footwork, *and* a hell of lot more mental and physical toughness he'd never make it to Division I football. Okay, some small college might pick him up, but that was about it.

Sticking his key into the ignition he muttered, *hell with it, they can all kiss my rosy red ass.*"

Rushing up the stairs Cleat was antsy as a small child on Christmas Eve. He wanted to review the brochures of his new school. Crashing through the doorway, he almost knocked Coon off of his feet.

"Whoa there big boy, I haven't seen you run that fast since Harvey Blake chased your ass."

Cleat grabbed Coon's shirt. "Brother, I've got great news…Coach Dunn got me a full scholarship to play football in North Carolina." Cleat dug into his back pocket and whipped out the literature on Wingate. The front cover of the brochure portrayed a picturesque campus with rolling hills and old colonial red bricked buildings. Book-laden coeds dressed for cold weather walked among a scattering of large oaks and pines that dotted the landscape. In the distance a chapel could be seen with high, arching windows featuring colorful stained glass. One side was configured with a sunburst and crucifix, on the other side was a shinning star glowing in the heavens surrounded by angels.

Coon stood to the side looking around Cleat's shoulder at the college's layout. "You know, it kinda looks like a smaller scale of Florida State's campus."

"Yeah, you're right…it sort'a does."

"Cleat, you think the coach could get me one, too?"

"What...are you crazy? You've got a full ride to Auburn...I'm the one who lost his scholarship, not you."

"Yeah, but I'd rather go play ball with you. We've been playing together since we were eight-years-old, and I don't feel like changing now. Besides, who's going to look after you if not the old Coon-dog?"

Cleat was touched; he never expected his friend to give up a chance to play Division I football and follow him to a small junior college set in the hills of North Carolina. "This isn't some big ass school, hell it's Podunk, USA for Christ's sake. Are you sure that's what you want?

"Your asshole stinks doesn't it?"

"Yes, it absolutely does."

"Well, that's my answer, too." The thought of being separated from Cleat caused Coon to break out in a cold sweat. Goose bumps the size of pinheads covered his body.

"That's great Coon, it'll be like ol' times." Cleat grabbed Coon by the shoulders before giving him a hug. "You and me brother, we'll go together."

Five days after Cleat was notified he successfully passed the GED their package deal to Wingate Junior College was signed, sealed and delivered. The duo from Lakewood would be heading to North Carolina in July. After Coon's graduation they relaxed at the beach house chasing girls and lying in the sun enjoying their fraternity of two. Time away from Lakewood was just the right medicine for Cleat. Over the years while spending their summers at Daytona Beach they acquired close friendships with kids who lived in the surrounding area year-round. Within the first hour of their arrival the locals knew they were back in town and a party was set for that weekend. Although they played a lot, the boys stuck close to an exercise regimen that consisted of running on the beach twice a day and lifting free weights set up in the garage.

Mrs. Davis thought it was prudent for the family to forgo spending the entire summer in Daytona Beach so the boys could have fun and relax. Her sentiments were especially formulated for Cleat, for she knew his compassionate side and his sensitive nature. He needed to get away from Lakewood and all of the hateful, mean-spirited gossip. Spending the summer at the beach house with Coon would give him the opportunity to gather his thoughts and composure. The rest of her family would still make periodic trips on the weekends, but sparingly so…all but her husband. He always seemed to have a last minute excuse for not coming.

Cleat and Coon's nights usually lasted till the wee hours of the morning and their days began around 11:00 AM or thereabouts. Bo Collier spent a rip-roaring week with them and several friends visited on the weekends, but their most unusual and unexpected visitor was Harold "Big Oak" Trim. They were surprised and glad to hear he received a last minute scholarship to Indiana State. Since then he'd been working out in the weight room at LHS and running six miles a day. In the process he lost forty pounds of body fat *and* added twenty pounds of muscle. Big Oak's appearance had changed considerably.

He came up for the weekend and stayed eight days. His lengthy stay began on a Friday night during one of many parties held at the beach house. He met a buxom blonde from Wisconsin who was vacationing with friends before attending college at summers end. She was on scholarship to play softball for the Badgers *and* she was big…really big. Mirabel was a Germanic farm girl from the dairy lands and conservatively speaking, she weighed at least two hundred. She towered over Coon *and* she could look Cleat dead in the eye while standing flatfooted on extremely large feet. On the following Tuesday, Mirabel moved into the guest bedroom with Big Oak. The grunting sounds, animalistic noises, and squeals of delight emitting from the room would have kept most people awake, but Cleat and Coon were too busy to pay it any mind.

Everyone fell in love with Mirabel. In many ways she became one of the guys. Growing up on a farm in Wisconsin and having four older brothers and three younger brothers, she regarded the human body for what it was…a human body. At first it was hard getting used to hearing a girl burp, and God forbid fart, but that was Mirabel. As far as nudity was concerned…she wasn't concerned. She would just as soon undress in the privacy of her bedroom *or* in front of them. Mirabel was far different from any girl they had ever known, much less heard of. She could drink them all under the table and piss standing up. Once her uninhibited ways became customary it was no big deal.

The beast had found *his* beauty. Mirabel was Big Oak's first love, *hell* she was his first everything. The day he had to say goodbye they both cried, and when his two best friends joined them in a lasting embrace…he cried even harder. Big Oak and Mirabel pledged to continue seeing each other when they arrived at their universities. It was a promise they would keep and a lifetime they would share.

Both Cleat and Coon had summer romances, Cleat more than Coon, but they were only flings to occupy their vacation. Harvey Blake drove his 1960 ford pick up and made a five day pit stop before heading to South Bend, Indiana, and the home of "The Fighting Irish". The three of them spent their nights rounding up girls at the Surf Bar, Club Martinique, and The Beach Comber. Despite their morning hangovers they raced on the beach, and lifted weights in the afternoon, each pressing the others endurance. Their friendship grew, along with their respect for each other. After bidding farewell to Blake, their endless summer came to an end. It was time for them to go home and pack for Wingate. They made a nostalgic inspection inside and outside to make sure the beach house was in order before heading back to Lakewood.

CHAPTER 10

Cleat stepped through the den door and was summoned by his father before his eye's had a chance to adjust. He was waved to the sofa next to where his father was sitting in the familiar brown leather chair. Cleat dreaded what was coming, even though he did not know what it was, he knew whatever his father had to say was going to be derogatory, or he was going to have to sit and listen to one of his lectures about being a man and showing responsibility.

"Have a seat son." Mister Davis laid his pipe on the marbled antique smoke-stand and waited for his son to settle. It was an understatement to say things had been cordial between the two of them as of late. He could not remember the last time a kind word had passed between them. The disappointment of his son's senior year was embarrassing and hurtful. The loss of his son's scholarship to Auburn was painful...he had such high hopes for Cleat *and* of course for Coon too.

Three days following their return Cleat made dozens of attempts to contact Mandy, but all ended in dismal failures. Cleat used every means possible, as a last desperate ploy he plied Coon into acting as an intermediary, but it was unsuccessful. Early Saturday morning they said their goodbyes to the family and headed north. On the outskirts of town Coon asked Cleat to drive by his dad's house so he could check on him before leaving town.

Cleat turned down the cheerless dirt road lined with rundown shanties. A dozen or so racially mixed kids ranging in ages from toddler to maybe six- or seven-years-old were dressed in rags playing a game of tag. The thought of his friend's living conditions prior to moving in with his family broke his heart. At the end of the road he parked beside a beat-up mailbox in front of a dilapidated structure with a rickety open porch.

Taking the place of a missing corner post meant to hold the roof up was a rusted piece of steel pipe. On the wooden floor leaning against a clapboard wall was Coon's shoeless father, busy picking his nose searching for an object of discontent. He must've found it because he withdrew the probing finger and began rolling his left forefinger and thumb together in a circular motion. In his right hand he raised a clear bottle of booze to his lips and took a long, hard pull.

"I'll be back in a few minutes."

Cleat patted his friend on the shoulder, "Take your time."

Coon stepped on the concrete blocks substituting for rotted steps. Once on the porch he almost gagged from the stench of sweat, stale urine, and vomit; it was so overpowering the smell of alcohol wasn't detectable.

"I...I see th...the prodigal son has returned to gra...grace my threshold. Wh...what happened...your surrogate fa...family...throw your worthless ass on the streets?"

"No sir, I've come to say goodbye before going off to college."

"Good rid...riddance...you ain't been nothing but tro...trouble since th...the day you wa...was born. If it ha...hadn't been for you...my wife wouldn't have run off." His alcohol voice was barely audible. A grimy T-shirt covered in stains drooped over his shoulders and hanging loosely around his waist was a pair of dirty, gray cotton slacks held in place by a rope. The cuffs were frayed and worn almost black from months of neglect.

Coon sat on the planked floor and watched his father slowly drift into an alcoholic slumber. His eyes were dilated and Coon knew it wouldn't be long before his wretched father passed into unconsciousness. Standing up, he moved to his father's side and lifted him from the floor...he was surprised how little his father weighed...the man was nothing but skin and bones. In the bedroom he laid him on soiled sheets and pulled the top cover up to the old man's whiskered chin...he looked ten years older than his age. Coon leaned over and kissed his father's tortured brow. "Goodbye dad."

When Coon returned to the car all that was said between them was a simple "thank you" and "you're welcome." Several hours passed before any semblance of normal conversation started. Cleat didn't want to press, and Coon wasn't in the mood, but once they crossed the Florida-Georgia line their spirits were lifted substantially. When they rolled into Savannah, Georgia they found a beachfront motel and spent a peaceful night exploring the historic port city. Morning came early, and after breakfast they took a refreshing dip in the pool before continuing their journey northward.

At 2:35 PM they turned left off of US-74 onto Camden Road and drove up the hill leading to the rolling campus of Wingate Junior College. It was unexpectedly more beautiful than the brochure. A red brick archway stated the school was founded in 1897. They sat for a few moments taking it all in, the trees and buildings were just like the pictures, and across the way they recognized the building that was on the cover of the brochure. It was the first time the two of them had been this far from home unsupervised. Both were excited over the prospect of being away from home and having the freedom to do whatever they wanted without the fear of someone looking over their shoulder. *They* were soon to have a rude awakening.

Having arrived two days earlier than anyone expected, neither had the foggiest idea where to go or what to do. They decided to drive around campus and see their new digs. Taking a right at the end of the street they traveled down the hill, passing the Sanders Sykes Gymnasium with its large domed roof. At the bottom of the hill you could see the football stadium, it reminded them what they were there for.

Parking the car near the front gate they raced one another to the playing field. Both of them stood on the fifty-yard line huffing and puffing and dreaming of thrills to come. It was a new era, and they were strangers in a new land, but in the coming months the stadium would be filling with faithful fans screaming out their names as they triumphed on the football field.

"Hey you down there...come up here." A medium size man dressed in dark shorts and a gray T-shirt was standing by the locked gate they squeezed through only minutes ago.

"Who do you think that is?"

"Shit, Coon...how the hell am I supposed to know? I can tell you who it *isn't*...it's not Bob Hope, Bing Crosby, John Wayne, or Mickey Mantle."

"Very funny asshole."

"But whoever it is we'd better get our ass up there and see what he wants."

The closer they got to the man the more he resembled a coach, a gray shirt stenciled with "Wingate Football" and the whistle dangling around his neck were dead giveaways. His physique and demeanor were two more.

"Yes sir, you called for us?" Cleat smiled his most pleasant smile.

"What were y'all doing down there on my field?"

"Just looking around, we kinda wanted to get the lay of the land." Cleat answered with a wide smile spreading across his face. He liked the man at first sight.

Coon nodded his head before adding, "Yes sir, we wanted to check out the thickness of the sod and how level the field was. You got some good grass down there and I guess from the looks of things you have an adequate drainage system in place."

"You boys ain't from around here, are' ya? School isn't in session for another five or six weeks, so tell me what the hell are you doing here?"

"We've come to play football, Coach." Cleat held out his hand, "I'm Cleat Davis and this is John Truman."

"I'm Coach Baughman, the assistant head coach." His dialect had a pleasant Irish dance.

Coon was next to shake the coach's hand. "Coach, if you got some linemen that can open some holes, and a quarterback that can throw the ball, we'll show you the most excitement you seen in a long time."

"You're the two boys we recruited in Florida. Hell, you weren't supposed to check in 'til Wednesday noon with the rest of the team. There's nobody here but the coaching staff and a few other personnel." Coach Baughman scratched his head before coming to a decision. "Come with me and meet the head man."

Stepping into the cool gymnasium was a welcome relief to all three. At the far end of the court were four men shooting hoops. One of them was several inches taller and seemed much younger than the other three.

"Hey Coach Danielson, the Florida connection is here."

Everyone turned in their direction. A balding man of middle age let the basketball roll out of his hand and dribble across the floor. He was about six feet tall and weighed in the neighborhood of two hundred pounds. There was a livid scar that began at the corner of his right eye and traced over the bridge of his crooked nose.

"This here's Cleat Davis and the shorter one's John Truman."

"I'm Coach Danielson, boys, it's good to have you with us." The head coach shook both of their hands. "Y'all play much basketball?"

Cleat smiled at the youngest of the four standing off to the side. "A little...not much, we're mostly football jocks, but we..." He started to add more, but Coon nudged him with an elbow.

"All right then, we got us a game. It'll be the young guys wearing skins against the old farts. Robert, this is Cleat and John, your new teammates." Coach Danielson smiled at the new boys before explaining, "Robert Purdy is our sophomore quarterback...this will be his second year as a starter. He has a full scholarship next year to play ball for North Carolina State. We struggled to a seven and three season last year, but if we'd had players who could've caught the damn ball nobody would've beat us."

"Hey Cleat, Coach told me about you guys. I'm really looking forward to playing with y'all this year. Last season I didn't have any receivers that could catch worth a shit."

The basketball game, if you could call it that, was a slaughter. The first team that reached ten baskets and was up by two would be declared the winner. The final score was 10-2. Cleat, Coon, and Robert played like they'd been playing together for years. Not only was it no contest, the younger boys didn't even break a sweat.

Coach Danielson was bent over with his hands on his knees, droplets of sweat dripped from his chin and splattered on the hardwood floor. When he looked up his face was flushed beyond red. "There ain't gonna be no best outta three. I concede y'all gave us a good old fashion country ass-whipping." He pointed a finger at Cleat and Coon. "Y'all said you weren't much on basketball, I beg to differ. Y'all put one over me, don't go for twice." With a wink he peeled his shirt over his head and mopped his face. His upper body was covered with brutal gouges and scars; some of them appeared to be bullet wounds.

Robert clapped his new teammates on the back, "Y'all come with me and I'll get y'all squared away. Cleat and Coon became roommates thanks to Robert Purdy. They usually paired a sophomore with an incoming freshman to help them become acclimated to college life.

So far junior college football was far more grueling then expected. Instead of the two-a-days they were familiar with in high school…three-a-days were a real ball buster. Two weeks of brutal drills and calisthenics weaned the team from the want-a-be's and left the coaches with a hard corps of determined players.

"Christ on a crutch Cleat, did you think it was going to be like this?" Coon sat on a locker-room bench wearing nothing but a jockstrap while rubbing his tender feet.

Cleat was standing by his locker with a towel wrapped around his waist, he hadn't bothered to dry off…he was too damn tired. "Hell no, it's been a bitch from the start, but good riddance to those who couldn't hack it. We need guys around us we can count on, and the quitters weren't willing to pay the price. The ones that didn't quit are guys that love playing football as much as we do and I'm proud to call them our teammates. We've survived the tough part…the rest of the way will be fun."

"I'll amen that brother."

Prior to and during football season the carefree college life they often dreamed of was nonexistent, more so than the naivety of a child's belief in fairytales. Their world consisted of blood, sweat, bruises, sore muscles, and hours of sitting in the whirlpool to ease the pain. It began at 5:30 AM and it arrived at the same time everyday: to damn early. When the coaches and team captains performed their mandatory 10:00 PM bed check, they found most of the players already sound asleep. The playbook was two inches thick, comparing it to Lakewood's notebook it looked more the size of Shakespeare's entire collection, and it was harder to read. If they weren't on the practice field spilling their guts they were either in the classroom studying plays or lifting weights. The only breaks were showers, meals, and weekends.

Weekends were mostly spent doing laundry and catching up on sleep, and when they weren't doing that you could usually find them at the rec-hall playing ping-pong or cards. The trips to Monroe, a little town located just down the highway, were a rarity because there wasn't much to do except go to a movie or drive by the Dairy Queen trolling for the opposite sex.

Cleat and Coon were measurably impressed with the size and speed of their teammates. The caliber of athletes surrounding them wasn't at all what they expected to find playing junior college football. They presumed the team would consist of players not good enough to play for colleges with four year curriculums. Under normal circumstances they would've been correct in their presumptions, but there was nothing normal about Wingate's athletic department. Most of their teammates had been offered major scholarships, but personal trouble back home *or* failing university academic requirements left them in an athletic purgatory. The hallowed halls of Wingate offered the refuge of lost souls and broken dreams a second chance to fulfill their aspirations of playing Division I football.

During their six weeks of hell the campus was like a ghost town. The football team and coaches were the soul residents, if you discounted fulltime employees, and some of the administrative staff. It was worse than being at home; at least you could associate with friends not related to the world of football.

Cleat and Coon blended in with their teammates as if they were old friends, and it wasn't based solely on athleticism. Cleat's leadership and driving personality to be the best at anything he deemed worthwhile drew the same response from others, making him one of the most respected members of the football team.

Coon's zaniness and his love for fun made him the most popular player on the team. His incredible ability to mimic Coach Danielson's idiosyncrasies and impersonate the coach's voice was hilarious, and constantly in great demand. One evening pretending to be the head coach he phoned the lovable Coach Baughman. He demanded him to go to the equipment room and paint the footballs white so the receivers could see them better. That morning when the trainer dumped the bag of balls on the ground, Coach Danielson went nuts. He ranted and raved, wanting to know who the guilty party was. When Baughman whispered in his ear you could tell he was suppressing a laugh. Slowly his eyes singled out Coon.

"Truman, I'd like to see you after practice."

"Yes sir, at your command, sir." It was impossible not to register the snickers and guffaws of his teammates.

At 4:30 the football team hung around until Danielson was through chewing Coon's ass. When it was finally over Coon joined his teammates and informed them he was to run laps around the field until the stadium lights came on, which would make it somewhere on the other side of 7:30 PM.

The coaches were off to the side in an impromptu meeting when they witnessed the entire team fall-in beside Coon and begin to run the laps as one.

"Men, I've never been more excited to begin a season. Maybe once in a lifetime you are privy to coach a team destined for glory, congratulations gentlemen, you have been chosen."

Wingate won the conference championship with an undefeated season, *and* they won the JUCO National Championship against Coffeeville 31-10. In the national championship game Cleat caught eleven passes for two hundred and twelve yards; three of the receptions were touchdowns, his longest went for seventy one yards. Coon had one hundred and seventy four yards of combined yardage: one hundred and thirty four rushing, and forty in receiving. On the Bulldog's first drive Coon scored a touchdown on a twenty three yard screen pass that gave Wingate a lead they never relinquished. Once again Cleat was in the national headlines, and even John Truman's name was mentioned. Wingate football was bigger than ever and nationally recognized. College recruiters from around the nation flooded the campus openly salivating over the host of prospects. Cleat and Coon's teammates benefited greatly from the notoriety.

When their championship season came to a close basketball season was already in progress. Coon eagerly joined the team and pleaded with Cleat to join him, although Cleat briefly entertained the thought, he chose to pass up the opportunity. From the time he was eight years old he'd played all three sports year-round, plus the years between eight and fifteen when he and Coon boxed in the Boys Club's Golden Gloves program. He never lost a bout and Coon only lost three before it was discontinued after a boy suffered severe head injuries, surely there must be more to this world than athletics. He was tired of the strict regimen that went hand-in-hand with organized sports, and especially the roll of leadership that was always thrust upon him. It was time to take a breather and enjoy campus life.

At the conclusion of basketball season Coon couldn't stand the thought of being idle so he tried out for the baseball team and easily made the final roster. Once again he tried talking Cleat into playing, but all Cleat wanted to do was hangout with his latest cutie. Coon had lost count which number she was. Hell, he couldn't even recall the girl's name. Cleat wasn't the proverbial BMOC, (big man on campus)…he was the reigning *King*.

Coon sat on his bed rubbing a light coat of Hiram's Linseed Oil on his baseball glove. He was worried about his best friend, as of late he couldn't even get Cleat out of bed to go to class. It was like fame had gone to his head and he didn't have *or* want any responsibilities. Granted, they both achieved notoriety playing football. Cleat had broken every conference receiving record, and Coon had rushed for over eighteen hundred yards to share some of the gridiron glory. Naturally the press *and* the girls flocked to Cleat as if he were a movie star; sadly the girls were like moths to a bright light…once they got too close they were burned.

Finals were coming up, and he knew Cleat hadn't cracked a book in months. Coon was the only one who understood Cleat, and that caused him even greater concern, because he knew Cleat was in a state of depression. Outwardly he exuded confidence, but Coon was aware of the times he tried to call Mandy at Florida State and not once would she receive his calls. Letters didn't get any results either, *all* of them were returned with the seal unbroken. Considering Cleat's past treatment of Mandy some might think Coon's devotion was undeserving, but his love was unconditional. Coon wanted to ease his friend's pain, but try as he might Cleat wouldn't let him inside to help in his suffering. After football season Cleat changed into who he'd become…an asshole.

Wingate was a Baptist affiliated college *and* that meant no alcohol, or dancing, was allowed on college grounds. The college administration frowned upon and discouraged displays of affection between students. There was to be no kissing, holding hands, or any other expressive gestures that may be construed as sexual. It was more of a nuisance than anything else, and young, intelligent minds with active imaginations can circumvent most obstacles adults threw at them. They had good times going to parties off campus and hanging out at the Klondike eating fried egg sandwiches and dancing in the back room. Occasionally a panty raid would occur, but the most brazen act was to sneak a girl into your room without anyone's knowledge, except for your roommates.

Certain counties in North Carolina were wet, and the modified drinking age was eighteen *if* you restricted your preference to beer with an alcoholic content of 3.2%. The Last Chance Saloon was a stones throw across the county line and a local gathering place during the week, but on Friday and Saturday nights a live band rocked the house. On those nights dozens of Wingate students congregated at the watering hole to party. They rubbed elbows with underage high school kids carrying fake ID's, servicemen, bikers, and girls looking for a fun night out. Barroom brawls were infrequent, if there was an injury it was usually caused from slipping on peanut shells that covered the hardwood floors. The older women who graced the joint were wilder than wild.

Coon laughed out loud when he remembered the time Coach Baughman discovered their beer stash hidden inside the athletic dorms toilet tanks. By chance, the coach went into the bathroom to take a leak and found an open can of Black Label. Some ingrate left it sitting on a toilet lid in plain view. He immediately convened a team meeting inside the bathroom.

In an Irish brogue the coach began, "Men, my righteous foundation has been shocked to its very core. Inside the confines of these hallowed halls I've uncovered the root of all evil. Alcohol is the damnation of our souls. Its demonic power inhibits rational behavior and facilitates unchristian acts. I entrusted you fine men with the castle-keep and you saw fit to dishonor not only me, but your entire coaching staff *and* the fine traditions of Wingate. You did so in a shameful exhibition of callous disregard for all that's saintly in this world. You can't buy trust and integrity, but you can lose it." Baughman stared around the room looking each player in the eye; most of them couldn't meet his glare of disappointment. "Now if you boys would be so kind, I expect to find a can of Budweiser, not that Black Label piss, in number one stall each time I visit this holy sanctorum for the depraved and foolhardy."

It took a few moments for his last statement to register, but when it did the bathroom erupted in a chorus of shouts. Although they gladly complied with his wish, the can of Budweiser was never exhumed from its watery grave. Someone painted a four-leaf clover on stall number one's door and it instantly became a shrine to believers in goodness and fair play. From that day forward Coach Baughman became an icon to the athletes. He was a man among men, and they loved him for all his Irish ways.

In late January an incident occurred that went far beyond any one's intentions. It started when the circus came to Monroe and set up shop down by the railroad tracks close to Morgan Mill Road. They were in the process of setting up the Big Top when Cleat, Coon, and several members of the football team inquired about student pricing. When the burly handler told them there weren't any discounts to be had Cleat tried to explain to the tough looking guy that they'd just won the national championship and it would probably be good advertisement if they would make an exception. The man's only response was telling them to get lost, or pay the full price like everybody else.

Coon wasn't sure whose lame idea it was to take one of the large ropes attached to the huge tent and tie it to the trains caboose, he only knew that it wasn't his or Cleat's. Twenty minutes later the train began rolling down the track, and when the rope became taut the noise from ripping canvas and the popping sound of stakes being jerked out of the ground created a frantic scene. Circus people were running around screaming in horror as the Big Top collapsed and followed the train out of town. The boys were well on their way back to school before the commotion died down.

Within a week everybody remotely considered to be affiliated with the football team was under investigation. At first the campus police handled the inquiries, and most of the players thought it was a big joke. When it was turned over to the sheriffs department it became more serious. After two weeks of getting nowhere they called in the North Carolina Department of Law Enforcement, who in turn invited FBI agents to assist. Coon was so nervous during the interview he was afraid they would consider him one of the guilty parties. Three days later he almost shit his pants when he was one of the few to be recalled for an additional interview. Thankfully, whoever the true culprits were escaped all of the scrutiny, and the team was left alone. Coon wasn't sure of the lesson learned, but was sure something was learned.

Sometimes there were days when he and Cleat rarely saw each other, and it had been weeks on end since they had had any meaningful conversations. They weren't intentionally avoiding contact; it was more to do with circumstances. Baseball took up a lot of Coon's time, and when he wasn't practicing, or playing, he was studying. On the other hand Cleat partied most nights drinking way too much, and slept during the day. Occasionally he attended a class or two just to keep up appearances, but ever since the football season ended he'd lost all interest in school.

During finals Cleat and most of his rowdy friends spent the week at Ocean Drive, South Carolina. They partied for two weeks at a beach house belonging to one of the player's parents. Coon couldn't believe his friend's lack of responsibility, but what the hell, by then Cleat literally became a stranger. Cleat was definitely out of control, and Coon feared he didn't have the expertise to bring him around, or at the very least modify his friend's behavior before they went home for the summer. Cleat couldn't have passed the last semester even if he'd aced the exams, which he never bothered to take in the first place. Cleat had way too many unexcused absences to save him from his father's wrath.

Coon sat on his bed staring at the suitcases and boxes he packed on Monday. It was now Friday and Cleat should've been back four days ago. Coon turned in their bed linen on Monday, which was supposed to be their final day of the school year. Ever since then he had been sleeping on a bare mattress using a worn-out blanket he scrounged for a cover. Coon had been given an extension to stay a few days longer, but if Cleat didn't show up by Sunday he would be out on his ass.

Daddy "D" had opened a joint checking account for the two of them at the local bank. Mister Davis roughly figured the sum of two thousand dollars would equal to approximately twenty-five dollars a week spending money for the two boys. Cleat, with his partying ways went through most of the money set aside for both of them. Coon didn't mind, the ten dollars a week the athletic department paid them to monitor the football field was more than enough. It was a job in name only, since ground crews worked year-round fertilizing and mowing the field, plus there was an automatic sprinkler system to take care of the watering.

Forty dollars a month was more than enough for Coon, since he didn't date on a regular basis and if he got low on funds he would dip into the account for five or ten dollars now and then. When Cleat didn't show on Monday he waited until Wednesday before going to the bank and draw enough money to pay for a train ticket or bus fare home. The teller notified him that the account was overdrawn, showing a deficient of two hundred and fifty-five dollars. That's when he really started to worry about his plight. He sure as hell wasn't going to call the family and ask for money, because Cleat was going to be in enough trouble as it was. His only option now was to hitchhike. Curling under the blanket he said a silent prayer for his friend.

"Come on Coon...get your ass outta bed, its time to head back to Lakewood."

Before he could sit up and get his bearings the old moth-eaten blanket covering his naked body was snatched from the bed. "What the hell...?"

"Jesus Christ, put some clothes on. It's too early in the morning for a sight like that. I find it rather disturbing, if I do say so myself. I've had two weeks of naked women and enough beer to float a battleship, dammit man you should've come with me."

"Well now let's see asshole, first of all it was during finals, and secondly I wasn't invited." Coon turned his back and slipped on a pair of white jockey shorts.

"Since when do I need to send an engraved invitation to my brother?"

Pulling a T-shirt over his head, Coon gave Cleat a hard look. "I wouldn't have gone anyway, so don't worry about it."

"What crawled up your ass and took a dump?"

"You don't want me to even get started, Cleat."

"Well, the hell with you *and* your holier than thou attitude. If you got something to say then spit it out, or have you lost your balls along with your desire for fun?"

"You ain't ready for what I got to say."

Cleat picked up Coon's suitcase and threw it across the room. "Dammit...we ain't leaving till I hear your sermon."

Coon held his rage in check, they hadn't fought each other since they were twelve-years-old, but he was ready to deck the son-of-a-bitch right where he stood. "Cleat, you've turned into a stranger, and not a very nice one at that. You're like a brother to me, and I love you regardless of what you've become. If..."

"Hold it right there asshole...what do you mean by *what* I've become?'"

"Cleat, I know this isn't the real you, not the same caring person I know and love. You've been through some hard times, but that doesn't justify your actions. You can't bury your head in the sand and pretend everything is okay. When we get home you're gonna have to face the consequences of your misconduct." Coon slipped into his Levis and sat on the bed to lace up a pair of scruffy tennis shoes.

"Misconduct! What's with you? Damn Coon, you sound like my fuckin' councilor instead of my best friend." Cleat picked up Coon's winter jacket off his student desk and angrily tossed it across the room.

Coon caught the fleece-lined leather jacket in midair. "I am your best friend, that's why you need to listen." Coon lifted his suitcase off the floor, "Ever since we won the JUCO National Championship you've been running wild like there's no tomorrow. Let me be the first to bust your bubble: there is a tomorrow *and* it's gonna bite you right in the ass."

"Come on Coon, college life is supposed to be fun. That's one of the reasons we decided to come up here together."

"Cleat, we both know there's more to college life than drinking and staying out all night. It's also about higher learning and assuming responsibilities without parental guidance. Not only have you failed in those aspects, you've also failed in your studies. What in the hell were you thinking? Did you think going to classes and meeting your academic obligations were beneath you?"

"Don't worry about it. The coaches fixed it so I can make up the finals. All I have to do is report a week early and take the damn exams."

"Oh shit, I forgot you're somebody special. Pardon me if I don't bend over and kiss your hairy ass."

"Hey jerk-off...if it wasn't for *me* we wouldn't have won the conference championship *and* national championship."

"Christ, listen to you. You've *never* put yourself above the team before. *You* didn't win anything. The team won and without the team *you* are nothing. Prequel to becoming a superstar you were a decent human being, but now you're an arrogant, egotistical asshole that thinks his jockstrap doesn't smell. I thought I knew you, but over the past few months you've become a complete stranger and not a very likable one at that."

"Fuck you. I don't need to stand here and listen to your condescending bullshit. Why'd you wait on me anyway? You coulda taken the train or bus."

"Believe me I would've, but when I went to the bank to withdraw enough money to buy a ticket I found the account overdrawn by almost $300.00."

"No sweat, I've got enough on me to get us there and back."

"Cleat, I know the loss of Mandy has been devastating, and I feel your pain, but hanging onto false hope will only make it worse. You have to consider the distinct possibility of having to face life without Mandy."

"You fuckin' asshole." Cleat lunged forward, sticking his finger in Coon's face. "Who in hell are *you* to say that Mandy's out of my life. *You* don't know shit."

Coon stood ramrod stiff staring at Cleat's finger. He had to summon every ounce of self-control not to snap it off and ram it up Cleat's ass. "You might think you know Mandy better than anyone, but I beg to differ. I know her for *who* she is. She's used my shoulder as a crying towel for years. Her beauty belies the fact she's full of self-doubt and..."

"She still loves me dammit; can't you get that through that thick skull of yours? You of all people should know how much we love each other."

Coon placed his hand on Cleat's shoulder, "Sometimes love isn't enough. Love is a word with many dimensions, and if you confuse it with emotions it's never lasting."

"Christ Coon, you sound like professor Ludlow spouting ethics. I know the meaning of love. It's what Mandy and I have."

"When's Mandy's birthday?"

"What?"

"Who's her favorite poet? Who's her favorite writer? What kind of books does she read?

"Why?"

"What's her greatest fear? What's her major in college? How many children does she want to have?"

"This is crazy, why are you asking me all of these questions?"

"Do you know the answer to any of them?"

"Her birthday's in August."

"When?"

"I don't know…somewhere towards the end." Cleat was uncomfortable with Coon's expression. "I suppose you know all of the answers."

"As a matter of fact I do. That ought to tell you something."

"What?"

Coon shook his head, "Brother, if you don't know then it ain't worth telling."

"Fuck your questions, they don't mean shit. I'm not going to give up on Mandy. All she needed was some time and space. It's been almost a year since we've seen, or talked to each other. When I get back home and see her face-to-face things will be back to normal. It's all gonna work out, you just wait and see. It has to, because I can't live my life without her in it."

"I hope for your sake that's what'll happen, because all I want is what's best for you. I've experienced the pain of losing someone you love. I lost my father years ago and even though the memory of my mother is vague, there are glimpses of the past I hold dear. During moments of despondency I can still smell her scent and feel the warmth of her caresses. Periodically she enters my dreams floating on billowy clouds beckoning with open arms. With a purity of voice she professes undying love and pleads for forgiveness. When I awake her haunting last words echo in my mind, *I love you John. You are not to blame.*"

Cleat's animosity waned, and a great sorrow filled the void. While trying to bury his troublesome doubts he had forsaken his best friend. "I'm sorry Coon, you're right. I haven't been myself lately. What I said earlier was pure bullshit, but this thing with Mandy is driving me nuts." Cleat wrapped his arms around Coon and gave him a brotherly hug. "I love you man, don't *ever* forget that."

"Yeah, I know, and I love you too. You're the closest thing I'll ever have to a brother."

"Yeah, I know."

On the return trip they decided to drive straight through, and most of the way their conversation had been light, or nonexistent. Coon was preoccupied over the upcoming confrontation between father and son. When the inevitable happened he didn't want to be anywhere around. Unjustly so, his devotion to Cleat shouldered the blame for not hounding him into going to class and accepting responsibility.

Cleat's thoughts were of Mandy. Would she see him? Would she forgive him? He prayed she would understand how much he truly loved her and made a vow to become monogamous if she would take him back. When they crossed the Florida-Georgia line a little after 11:00 PM, Cleat let out a bloody "hurrah" that awakened Coon from a deep slumber.

"Coon Dog, in a little over five hours we'll be home for the summer, and I bet'cha a dime to a doughnut I'm still on everybody's shit list."

The intrusion startled Coon; Cleat hadn't called him by his *full* nickname since grammar school. "Yeah, you're probably right, but it'll be good to be home again."

Several minutes of uncomfortable silence elapsed before Cleat probed for a more meaningful conversation. "I can't do it, Coon."

"Do what?"

"I can't put Mandy out of my life. I've always loved her. At first it was adolescent love with stolen kisses and explorations, but it grew into so much more. It's taken a horrendous mistake on my part to realize how much I truly love her. There's got to be some way to make her understand that I've learned my lesson. She can't sentence us to a lifetime of isolation. She's *got* to give me another chance."

"Cleat, I hope you're right, but if it doesn't come to be, life goes on. You make the best of what fate deals you, and go from there."

Cleat rubbed the top of his friend's head affectionately. "I'm sorry for the things I said earlier. You know how much your friendship means to me. You're gonna forgive me, right?"

"I'll give it some thought."

Cleat laughed. "Were you born an asshole, or was it something you strived to achieve?"

"It's a gift from God, what can I say."

On the outskirts of Jacksonville they pulled into Harley's Truck Stop for gas and something to eat. There were very few people inside the dinner, a trucker or two, and a couple of travelers. They chose one of the red vinyl booths midway down the row of a dozen lining the wall. Cleat slipped a quarter into the miniature jukebox and selected three songs. "Are you Lonesome Tonight" by Elvis was the first of his random selections.

A waitress in her early twenties wearing too much makeup sashayed over to their booth with a red lipstick smile on her face. She was easy to look at in her light blue uniform showing every tantalizing inch of her curvaceous figure. Her dark hair was tied in a relaxed ponytail, belying her age. "Well, is it true…are you boys lonesome tonight, or just passing through town?"

"I was feeling mighty lonesome until a beautiful girl suddenly appeared before me." Cleat smiled his most charming of smiles.

"Oh, aren't you a charmer. I bet you say that to all the girls."

"Only to the pretty ones Misty." Cleat read the nametag pinned above her left breast.

Misty pushed a loose strand of hair off her forehead. "Thank you, I must look a sight after a twelve-hour shift, but flattery will work every time. What'll you gentlemen have tonight?"

"That's a leading question, Misty, and I must say extremely tantalizing."

"I was talking about your order, silly." Misty laughed playfully. "I bet you're naughty whenever you have the chance."

Cleat placed a hand over his heart. "I'll have you know in my misspent youth I was a boy scout in good standing, and I'm overly offended that a beautiful woman such as yourself would haphazardly, and with absence of feeling or remorse, slander my character without knowing the purity of my soul. I am deeply hurt."

Misty slowly raised an eyebrow as she scrutinized the good-looking young boy sitting at her station. His ice-blue eyes were captivating and he was certainly different than the normal traffic of customers. She'd become impervious to the usual crude overtures of tired truck drivers and drunks, but there was something unique about blue-eye's flirtations that intrigued her. It had been a long time since she'd been stimulated by anyone other than her fantasies, she couldn't remember the last time she spent an evening without wishing she were home in bed *alone.*

After divorcing her high school sweetheart six months ago life had been difficult to say the least. Trying to make ends meet while attending Jacksonville Junior College and working weekends was extremely hectic. She just didn't have the time or patience to deal with adolescent behavior. At twenty-two she felt like a fish out of water mingling with a student body mostly comprised of acne infested teenagers struggling for adulthood. This young man was a welcome relief from the post-puberty crowd hitting on her Monday through Friday.

"Where are y'all headed?"

"Lakewood."

"Really, I have an older sister who teaches school at Highland Elementary."

"No kidding, do you ever visit her?"

"Occasionally, but she's married with a couple of kids and stays pretty busy. Her husband's an engineer with the electric company. He's the one that got me interested in electrical engineering. I'm a student at Jacksonville Junior College during the week. School's out for the summer, but I have to make-up a lab final on Wednesday because I was out with the flu. Next weekend I start back full-time at Harley's until classes resume this fall, then its back to the same old grind." Misty smiled at Cleat, "Y'all better put your order in, because I'm off in twenty minutes."

Fifteen minutes later Cleat and Coon were finishing their last bites of steak and eggs when Misty dropped by to see if they were doing okay before punching the clock. "Anything y'all need before I go home?"

"My, my, another leading question. What am I going to do with you, Misty?"

"I could say something, but I won't." God, she couldn't believe those words came out of her mouth.

"Hmm, how about a refill on coffee, *and* if it's not against policy how about sitting with us and make two lonely travelers feel special before you go home?"

"It's not, and I will, but only for a few minutes."

They watched her retreat through the swinging doors, both of them sharing the same thoughts although Coon knew he wasn't a player. The eye contact and conversation was solely between Cleat and Misty, but what the hell, he had as much right to wish as anybody.

The three of them laughed and talked for more than an hour when Cleat decided they either needed to get on the road, or ask her something he'd been thinking about for the past thirty minutes. "How in the world has a beautiful girl like you stayed single?"

"As of six months ago I wasn't. I married my boyfriend the weekend after we graduated from high school, but within the year it started going sour. After two trial separations I'd had enough. I just thank God we didn't have any children."

"When's the last time you've had a vacation, or had some relaxing downtime to enjoy life?"

"You're kidding, right?"

"Not at all."

"Well let's see, my best guess is when I was twelve-years-old, which would make it the summer before my parents divorced."

Cleat reached across the table and placed his hand on top of hers, "John and I are planning on spending a few days at our parents' beach house in Daytona, and we would consider it a privilege *and* an honor if you were to grace us with your presence."

As Misty made an abrupt move to leave, Cleat quickly slid from the booth, "Wait…please you mustn't misconstrue my proposal. I know how it sounded, but it's strictly an invitation to enjoy the beach. It's a big house with separate bedrooms, and you can even invite a friend if it would make you feel more comfortable."

Misty tried to read something more sinister in his eyes other than a friend-ly invitation, but his offer seemed surprisingly sincere. "Even if it was my older brother I invited?"

"Sure, he could act as your bodyguard, but I promise there's no ulterior motive in my offer. Heck, you can even invite your mother if it makes you feel better."

Misty laughed, "I don't think that'll be necessary. My brother and I share an apartment together, so I'll give him a call and let you know the answer in a few minutes."

The two boys anxiously watched her disappear around the corner.

"Shit Cleat, I thought you had something going until she mentioned her brother."

"Yeah, but I meant what I said. You can look in her eyes and tell that she needs a break. Hell, I wasn't looking forward to seeing dad go nuts over my grades anyway. Catching up with old friends at Daytona and allowing Misty to enjoy a few days of much needed relaxation isn't a bad combination."

Ten minutes later Misty rejoined them wearing a white halter-top, faded jeans, and a scuffed-up pair of tennis shoes. Her brown wavy hair was brushed into a long flowing mane that fell below her shoulders. She looked five years younger and twice as attractive.

"He said okay, but the two of us want to take my car in case we want to leave early. Follow me to our apartment…by the time we get there he'll be ready. Are you *still* sure this is what you want, because I don't want you expect-ing anything else. My uhh…Jake just finished a four year hitch with the Marines and he's overly protective of his little sister."

"Absolutely, scout's honor, we'd be glad to have your brother as our guest." Cleat saluted, using the Boy Scout's universal three-fingered salute.

"Then follow me…my cars parked out front."

They'd been parked behind Misty's 1960 green and white four door Impala for twenty minutes waiting for them to come out of the small duplex. In the distance they could hear an old tomcat prowling the lower income neighborhood for some companionship. Without warning the stoop light came on, casting long shadows from a large Camphor tree. Misty was the first to appear in the doorway carrying a small overnighter; following close behind was her brother. At first glance he looked too frail and feminine to be a Marine. Their jaws dropped when Misty stuck her head in the passenger side window.

"My brother decided not to go at the last minute so Debbie's taking his place, if that's all right."

"Sure, it's fine with us, but I was really looking forward to meeting your brother." Cleat got out his car. "Before we leave do you mind if I introduce myself to him? I'd sure like to know what it was like serving in the Marines Corps."

"I don't think it would be a good idea, he just got off the late shift, and he's probably gone back to sleep."

"What'd you say his name was?"

"Uhh…his name's Bobby."

"Well I'm sure Bobby, or was it *Jake*, wouldn't mind if I woke him up."

"Ohhh okay…I told a lie. I don't have a brother."

"Oh, so you were testing me? Well, did I pass?"

"We're here, aren't we?"

"Well, get in and let's go."

"Should I sit up front with you?"

"I wouldn't have it any other way."

Misty waited for Coon to hop in the back seat before she introduced Debbie. "John this is Debbie, my cousin and best friend. We go to school together."

"Hey Debbie have a seat, I promise I won't bite." He was immediately impressed with Debbie. She was around five foot three with short brown hair and great tits.

When Debbie crawled into the back seat with Coon she slid close to him and smiled sweetly, with a modicum of shyness. "Hi John."

Coon slipped his arm over her shoulder and smiled. "Hi Debbie."

On their first night in the beach house Cleat and Coon were sleeping in separate bedrooms while the girls shared the guest room in the rear of the house closest to the road. The mini vacation turned out to be a blast for all four of them. The girls were terrific in every way. Their first day was spent playing in the sun and getting to know each other. It was purely coincidental how well the couple's personalities coincided. Their first night out they went to the Surf Bar and stayed for a couple of sets listening to the soulful sounds of rhythm and blues. Their last stop was Club Martinique where they spent an hour or so dancing before calling it a night. Both of the girls were impressed with the boys' dancing abilities and said so. Cleat and Coon thanked them, but failed to mention the hours of secret lessons they'd taken from Arthur Murray's Dance Studio when they were sophomores in high school.

By Sunday night the girls decided it was time to abandon their charade and move into the boys' bedrooms. The next few days and nights ran together in a whirlwind of enormous fun and sexual gratifications. Regrettably Tuesday afternoon arrived much too soon, and no amount of pleading convinced Misty to forgo her make-up exam. Cleat and Coon would've been more than glad to stay for as long as they so desired, but unfortunately all good things have to come to an end, or so they'd been told.

Even though they'd only known each other for a few days it was tough saying goodbye. The small amount of time they'd spent together was memorable, especially to Cleat and Coon. They learned more about the female body and its cravings than either of them ever dreamed possible, especially Coon. Both of them were inwardly shocked over the girls' sexual enlightenment. It wasn't until they were headed back to Daytona after taking the girls' home that they were able to compare their experiences in the bedrooms. It was then they realized how little they actually knew about a woman's wants. How stupid of them to think there had been nothing more to learn. They proved as willing participants and absorbed a vast amount of knowledge in the carnal arts of pleasing a woman. Don Juan would've been proud.

Early Friday morning they were homeward bound, each anticipating their family reunion with mixed emotions. Cleat could hardly wait to speak with Mandy and try to patch things up; surely it had been long enough for her to forgive and forget. He tried talking to her during Christmas vacation, but she'd avoided him like the plague, as did most of her friends. This time he hoped it would be different.

Coon was fidgety; he knew it was only a matter of weeks before Cleat's grades arrived and when they did all hell was going to break loose in the Davis household. *Damn, all Cleat had to do was go to class. Christ, he's twice as smart as I am. With his damn near photographic memory all he had to do is sit in class and absorb whatever came out of the professors' mouth. Now me, I have to study my ass off and hope*

I've retained enough to pass the next test.

He was totally aware that his feelings of guilt over Cleat's dilemma were misplaced and self-destructive in nature, but feelings were just that, feelings. Cleat was to blame…not him. He thought of how many times he tried to dissuade Cleat from neglecting his studies and go to class, but it was like talking to a brick wall. A shiver went down his back when he thought of Cleat's grades arriving at the Davis household. Mister "D" was going to hit the freaking roof and rightfully so. Cleat's maniacal self-absorption was going to fuck up their entire summer.

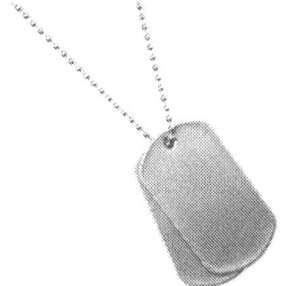

CHAPTER 11

Things were going poorly for Cleat, as his every attempt in reaching Mandy had failed. Her parents intercepted his phone calls, and refused to relay his messages. None of her friends were willing to help with his impasse, nor would any of his. For that matter he wasn't sure he had any friends, except for Bo and Coon. When they were home for Christmas vacation Bo was the only Christmas party he and Coon were invited to. It was like he had a "Scarlet Letter" burned on his forehead, and due to their friendship Coon was being punished as well.

The following Sunday after their return he and Coon were driving around Lake Holley when by chance Cleat saw Mandy walking their Labrador "Ketch" around the lake. He recognized this as his chance and pulled onto the grass twenty feet behind Mandy. Getting out of his car he quickly ran the short distance to confront her. His heart was racing a mile a minute when he approached her from the rear.

"Mandy, wait up." His heart skipped a beat when he saw her turn to face his plea. She was more beautiful than ever. "We have to talk."

"No, no we don't. I never want to see you again, and furthermore I want you to quit calling my house and making a nuisance of yourself."

"Mandy, please…you can't be serious. I love you with all my heart. You can't dismiss what we've shared together."

"Leave me alone, Cleatwood Davis. Once and for all you are out of my life." She turned her back and began walking away without a backward glance.

Cleat felt a cold stab of pain dig deep into his chest. He couldn't let this happen; reaching out he grabbed her arm and forcefully restrained her. "You don't mean that, Mandy…I know you can't possibly mean that."

"You're hurting me, Cleat. Let go of my arm this second or I will scream."

Cleat did as he was asked. "I'm sorry, but please don't walk away until we work this out." Cleat noticed the welts on her upper arm outlining the imprint of his fingers.

"There is nothing to work out, Cleat. You are out of my life forever and always. I've met someone at school that I care for very much, and thank God he's nothing like you. He's kind and decent, and most of all I trust him with all my heart. It's time to grow up Cleat, whatever we had between us you destroyed. It will never be the same again, it's lost in the past and there it shall remain. If you ever loved me then I ask you to please leave me be. Move on with your life as I have with mine. Goodbye, Cleat."

Mandy turned away before she changed her mind. She knew that her broken heart would be exposed if she didn't leave immediately. His pleas were captivating and the desperation in his eyes threatened to melt the emotional barrier she had been hiding behind. She had done everything in her power to avoid such a chance encounter, but now it was over...she survived. There would always be a place in her heart for Cleat, but she would bury it deep and throw away the key. As of this day her new life would begin.

Her parting words brought a lump to his throat. His last image of Mandy was her eyes flooding with tears, and it gave him a breath of hope. He didn't believe a word she said. If their love was real a year ago then somehow they could get past this crisis. The longest walk he ever took was back to his car...*alone.*

When Coon and Cleat entered their home through the den doorway Mister Davis was standing in the center of the room with an open letter in his hand.

"Coon, would you excuse us a moment please?"

"Sure thing, Daddy 'D'...no problem." He thought, *Doomsday has arrived early and hell is upon us.*

Mister Davis waited until they were alone. "Cleat, do you know what I have in my hand?"

"Looks like a letter. Why?"

"Actually, to be more precise there are four letters. The first one illustrates your poor excuse for grades, and here's one from the Dean's office stating you are hereby on academic probation, and they further imply a strong desire for you *not* to return to their halls of academia. The last one is a notification from the Athletic Department stating that prior employment arrangements are subsequently nullified. I'm not sure what they are talking about, but it further states your scholarship is in suspension. If you desire to have it reinstated, you may do so by attending summer session at your own expense. If you pass the required courses your scholarship will be reinstated and you will be eligible to play football this coming fall. The last letter is an official notification from the First City Bank of Monroe stating that yours and John's bank account is overdrawn by a substantial amount. Being that I am the sole bearer of said infraction that leaves me personally responsible for the overdraft. I find it highly unlikely that John has any responsibility in this matter. This has your misdoings and lack of respect written all over it."

Mister Davis waved the letters angrily, "I can't tell you how disappointed I am. For the life of me I don't understand why you are not a responsible young man like your brother. Never once has he shamed the family, and you seem to go out of your way to do so. First you impregnate the daughter of one of my best friends, and instead of facing the consequence for your indiscretion you chose the coward's way by running off. Not many people get a second chance in life, but Coach Dunn gave you an opportunity to prove your worth and once again you failed. I had hoped you would change your ways, but apparently they were false hopes." Mister Davis shook the letters in Cleat's face. "Can you explain your actions, or does it even matter that you continually discredited your family?"

Without waiting for an answer he continued, "If it's not one thing or another, you somehow manage to find ways to bring disgrace to the Davis name. You are no longer a child, but you are far from being the mature individual your mother and I dreamed of you becoming. Your life is an immoral playground infested with amoral games played by adolescents who have no conception of what respectable behavior is. Courtrooms and jails are filled with people who rebel against society and wallow in self gratification."

"Dad, I'm sorry that I've…"

"I don't want to hear apologies, nor will I listen to excuses. Christ almighty Cleat, you are nineteen-years-old *and* supposed to be a man. I find your actions despicable and your lack of common sense deplorable. The apathy you display to those who love you is callous and undeserving. As a father I have failed you, but I will not hold myself solely accountable. You were taught right from wrong and good from evil, you were rewarded for good behavior and punished for misbehaving. We provided you with food, clothing, and a roof over your head without unjust demands and yet you chose malfeasance over scruples. I will no longer support any of your future endeavors, nor will I allow you to live under my roof while you throw your life away. By the end of the week I want you out of my house. I pray facing the harsh reality of the real world will expedite your growth into manhood." Mister Davis took a deep breath, waiting for his son's rebuttal, after a long pause he realized there would be none forthcoming and proceeded, "Do you have any explanation for your irresponsible behavior? I warn you, standing mute is not a good defense."

"I'll be gone in less than a week, and I apologize for being such a failure in your eyes, it was never my intent." Spinning on his heels, Cleat left the room and went upstairs to his room. He found Coon sprawled on the bed.

"Did you hear?"

"Yeah, I knew it was going to be the shits when he found out, but I never thought it'd be that bad."

"Well, at least he finally expressed his true feelings."

"Hell Cleat, you can't blame his disappointment, but he didn't mean what he said, give him some time to simmer down, in a few days it'll blow over."

"Forget it…I'm going for a ride."

"You want me to go with you and talk it out?"

"Thanks, but right now I'd rather be by myself."

Cleat drove aimlessly down one street after the other reflecting on his life. Could he possibly be the loser his father so verbally described him as? Some of what his father said was painfully true, but in all honesty he couldn't be as bad as his father portrayed him to be. Although he was forced to admit he hadn't a serious ideation in months when he wasn't the focal point. Had he become so self-centered that nothing else mattered unless it revolved around him? How pathetic had he become?

Before leaving school Coon stated he had become a stranger who he didn't like very much. Was Coon right? Had he forgotten who he was, or who he *thought* he was? He had always been well liked in school, with more friends than he could count. Now he had none to speak of, except for Coon. In retrospect he didn't even like himself, so how could he expect anyone to give two shits about him?

Almost a year and a half ago he had abandoned Audrey in her greatest time of need. And how did the great Cleatwood Alexander Davis, athlete extraordinaire, react? He ran away from home like a scoundrel in the night. It was a shameful cowardly act, and now he had the audacity to be pissed off at people for treating him like shit. Even Papa Nick didn't approve, and he was one of the most honest, fair-minded people he ever met. Now, in the most recent chapter of his misbegotten life, he was angry with his father for reading him the riot act over his irresponsible conduct. Even Cleat had to admit it was time for change…somehow he had to find the person he used to be before that person was lost forever.

On the north side of town he found himself at the corner of Wabash and Seymour Street waiting for the light to change. Until then he was oblivious to his whereabouts. When the light changed he decided to pull into Alfonso's Liquor Store and buy a pint of Seagram Seven. Flipping out his wallet he casually offered the same old fake ID he had been using since his junior year of high school. If you went by the old beat-up Florida driver's license, he was twenty-four-years-old with a birthday on the horizon. Same as always, the purchase went without a hitch. It was nice to know that some things never changed. After swallowing a mouthful of the warm liquid his body shook with spasmodic shudders. The warm liquid burned a fiery path as it slid down his throat. His head quivered over the awful after-taste and considered pouring it out. As an afterthought he decided Coon's dad would find a better use. The intersection was only two blocks from Mister Truman's house and he knew his gift would be appreciated. The old man drank all of the time anyway so it wasn't like contributing to his ill health.

It was 10:46 PM when he pulled his Chevy to a gradual stop in front of the shack. He could see Coon's dad sitting on a front porch rocker. From a distance Cleat couldn't tell whether he was asleep or just resting. Walking across the weed-infested, overgrown yard he sidestepped dozens of beer cans and empty bottles. "Mister Truman, are you awake?"

"Zat you Cleat…I th…thought I recognized your car. You got John with ya?"

"No sir, it's just me."

"Well, come on up and sit a spell."

"I brought you a pint of Seagram Seven." Cleat handed the bottle to Mister Truman.

"Glory be…there are angels in this world after all. Thank you for the kind thought, son. Uhh, there ain't nothing wrong with John is there?"

"No sir, he's doing just fine."

"Good…that's good to hear. Now you sit down and tell me what's troubling you son."

If Cleat didn't know better Mister Truman seemed sober, at least more sober than he had ever seen him. Cleat began with Audrey's pregnancy and ended with his father's castigations earlier in the day. Why he was telling his troubles to Coon's dad he hadn't a clue, but he let it all out, leaving nothing unsaid. When he was through he felt better just getting it off his chest; somehow it had drastically improved his sullen mood.

"Son, sometimes fathers can be hard…I know because I've been that way with John. My reasons are different than your dad's…mine have been to distance myself from John because I'm just a no-good drunk who ain't long for this world. I've tried to destroy whatever love my son ever had for me so he'll have a chance to become a better man. It's been heartbreakingly difficult because he's a decent boy, unfortunately he continues to have childish thoughts there is good in everyone, but he's dead wrong. There is evil in this world, and when you meet the devil you damn well better be prepared to deal with him, or by all that's holy he will devour you without a second thought. God was looking over John when your family took him in. There is no way I'll ever be able to repay them for their kindness. But let's get back to your father, you've done some things that you can't possibly be proud of, and for that you owe your family and friends a profound apology." Mister Truman took another long swallow from the bottle.

"Cleat, there's something different between a father and son than there is between fathers and daughters…I'm not smart enough to know what it is exactly, but I do have my own notions. A father's love for his daughter is based on the purity of love without conditions. She is worshiped for the pure pleasure she brings into his life, nothing is too good for her and often times she can do no wrong, but with a son it is a prideful thing. A son honors his father by being a testament to his strength and virility. He is held to a higher standard, for he will always bear the family's name, and be responsible for carrying its crest to future generations. A father's greatest fear is for his son to be looked upon as a failure. Demands and expectations are often set too high to be attained, but fathers before fathers through the passage of time have wanted more for their sons than they've ever wanted for themselves, and so the cycle continues for all generations to come. I know John doesn't think I care a hoot about him, but he could never be more wrong. With the help of you and your family I've watched him grow into a proud young man. He especially looks up to your father, and rightfully so. He's one of the pillars of this community, *and in the State of Florida.*" A coughing fit briefly interrupted his dialogue.

"Your father is a good man, he's pure of heart, and one day you will dis-cover this on your own accord when you least expect it. When you begin to understand who your father is you'll feel foolish for taking so long to recognize his virtues. At first he will seem a stranger, but you'll grow to love and respect him as a father, mentor, and friend. In the meantime, before you mess your life up anymore than you already have, ask yourself one rudimentary question: Will your father be proud of your future actions? If your answer is no then God in heaven change your ways. It's that simple, and in the meantime it'll keep you out of a lot of trouble." Another spasm interrupted Mister Truman, and this time it lasted much longer.

After clearing his throat he continued. "Don't tell John this, but I haven't missed a high school football game since John's been playing. It was the only sport he played that I could get lost in the crowd without him knowing I was ever there. I've saved every write-up that's been written about him playing foot-ball, basketball, and baseball, but it's something I never want him to know, not while I'm alive anyway."

Mister Truman placed a caring hand on Cleat's shoulder, "Son," he con-cluded, "my best advice is for you to get away from your family as fast as you can; your dad needs some time to let his emotions calm down. There's an old saying that makes more sense than most: *absence makes the heart grow fonder.* Join the Army, as fit as you are you're going to have to serve sometime anyway, and there's no time like the present."

On Cleat's way home Mister Truman's advice played over and over in his mind. The more he thought about enlisting in the Army the more it sounded like the answer to most of his problems except, of course, for Mandy. He was-n't going to make any inroads in her present state of mind. Maybe he could convince her not to do anything stupid until he got out of the military.

It was almost one o'clock when he quietly opened the door to his bedroom. Coon was between the sheets snoring. Cleat was so excited over making such a monumental decision that he felt like waking his friend and let him in on the news, but on second thought he decided tell him in the morning. He tiptoed down the hall hoping a hot shower would help him relax and unwind.

While Cleat was busy drying from his shower he remembered Mister Truman's request not to speak of their conversation about how much he truly loved his son. It didn't seem fair that Coon's father wanted to keep him in the dark until after his death. Coon needed to know now, not when it too late for father and son to make amends. Cleat wanted to tell Coon, but if that's the way Mister Truman wanted it then he would not go against his wishes. He had already made enough mistakes to last a lifetime.

"Hey, get your lazy ass out of bed. I can smell Mama Marie's blueberry muffins all the way up here." In a single motion Coon grabbed Cleat's top sheet and yanked it off the bed. "Where'd you disappear to yesterday, and what time did you get in? I waited for you until around 11:30."

Cleat rubbed the sleep from his eyes. "I've got some news that's going to blow your socks off."

"Don't tell me you and Mandy got back together."

"I should be so lucky, but that's not it. Today, I'm going down to the Federal Building and enlist into the United States Army."

"You gotta be kidding me."

"Nope, I'm heading down there right after breakfast to sign my "John Henry"."

"Have you thought this through?" A wave of nausea did back flips in the pit of Coon's stomach.

"Hell yeah I have. It's all I've thought of since I left the house. I've gotta go sometime, so why not now? I'll have a roof over my head and three squares a day, that's more than my dad's offering."

"I'm going with you."

"Sure, I don't mind you riding along."

"No, I mean I'm joining the Army too."

"Are you crazy? I'm the one on everybody's shit list, not you."

"Hey, we're brothers, wherever you go I go. When we were at Wingate I heard JP talking about a couple of his friends signing up right out of high school on something called the buddy system."

"What's the buddy system?"

"It's when you sign up with a friend so you can stay together during your enlistment."

"You don't have to do this Coon. Dammit man, you made your grades and can go back. Dad didn't give me much choice. If I hadn't been such an ass at Wingate we'd be going back together."

"I go where you go and that's final."

Cleat got out of bed and hugged Coon, "I love you, brother."

"Hey you freaking homo don't get all mushy on me. I've got my reputation to protect."

After breakfast they almost ran to the car. Fifteen minutes later they were parked across the street in front of the Federal building. The four storied red and white brick colonial structure featured huge gothic columns, and was the third highest building in town. Engraved on the granite above massive double doors was the date: 1873. Inside the foyer it was cool and dark and the only lighting was coming from five smoked glass globes dangling from the ceiling. At the end of the hallway a soldier dressed in kaki was standing outside the recruiter's office smoking a cigarette. His back was turned, but he must have heard them approaching because he stuck his half-smoked cigarette in an ashtray stand filled with sand and spun around.

"You boys come to join up?"

"Yes sir," they answered in unison. Their eyes never left his chest full of ribbons.

"I'm Master Sergeant Crawford, step into my office and I'll see what I can do."

Inside the sergeant's office a window unit was blowing ice-cold air. The glass windowpanes were wet from condensation. Along the walls were framed pictures of past battles representing centuries of wars. One of them was of Custer's famous last stand. In the corner behind his desk were an American flag and a Florida state flag. On his desk was a bronzed miniature tank.

"Well, you boys certainly look old enough *and* fit enough to join my Army."

"Yes sir, I'm Cleat Davis and he's John Truman. We want to sign up on the buddy system."

"You boys ain't queers are you?"

"Hell no!" Coon blurted.

Sergeant Crawford slammed the wooden desk with the palm of his hand, startling the two young men. "Good, because if you *were* I'd have to send you to those Marine faggots down the hall. What part of the Army are you hankering for?"

"I'm not sure what you mean, Sergeant Crawford." The question was more than confusing to Cleat.

"You know, what kinda outfit do you want to serve with?"

"We want to serve with the toughest and the best," Cleat responded.

"You mean like that over there?"

Cleat and Coon followed the sergeant's pointing finger to a manikin in the far corner of the room dressed in combat gear with something hanging off his back and lots of strapping. "What's that?" Cleat queried.

"That is a replica of the finest fighting soldier in the world…a United States Army Paratrooper."

They walked over to get a better look. They were both impressed. Neither had taken the time to consider different aspects the Army had to offer, but both of them knew instantly they wanted to be counted among the best.

"What do you think, Coon?"

"Shit Cleat, that's for me if you're game."

"I was hoping you'd say that." Cleat faced the sergeant, "That's what we want, Sergeant Crawford, the paratroops."

Sergeant Crawford laughed. "It's called Airborne, sonny boy, but you two are perfect specimens. If you want the badest of the bad then you'll want to volunteer for Airborne Infantry."

"Where do we sign up, and when can we leave?" Coon asked excitedly.

"First you boys will have to fill out some paperwork, take a test, and a physical. It shouldn't take more than a couple of days before you can take the oath. After that you're off to Fort Jackson, South Carolina for in-processing."

Standing outside the federal building Coon took a deep breath and exhaled loudly. "Man, we've gone and done it now."

"Tell you the truth Coon I'm kind of excited. No, that's not true, I'm really excited. I feel like the weight of the world has been lifted off my shoulders and I can't tell you how much it means to me you're going with me."

"Somebody has to look after your ass. Without me by your side you'd be lost."

"Yeah, right, how would I ever manage? You know, I've been giving this a lot of thought, when we actually enlist and go to basic training we need to treat this like a game. The Army's a lot like athletics, by that I mean sports. It's all about teamwork, but on a grander scale than we're used to. If you break it down to a more personal level it's about men working close together towards a common goal. We've worked under a team concept most of our lives and it's an environment we've excelled in. Speaking hypothetically, the Army shouldn't be any different."

"Yeah man, I can dig it."

Three days later they were on a train bound for Fort Jackson carrying nothing but the basic essentials Sergeant Crawford advised them to take. The only exceptions were a couple of magazines and a paperback Zane Grey western Coon was reading. The trip itself was uneventful, but it gave the two friends an opportunity to talk about old times and what their future might hold. The talk of war was in the air and every war movie they had ever seen flashed through their minds as they tried to sleep.

At the station several hard-ass NCO's were yelling and screaming for the group of fifty or more to climb on a dark green military bus parked beside the terminal. Cleat mused all the shouting was completely unnecessary, unless the sergeants thought the new inductees were from a school for the deaf. Smiling, he mingled with the rest of them clamoring aboard.

"Wipe that smile off your face maggot you ain't going to no summer camp." A large black sergeant with dark brown eyes stood inches from Cleat's face daring Cleat to say something stupid.

"Yes sir, Sergeant." Cleat noticed the nametag over the sergeant's pocket read 'Talbot'.

"Don't address me as sir maggot, I ain't no candy-ass officer. I work for a living. You will answer an NCO with a 'No Sergeant' or 'Yes Sergeant'. Are we clear, shit-for-brains?"

"Yes Sergeant Talbot."

"I'll be damn Sergeant Stafford," the black sergeant hollered to a white

NCO standing in front of the bus, "at least one of these dumb-ass maggots got some sense. Are you a college boy maggot?"

"Yes sergeant."

"You a bright boy ain't 'cha maggot. Do ya' think you're smarter than me?'

"No sergeant." Beads of sweat started popping out on Cleat's forehead. The midmorning sun wasn't the only thing that was making Cleat uncomfortable. The black sergeant had a menacing sneer and there was something in his black eyes he found troubling. He'd seen the same look in his Uncle Wade's eyes and others like him who had seen war and tasted its bloodletting.

"Are you buttonholing me maggot?"

"I uh...I don't understand sergeant."

"Are you trying to butter my backside, cuz if that's what you're doing I'll squash you like a bug."

Cleat's eyes almost bugged from there sockets. "No sergeant, not at all."

The sergeant leaned forward until their noses almost touched, "You don't like me do you maggot?"

"Yes sergeant." Cleat regretted the smile that singled him out among all the rest, and swore that he would never smile again while he was in the army.

"Yes you like me *or* no you don't like me, which is it college boy?"

Cleat knew whichever way he answered the sergeant's question would end up being a bad choice. "I uh...I like you sergeant."

"Are you queer for me college boy?"

"No sergeant." Cleat had the greatest urge to pee.

"Drop and give me a gig maggot."

Cleat blinked when spittle from the sergeant's fat lips splattered him in the face. *This is crazy, all I want to do is get on the bus and end this inane inquisition.*

"I said drop and give me a gig."

"I uh...uh...I don't know what a gig is sergeant." The sergeant's breath was staggering and his urge to pee increased to tenfold.

"Listen up maggots. A gig is ten pushups. When an NCO orders you to drop and give him a gig, you will immediately stop what you're doing and fall to a leaning rest position. Once in the proper position you will commence with your punishment by counting out loud. When you reach said number you will do an extra pushup for airborne and holler clear sergeant. Only until the sergeant answers in kind may you return to attention. IS THAT CLEAR MAGGOTS?" The sergeant was dissatisfied with their weak response and asked again, and yet again. Stepping back he glared at the recruits and hollered, "GIVE ME A GIG MAGGOTS!"

The recruits fell into a leaning rest and began counting. When they were through the sergeant grabbed the back of Cleat's Izod shirt and held him in front of the mingling young men. "This here college boy is going to be in charge of you maggots until we reach our destination. You will hereby refer to him as Sergeant Maggot, is that clear?" A chorus of yes sergeants echoed through the ranks. Still holding firmly to Cleat he yanked him closer. "You're in charge of these scumbags until we get to your barracks, now Get outta my sight, maggot."

"Yes Sergeant." *Shit*, Cleat thought, *here I am, in charge again. When will it ever end?*

The next five days were spent measuring for uniforms, boots, drawing equipment, getting shots, and more testing. When they weren't learning about military procedure, they were conscripted into providing manual labor such as policing the area, guard duty, and KP. They learned firsthand that KP stood for (Kitchen Police) which in turn meant washing pots and pans, cleaning grease traps, and a dozen other tasks not worth remembering.

Cleat, Coon, and five others in the group scored high enough on their entrance exams to further test for Officers Candidate School. Cleat, Coon, and one of the others qualified, but the two friends declined the Army's offer. Coon was interested, but Cleat didn't want the additional responsibility of being an officer, all he wanted to do was serve out his enlistment and go back to college.

The next afternoon the duty roster was posted and they were scheduled to report for KP duty no later than 0400. The long grueling day lasted until 0200 the following morning, when they climb the stairs to the platoon bay they were too tired to shower. The only thing good about their ordeal was they had the rest of the day off. They awoke midmorning, showered, dressed and went downstairs to await chow. Even though they had free time there wasn't much to do without money and transportation so they migrated to the dayroom to shoot some pool. Brushing through the double swinging doors they were surprised to find it almost empty, and even better, the pool table wasn't occupied. In the corner of the room a TV was blaring to an empty audience. On the far side three blacks were involved in a card game of sorts.

Cleat gave them a friendly nod, but received no recognition. "I'll rack 'em for eight-ball while you pick us out a couple of cue sticks."

"Sure thing Cleat, I'll make sure and find a crooked one for you."

"That'd be just like you." Cleat laughed.

Cleat stooped over and retrieved the rack hanging underneath the table. When he started gathering the balls he noticed there wasn't any chalk on the table and called out, "Hey Coon, bring us some chalk."

"Hey honky, who the hell you calling *Coon?*" The largest of the Blacks rose slowly from his chair. The others joined him as they approached Cleat in a threatening manner.

"Oh, uh...I'm sorry about that. I was referring to my friend...that's his nickname."

"Man...is I supposed to believe that shit white-boy?"

"Yeah, as a matter of fact you are, because it's the truth."

"Bullshit, I'm gonna kick yo' *ass whitie.*"

Coon interceded, "Hold-on man, he's right man. Shit, I've been called that since I was ten years old. My whole nickname is Coon-Dog."

"Shut the hell up little man or yo' ass is next."

The soldier with the mouth was the alpha male and he was fifteen feet away from invading Cleat's space. Cleat said all he was going to say in the matter, and his eyes never left the black's cold black stare. He was prepared for battle if that was what the antagonist was looking for. Cleat read the black's intent the moment he got out his chair. They were approximately the same size and weight, although Cleat was a couple of inches taller. He could tell by his opponent's slow deliberate movements that he was an experienced fighter. The only thing worrying Cleat was the soldier's enlisted rank of Specialist Fourth Class. Would getting into a fight with someone who outranked him generate into something more serious? Cleat didn't know for sure, but he wasn't going to back down from the asshole.

When the soldier came within five feet Cleat warned him, "That's far enough."

"So, you think you're some kind'a badass now, is that it?" The black continued his approach and walked into two lighting quick left hooks high on the cheekbone and a solid right-cross to the jaw. The Spec-4 staggered backwards several feet before regaining his balance. Blood dripped from a small cut under his puffy right eye.

"Goddammit James, kick his white-ass."

"Yo ass is mine muthafucker." James Warren wiped the blood from his face, and moved in using more caution.

Cleat stood on the balls of his feet shuffling them from side to side waiting to counter James's first move. He had given the guy a break by not taking him out right away. Usually he pressed the attack until his opponent was either knocked out *or* simply gave up.

"We don't need to do this Specialist. I made my apologies." He knew his words fell on deaf ears. The guy was embarrassed in front of his friends and he sought retribution. Cleat remained vigilant, patiently waiting for an opening.

"Ya' done picked the wrong brother to mess with *whitie*. I'm gonna make you pay."

"That's right James, you da' man." The tallest of the three coaxed.

When James dropped his shoulder and threw a lazy left jab Cleat quickly parried the punch and came over the top of James's low shoulder with a straight right that caught James flush on the mouth. He heard the loudmouth grunt, but paid little attention to the grimace of pain and continued his onslaught. Cleat easily ducked underneath a wild right hand lead and threw two stinging left hooks to the kidneys and finished the combination with a solid right uppercut to James's jaw. Cleat was prepared to proceed with his attack, but when he saw the glassy look in James's eyes he backed off.

The Specialist wobbled on rubbery legs for a couple of seconds before collapsing face first onto the hard linoleum floor. His head bounced twice and then came to a rest.

When James's buddies recovered from their dismay, they began to move toward Cleat with their hands raised in a threatening manner.

Coon stepped beside Cleat, "Y'all are fixing to step into a world of hurt, because I can whip this punk with one hand tied behind my back." Coon pointed at Cleat never taking his eyes off of the two blacks. "My best advice is for y'all to pick your friend off the floor and get the hell out'a hear before you really piss us off."

The two hesitated briefly before taking Coon's advice and dragged their friend through the double swinging doors.

"Dammit Cleat, I told you not to call me that. The blacks in the Army are gonna take it the wrong way every damn time."

"Sorry Coon...uh...I mean John, I let it slip."

"Well don't do it again, cuz you almost got me into trouble."

Cleat held an incredulous look on his face until he started laughing at Coon's fluttering eyebrows, Coon quickly joined in. After regaining their composure they decided it was prudent not to hang around the dayroom. More of James's friends might show up.

The following morning a Pfc. bustled into the platoon bay, after pausing a few seconds his eyes expressed recognition when they fell on Cleat. The corners of his mouth curled with a hint of a smile as he walked down the center aisle and came to a halt in front of the recruit he was searching for. "Private Davis, Sergeant Talbot wants to see you in the orderly room. My instructions are to escort there post haste.

Cleat thought, *Oh shit, I was afraid of this.* "Do you know what he wants to see me for?" Cleat consciously looked at the Pfc.'s nametag: Hargrove.

"Nope, but it ain't never a good sign to be singled out by an NCO. My advice is to keep your mouth shut and follow me."

When Cleat fell-in behind Hargrove, Coon approached them with a quizzical expression and impeded their progress. "Hey what's up? Where're you going Cleat?"

"Pfc. Hargrove has notified me that Platoon Sergeant Talbot requests my presence in the orderly room."

Coon's brow wrinkled, "Hargrove, what's the sergeant want with Cleat?"

"Beats the hell out of me, I'm just following orders. Sergeant Talbot told me to go find Private Davis and escort him to the orderly room."

"Is it alright if I tag along?"

Hargrove shrugged his shoulders, "Suit yourself, but if it was me I'd stay clear. The sarge didn't seem like he was in a good mood."

"Well I'm not you, so let's go."

Cleat grabbed Coon by the arm, "He's right Coo...uh John. There's no reason for you to be there. I think I know what this is about and it doesn't concern you."

"That's bullshit and you know it. We signed up on the buddy system, so whatever goes down I'm part of it."

Cleat knew any further discussion was useless. "Okay Hargrove, lets go see the man."

Cleat and Coon stood inside the orderly room patiently waiting for Hargrove to reappear. He had been behind closed doors long enough for them to scrutinize the small space. It certainly wasn't designed for comfort *or* visitors. The only chair in the room was behind the orderly's green metal desk. In one corner was a five-drawer metal file of the same standard color as the desk. In the opposite corner were two flags, one was an American flag and the other flag displayed the Army Crest. An array of military pictures hung on the wall and an old air conditioner rattled in the solitary window.

Cleat and Coon snapped their heads towards the sergeant's door when it suddenly opened. Hargrove closed the door and turned to the two privates, "Knock twice and wait for permission to enter. Good luck."

"Thanks." Cleat rapped twice and dried his sweaty palms on the sides of his fatigue pants. He heard a gruff "Enter" and reached for the door handle. When he turned the knob it was slippery to the touch. Not knowing what to do or what to expect they entered the office and came to attention in front of the sergeant's desk, Cleat was the first to speak. "Private Davis and Private Truman reporting as ordered Sergeant."

Talbot leaned back in his chair and surveyed to two privates, he'd been in the army long enough to recognize potential soldiers. It made him yearn for the days when he was a drill sergeant. "At ease maggots." He watched them come to parade rest and almost smiled. "You're taking the buddy system to the extreme Private Truman. If I'd wanted to see you I would've sent for you." He waited for an answer, but when he realized the private was too savvy to open his mouth he continued. "Private Davis, it has been brought to my attention that you made a racial slur and caused bodily harm to one of my enlisted men. Any form of racism will not be tolerated in this mans army, and it's my duty to inform you these allegations are very serious. For that matter it's a court-martial offense. What do you have say to say in your defense, before I send this up the chain-of-command?"

Cleat's knees weakened when he heard the word court-martial. *My God, is trouble going to follow me into the Army?* He tried to clear the frog out of his throat before replying to the sergeant's question. "It was all a misunderstanding

Sergeant Talbot."

"You'll have to do better than that Davis, or you'll be seeing the inside of a courtroom and most likely receive a General Discharge from the Army. Receiving anything other that an honorable discharge or a medical discharge will hound you for life."

Coon stepped forward a pace, "Sergeant Talbot, if I may intercede on my buddy's behalf I'm sure that I can bring clarity to the unfortunate incident that has been brought to your attention."

Sergeant Talbot laughed, "Are you some kind of lawyer Private Truman?"

"No Sergeant, but my father is."

"I'm all ears maggot." The story Specialist Warren told of the altercation in the dayroom didn't ring true and the truth was what he was after.

Coon eloquently told the story of how he acquired his nickname from Mister Davis, but referred to him as *his* father. When he was through he gave the sergeant a sly grin and added, "Sergeant Talbot, that's the truth so help me God."

Talbot suppressed the laughter forming in his throat. He knew from the start Warren was lying through his teeth. The troublemaker had been a pain in the ass since he was assigned to the company. "For some ungodly reason I believe you Private Truman. You are dismissed. Davis you stay here."

Coon hesitated, pondering if leaving Cleat's side was the right thing to do. The sergeant's next words speeded his decision and hastened his departure.

"Private Truman, if you're not out of my sight in three seconds you'll be doing KP for the remainder of your enlistment." Talbot waited until the door closed behind the private.

"Davis, was what your friend said the truth and nothing but the truth? If you lie to me I'll see the both of you face charges."

Cleat gulped, "Most of it Sergeant Talbot."

"I'm listening."

"Well the part about what happened in the dayroom was and that's what's important."

"Private, you let me make that distinction."

Cleat explained in depth their unique relationship and John's background before they became like brothers. Sergeant Talbot liked the young private and became involved in a friendly conversation covering a wide range of topics. When the subject of sports came up they discovered their lives paralleled somewhat. An hour later the sergeant brought the meeting to a near close.

"Davis, you're lucky to have a friend like Truman, and I believe you deserve his allegiance as he does yours. I also understand your reluctance to be a leader, but I'm afraid you're gonna have to shoulder that responsibility in the Army as well. Most leaders are born, *not* made, and whether you like it or not…you were born to lead. I knew you were a natural leader the first day I laid eyes on you. The Army can turn boys into men, but leaders will always lead and followers will always follow. You can try and shirk that role, but the Army has a knack for picking the right man for the right mission. They've been at this for a long time and its not often they screw up when it comes to leadership. Without a leader, good men will flounder and die before their time. Son, mark my words' you will be chosen, and when that day comes I expect nothing but the best from you as will your men."

"I hope you're wrong Sergeant. I have enough personal problems to keep me occupied than having to worry about everyone else's."

"Son, if you try and run from it you'll be running for the rest of your life. The best thing for you to do is face it head on and accept the inevitable. To help facilitate your transition I'm placing you in charge of all the recruits assigned to your basic training outfit. That is all, you are dismissed."

On Thursday afternoon they received their orders to report to Fort Hood, Texas for basic training. They would be flying out the following morning at 0945, and much to Cleat's chagrin and true to Sergeant's Talbot's word, he found himself in charge of twenty-four other recruits making the trip. It was his job to ensure everything went smoothly, starting from when they received their orders until reporting to the NCOIC (Non-commissioned Officer in Charge) at the airport.

Was Sergeant Talbot's prophecy a revelation? Could he not hide from responsibility in the Army? Would not the masses shield him? Why couldn't he melt into the nameless faces and become a nonentity? Surely he wasn't branded forever and always. It wasn't fair, for as far back as he could remember the onus was either thrust upon him by authority figures or his teammates He had hoped the Army would be different, but here he was in charge of his peers once again.

Since Cleat and Coon were in superb shape upon entering the Army basic training was a breeze for both of them, although the DI's did their best to make it as tough as they could without killing anybody. There were the usual malingerers and bed-wetters' trying to get out of the Army, but all-in-all the platoon tried to do their very best. The Southern boys were having more difficulty adjusting to Army life than the Yankees simply because it was the first time most of them had ever been exposed to blacks. There were a few whispered remarks made by both sides, but nothing serious until the beginning of the third week. It began when Thurston, a big athletic black guy from the ghettos of Chicago threw his boots down on Sorenson's footlocker. Sorenson was a smallish, bucktoothed white boy from White Haven, Mississippi.

"Polish my boots, grey-boy, and be sure to give 'em a good spit shine, or I'll kick your skinny white ass."

"Fuck you Thurston. I ain't polishing nobody's boots but my own." Sorenson pushed the boots onto the floor. Before he could protect himself, Thurston slapped him in the face so hard it knocked him off of his footlocker.

"I'm gonna kick your punk-ass, whitey." Thurston lifted the kid off the floor with one hand. A sinister grin spread across his face. Several blacks began chanting encouragements.

Richard Armstead quickly rushed to intercede. He was chosen the acting platoon sergeant because he had two years of college ROTC. "Put him down Thurston, before you get us all in trouble."

"Back off Armstead… or your ass is next." Thurston pointed his finger between Armstead's eyes. "Open your mouth again and I'll shove a fist in it."

Cleat and Coon were four bunks down watching the confrontation. "Shit, I was hoping something like this could've been avoided." Cleat dropped the brush he'd been using to buff his boots. "Watch my back, John."

"You got it, Cleat."

They walked side by side down the platoon bay aisle. Cleat was wearing shower shoes and a pair of fatigue pants. Coon had on a pair of boxers and was barefoot.

"How about putting him down, Thurston?" Cleat asked as nicely as he knew how.

"What's the matter, Davis…you his mama, or just queer for dis' piece of shit?"

"You're wrong on both counts, but he's a member of this platoon and that makes it my business so back off."

"You ain't telling me what to do. You don't mean shit to me."

"Leave him be. I'm telling you up front, you don't want this kinda trouble soldier. We are not going to fight amongst ourselves; your bullying days are over."

Thurston shoved the kid aside. "Sorenson don't mean shit to me anyway, but you, cracker-head…I been wanting a piece of your redneck ass since the first day I saw you. You be's acting you is better than us…like we ain't worth spit."

"That's not true, and you know it." Cleat was through talking.

"You be's saying I'm a liar?"

"What's going on in here?" Platoon Sergeant Stamps hollered from the platoon doorway. The black Sergeant First Class was tall and thin, but looked as lethal as a King Cobra. He hailed from Harlem and was a career soldier. His opening statement to new recruits was always poignant and to the point. He demanded obedience and didn't play favorites. To his puzzlement he drew more respect from the whites than he did with the blacks. For some reason they thought he would be easier on them because of their skin color and when they found out that wasn't the case they held a deep seeded resentment towards him. The color of *his* Army was green and *anybody* that stepped out of line was gonna get a boot up their *ass*.

"You two *cruits* have a disagreement?" The sergeant stood with his fist resting on lean narrow hips. "All right…we can settle this the Army way. I've been itching for some excitement around here. I want every swinging dick to fallout on the grassy knoll behind the barracks. We gonna have us a ringside seat to a boxing match." The platoon bay erupted in a chorus of excitement. The men were up for anything that would help them escape the mental and physical drains of basic training.

On the grassy summit two combatants stood bare-chested less than ten feet apart, silently facing each other with old worn-out sixteen-ounce boxing gloves that had seen better days. Thurston was approximately six feet tall and outweighed Cleat by a good twenty pounds, the guy looked more like a professional linebacker than a soldier. Cleat tried liking the guy when the platoon was first formed, but like all bullies Thurston used his size to intimidate people. Cleat didn't think the black platoon members cared for him either, but through primal fear and race they aliened their allegiance with Thurston.

Sergeant First Class Stamps positioned himself between the men. "Here are the rules maggots: there will be no kicking, biting, gouging, grabbing, poking, or spitting. If one of you is knocked down and wants to continue the fight, then he has the right to regain his footing without being encumbered. There are no rounds in this match; you will fight until one of you quits, injured, or deemed incapacitated." Stamps looked from one to the other, "Do I need to repeat the rules? If not, you may begin on my whistle."

When the whistle blew Thurston stepped forward and wasted no time by throwing a wild roundhouse right that Cleat easily evaded. Cleat came in low with a hard left-right to the bigger man's exposed ribcage. He heard the breath whoosh out of Thurston's lungs as he staggered backwards trying to maintain his balance.

Wheeling around to face Cleat he snarled, "You be a dead man, whitey."

Cleat stayed light on his feet warily on guard as he anticipated Thurston's next move. Without a doubt he knew it was going to be another out of control charge. Cleat could tell by Thurston's body language that he had no formal training in the ring. The muscular black youth was the consummate bully who relied on strength alone to overwhelm his opponents. Cleat knew most bullies were either cowards or overconfident in their abilities. His Golden Glove experiences would soon tell which category Thurston fell into.

Thurston's next move surprised Cleat. The big man closed the distance slow and easy in a more classical style, but he carried his hands far too low to stop the straight left hand jab that busted him in the mouth. Thurston wasn't quick, or agile enough to prevent Cleat's speedy left hook that struck him squarely on the cheekbone. Cleat's third part of the combination was a solid right to the jaw that sounded like a rifle shot. *That* was the crowd pleaser. Thurston's eyes rolled to the back of his skull before falling face forward onto the grass hillock. It was over so suddenly the onlookers were shocked into silence, all except for Coon.

"Hot damn, another one bites the dust. What's that make Cleat, 24 and 0 in the ring? Jesus Cleat, you are one badass dude."

"Is he dead?" one of the blacks asked.

"Kiss my black skinny ass, man. Did you see that brother go down? I ain't nevuh seen nobody get hit like that. Shit, that grey-boy done hit Two-Ton so hard it hurt my own black ass."

Sergeant Stamps clapped his hands together. "All right…some of you men pick him up and take him to the showers. Davis, I want to see you in private."

"Yes Sergeant."

"Move out, you maggots. Chow's in twenty minutes."

Sergeant Stamps grabbed Cleat's fatigue collar and pulled him to the side. "Are you a professional boxer, son?"

"No, Sergeant"

"Don't hand me no line of bullshit Davis, I heard your buddy loud and clear about you being 24 and 0."

"Permission to speak Drill Sergeant?"

"Permission granted." Sergeant Stamps liked this young man and saw potential in the raw recruit. He had an air of leadership. It was against his better judgment choosing Armstead over Davis. He should have gone with his gut and made Davis the acting platoon sergeant and Armstead one of the four acting squad leaders.

"As a kid I did some boxing with the Boys Club Golden Gloves youth program."

"You must've been pretty damn good because I would've put all my money on Thurston. Hell, I thought he'd rip you a new asshole. I was even primed to step in and stop the fight if it got outta hand. "

"Looks can be deceiving, Sergeant Stamps."

"They sure as hell can, son. Now my next question is this, why did you take it easy on Thurston when you could've prolonged the fight and cut him to pieces?"

"It's simple, Staff Sergeant, he's a member of my platoon."

Stamps looked at Cleat for several moments, trying to figure out if he was being snowballed…he decided he wasn't. "Davis, as of this moment you are my new acting platoon sergeant. I'll inform Armstead that he'll move into your slot as squad leader. I got my eye on you, so you better not let me down."

"Yes Sergeant, you have my word."

"Now get out of my sight maggot, before I change my mind."

After evening chow Cleat held a platoon meeting. "Sit on your bunks, foot-lockers, or on the floor, for now it doesn't make a difference." He stood before them waiting patiently as they made their choices. "Alright get squared away and knock it off." Cleat ignored the grumbling and gave them a few extra min-utes. "As you know I'm the new acting platoon sergeant. I didn't ask for the job, nor did I want the damn thing, but while its *mine* we're gonna start acting like *soldiers.*" He paused and gave each face a few seconds of his time. "As of tonight there's gonna be some changes made. First of all the chain of command will be strictly obeyed. If you wish to file a grievance take it to your squad leader, if he can't handle it within the squad he will bring the complaint to my attention. If for some reason it falls beyond my expertise I will see Sergeant Stamps over the matter. Is that clear?" His answer was a conglomeration of yes's, a scatter-ing yeah's, and one blow it out your ass. A slow crooked grin stretched across his face.

"That's the kind of response I expected from you malcontents, and tonight that kind of shit is going to stop right here and now. I don't care whether you guys like me or not, that's not part of my job description. I don't even care whether you respect me, but by God you will show due respect to this arm-band I'm wearing. From here on you will answer me as: yes sergeant, no ser-geant, or clear sergeant. Is that clear?"

When he didn't receive the enthusiastic response he was looking for he raised his voice. **"Is that clear!"**

"Clear sergeant."

"If any of you played team sports in high school raise your hands." He was pleased at the show of hands. "Good that's means almost half of you know what it takes to be a team player. A platoon is no different than a team. Each individual has to sacrifice for the betterment of the team. If someone falls behind or is slacking off then his teammates will come to his aid. No one indi-vidual will be allowed to jeopardize the team. As of this moment the only con-cept that is important to us is teamwork. A team that works together wins together…is that clear."

"Clear sergeant!"

God he hated this. He sounded like an asshole. "Okay, I want all but the squad leaders to line up so I can pick new bunkmates. Some of you will end up in dif-ferent squads and bunks than you were originally assigned to, but that's the way it's gonna be. We'll have it all worked out before lights out."

Cleat went down the line assigning blacks to whites when it was possible, and when it was no longer applicable he mixed southerners with northerners and teamed Hispanics with those he thought best suitable.

"Okay, I want y'all to fall in with your new bunkmate and line up." When he was satisfied he went down the line of soldiers and counted out the first ten. "You men are first squad." He followed the procedure until forth squad was formed. "Whoever needs to switch bunks and lockers do so now. You have ten minutes before the next meeting."

A tall white boy from Tomlinson, Georgia complained, "Sarge, I don't see why we have to…"

"Who is your squad leader Travis?"

"Private Truman's my squad leader Sergeant Davis."

"First of all you will refer to your squad leader as *corporal* and secondly you will register your complaint through the chain of command. Is that clear Private Travis?"

Travis snapped to attention, "Clear Sergeant Davis."

In less than ten minutes the men were standing on either side of their foot-lockers waiting for Sergeant Davis to commence with the scheduled meeting.

Cleat used the center isle as his stage. He walked from one end to the other before saying a word, and continued pacing as he began his preconceived speech. "Men, I'm sure you've noticed that your new bunkmates are either different in race, creed, ethnicity, national origin, or geography. In the real world that may be so, but in the Army he's none of those things. The man standing next to you is a soldier; he's also your comrade in arms, your brother, and your teammate. You will watch out for his well being and he will do the same for you. I want you to get to know each other and your teammates. Understand his strengths and weaknesses. Learn to rely on each other and help those who need help. In the eyes of those who passed before us we might be looked upon as shit birds, maggots, cruits, scumbags, but we will rise above these derogatory labels and become the best we can be. We're gonna have pride in ourselves and earn the respect of others." A dozen or so *uhhhraaahs* exploded among the men.

"Tonight we have formed a bond that no one can break. We are a team and as a team we are one. Self-sacrifice is our motto and pride is our fuel. When we awake in the morning we will do so with a new fervor that will carry us through days of trials and tribulations. That is all…you are dismissed."

To a man they stood and shouted choruses of *uhhhraaahs.*

Coon was impressed and pulled Cleat to the side. "I guess you were right when you said treat our time in the Army as a game. Shit, you sounded just like Coach Dunn."

Cleat laughed, "Yeah, he was my inspiration. Do you think they bought it?"

"Hell yeah, I even bought into your line of bullshit."

"It wasn't bullshit Coon, I meant every word I said and I'm counting on you to back me up."

"Name me one time I didn't cover your ass."

"I can't."

"Then there you have it ol' buddy. In time of need ol' Coon Dog will be present and accounted for."

Staff Sergeant Stamp's face was beaming with pride as he stood at attention in front of his recruits, minutes before he had accepted the coveted award for having the outstanding platoon during basic training. All of his men made it through training except for Private Briscoe. The left footed son-of-a-gun fell down the stairs in the middle of the night and broke his leg while executing a fire drill. His platoon finished first in every phase of training, and he knew without Private Davis's help there wouldn't have been a trophy. Davis taught him more about leadership than any NCO school he had ever attended. The young man was a natural born leader, and he assumed the role as if it was expected of him. Granted, he led the men more by example than anything else, but there was a quality in him that drew tremendous respect from the men. While not all of them liked Davis, they nonetheless gravitated toward him like a bear to honey. Every last one of them would follow him through hell and high water if asked. The strangest thing of all was Thurston and Davis became friends soon after their fight on the grassy knoll. To his surprise Thurston became a better soldier and helped tremendously with race relations.

One of Davis's many attributes was being able to read men and get the most out of them. In his fourteen years of service he'd never seen anybody recognize and evaluate individual strengths and weaknesses with such proficiency. During Davis's first day as acting platoon sergeant he busted up the squads and reorganized the platoon into a buddy system. He paired as many blacks with whites as he could, and held them accountable for their actions. Another thing he instilled was squad competition, which led to the whole platoon striving to do their best. In the beginning there were a few altercations, but they were dealt with swiftly by assigning extra guard duty to the guilty parties regardless of who they were. Even his friend Truman pulled extra guard duty on more than one occasion.

When Thurston saw Cleat played no favorites he began to realize his own potential and became a soldier and co-leader of the platoon. Within a week the platoon settled into racial harmony, or at least they learned how to coexist with one another, and some actually became friends. Once or twice a year he was lucky enough to have somebody pass through his platoon similar to Davis, but never anyone quite like him. The young man was a born leader of men.

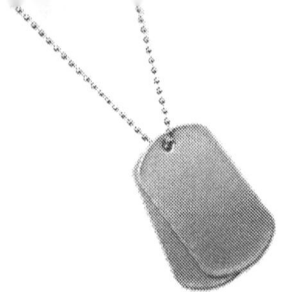

CHAPTER 12

The next eight weeks of training were spent in Advanced Infantry School refining their skills to become proficient in killing the enemy and learning how to survive in combat. They spent a tremendous amount of time in the classroom learning about weapons, techniques of patrolling, map reading, radio procedure, and ambushes. Thankfully, there was enough field time dedicated to keep their interest heightened. Strangely, their second eight weeks of training flew by rather quickly, and before they knew it they were approaching their last week before graduation.

On the following Monday a runner caught up to them in the chow line and told them to report to the company commander's office on the double.

"Dammit Coon, what kind of trouble have you gotten us into now?"

"Hey brother, I ain't done a damn thing. If he wants to see us it's not because of something I did."

"Yeah, right, and I still believe in Santa Clause."

When they entered the orderly room they were told to go knock on the door, the ol' man was waiting on them.

Cleat was sweating profusely. They were so close to graduation he could taste it and the thought of being recycled was nauseating. He knocked lightly on the door and the two of them entered when they heard a gruff voice granted their entry.

"Private Davis and Truman reporting as ordered sir." They stood two paces from Captain Cozart's metal desk. The captain's hair was shorter than most recruits and his stature was ramrod stiff. He was of medium height with dark green eyes set close together underneath a pair of bushy eyebrows. A narrow nose was positioned at a deviated angle above thin menacing lips and his ears were oddly shape, otherwise he could easily pass for downright ugly.

"At ease soldiers. I am pleased to announce the two of you have been chosen as honor graduates and are hereby promoted to grade E-3, private first class. It has recently been brought to my attention both of you qualified for OCS, and I would like to know why the Army's offer of turning you into officers and gentlemen was declined"

Neither Cleat nor Coon were willing to be the first to speak, as the pregnant pause continued the captain became impatient.

"Private Davis if you will please."

Shit, why me? "Well sir I suppose it has more to do with my decision than Private Truman's. We attended college together on football scholarships and when I flunked out of school we joined the Army on the buddy system. Although we both would consider it an honor to serve as officers, unfortunately the time constraint intercedes with our desire to return to the halls of academia."

Captain Cozart's thin lips curled into a slight grin. "Have you ever thought of attending West Point as a career choice and achieving your goals? Your scores indicate that could be a possibility."

Cleat took a deep breath, "Sir with all due respect officers lead and I'm tired of leading. It's something that's been expected of me all of my life and psychologically speaking it's become an albatross."

"What about you Truman?"

"Sir, whatever Cleat says I'm down with. We've been like brothers since I was eight years old. Somebody needs to look out for him and it would be dereliction of duty if I didn't personally assume the responsibility of seeing he stays out of trouble."

Captain Cozart opened one of the files lying on his desk and scanned some of the pages inside. The captain returned the pages and chuckled before looking directly into Coon's soft brown eyes where a persistent twinkle always seemed to reside. "I've read all about you Pfc. Truman. It seems to me it's the other way around. With a little imagination and creative latitude a novel of great magnitude could be written about your escapades. If the senior NCOs' hadn't vouched for your credibility and run the risk of jeopardizing their careers you wouldn't be standing in front of me today. How you've managed to remain in this mans Army speaks volumes. Your efficiency reports are outstanding, but your regard for authority is dismal and unacceptable. I would like to hear your reasons for such actions."

Cleat thought, *Oh shit here it comes.*

"No excuse sir." Coon's boot heels clicked when he came to attention.

"That's the best answer I've heard in awhile, but not the one I was hoping for. Now stand at ease soldier. Whatever is said in this office stays here. I want to know what makes the real Private First Class John Truman tick."

Coon relaxed somewhat and wondered where to begin. "Sir, I've pulled some pranks and skirted on the edge of trouble, but I can honestly say that I've enjoyed Army life. It's a lot like playing football. Even though each player is an individual they must function as a team to be successful. You need to become proficient in your designated roll *and* learn to depend on your fellow teammates to accomplish the mission. Everyone has to be on the same page and the drills, exercises, and regimens the Army subjects us to are not unlike football practice. Its purpose is to teach individuals the importance of teamwork and the byproduct of their effort is self-worth. It is imperative for each individual to believe he is an integral part of the team to establish a cohesive unit. To achieve excellence we willingly shed our blood, sweat, and tears to reach a common goal and when that goal is achieved we are rewarded with a sense of pride that we did it together as a team. Therefore I ascertain that all work and no play are detrimental to attaining the lofted ideals set before us, so I bring levity to a Spartan environment to increase productivity."

Captain Cozart couldn't contain his composure, several minutes passed before he was able to readdress the men. "Well said Truman, a West Point cadet couldn't have pontificated more eloquently. I believe the two of you are making a grievous mistake by not going to OCS. The Army needs men like you, and assuming that you will escape responsibility by remaining in the enlisted ranks is sorely naïve. The Army has a certain knack for recognizing outstanding leadership and both of you are earmarked to become leaders. If you change your minds put in a request to attend OCS at your next duty station, dismissed."

"I hope you realize you're nuts." Cleat stood outside the orderly room shaking his head.

"Tell me something I don't already know. If I hadn't followed your ass into the Army I'd be playing football at Wingate and rolling in the sack with beautiful girls."

"What, and miss out on all of the fun?" Cleat playfully shoved his friend sideways.

"You know what, it has been kind of fun in a weird sort'a way. The real drawback is no women. How long has it been?"

"It's been waaaay toooo long brother." Cleat didn't want to count the months.

"I heard that. By the way, how did you like my Coach Dunn impersonation?"

"Not as good as mine, but passable."

Cleat, Coon, and a guy from another platoon were selected to attend NCO school. Once again Cleat wanted to pass, but Coon was able to talk him into accepting.

Noncommissioned Officer's School was a long, tedious indoctrination into the intricacies of leadership among the enlisted ranks. Much of the schooling had to do with military protocol, which *most* of the class found extremely boring. When elements of infantry tactics were introduced the cadets' interest peaked and richly coincided with their enthusiasm. Cleat and Coon excelled in the classroom, and no one exceeded their accomplishments in the field. The two of them treated NCO school as a personal competition, just as they had athletics, and they were either one-two in every aspect of training.

Midway through the course a ponderous of news concerning the Vietnam War monopolized the media and intensified weekly with visual combat footage. Not a day went by without communiqués of Americans dying in Southeast Asia. Combat correspondents traveled with line companies filming skirmishes and its aftermath. Between the hours of 1800 and 1900 the dayroom was filled to capacity with onlookers glued to the television set.

Coon's eyes were glued to the TV when he asked, "Christ Cleat, do you think we'll end up in Vietnam?"

"Maybe, I don't know." Cleat watched in dismay as two Marines dragged a wounded buddy through the jungle out of the line of fire. A blood-soaked bandage was wrapped loosely around the man's forehead, and his face was contorted in agony. The scene was unlike the Hollywood movies portraying Marines fighting in the Pacific during WWII. This was too graphic and realistic to be staged. This was the real deal. There was a distinct similarity to the old color films he used to watch on the TV program "Victory at Sea".

Terry Smith overheard Coon's question and Cleat's answer. "Shit, man that war will be over with by the time we graduate and sew on our stripes. The bitch of it is I hope the damn thing lasts long enough so I can get over there and earn the CIB. Man, would I like to wear that piece of tin over my jump wings."

Coon looked at Smith as if he'd lost his mind. "Be careful what you wish for Smitty, it just might come true. You do realize those are real bullets they're shooting over there."

"Yeah man, what a rush…real cowboy and Indians. Every generation needs a war, don't you know that?" Smitty slapped Coon on the shoulder.

"I know people die in a war *and* I don't want to be one of them."

"That doesn't sound very patriotic to me. What in the hell did you join the Army for if you're not willing to fight for freedom." Smitty's eyes narrowed as he took a closer look at Coon.

"I'll go wherever my country sends me, *but* I ain't anxious to get my ass shot in a place I never heard of until a year ago."

Cleat wasn't listening to his friend's conversation; he was wondering whether or not he was capable of leading men into battle. The big question was: how would he react under fire? Did anyone ever know until that moment in time presented itself? He sure as hell didn't. His biggest fear was becoming a coward when the bullets started flying. If that happened he wouldn't be able to live with himself, much less face his family and friends. Shakespeare's King Henry V Saint Crispen's day speech came to mind:

> We few, we happy few, we band of brothers;
> For he to-day that sheds his blood with me
> Shall be my brother; be he ne'er so vile,
> This day shall gentle his condition;
> And gentlemen in England now-a-bed
> Shall think themselves accurs'd they were not here,
> And hold their manhood's cheap whiles any speaks
> That fought with us upon Saint Crispin's day.

He couldn't remember the rest *or* the beginning, but at that very moment he made up his mind dying would be better than letting fear control his emotions.

When graduation neared it was a dead-heat between Cleat and Coon on who was going to be the top graduate. The cadre had to decide who was the most deserving. If it was a popularity contest Coon would've won hands down, but his high jinx and pranks were his downfall. He even got blamed for actions perpetrated by others. On more than one occasion the instructors considered booting him out, and they would've done so if he had not excelled at every facet of training. Cleat, the more serious minded cadet hung onto every word that came out of the instructors' mouths and won the honor, *but* Coon became a legend. Graduation ceremonies concluded at 1430 hours the following Friday and their official leave began at 2400.

Cleat stood in front of a full-length mirror admiring his three stripes of gold. He finished tightening his tie and made sure his gig line was straight before turning to Coon, "How do I look?"

"Like a little snot-nosed kid dressed up for Halloween. Hell, all you need is a trick-or-treat bag and you'd be all set."

"Fuck you."

"That reminds me, Anne answered my letter and wrote that she couldn't wait to see me while we're on leave. She'll be home for Christmas break at the same time we're there. It'll be nice to see a friendly face."

"At least you have someone looking forward to your return. I can't imagine anyone glad to see me back in town."

"Shit Cleat, it's been almost two years since all that shit went down…it's water under the bridge by now my friend."

"There's nothing back home for me anymore Coon…except family. Without Mandy in my life *home* is just a word that has very little meaning."

"Damn Cleat, you've got the greatest family in the world and they can hardly wait to have you home for Christmas. Come on man, you can't go home dragging your tail between your legs…life's pretty damn good."

Three days before Christmas Cleat let Coon talk him into going to Bo's annual Christmas party. It took some persuading, because Coon was escorting Anne and he was gonna be the third wheel, besides he wasn't looking forward to reminiscing with any of his so-called friends. When they pulled into the circle drive they were met by a valet who gave Cleat a claim stub.

Coon put his arm around Cleat and Anne, "Bo's parties are always first class."

"I've never been to one before. My goodness, I never dreamed that Bo lived in such an elegant house. I hope I'm dressed for the occasion." Anne's voice was filled with self-doubt.

"Don't worry Anne, your beauty will suffice."

"Coon, you say the sweetest things."

As they walked to the front door sounds of a live band filled the festive night. Cleat's knock was answered by a properly dressed butler and they were politely ushered into the foyer. Within two minutes Cleat understood his place, as expected he wasn't the most popular guy there, although he was probably the most talked about. He saw their snide looks as they stood in small groups whispering and stealing stolen glances.

Cleat thought, *Shit, why am I here? Am I a glutton for punishment, or am I destined to pay penance the rest of my life?*

"Coon, we seemed to be somewhat underdressed. I don't believe our jeans and sweaters are the proper attire." Cleat surveyed the cluster of faces he once called friends. Of the males, he and Coon were the only ones not wearing a coat and tie, and even more ridiculous were the females dressed in their sophisticated party dresses. Some even had the audacity to flaunt their mothers' expensive stoles around their slender shoulders when it was 72 degrees outside. Was that pretentious or pathetic? *My God, have we been gone that long? What happened to the old gang we used to hang with? Had they all rushed gleefully into adulthood? Didn't they realize they were mere pretenders?*

Cleat laughed out loud, "Would you look at these fools playing grownup."

"The hell with them Cleat. I came here to party, not hobnob with the upper-class. If they can't take a couple of soldiers crashing their party then by God they can kiss my rosy red ass."

Anne clasped onto Coon's arm and drew it close to her breast, "Don't be silly, y'all look just fine." She regretted forcing herself into her older sister's tight fitting dress. She felt like she was bulging at the seams, and any second the sides were going to split wide-open. Her diet was working, but oh how slowly the pounds were shedding.

"Y'all go on ahead and see your friends while I find something to wet my pallet and drown my embarrassment" Cleat slithered though the tangle of people with an occasional nod to fictitious friends. He felt awkward and hated every step of his way to the sidebar. A friendly looking black waiter wearing a white shirt, black bow tie and red jacket took his request. He accepted the drink and while lifting the rum and coke to his mouth a nostalgic laugh carried across the room. It was a sound he had been denied for almost two years. There were nights he'd dreamed of hearing her melodic laughter. It brought back so many memories filled with mirth and romance. An eternity had gone by without having Mandy in his life. Somehow he had to talk to her, smell her fragrance, and feel her warmth. He knew there was still a chance for them, there had to be, for in his heart he knew they were meant to be.

Placing his drink on a marble end table he wove his way through the crowd and suddenly came to a stop short of his goal. A guy he had never seen before slipped his arm around Mandy and pulled her close enough to plant a kiss on her cheek. He watched in awe as she smiled and nestled her head on his shoulder. A wave of nausea swept over him. It felt like someone had driven a hot poker in his stomach and twisted it in his gut. He had to find someone who was knowledgeable of the relationship between Mandy *and* whoever the asshole was. In a panic he searched for a friendly face that might be able to help, and was near hysteria until he spotted Bo, where else but in the kitchen.

When he entered the kitchen he grabbed Bo by the arm and sequestered him to the laundry room. "Who in the hell is that asshole with Mandy?"

"Good to see you too Cleat, Merry Christmas ol' buddy." Bo's eyes were glassy and his words were slurred.

Bo tried to wrap his arm around him, but he shrugged it off. "Yeah, Merry Christmas Bo. Who the hell is that jerk-off with Mandy?"

"Oh, him, that's Richard Hightower. He and Mandy are supposed be a real hot item up at Florida State. From what I hear they're supposed to be pinned over the holidays. Somebody told me he was a junior majoring in finance. He's been in town for a couple of days and everybody seems to like him."

Anger was his first emotion, but that was fleeting. Paralyzing fear was the predominate affectivity. His thought patterns were jumbled and incoherent. There was a roaring sound in his skull that threatened to rupture his eardrums. His mouth struggled to form words, but he was incapable of responding to Bo's cavalier attitude to his plight.

"Hey Cleat, you don't look so good man. How about some food, we've got a great buffet." Bo tore into a breast of southern fried chicken.

"Huh?"

"I said there's food in the dinning room fit for a king. Why don't 'cha go grab a bite, you look kinda peaked."

"Uh…no thanks, I'm fine. I think I'll have another drink."

"Okay, suit yourself." Bo slapped Cleat on the back, "See 'ya around buddy."

Cleat picked up somebody's full glass of booze off the countertop and slugged it down as he watched Bo disappear into the mingling crowd.

"I believe that was mine," Complained a boy of average size who Cleat didn't recognize.

"Find another one." Cleat growled.

The stranger puffed up, "Why don't *you* try getting your own."

Cleat grinned, "I'll tell you what asswipe, how about me ramming this empty glass up your ass?"

The startled young boy frowned, "You're a real…" but something in Cleat's eyes made him reconsider what he was about to say. "Uh…I don't think that will be necessary."

"Thanks for the drink." Cleat held the glass out until the boy took it from his hand. "Merry Christmas and good tidings."

"Yeah, thanks, same to you."

Cleat walked into the living room and looked for Mandy. He didn't see her, but he saw Richard Hightower talking to Bo and several of Cleat's former classmates. There was something about the guy's looks that rubbed him the wrong way. He was too handsome to be anything but a sissy, and his mannerisms were annoyingly effeminate. He couldn't stand the thought of Richard 'Dick Head' Hightower touching Mandy. His stomach twisted in knots watching a total stranger socialize with couples he used to considered life-long friends.

Straining his neck he searched for Mandy. She had to be somewhere close by, and then it dawned on him that she was more than likely in one of the bathrooms. Cleat hurried to the hallway where the nearest one was located, and knocked on the door.

"Just a minute please."

It was her, now what to do? He decided to wait until she came out and play it by ear. He didn't have to wait long. When he heard the door unlock he almost bolted down the hallway. No. He had done that once before, he wasn't running anymore.

"Hi Mandy, it's really good to see you?" *Brilliant, just brilliant,* he thought.

"Hello Cleat. I heard you were in town." Mandy's face was flush.

"Yeah, we're on leave until January sixth."

"That's nice, well it was good seeing you again Cleat, but I really have to go."

"No, wait Mandy. We have to talk."

"Cleat, we've already been through this, and I really don't care to relive our last meeting." Mandy tried to sidestep Cleat, but he blocked her way.

"Please Mandy, just a few minutes. There are so many things we need to talk about, and there are so many things I need to say. All I ask is a few minutes, you owe me at least that much."

"Cleat I don't *owe* you anything. You have nothing to say that I want to hear, and there's certainly nothing that I want to embellish upon. I want to leave now, so please move so I can rejoin my friends."

"No, I won't do that. I've waited too long for this moment." Cleat grabbed her by the arm and pulled her into the bathroom, locking the door behind him.

"Cleat Davis, have you lost your mind? Let me out of here this very instant."

"No, you have to listen. There're times I doubt my own sanity. Being apart from you is driving me crazy. I did wrong Mandy. I made a terrible error in judgment and I'm sorry. I love you and I think about you all the time. I know I filled your world with pain, but I've been living in pain too. Please understand my love for you, *and* my promise that it will never happen again." Tears were streaming down his cheeks as he pleaded with her. "Give me another chance Mandy…please."

"Cleat I'm sorry, but I can't. There is no future for us; you have to move on with your life and let me go." Her heart went out to him, but she couldn't let this continue. "What we shared in high school was wonderful, but that was high school. My God Cleat, that was two years ago, it's in the past."

"Your wrong Mandy, can't you see that? My love isn't in the past, and neither is yours. It is here and now in this very room. How can you deny what we both know is true? Remember how it used to be, the things we said and the moments we shared? How can you say our love is in the past" Cleat reached for Mandy, but she backed away.

"Oh Cleat, why must you make this so difficult. I'm truly sorry you refuse to accept reality. The plain truth is: we just weren't meant to be. From the very beginning thoughts of losing you haunted me. What would I do if it came to past? How would I go on? Could I even want to live without you? I don't blame you for what happened. I knew what I was getting into when I gave of myself."

Mandy took a deep breath to refrain from bursting into tears. It had to end now. "The pain you brought into my life was devastating, but somehow I managed to survive and become a stronger person. If there was…"

"Mandy if I could take back the pain I would, but what happened back then would never happen again. I've learned from my mistakes…I would never risk losing you again. We still have time…we have the rest of our lives."

When Mandy placed her hand on Cleat's cheek his hopes soared. Her soft caress was heavenly and the tenderness in her eyes swelled his heart.

"Cleat, dear Cleat, the love we once knew is no more. What we shared together was sweet and innocent, but since then our lives have grown apart. We're different people now. Whatever you feel towards me isn't love, it has more to do with how our relationship ended than anything else."

Cleat tried to hold the hand touching his face but she deftly escaped his grasp. "Mandy, you might be able to make yourself believe that, but I never will. Speak from your heart Mandy if you want people to listen."

"Cleatwood Alexander Davis, you are impossible. You are absolutely the most pigheaded, arrogant individual I've ever known *and* you'll never change from being that person. Ohhh, you make me so angry." Mandy threw her arms in the air. "Even if I *was* still in love with you, which I'm not, I would never risk becoming involved with you again. You're too dangerous."

"Dangerous, what in the world do you mean by dangerous? That makes no sense at all."

"Since I've been in college I've broadened my horizons, I've met knew friends, and one of them is very special. He's simply wonderful and he has goals in life other than his next female conquest. We share commonalities other than sex. On the other hand you continue to screw up your life and those who are close to you suffer the most. You scoffed at an education and joined the Army as if it was the most natural thing to do. Life isn't a party Cleat and the world isn't your cherry. You need to grow up and face responsibilities. What sensible girl in her right mind would be willing to risk everything for you, certainly not me?"

Cleat was dumbfounded and stood open-mouth as Mandy brushed by him, unlock the door and left the room.

"Hey, are you about through in there?" A voice hollered from the hall.

"No! Get the hell away from the door." Cleat kicked the door closed and sat on the toilet seat. Christ, is that what she thinks of me, a man going nowhere with no future in sight? Hell, she never gave me a chance to defend myself. Christ, can I be the loser she described? It sounded like something his father would've said.

Ten minutes passed before Cleat forced himself to give up the sanctity of the bathroom. His destination was the sidebar and it was there he became a permanent fixture. A few brave souls tried to spark a conversation, but those who cared *and* knew him well gave him a wide berth. The more he saw Mandy and her prissy date the more he drank and the more he drank the surlier he became. When he observed Dick walk out the backdoor alone, he placed his empty glass on the kitchen countertop and followed. Once he acquired his night vision he spotted the guy standing next to the trunk of an old southern oak shrouded by azalea bushes. Evil thoughts raced through his mind as he watched the asshole take a leak.

"Who's there?" Richard whispered over his shoulder as he shook his penis free of the last drop.

"Just me," Cleat answered in his deep, authoritative voice. Cleat's eyes narrowed as Dick turned around. He wasn't very big...not more than five foot nine and a buck-fifty.

"Hi, I don't believe we've met. I'm Richard Hightower." Richard held out his hand.

Cleat stared at the friendly gesture without moving a muscle. He was thinking how easy it would be to crush Dick's frail body.

"Oh...yeah, I just took a leak...sorry." Embarrassed, Richard quickly withdrew his hand. "Uhh...I don't usually take a leak outside, but the girls had all of the bathrooms occupied."

"I don't believe there's been any harm done, Dick."

"If you don't mind, I prefer Richard."

"Personally, I kinda think 'Dick' rather suits you," Cleat sneered; hoping the little shit would give him an excuse to bash his pretty little face in.

Richard was fuming; Mandy's entire group of friends had been really nice until this asshole showed up. He felt like reaching out and knocking the drunk on his sanctimonious ass, but no sooner had the thought registered an inner voice began screaming in his ear warning him of danger. "I don't believe I caught your name."

Cleat leaned forward bringing himself within inches of 'Dick Head's' face. "It's Cleat, Cleat Davis." He saw the startled look of name recognition freeze Dick's face in utter terror. Cleat emphasized his next words with a stiff poke of his forefinger to the center of Dick's forehead. "If—you—ever—hurt—Mandy—I—will—kill you." With each word spoken Dick's head rocketed backward. Cleat spun on his heels and left the party.

CHAPTER 13

January the 6th couldn't arrive soon enough for the newly commissioned sergeants, especially for Cleat. At least Coon had female companionship. They were due to report to Fort Campbell by the 6th, and start jump school soon after. Fourteen days was far too long a stay at home when so much had changed. Whoever coined the phrase: *"time stood still for no one"* knew what the hell they were talking about. He still hadn't gotten over how his friends had deserted him during his time of duress. The friends he once had no longer existed. They were too self-absorbed in their own inflated egos to care about anything else. He often asked himself if one of his friends had acted as he, would he have deserted them when they needed him the most, he thought not. A friend was a friend through thick and thin. In times of trouble they needed you the most.

Cleat enveloped himself in an invisible shield to prevent anyone from ever becoming close to him again. His persona was guarded, and to call someone a friend other than Coon was highly unlikely. The pain he was forced to endure and the damage to his psyche made seeking friendships less than desirable.

After Bo's party Cleat remained persistent in his attempts to see or at least talk to Mandy, but each of his efforts met with failure. She was incognito and incommunicado. Undaunted, he continued his quest until Mrs. Henson informed him that Mandy was no longer in town. She went on to say that her daughter was visiting at a friend's house for the remainder of the holidays. Cleat knew who the "friend" must be, and this discovery made him more anxious than ever to leave, but Coon was having a grand old time spending night and day with Anne. She'd lost a few pounds and looked terrific.

His dad was distant and reserved during the holidays, but it was nice to see the rest of the family. The brightest spot of all was the opportunity to renew his relationship with Randy. It had been years since they'd shared the same roof together, and from December the 23rd through January the 2nd they spent a lot of quality time catching up. Randy was in his first year of law school and excited over the prospect of practicing law alongside their dad. Cleat couldn't think of anything worse, but he didn't voice his opinion. Randy had always been close to their father and the fact that his brother was the favored son really didn't bother him anymore. He was tired of trying to gain his father's approval, besides no matter how hard he tried it turned to absolute shit, and what the hell, after what he put his family through he didn't deserve respect from any of them.

Coon walked into the family room dripping wet from the pool. He stood in the middle of the room shaking his hair flinging water everywhere. "Do you want to go out with Anne and me tonight? We're going to the Ames Theater and see Steve McQueen in "The Sand Peebles." It's supposed to be a really good movie." Coon looked at his watch, "She'll be here in a few minutes, so why don't 'cha go change?"

"Naw, three's a crowd. Y'all go and have some fun. Bo and I are heading over to the north side of town. There's a club called 'The Inferno' that's supposed to be loaded with chicks from all over the county. Hell, they've got a black rhythm and blues band that everybody says is great."

"Yeah, I've heard about the dive. You better stay out of trouble, because I hear it's a haven for rednecks and bikers. You're an NCO in the United States Army…mess around and you'll end up in the stockade with bare sleeves.

"Okay, daddy, I'll be careful."

"Fuck you, asswipe."

After Coon left he decided to go downstairs and catch the national news before picking up Bo. CBS news was coming on when his father walked in and sat heavily in his favorite chair. Walter Cronkite finished his introduction and led into a lead story covering the fighting in Vietnam. Color films of helicopters landing and taking off in open fields of tall grass filled the screen. American troops were jumping out of the machines and shouting orders as they rushed towards the surrounding tree line covered in varying hues of green. The correspondent and his crew were dressed in kaki safari attire and seemed to be flinching as rounds tore through the air. In the background you could see flashes of orange and black explosions throwing dirt and vegetation into the air. Balls of fiery napalm rolled through the jungle setting fires to everything it touched. The correspondent grabbed one of the soldiers nearest him, "What's your name and outfit son?"

The boy with peach fuzz looked at the man as if he'd been asked the dumbest question in the world. "Lance Corporal Billy Cathart, Second of the Third Marines, Charlie Company."

"Where are you from son?"

"Cats Paw, California." A silly looking grin spread across the Marine's face.

The correspondent smiled pleasantly, "I don't believe I'm familiar with Cats Paw. Where is that exactly?"

"It's between hello and goodbye…population I don't know."

The correspondent laughed at the Marines wit and cavalier attitude in the face of danger. "Aren't you scared son.

"Naw, not much…there's only three things to worry about over here."

A salvo of 155 artillery rounds landed somewhere in the distance causing the correspondent to visibly flinch. "And what would they be?"

"Watch where you step, your fellow Marines, and which end of the bullet you're on."

"Is there anything you'd like to say to the people back home in Cats Paw?" The correspondent held onto his Australian bush hat and pushed the hand-held mike close to the young Marine's mouth.

"Yeah, as a matter of fact there is. Tell 'em to send me a one-way ticket home. I'm not very popular over here."

A scruffy sergeant in ragtag fatigues yanked the Marine away from the news crew and shoved him forward. With a backward glance the young Marine from Cats Paw, California gave his new friends a halfhearted salute.

"My God Cleat, that Marine looked as if he should be running from the truant officer instead of dodging bullets in Vietnam."

"Dad, he's a Marine, and the military's full of men just like him. They are young, tough, and grossly undereducated *and* underprivileged, but most of them are proud to be serving their country's call to arms."

"I hope and pray you and Coon don't have to serve over there. Christ, of all things, I never dreamed of that damn war escalating when you boys joined the Army. For God's sake, we shouldn't even be over there. They have nothing to offer that's worth one American's life."

"I'm sure the terrorized people of South Vietnam don't concur with your convictions, and not surprisingly, I don't either."

"Son, our sacrifice won't mean a goddamn thing. All of Southeast Asia is going to end up being under communist domination no matter what we do. After World War II we tried to help the damn French in that part of the world and it was a waste of men, material, and money. We'll never risk a war with China or Russia, at least not in that part of the world, and furthermore they won't risk one with us in our hemisphere. God forbid, if they do send you to Vietnam please read up on your history before you go and know what you're up against."

"Yes sir." Cleat got up to leave.

"Where are you going?"

"No place in particular dad, just out and about."

"Well be careful."

"I will."

Cleat sat behind the steering wheel and took a deep breath. *My god, he's suffocating. I'll never be able to come home again and live under his rule.*

Their departure day finally arrived and Cleat was thankful that he and his dad hadn't had any confrontations. Randy's presence was a contributing factor, along with the entire family's awkward endeavors. Over the past few days interaction between father and son were cordial, at times you could've easily classified it as being friendly. The morning of their departure his dad surprised them all when he took over the kitchen and fixed them breakfast. Mrs. Davis hid her displeasure over the shambles her husband left behind, only because she understood his reason.

Cleat attributed the pleasantries to their time away from each other and the fact he was serving in the armed forces. Maybe Coon and Mister Truman were right…time heals all wounds of the heart. At 0930 he and Coon were putting their last piece of luggage into the trunk of his Chevy. Final goodbyes were said standing in the driveway outside the den door. It was extremely emotional, the women all cried as the men awkwardly shook hands. No one went back inside until the boys drove out of sight.

Mrs. Davis scowled at her husband of twenty-eight years, "It would've meant a great deal to me if you could've given your sons a hug. You and Cleat are stubborn beyond belief. I could just slap your face." With a huff she stormed back into the house with Mama Marie and Sissy following angrily behind.

Mister Davis stood in the driveway, vacantly staring at the spot he last saw his son drive away. No audible words were spoken, but if you could read lips you would've seen the words, "I love you son, and I love you too Coon. God be with you and keep you safe." As he was turning to go back inside and rejoin his family he noticed the morning newspaper lying in the driveway. Anxious to read about the local election for mayor and the sports section he hastened his steps. Once situated in his favorite chair he placed his reading glasses on the bridge of his nose, rolled the rubber band off of the paper and snapped it open. The bold headlines read:

ONE OF LAKEWOOD'S FINEST KILLED IN VIETNAM

By Leonard Gillespie

First Lieutenant Paul J. Arnold, Lakewood High School, class of 1959, was killed in a firefight near Tay Ninh, South Vietnam on January 2nd. He lettered in three sports at LHS, and after graduation he attended West Point. He graduated from West Point with honors in June of 1963. Lieutenant Arnold was serving as a platoon leader with the 173rd Airborne when elements of his company were overrun. He rallied his men and thwarted the enemy attack. While assuming command he received several wounds but continued to lead his men until he succumbed to a mortal wound. His Battalion commander has recommended First Lieutenant Paul J. Arnold for the Congressional Medal of Honor.

Paul Arnold is survived by his Mother: Elizabeth Arnold, Father: Daniel Arnold of 1126 Camphor Drive, Brother: James Arnold, Sister: Tabitha Arnold of the same address. Parental grandparents: Daniel and Mary Arnold of 714 Callaway Court, Lakewood, Florida, Jack and Carol Mooney of 3232 Cedar Circle, Orlando, Florida. Funeral arrangements will be announced at a later date.

Randle Davis's hands were shaking when he laid the paper in his lap. Paul had been one of Randy's best friends. They played sports together since little league and were constant companions. Paul had spent the night dozens of times, and Randy did the same at Paul's house. *My God, poor Liz and Paul, I'll have to do or say something, but how can you console friends when they've lost a child?*

Their devastation must be excruciating.

Randle Davis rose from his chair and lifted its cushion. He folded the paper into a square and hid it under the seat. Even though June rarely read the paper he didn't want to leave it laying about for her to see the headlines, besides the small community of Lakewood would spread the news like wildfire. He hoped that God would offer her a short reprieve; even a day would be appreciative.

"Honey, I'm going upstairs and lay down for a bit."

"Alright sweetheart, we'll be in the kitchen cleaning up your mess. If you need anything give us a holler."

"Thanks, I will." The climb upstairs was slow and laborious; entering their bedroom he knelt at the bedside and began: *Lord I know it's been awhile, but you know me not as a stranger, for I have called upon you many times. I ask not for myself, but for Cleat and Coon. They are good boys and know not of the perils in this world. I fear they will soon tread in dangers path and I pray that you will watch over them. Fear comes not from you, but from my lack of trust and faith. Help strengthen my belief for in my heart I know you are Father of us all and you want only the greatest good for each of your children. I lift up Liz and Paul and their family to your loving arms as they walk through this tragic loss into acceptance. Thank you for loving us. In the precious name of Jesus, Lord our Savior, Amen.*

The sign over the main entrance read:

HOME OF THE 101ST AIRBORNE DIVISION
(SCREAMING EAGLES)
FORT CAMPBELL, KENTUCKY

Under the bold, black letters was a large replica of the famous division patch. They waited patiently for the car in front of them to pass through the front gate. An overwhelming presence swept over them. They experienced an enigma so strong neither one of them could have put into words if asked. They were about to become members of the infamous Screaming Eagles, the same division that jumped behind the German lines in France preceding the Normandy invasion. Later in the war they held Bastogne during the Battle of the Bulge when the enemy counter attacked through the Ardennes Forest. They were surrounded by the Germans in a last ditch effort to defeat the allies.

The 101st held and became legends.

Finally it was their turn to move forward. One of the guards manning the gate stepped up to driver's side of the open convertible. It was 42-degree outside and you could see the soldier's breath as he inspected the occupants. He was dressed in a perfectly fitted Class 'A' uniform, his pants legs were bloused over boots laced with white bootlaces. The paratroopers webbing was also white, and held an Army issue 45 automatic. The white helmet liner he wore had MP stenciled on the front. But what stood out the most were the silver jump wings pinned over his left breast pocket.

"Let's see some ID cards and orders."

The two sergeants eagerly handed them to the MP.

"Hey, George, we got us a couple of new 'legs' over here."

A black, under sized E-6 came from the other side of the guard shack and briefly scrutinized their orders. "You 'legs' look too damn young to be E-5's. Shit, y'all ought'a still be suckling yo' mama's tit for Christ's sake."

Cleat's face turned red as a beat. "We're just a couple of 'shake n bakes' hoping to become American heroes, Sergeant. I realize it's against insurmountable odds for a couple of *legs* lower than whale-shit. Even though we are about to face horrific trials and tribulations, I can assure you that we will proudly crawl from the dredges of obscurity and join the legendary ranks of the elite 101st Airborne."

"Shit, you one intelligent dude, ain't cha? I wouldn't be talking that shit in front of the Black Hats though, or you'll be in a world of shit."

"Thank you Sergeant, I'll heed your advice, now if you would be so kind as to offer a couple of unworthy 'legs' directions we'll be on our merry way."

After three long days of hanging around the replacement depot shooting pool and watching TV they finally received their orders to report to Bravo Company, 3rd Battalion/187th Infantry Regiment. When they drove into the communal parking lot it was pleasing to see the modern, air-conditioned cement block buildings they were soon to be calling home. Dressed in fatigues they reported to the company orderly room with orders in hand. A specialist fourth class was sitting behind a metal desk reading the paper.

"Sergeants Davis and Sergeant Truman are reporting for duty specialist."

Showing annoyance and total disregard for their rank he meticulously tri-folded the newspaper and placed it neatly on his desk. "Yeah, we've been expecting youse guys…the Top wants to see youse ASAP." His New York accent was unmistakable. "Youse two hang tight while I let him know youse guys are here." He took their paperwork and disappeared down the short hallway, within thirty seconds he was back. "Knock once and go in."

Cleat and Coon came to a closed door with a highly polished bronzed plate signifying it was the office of First Sergeant A. Caitiff. As instructed, they knocked once and entered the First Sergeant's office, but before they could come to attention Top Sergeant Caitiff bellowed loudly, "Did you lower than whale shit 'legs' hear me give permission to enter?"

Cleat knew they had been had. "No First Sergeant…my apologies…it won't happen again."

"I don't want your apologies, only sissies, queers, and 'legs' hand out apologies."

"Yes First Sergeant, as I stated earlier it won't happen again."

"You can bet your ass it better not." For the next ten minutes the First Sergeant read over their files. "Very impressive. You two have finished one-two through all phases of training. We need men like y'all to strengthen our cadre of NCO's. We're losing four good troopers in the next few weeks…they'll be hard boots to fill, but it looks like y'all can fill 'em just fine." Sergeant Caitiff stood to his full height of five foot six inches and walked around his desk to shake hands with the new buck sergeants.

Cleat and Coon were surprised how short the Top was; from behind the desk he looked much bigger. Compared to the rest of the sergeant's body his head was so huge it was comical, and it was extremely difficult not to stare in awe at its grandiose size. Without knowledge of the other they both chose the sergeant's broad gleaming forehead as their focal point.

"You men are lucky to arrive when you did, because jump school's new cycle begins next week. If you'd of arrived any later y'all would'a been scheduled for three weeks of pre-jump training, and that's nothin' but good old fashion PT." Caitiff laughed, "I should'a been so fortunate when I came through here. The most important thing is to get you two jump qualified and assigned to one of our line platoons. Have a seat and I'll give you some pointers before you start hell week, I promise you'll find it to be most beneficial."

The first day of jump school they were marched in formation to a theater in order to view highlight films of all the horrors that might befall a paratrooper. The showing began with brutal combat scenes during WW II and Korea. They were so graphically explicit that it created a murmuring of self-doubt amongst the fledgling class of men aspiring to become paratroopers. Captured German films of Americans being shot out of the sky during Operation Market Garden in Belgium, and the Normandy invasion were grueling to watch. It was an emotional scene to witness paratroopers hanging lifeless in their harnesses as they drifted with the wind. The portion showing prolific injuries and deaths from jumping out of perfectly good airplanes during peacetime was the instigator that triggered a change of heart to many of the viewers. Approximately 20% of the original three hundred or so volunteers were quietly removed from the theater *and* from their prior commitment to attend jump school.

The first week of jump school was mostly devoted to weeding out the weak links that couldn't cut it under pressure. A lot of running, harassment, and yelling from the Black Hats made life miserable, especially if you caught their undivided attention. It was best to try and blend in with the masses, if for some reason you stood out above the rest you were asking for trouble. Your days were short lived if the Black Hats made it their personal responsibility to turn your life into a living hell. If you were unfortunate enough to be inside the Black Hats' Circle of Doom you were facing long odds of ever surviving the day. Once they had your number you were dead meat.

It began when an instructor singled you out for whatever reason and ordered you to give him a gig, in the middle of your pushups the vultures with black hats would form and begin screaming out separate commands. One would holler for sit-ups while another demanded squat jumps, and the original instructor would yell at you for not finishing his gig. It was an impossible situation and only the strong of heart and most determined survived the ordeal. Another 20% ended up leaving by week's end.

Thankfully there was less harassment during the second week, and more time was devoted to actual training, which included the thirty-four foot wooden jump tower and the *Suspended Agony* where you practiced in harness jumping off of a wooden platform simulating a parachute jump. If done incorrectly, an instructor would grab the legs of whoever preformed the less than perfect attempt and swing back and forth with all of his weight on the poor soul.

Invariably the straps between his legs would pinch your gonads causing excruciating pain, henceforth the nickname, "Suspended Agony." Amazingly, by week's end they'd lost another 10%.

Cleat felt sorry for the men who quit in the morning. Those that did had to wait outside the jump schools orderly room and see the First Sergeant. It was quickly learned and understood that the First Sergeant would not grant an audience before 1640. That meant they had to stand at attention on one of a dozen eighteen inch square concrete patio stones. After several hours of standing in place it wasn't uncommon to see men shivering and collapsing on the frozen ground. Cleat and Coon vowed if either one of them quit they would do so late in the afternoon, of course if you lasted that long there was no sense in quitting. The Army did have its ways.

The third week was jump week, five jumps and you were eligible for graduation and the pinning of your blood wings. During jump week they lost another 5% of their class either to injuries or refusing to jump. Jump masters had to forcibly exit several men who were frozen in the doorway, but only to those they deemed worthy to wear the wings. Inconceivably, six guys made their first jump and then refused to go up again.

Out of the original class of slightly over three hundred almost half of the volunteers failed to qualify. Cleat and Coon were among the ones who graduated. They were proud of their accomplishment, but jumping out of an airplane wasn't such a big deal compared to the constant harassment and physical torment the Black Hats put you through. They were especially rough on officers and NCO's, and well they should be if they were expected to lead men into battle. With callous due respect the instructors always made it a point to refer to the officers as sirs, but Black Hats showed little regard for the noncommissioned officers. Although none of the unfortunates deemed they were being treated fairly, they were smart enough to keep their mouths shut and endure the pain, and abuse.

Six weeks had passed since Cleat and Coon had graduated from jump school, and as fortunes fell they were still together, both of them were assigned to the second platoon as squad leaders. Cleat was a natural and easily assumed command and control of his men, but Coon floundered like a fish out of water. His qualifications had nothing to do with his lack of command and control over his squad. Coon had never been challenged with the awesome responsibility of leadership. He was used to everyone liking him. Rarely were his orders obeyed without someone bitching or castigating its validity. The squad members held little regard for his stripes and less for his leadership.

It was a festering problem that seemed to grow with each passing day. Cleat heard the rumors and jokes among the men and he was afraid it would contaminate the rest of the platoon if something wasn't done. It was hurtful to see Coon struggle, several times he felt like stepping in and knocking some of the instigators on their ass, but he didn't want to further weaken Coon's stature. At the end of every day Cleat hoped it would be *the* day that Coon would broach him with his dilemma, but days quickly turned into weeks. If the situation didn't drastically improve he had no other choice but to confront his friend. He would give him until the weekend.

Late Friday afternoon the two friends were sitting in the Normandy Club making plans for the weekend while nursing a couple of draft beers.

"You got any bright ideas Cleat?"

"Shit, I'm almost too tired to go anywhere or do anything."

"We could go to Evansville for the weekend and try our luck."

"Naw, it's too long of a drive, I'm for hanging around here. Maybe we'll try Hopkinsville tonight and Clarksville Saturday night."

"Sounds like a plan. Damn, Cleat, if I hadn't lost Tammy's number we could've had a sure thing."

"No thanks, her girlfriend wasn't my type."

"Are you crazy, Becky fell head over heels for you? She's a nice girl man, and she was a knockout."

"That's the problem Coon; from now on I'm through with nice girls. The raunchier they are the better they are. I've hurt too many girls like Becky. They want more than I can give them, and I refuse to be the object of their discontent."

Coon put his mug down and stretched his hand across the table, "I'm sorry, let me introduce myself, my name is Sergeant John Truman and yours is…?"

Cleat laughed as he slapped at Coon's hand, "Very funny asshole."

An awkward moment of silence ensued when Coon swallowed a mouthful of beer. After wiping the foamy residue from his lips he looked at Cleat with sorrowful eyes. "Cleat, this sergeant shit ain't all its cracked up to be. It's a chore for me to roll outta my bunk in the morning." Coon rubbed his face and let out a sigh. "Hell, I thought jumping out of planes and running through the woods would be a blast, but its not. I should've never gone to NCO school. For Christ sakes, who was I kidding? I can't lead my own damn self much less anybody else. I don't know what to do, I'm telling you man, this really sucks. As hard as I try nothing seems to work. They don't show me or my rank any respect, it's like I'm an outsider looking in." Coon shook his head in disgust, "I ain't cut out for this shit."

"Coon, I know what your problem is and its solution, but you're not going to like hearing it, especially from me."

"Hellfire, don't worry about hurting my feelings. I'm at my wits end so give it to me straight."

"First of all you're too easy on the men. You don't control them, they control you and what's worse…they know it. Your job isn't to be a nice guy, or the most popular. You are a squad leader, so by God you better start acting like one. These men don't need a friend and you can't afford the luxury of becoming one. Rank is a symbol of authority and you've shown them none. They need discipline and leadership, but you kowtow to them like they were your best friends. They're not your friends and they never will be. Those three stripes on your sleeve make them your subordinates and if you treat them any differently you'll only confuse them and subject yourself to insubordination. I'm not saying that you have to act like some demigod, but you have to demonstrate leadership. These soldiers aren't your ordinary breed, they are hard charging paratroopers and they expect more from you."

"Christ, what am I supposed to do? They don't show me any respect at all."

"Coon, respect isn't handed out, it's earned. Until you show them whose boss the problems you're facing now will only escalate. Time in service doesn't mean a damn thing when it comes to leadership. You have second lieutenants too young to vote leading NCO's who are old enough to be their fathers. Leadership comes from within and by example. The men in your squad are taking advantage of you because you worry too much about being a nice guy. You hang around their bunks telling jokes and laughing at their bullshit lies as if you were one of them. Those sergeant stripes exclude you from their club. If you want to socialize then do it with fellow NCO's and leave the lower four alone."

"Damn, Cleat, that sounds kind of cold and rather snobbish."

Cleat shook his head in wonderment. "This isn't civilian life where friendship is important, and we're not living in a democracy. This is the United States Army where discipline rules. Without discipline the armed forces would be a mob of anarchist laced with bedlam."

"How do I begin?"

"Have a squad meeting and issue a warning that kindergarten is over. Let them know what they can expect from you *and* what you expect in return. After that if anyone gets out of line send them to KP, police call, guard duty, or take some other form of disciplinary action. I promise it won't take them long to realize a new sheriff is in town."

After digesting Cleat's lecture on leadership and coming to grips with the multitude of mistakes he'd made, Coon could hardly wait for the uneventful weekend to conclude. His mind had difficulty focusing on anything other than meeting with his squad Monday morning after breakfast. Hundreds of thoughts raced through his mind and he was angst over how he was going to address his men. He had time to work it out, but the bottom line was: things had to change, not only that, they were going to change.

Coon stood under the window of their two-man sleeping quarters waiting patiently for the men to settle down. It was a small room and it was overly crowded with the additional bodies, but it was private. When he deemed enough time had passed he began with, "Knock it off and listen-up." Once again it took longer than necessary for the squad to get squared away. "The next person that says a word without my permission will end up on KP duty for a week." That got their attention.

"This squad is the sorriest squad in the platoon, the company, and quite possibly the entire battalion. I'm your squad leader and I take full responsibility for your sorry asses. I've called this meeting to give you a heads up, starting today your attitude is going to change."

"Come on Sarge, lighten up, we ain't that bad." Pfc. Adams laughed

"Adam's, report to the mess hall and offer your services to the spoons for the next seven days." Coon paid little attention to the sharp intake of breaths. "Leave now before I make it fourteen days."

Adams started to object but caught himself before making another error in judgment. Weaving through his fellow squad members he exited the door without a backward glance.

"Damn it, you men are elite paratroopers and I swear to God you're going to starting acting it. We are members of the 101st Airborne, the best of the best and I'll not leave a man standing that disagrees. This squad is going to personify the meaning of unit pride. I will no longer put up with any bullshit or excuses...those days are over. My orders will be obeyed without question, anyone failing to do so will suffer the consequences. You will demonstrate military protocol at all times. If you have a gripe approach your fire team leader, if he can't handle the matter he'll initiate the chain of command. Future warning: I suggest the issue to be warranted before it reaches me." Coon gazed over the huddled men and recognized Alpha team leader, Spec-4 Henderson with his hand held high.

"Sarge, what brought this about?"

"If you need to ask then maybe you shouldn't be a fire team leader."

"Clear Sergeant." Ralph Henderson's felt the blood rush to his face. He was dressed down and didn't like it, but he had hopes of making E-5 before his enlistment ran out and he sure as hell wasn't going to muddy the waters. If this was what Truman wanted then that was the way it was gonna be.

"Does anybody else have any questions?" Coon waited long enough to see there were none forthcoming, "This squad has a lot of catching up to do and we're gonna start today." His statement was met with groans of displeasure. "This is the United States Army, not the Boy Scouts. You are at my disposal seven days a week twenty four hours a day if I deem necessary, so get used to it. I have Platoon Sergeant Madera's and Lieutenant Massey's permission to use my own discretion in getting you men STRAC. At 1800 hours your training begins with a class on light infantry weapons. Sergeant Madera will assist.

Coon had to enforce disciplinary actions during the first week, but by the end of the second week he had his squad walking the straight and narrow. When Sergeant Truman barked commands they answered him with a yes sergeant, no sergeant, or clear sergeant. Although their awakening was abrupt and demanding, none of them would willingly admit to the plain simple truth...they were glad. Coon could finally sleep at night and in the mornings he looked forward to a new day.

Once Cleat decided Coon's squad was squared away, the competition began. As the rivalry between them intensified it quickly spread to the other squads and then leapfrogged throughout the company. Within the month the entire battalion was obsessed with being the best of the best.

Coon dropped his last boot on the floor and began rubbing his soar feet. "All of this is your damn fault."

"What's my fault?" Cleat lay on his bunk wondering if he would ever be able to walk again.

"The goddamn force field march jerk-off." Coon pulled off his bloody socks and held them in the air. "This blood is on your hands."

"Coon, contrary to your beliefs everything in this world that turns to shit *isn't* my fault."

"Well this sure as hell is. If you hadn't started a competition between our squads this shit would've never happened."

"I suppose the general has confirmed your allegations, *or* is this merely supposition?"

"Cleat, I swear sometimes you're just plain irritating."

"Coon, ol' buddy, I never claimed to be the personification of perfection." Cleat made it a point not to move any unnecessary muscles. He was so sore even his eyelids hurt.

Coon rolled over on his bunk, "You're one lucky asshole, because I'm too worn-out and crippled to come over there and kick your ass."

"You better bring some friends…oh I forgot you don't have any." Cleat was laughing at his own joke when a boot sailed across the room scantly missing his head and slammed into the wall. "Dammit to hell, you're about to piss me off. If I had enough energy to throw the damn thing back I would."

"Hey, if you're feeling froggy then by God jump your ass over here and…"

"I'm surely tempted to do just that, but for now I'm contented to lay here and wallow in my own self-pity."

"So ass-wipe, you admit that…" A sharp knock at the door interrupted Coon's chastening.

Sergeant Madera opened the door and thrust his head inside, "Hey, have you two heard the latest?"

"Lay it on us Sarge." Coon threw his bloody socks across the room towards his wall locker.

"The Rakasans are deploying to Viet-by-God-Nam in ninety days. Notify the rest of the platoon while I spread the word." Madera disappeared from the doorway as suddenly as he appeared. You could hear his boots slapping the hall tile as he rushed down the hallway.

"Holy shit Cleat, do you think it's for real this time?"

"Probably so, it's not like we haven't been expecting it. Half of the Division's been over there slugging it out for awhile. Our turn was bound to come." Cleat swung off of his bunk and planted his feet firmly on the floor.

"Man, we're actually going. Wow, all of our training is finally going to pay off."

"Coon, training isn't enough to prepare us for what we're about to face."

"For Christ sakes Cleat, what're you saying, we're paratroopers...the best there is."

"Training is just that, training. It teaches us the art of combat, but nothing can simulate the horrors of war. Have you talked to or even listened to the senior NCO's? I'm talking about the ones who experienced combat in WW II and Korea."

"No, but that doesn't mean I won't. Hell, going to war isn't something I'm looking forward to, you know me better than that, but damn it to hell, you have to admit the prospect is exciting."

"No, I'll admit to no such thing. While you've been hanging around bull-shitting with the troops, I've been listening and talking to the senior NCO's who've been there and back. It's going to be bad Coon...real bad. When we go to Vietnam it's for real and the loser pays the ultimate price." Cleat reached for a book on his dresser and tossed it to Coon. "Here, I suggest you read this before we land in Vietnam, it'll give you an insight and a better perspective of our mission."

Coon caught the book and looked at the cover, "Shit, man, what the hell is this "Street Without Joy" about?"

"It's about the French Indochina War, how it came to be and what happened to the French after WW II when they tried to reclaim Vietnam as a Colony."

When rumor of the 3rd Battalion's deployment was confirmed the ready-alert intensified and time in the classroom increased. The Rakasans were preparing for battle. Requisitions were submitted covering everything from toilet paper to ammunition. Every waking moment was an opportunity to refine their skills. Senior NCO's haggard the troop's night and day on company, platoon, and squad tactics. Classes were given on ambushing, patrolling, intelligence gathering, radio procedures, first aid, weapons, hygiene, and everything else they deemed necessary for survival in a combat zone.

After noon chow Cleat and Coon were told to report to the orderly room along with three other NCO's. The runner quickly ushered them into Captain Spangler's office. The CO greeted the NCOs with a smile and promptly informed the sergeants of their involuntarily enrollment in Jungle Warfare School. They were joining an additional forty-five enlisted personnel in the battalion and traveling to Fort Sherman, in Panama. SOP for the school was a three week course, but the Army decided to initiate a two-week prototype designed especially for elite troops headed to Vietnam.

Since the schools instructors were willing to acknowledge the men from the 187th were already in peak physical condition the normal screening process for applicants were waved. Upon their arrival the Commandant of the school divided the men into ten five man teams with an instructor assign to each group.

Cleat and Coon's class was the first to be indoctrinated into the new program and following their completion four subsequent classes were slotted to closely follow theirs. It was intense from the word go...no rest for the weary and very little sleep. It was two long insufferable weeks of hell, but there were no injuries, or quitters among the hardened paratroopers.

Not only did the instructors teach their students how to conduct war in a jungle environment, they also taught them how to *survive* in the jungle. Classes were given on which types of plants were known for water retention, and the classification of vegetation and roots you could safely eat in the tropics between Cancer and Capricorn. A full day was spent teaching the fledgling jungle fighters how to trap small game. As youngsters Cleat and Coon acquired a vast amount of experience catching game in the Florida woods and swamps, even so, they were about to experience the true meaning of survival.

A stocky instructor sergeant dressed in camouflaged fatigues entered a circle of loosely scattered men resting on the jungle floor, wrapped over his shoulders was a large snake from the constrictor family. In one hand he held a fighting knife and in the other were two palm fronds. He knelt on the ground and made a great production out of placing the lifeless snake on one of the fresh-cut palms. Ignoring the ohhh's and ahhh's he severed its head and slit the reptile from one end to the other. Using his knife he scraped the filet clean and lastly pealed away the skin. Rising to his feet he held the long piece of white meat high overhead for all to see. "Gentlemen, you are about to feast upon the harvest of my labor. Mother nature has provided you with a bountiful meal." Grinning from ear-to-ear he laid the freshly skinned meat on the remaining frond and began slicing it into two inch sections.

"You've got to be kidding." A tall lanky sergeant from Tennessee moaned.

"No freaking way Jose." A New Yorker bellowed amidst the groans and moans of the wide-eyed students.

While snake-man was busy slicing and dicing another instructor stepped from the inner circle and used his bush knife to whack-off several limbs from a nearby tropical plant. When he was through the instructor hauled the branches next to the chef and stripped them bare. Gathering the dark green, palm-sized leaves he placed them off to the side in a neat pile.

Coon leaned over and whispered to Cleat, "Man, can you believe this shit?"

"Yeah, I just hope it doesn't taste the same."

"I'm hungry, but I don't know if I'm *that* hungry."

"Unfortunately, I don't think we have a choice…not if we want to graduate."

"I guess its time to hold your nose and close your eyes."

"Sounds like a plan to me." Cleat rubbed Captain Nick's crucifix hoping the silent prayer would enable him to pass the test without his queasy stomach rejecting the meal. Little did he know the worst was yet to come.

The following day they were truly put to test. Next to a nearby stream the paratroopers were ordered to search for grub worms and other delectable creatures they might find underneath rocks and rotting limbs scattered about. Less than excited, the foray commenced and when enough of the creepy crawlies were gathered in their soft covers they reported back to the instructors.

"Gentlemen, if you will, please remove your canteen cups and empty your next meal into the container. When you have completed said task, use the butt of your KA-BAR to mash the contents into gruel, add water and stir vigorously. Now the good part…you do have a choice. You can savor the meal as a tepid delicacy, as the French prefer, or use heat tabs to enjoy a hot, protein enriched soup.

Cleat was hesitant, but he mentally counted to ten and brought the cup to his lips. As he was about to take his first sip Coon nudged him on the shoulder.

"Hey, Cleat, this shit ain't half bad."

When he turned to face Coon his stomach did a backward flip. A brownish substance outlined Coon's teeth in a ghoulish smile and there was an equal color of drool dripping from his chin. "For Christ sakes, close your mouth when you talk." Cleat lowered his cup in a brief reprieve. He would have to start his count all over again.

Sergeant Wayne Whitehurst was sitting to the left of Cleat and chuckled, "Here, try this."

Cleat took note of the half-hidden, small bottle of Tabasco sauce the sergeant was offering him. "What will that do?"

"It'll do wonders. Just shake a little on and you'll see what I mean. This little bottle is full of miracles, and it's a *must* have when you're in the field. Hell, I wouldn't be caught dead without it."

"Thanks, I'd be willing to try anything if it'll disguise the taste of what I assume to be awful."

"It will, and when we deploy to the Nam be sure and put some in your B-4 bag before we ship out. Other condiments such as garlic powder, lemon pepper, and onion salt, are good, but you can't do without Tabasco. Mark my words and you'll thank me later."

"I'll keep that in mind." Cleat took the bottle and added several drops to the brown, lumpy liquid *and* added one more for Airborne. As expected, it was nasty and he could barely keep it down. He couldn't imagine what it would've tasted like if he hadn't accepted Wayne's offer. If there was ever a next time he promised to make sure it was lump-free.

"Here, let me try some of that stuff." Coon motioned Cleat for the hot sauce.

"I thought you said it wasn't half bad?"

"I did, but maybe this shit will make it taste even better."

Classes were held at any given time and under the darkness of the jungles canopy it became increasingly difficult to distinguish when one day ended and a new day began. Sunrise, sunset and moonlight were merely events that took place and were not to be confused with a twenty four hour period. Leeches and mosquitoes were a constant menace. They harassed you day and night along with an unknown variety of insects that, crept, crawled, wiggled, and flew. The pests were continually feeding on your flesh and exploring inside your clothing. The ever present danger of poisonous snakes, wild boars, and rumors of large jungle cats dragging you into the night was enough incentive to keep even the sleepiest trooper vigilant.

The biggest threat to survival weren't any of these living creatures…it was dehydration. Contrary to what most people believe, jungles aren't inundated with beautiful lagoons, winding rivers, trees bearing fruit, and trickling streams. The life-giving water that provides the ever-thirsty rainforest its nourishment comes from tropical storms and seasonal showers. Overhead canopies are pelted with rain and the excess gravitates through a thick latticework of branches, leaves, ferns, fronds, and creepers. The overflow from this highway of vine-twined trunks saturates the rotting compost and feeds its underlying root system.

During the accelerated two week cycle of jungle warfare training the only incident of note took place in a forty-by-forty sawdust pit. A young first lieutenant conducting a class in hand-to-hand combat selected Cleat as his reluctant participant. The lanky, toe-headed lieutenant summoned Cleat to center stage and enticed him to initiate an offensive move, but Cleat was unwilling and hesitant to strike an officer.

"Goddammit, Sergeant Davis, I order you to attack me in aggressive manner." Gaining no response other than a silly nervous grin, the lieutenant became enraged and shoved Cleat in the chest, driving him backwards several feet. "You chicken shit paratrooper, I'm going to kick your ass out of my school if you don't do something besides stand there with your thumb up your ass."

"Sir, I don't feel right about this."

"Sergeant, I don't give two shits about your feelings." The lieutenant's forearms suddenly rocketed forward with a pair of balled fists striking either side of Cleat's chest. The first and second knuckles of each hand stabbed like daggers into muscle and bone.

Cleat staggered from the painful blows. Bracing himself, he glared into the eyes of the abrasive lieutenant and snarled, "Don't try that again."

The lieutenant grinned, "At last, I finally have your attention, that's excellent." Reaching out to shove Cleat again, his hand was parried and two unbelievably quick left jabs collided with the left side of his face. The devastating blasts were quickly followed by a crashing right that rang a bell somewhere deep within his skull. When the lieutenant threw his hands up to ward off further punishment, he felt a battering ram burrow into his midriff driving every once of breath from his lungs. Grabbing his stomach to hold his organs in place, a right uppercut caught him under his exposed chin, slamming his teeth shut with an audible "clack." His brain exploded into a kaleidoscopic of colored starbursts just before a dark abyss swallowed him whole.

It was just under three minutes before the lieutenant regained consciousness, and only then because one of the instructors threw water in his face. Rising from the soggy pit on wobbly legs that tried desperately to hold him upright, he faced the reluctant young man who'd just knocked his ass out. He forced a smile and motioned the sergeant nearer. Looking into the young soldier's eyes, he saw no fear, only confusion, and maybe a touch of apprehension.

"Trooper, we're gonna have to try that again...now take another swing."

On that particular day Cleat learned all there was about leverage and balance as he flew through the air time and time again. Most often he landed hard on his back with the wily lieutenant sitting on his chest ready to deliver a deathblow. From then on Cleat absorbed everything he could when it came to hand-to-hand combat.

For the first time Cleat and Coon didn't finish one-two in their graduating class. They ended up two-three. Sergeant First Class Wayne Whitehurst from Alpha Company won the honor. Whitehurst served as a member of the Military Assistance and Advisory Command (MAAG) in Vietnam between 1963 and 64. He was assigned as an advisor to the country's ill-led, unmotivated, under-equipped army. His mission was to train the ARVIN (The South Vietnamese Army) into becoming a more efficient combat arm in thwarting the communist aggression raging in the South. In his roll as an advisor he held no real authority and his duties were regulated to giving advice only, thus, mission success became unfulfilling and unattainable. During his tour of duty he was awarded the Soldiers Medal, Bronze Star with "V" for valor, and a Purple Heart. Every opportunity that presented itself Cleat and Coon queried Whitehurst.

After returning from Panama the Rakasans training continued in earnest. It was a time when even the slackers became more serious about being the best they could be. No more was the Monday thru Friday mandatory run around the 'Horn' bemoaned or taken lightly. The prescribed uniform for the 0530 formation never varied, no matter what time of year or weather. They fell out in jump boots, fatigue pants, white T-shirts, and soft covers...period, no exceptions. With the 187th you ran everywhere, even to sick call, unless your leg was broken, or you had a fever over 101 degrees. A medic was always on standby to make sure you qualified for a free ride. All officers were saluted with a loud, "All the way, sir", and the enlisted were saluted identically except for the *sir*, in place of sir 'trooper' was used.

Cleat and Coon were sitting in their small, two man quarters cleaning their weapons after spending two weeks in the field acting as aggressors against the rest of the battalion. They'd just finished laughing over their last raid when there was a knock at the door.

"Come in," Cleat hollered.

"Captain Spangler wants the two of you in his office right away." The runner from the orderly room gasped for breath. The private first class was a member assigned to the 1st platoon, which was commonly called the "Ghost Platoon." It was where all non-qualified personnel were assigned until they completed jump school.

"Okay, tell him we'll be there in a few minutes."

"Sarge, he...uh...said right away, to come as you are as long as you're wearing at least a pair of regulation Army issue boxers."

"Christ, Coon, what have you done now?"

"Shit, I ain't done nothin'. You don't think it's about that last raid we pulled on Head Quarters Company do you?"

"God, I hope not, destruction of government property is a pretty damn serious offense, and they won't give a shit if it was an old WW II tent with holes in it."

"Man, I sure have gotten used to these stripes. I sure as hell don't want to end up being a slick-sleeve again."

"Me neither, Coon."

The two of them were dressed alike, shower shoes, Army regulation boxers, and T-shirts when they reported to their company commander. Whatever it was the captain wanted with them couldn't possibly match the abuse thrown at them while descending two fights of stairs to his office. It seemed like everyone in the Company caught them in their underwear. They could still hear the laughter and catcalls as they approached his door.

"Enter," the captain's squawky voice commanded. He couldn't help but smile when he saw his sergeants' mode of dress. "I see you took my orders literally."

Captain Spangler was well-liked among the troopers, despite his credentials as a West Point graduate. His demeanor as a no nonsense disciplinarian was legendary, but he was fair, and asked no more of his troopers than he was willing to do himself. Being slight of build, it was hard to imagine he was a second team All-American defensive back.

"Yes sir," Cleat answered for both of them as they stood at attention.

"Are you sergeants the subject of all that laughter I hear outside my office?"

"Yes sir…I'm afraid so."

"Good, because I thought I was missing out on something. Thank you…I feel much better now."

"Glad we could be of assistance, sir."

"Please, stand at ease." The smile was still in place as he watched his sergeants come to a more relaxed position. "I've received orders from the Battalion Commander to select two of my sergeants to attend Ranger School at Fort Benning, Georgia. There are several reasons the two of you are my first choice. I could say it was because you're single, and therefore less stressful than sending married sergeants, but the real reason is you are among the finest NCO's in the Battalion. If you men do well, as I'm sure you will, it'll make Bravo Company stand proud, and in turn show the brass I *do* know my ass from a hole in the ground." Spangler paused briefly, trying to read what was going through their minds. "This is voluntary and if you men need more time to consider then report back to me at 1600 hours with you answer."

Cleat knew immediately that he would accept the challenge to become a Ranger. He had committed to serving with the best when he first enlisted, and the opportunity to display the coveted black and gold rocker above his 101st Airborne patch was too much to pass up. "Sir, I consider it an honor to be selected, I will do my best to represent you, and Bravo Company."

"Me too, sir…I go where Cleat goes."

"Outstanding, your orders will be cut this week and you'll report to Fort Benning by Friday 1430 hours." Captain Spangler came from around his cluttered desk to shake their hands. "You make me proud to command."

Ranger School comprised over sixty twenty-hour days, seven days a week of pure hell with little food and sleep. The school itself was divided into three different phases, each phase at a different locale. The first phase was twenty days at Fort Benning, where you spent the first week proving you had the skill and mentality to finish the course. In the second week, training began in earnest by heightening your skills into becoming proficiently functional in fighting and leading close combat operations under mental and physical stress you would normally find during wartime. The second phase was the mountain course conducted out of Camp Frank D. Merrill near Dahlonega, Georgia. It was basically more of the same shit consisting of simulated combat stress, except for the mountainous terrain and learning the art of repelling. The third and final phase was in Florida operating out of Camp James E Rudder near Eglin Air Force Base.

During this phase they slugged through the murky waters of the Florida swamps day and night struggling with the fear of alligators lurking beneath the surface, and snakes of any kind. Their most prevalent annoyance besides fatigue and hunger were the mosquitoes that dive-bombed them at dusk and dawn. There was hardly a man in training that wasn't covered with cuts, scratches, and bruises. During each phase several men dropped out on their own accord, or failed to pass the cadres requirements to "Go" forward. Several were forced to withdraw because of injuries, but were given the option of recycling once they had medical clearance…some accepted and others opted out. The compass course was a bitch and probably the biggest determent in qualifying. By graduation over 40% of the class had failed to make the grade. Those that *did* couldn't believe they survived the arduous test and stood more proud than ever of their accomplishment.

Before leaving Fort Benning the graduating Rangers were notified of an unscheduled meeting. As they filtered into the operations room there was no one present, the only thing that greeted them was an unmanned podium situated in the front of the classroom. The room buzzed as the newly anointed Rangers sat in metal chairs speculating why the meeting was called.

"Attench-hut!"

The graduates snapped to attention as three NCOs wearing green berets and class-A's uniforms bloused over jump boots marched instep down the center isle. When they reached the podium, one stood on either side at parade-rest while the ranking NCO stood directly behind the rostrum. The hard-core veteran gazed at the sea of faces without showing any emotion. His stature was granite-like and his facial features were chiseled.

"Take your seats. My name is Master Sergeant Hans Dieter, and I'm with the 5th Special Forces Group stationed at Fort Bragg, North Carolina. I would like to…"

Gradually the Master Sergeant's Germanic accent faded as Cleat sat mesmerized by the three NCOs. He was awed by their headgear and their air of superiority. He had heard of the mysterious soldiers, but this was the first time he'd ever seen any. Besides the berets, what stood out the most was the Combat Infantryman Badges over their chest-full of ribbons. "Secondly, I would like to congratulate you upon the completion of Ranger School. That makes you a rare breed *and* an elite soldier. I would also like to thank you for being here. Before I go any further I'd like to ask those who aren't bilingual to please stand." The sergeant waited while almost 80% of the class rose to their feet. "Once again, congratulations. When you men return to your units be sure and share the knowledge you've gained at Ranger School, as for now, you are dismissed." A murmur rolled through their ranks as the men standing filed out of the room.

"What's going on Cleat?" Coon whispered without moving his lips.

"I'm guessing they're looking for volunteers."

"Shit, Special Forces, I don't know, man. That's some heavy-duty shit Cleat."

"Yeah, but if that's what they're looking for I'm game."

"Man, oh man, you're crazy."

"So I've heard." A crooked smile crept across Cleat's face.

Master Sergeant Dieter peered over the file he was holding in his hands and scowled. The young paratrooper sitting across from him was almost too good to be true. "It say's here that you speak French and Spanish fluently…is that correct?"

"Clear, Master Sergeant." Cleat sat in his chair stiff and upright.

"Why do you want to volunteer for Special Forces?"

Cleat sat for a moment to consider his answer. "When joining the Army I wanted to serve with the toughest outfit there was. When the recruiter told me that would be Airborne Infantry I volunteered, of course that was before I ever heard of the Special Forces." Cleat was pleased with his answer and was surprised there was no visible response from the sergeant. Several uncomfortable moments of silence passed before the Master Sergeant decided to speak his one word reply.

"Why?"

Why, shit. Why did I want to serve with the toughest? I don't know why. What kind of question was that? Cleat wasn't sure how to answer a question he'd never considered before. Was it prestige, pride, ego, or a test of manhood? None of those seemed the right answer. "At first it was ego, but later I learned it was the right choice for me."

"Why?"

Why, there it is again...Christ-on-a-crutch. "If I go into combat then I want to be able to count on the man next to me, with the 101st Airborne I can do that." Cleat wondered if his answer was as hokey as it sounded.

After thirty minutes of probing questions the interview was concluded with Master Sergeant Dieter accepting Cleat as a candidate to the Special Warfare School.

"Thank you Master Sergeant, but before volunteering for Special Forces I have a request and it's conducive to my acceptance."

Dieter's eyebrows furrowed, "Is that a fact? Its not often we're given ultimatums, but you've peaked my curiosity, so let's hear it."

Cleat came to attention, "Sergeant John Truman and I are like brothers, and he's been with my family since he was ten years old. We joined the Army on the buddy system and we'd like to stay together. He's in the outer office waiting to be interviewed."

Sergeant Dieter raised his left eyebrow and shuffled through the files lying on his desk. "Is he anything like you?"

Damn, another question. When will they ever end? "Yes, Sergeant, uh...kind of...sort of."

Dieter found the file he was looking for. "That's a weak affirmative Sergeant Davis, care to embellish."

"I prefer that you form your own opinion Master Sergeant."

A slow smile tweaked the corners of Dieter's mouth, "If the shit hits the fan would you want him next to you on the firing line?"

"I know of no one that I'd rather have by my side than Sergeant Truman."

"That's good enough for me...send him in." Dieter's lips actually turned into a full-fledged grin. *God, thank you for this blessing, looks like I owe you another one.*

Cleat paced back and forth outside the front office and looked at his watch for the tenth time in as many minutes. Coon had been with Sergeant Dieter for over an hour and a half, which was a hell of a lot longer than he'd spent with the sergeant. What could possibly be taking so long? Earlier he could've sworn that he heard muffled laughter coming from the office, but he shrugged it off as being far beyond the realm of possibility. Suddenly a roaring of laughter stopped him dead in his tracks. What in the hell could they be laughing at? He couldn't imagine Dieter laughing at anything.

When the door finally opened Coon wiped his tear-stained face with the heels of his palms and turned inward, "That was a good one Sarge. I'll see you later."

As soon as Coon closed the door Cleat grabbed him by the arm and pulled him off to the side. "What the hell went on in there?"

"What...with Hans?"

"Hans? You mean to tell me you're on a first name basis with the Master Sergeant?"

"Yeah, man, he's one hell of a nice guy. What's the matter with you? For Christ sakes Cleat, he ain't God."

"He sure as hell had me fooled. What were y'all doing in there that was so damn funny?"

Coon cackled, "Man, I tell you what, that guy could be a comedian. He's got more jokes than Jack Benny."

"That's all he did was tell jokes?"

"Yeah, after he went over my 201 file and asked me a few questions. We shot the shit for awhile and then started trading stories and telling jokes. He got a real big kick out me telling him about painting those footballs white up at Wingate. Shit, you should've heard the last joke he told me, it was the funniest damn thing I ever heard. It's about this salesman whose car breaks down in front of this old farmhouse out in the middle of nowhere and this farmer's daughter comes out to see if..."

"Stop right there, I don't want to hear the damn joke, or any of his other jokes. What did he say about Special Forces?"

"We're in, if that's what we want. What'ya think? We gonna do it?" Coon wiggled his eyebrows like Groucho Marks.

"I don't know...I sorta have mixed emotions. While you were in there shooting the shit with your good buddy Hans, I've been thinking about our guys back at the Company. It'll mean we'll probably never see them again and I kinda feel like we're abandoning them *and* letting Captain Spangler down. Also, we'll have to add an additional six months to our enlistment if we volunteer for Special Forces."

"Yeah, I've thought about that and it bothers me some too, but man, oh man, those Green Berets are bad as shit. I kinda dig'em and besides we wanted to serve with the best and there ain't nobody better than the Special Forces."

While waiting for their transfer orders they learned more about the Special Forces when they became friendly with a couple of Green Beret Staff Sergeants at the NCO Club. After engaging in some inquisitive conversation over a few pitchers of beer their excitement grew. The camaraderie and professionalism in the Forces was what they were looking for. They listened to their advice and relished in their words of encouragement.

A stout sergeant with a square jaw shoved the beret further off of his forehead and raised his mug, "You guys would have to be real screw-ups to be booted out. With the training you've already received and being fluent in three languages is exactly what the Forces are looking for. The main SNAFU that keeps us from filling our ranks is being bilingual. To most of us, English is our second language and once you're in you'll see what I'm talking about. You'll find the Special Forces have an enrollment of men from Eastern Europe and a preponderance of men who are Hispanic.

Cleat smiled, "Zwolinski, you and Ayala's nametags certainly affirm that statement."

Sergeant Ayala poured a refill from the half-empty pitcher of beer and took a long pull from his mug before grinning at the newly christened Rangers. "Shit, if you amigos could speak Chinese they'd probably make you officers."

Cleat shook his head, "No thanks, officers face too much responsibility and we kinda like staying under the radar."

"Shit, man, you've gotta lot to learn." Ayala drained his glass and slammed it on the table. "This mans Army is run by NCOs and its especially true in the Forces. If you're looking to shirk responsibility then you better rethink volunteering for the Special Forces."

Coon jumped when the sergeant's glass hit the table. "Hey, come-on Sarge, Cleat didn't mean it like it sounded. We just want to stay enlisted and not have to rub elbows with prima donnas and West Point pricks."

"You ain't gonna find officers like that in SF. Some might slip-in, but they ain't gonna stay long. The NCOs will run their asses off." Zwolinski laughed as he waved to a waitress for another picture of beer.

Zwolinski and Ayala were right on several counts. The Special Forces were desperate for qualified officers. Before Cleat and Coon's training began they were asked to reconsider attending OCS. The regular Army, and especially field grade officers, frowned upon anyone involved with the Special Forces, thus it was considered to be a bad career move. In some ways the Special Forces were better off. The dedicated officers that filled their ranks were men who willingly put their careers in jeopardy for the better good. Most, but not all of the officers were mavericks (enlisted personnel who attained a commission) or men whose nationality was different prior to becoming a US citizen.

Phase I at Special Warfare School was primarily consistent with schooling they'd already been through. Granted it was more intense, and more advanced, but nothing beyond their expertise or capabilities. Phase II was a different story altogether. It would be the first time Cleat and Coon would be separated. In order for them to stay together after training they had to go to different specialty schools. Cleat was attending a twenty-four week course to become an 11C (Weapons Sergeant) and Coon was assigned a like amount of time to become a 12B (Engineering Sergeant).

Their six months of classroom training and grueling field training exercises (FTX) passed quickly. At the courses end Cleat and Coon felt invincible and with that came an intense feeling of pride in ones self and that of the Special Forces. The day after winning their berets they were granted a fourteen day leave to spend Christmas holiday's at home.

CHAPTER 14

The familiar lamp posts in front of the Davis's home were shinning brightly as Cleat pulled his Chevy into the driveway and coasted to a stop. It was the wee hours of the morning and not a soul in the household was awake. They grabbed their AWOL bags, opened the den door and snuck quietly upstairs. Side-by-side they stepped over the loose step that always creaked and eased their bedroom open. They jointly decided to surprise the family of their arrival after catching up on some much needed sleep.

"Christ, its good to be home." Coon groaned as he lay in bed stretching his arms overhead.

"Yeah, nothing has changed, but yet nothing remains the same."

"There you go getting deep and philosophical on my ass again. For God sake, can't you just lie back and relax?"

"I am relaxed."

They were startled awake when Sissy burst into their room. "Cleat…Coon, why didn't y'all tell us you were coming home?"

"Damn, Sissy. What time is it?" Cleat rubbed the sleep from his eyes.

"It's after eight o'clock in the morning."

"If that's not Sandra Dee you're talking to then tell her to get the hell out of our damn bedroom." Coon rolled over and faced the wall.

"Ohhh, I'm gonna tell Mom and Dad y'all are cussing." Folding her arms under blossoming young breasts she pouted and began tapping her foot.

"Give us a few minutes and we'll be down to greet one and all."

"Dad's not here, he's in the Miami office till the end of the week."

Thank God for small favors. "Okay, but tell Mom and Mama Marie we'll be hungry for some home cooking when we come down."

Sissy sat on the edge of Cleat's bed and brushed her hand over the top of his close-cropped haircut. "I'm glad y'all are home for the holidays. I've missed y'all so much."

"Yeah, I'm glad we're home too, it's been a long time."

Most of their high school friends were home for the holiday's, including Mandy and Anne. Coon hooked-up with Anne right away, but Cleat was less fortunate with Mandy. He tried to call her several times to no avail, but caught fleeting glimpses of her around town. It wasn't until Bo's annual Christmas party that an encounter was made possible.

Cleat and Coon chose to wear their Class-A uniforms with all its regalia to the party, at first they felt conspicuous, but after awhile they were pleased with the commotion it caused. Everyone was curious over all of their patches, medals, and what they stood for. Their green berets were the *peace de resistance*.

Anne snuggled up to Coon, "My God, Coon, you're soooo striking in your uniform."

"Hell, all this time I thought that I was striking without it."

"Oh silly, you know what I mean."

"Speaking of being out of uniform, why don't we go somewhere and let me show you how striking I can be?"

"Shush! Somebody might hear you." Anne felt her face flush as she looked around the room.

"It's been a long time Anne, and I've thought of no one but you."

"Oh Coon, I want you too, but we have to stay a little while longer. If we leave too soon everyone will know."

"Who gives a shit, I sure as hell don't."

"Silly you, I have my reputation to consider."

"Anne, I don't know how to break this to you, but I'm afraid being with me your reputation is already destroyed beyond repair."

"I don't believe that for a second. Everybody likes you, and well they should."

Cleat stood by the wet bar nursing a rum and coke while observing Mandy across the way. She didn't seem to be with anybody, or if she was he hadn't arrived yet. Twice he started to walk her way, and both times he was stopped by inquisitors. It was kind of strange, he could tell most of his old friends were still standoffish, but their curiosity got the best of them. As far as he was concerned they would never be considered friends again, and he wondered if they ever were. High school kids were hangers-on and would do anything to be with the right clique. If you were one of the chosen then getting next to you was their calling. Nothing was more important in high school than being part of the in-crowd. Teenagers were supercilious and they always would be. It wasn't until you grew out of those awkward, know-it-all years that you realized how superficial your world was.

"Hey soldier boy, are you home on leave, or just trying to impress the female gender?"

Cleat turned around and came face-to-face with Mandy. She was more beautiful up close than he remembered. *My Lord, she was no longer a girl…she was a young woman.* "I…uhh…like your hair." *Brilliant, absolutely brilliant, she's been in your thoughts forever and that's all you can come-up with.*

Mandy laughingly reached out and touch his shoulder, "My mother had a fit when see saw how short they cut it, but I like it too."

"Yeah, it's really nice." Mandy's hair barely covered her ears, but the new style was becoming. It gave her an aura of sophistication and a touch of mystique. Cleat was aware that her hand remained on his shoulder and its presence burned like a hot poker.

"You're as dashing in uniform as I imagined you'd be."

"You look great Mandy, you really do. There's so much I want to say to you, and…"

"Lets not go there Cleat, what happened is in the past. The reason that I came over here was to let you know that I've forgiven you and I want more than anything to be friends again. We've shared so much of our lives together it's positively insane for us not to continue our friendship."

Cleat's gut wrenched and his heart felt like it was going to rupture. "I love you Mandy."

"I know Cleat", she squeezed his shoulder, "and I love you too, but not in the way you want."

"Is it Richard?" He hated to ask for fearing the answer.

"Richard, heavens no, he's old news, I'm not seeing anyone. It seems the only thing I have time for is studying and more studying. College is much more demanding than high school."

Cleat placed his hand on hers and brought it to his side. "Can we go for a walk?"

"Cleat, I'm not sure that's a good idea. I don't want to give you the wrong impression; I just want to be friends."

"And all I want is to talk privately without all of these people around."

Mandy followed his lead knowing she should have let well enough alone. What was it about Cleat that compelled her to reach out to him? She refused to be drawn into another disastrous relationship with Cleat. She'd been destroyed in high school with Cleat's promiscuous philandering and cheapened by Richard's lies and deceit. God, what a horrible experience Richard turned out to be, at least she knew Cleat loved her. If she ever fell in love again then it would have to be with someone she could trust explicitly.

Once they were outside Cleat led her to the side yard where he found a secluded spot beneath a Giant Oak festooned with layers of Spanish moss. They stood in resonate silence for several moments as each conjured private thoughts. Cleat broke the reverence by professing his undying love and pleaded for a second chance to prove he was worthy of hers in return.

"Oh, Cleat, I'm sorry. I knew this would happen. What we had was wonderful, we were young and foolishly in love. The experiences I shared with you will be treasured for a lifetime, but lets not dwell in the past. We must live in the present and look toward the future. We're all grownup now and those years betwixt adolescents and young adulthood were truly glorious wonders. Our dreams were merely dreams and what was, will never be again. You will always be in my thoughts and in my heart, but…"

"Please Mandy, don't say anymore." Cleat gently pressed his fingertips to her lips, "I don't want to hear finalities. Leave me a window of hope. I've changed Mandy and I understand completely if my words sound empty, but it's the truth. I didn't realize what I had until I lost you. God, Mandy, we were so good together…you can't deny the love between us." Cleat placed his trembling hands on either side of her face and stepped closer. "There has to be some way I can overcome my mistake. I promise to never hurt you again, or cause you any more pain. I don't blame you for losing faith in me, but you can't shut me out of your life forever. You mean more to me than…"

Please Cleat, don't." Mandy wrapped her hands around Cleat's and lowered

them to her side. "Too much has already been said and I'm afraid if it continues I'll only disappoint you. Let's go back inside before it goes any further."

"Will you hold my hand?"

Mandy paused briefly, "Yes, but only until the front steps."

Cleat breathed a sighed of relief, if she had said no he would've been
crushed. Although the brevity of the walk was less than desirable, the eupho-
ria of holding Mandy's hand was the most serene pleasure he had experienced
in over two years.

"No luck?" Coon sat beside Cleat on the leather couch and rested his sock
feet on a heavy Spanish coffee table.

"Hell no, they're screening my calls." Cleat slammed the receiver onto the
cradle.

"Come on, don't get paranoid on me. You can't possibly know your calls are
being screened."

"Shit, she's out shopping every time I call. She's shopped enough to buy out
all of downtown Lakewood. You'd think her parents would come up with
something a little more original. How about the beauty parlor or visiting relatives, anything but shopping every damn time I call. How stupid do they think
I am?"

"Sounds to me like they think you're pretty damn stupid."

"If I didn't love you like a brother I'd kick your hairy ass."

"You been looking at my ass again, what'd I tell you about that?"

"Seriously, Coon, what am I supposed to do? We have to leave for Bragg
on New Years day and that's only four days from now. I haven't talked to her
since Bo's party."

"I wish I had the answer brother, but your guess is as good as mine." Coon
stood up and stretched, "Hey, Anne and I are going to catch a movie and run
by Pip's afterwards, why don't you go with us?"

"Naw, I don't much feel like it. I think I'll just hang around here and spend
some time with the family.

Besides being unable to get in touch with Mandy, his other disappointment was learning that Randy wasn't going to be home for the Christmas
Holidays. He was spending his vacation hunting with friends in Alabama.

Even though they had drifted apart when Randy turned sixteen, Cleat still idolized his older brother. He was also jealous of his brother's relationship with their father, but not as much as he used to be. He'd quit trying to please his father the day he was inducted into the Army.

New Years Eve came and went and Cleat was dismal with his failing attempts to contact Mandy. While the family stood outside saying their good-byes a yellow 1966 Mustang convertible pulled into the driveway. Cleat was shocked to see Mandy crawl out of the bucket seats.

"Cleat, Coon." Mandy ran down the drive with open arms. "I was scared to death y'all would be gone before I got here." She leapt into Coon's arms and hugged him with all her might. "Anne told me that y'all were leaving for Vietnam soon. Ohhh, Coon, y'all be safe and watch over each other. I couldn't stand it if anything happened to y'all."

"We will Mandy, we'll be just fine."

Mandy broke from her sisterly embrace and smiled sheepishly at Cleat. "Could I speak to you in private?"

"Sure." Cleat grasped Mandy's hand and led her to the front yard.

"Late last night mother informed me of your calls and I apologize for the way she's treated you."

Cleat squeezed Mandy's hand, "In a way that's good news, because I was afraid you were trying to avoid me."

Mandy avoided Cleat's statement realizing it would lead to where she didn't want to go. "I wanted to say goodbye before y'all left. Please, be careful in that dreadful place, and come home safe. I…I…don't know what I would do if something happen to y'all." A tear welded in each of Mandy's eyes. "You both mean so much to me."

"It'll be okay Mandy…we'll be back before you know it." Cleat drew her into his arms and held her tight. He felt as if a great weight had been lifted from his chest. "I love you Mandy."

Mandy stiffened and pulled away. "Oh, Cleat, what am I going to do with you? You just don't give up. I'm afraid you've misconstrued my meaning. I want you home safe for your family and me, *not* for us. Our lives are separate now, but you will always be in my heart. Please understand I don't mean to hurt you, but it's for the best."

Cleat was stunned. He thought Mandy's presence meant they were back together. "I thought that..."

"Cleat," Mandy laid her forehead on his shoulder and sighed, "I'm sorry if my coming over here gave you the wrong impression. I should've known better, but I had to see you before you left. If I've brought you more pain it wasn't my intent."

Cleat grabbed Mandy's shoulders and held her at arms length. "Mandy, I'm coming back for you. Before this is over I'm going to make you believe in me again."

Mandy smiled, "You're impossible as ever, and you expect me to believe you've changed."

"Just wait and see Mandy, just wait and see."

Two weeks after returning to Fort Bragg Cleat and Coon found themselves on a flight to Vietnam. They were flying in as replacements for an A-Team located near the Cambodian border. They were to catch a hop to Na Trang and report to 5th Special Forces Group Head Quarters for several days of indoctrination. It was hard for them to contain their excitement, but they both privately wondered what had happened to the men they were replacing. Vietnam was in the news everyday with live pictures of real combat and the ever-growing numbers of dead GIs. They knew it wouldn't be long before all of their extensive training would be put to good use.

Their flight seemed to last forever, and between catnaps their excitement ebbed. When someone wakened them shouting they could see the coastline of Vietnam their previous enthusiasm rejuvenated.

Cleat looked out the window, although the jumbo jets massive wing obstructed most of his view he could make out the greenery of Vietnam and its azure blue sea. In the water were hundreds of ships, some large while others appeared to be quite small. He could easily identify one as being an aircraft carrier.

"Hey, don't hog the view brother." Coon leaned over Cleat's lap and pressed his nose against the thick glass. "Holly shit...would you look at that. Fuck me man, we're actually here."

Once on the ground they were ferried to the terminal in a green Army bus with chicken wire covering the windows. They were met by a friendly Master Sergeant by the name of Jankowski who was assigned to Command and Control in Na Trang. He filled them in on what to expect during their three days of indoctrination before being transported to their new home. The next morning they caught a C-130 to Na Trang. After being assigned to their billet they were free to do whatever they wanted until 0800 the next morning.

After chow they went downtown to check out the sights, and were pleasantly surprised at how modern some areas of Na Trang were. The hustling crowd of Vietnamese and foreign troops were at a frenetic pace, everyone seemed to know precisely where they were going except them. They wasted a couple of hours following different groups of GI's into some local bars, but found the establishments to be overly crowded with lousy rock-in-roll bands being preformed by less than adequate Vietnamese musicians. Disappointed, they ventured on their own and stumbled into an American style bar playing country and western music from a jukebox.

It wasn't particularly their type of music, but it suited them because there were fewer customers, and not near as nosey. Walking down several steps to a horseshoe shaped bar they took little notice of the other patrons. They approached the bar and sat on some vinyl covered stools. When the attractive female bartender asked for their orders they both requested a couple of cold beers. She bowed politely and served them with a smile. Before they could raise their chilled glasses a gravelly voice from the rear made an unwarranted snide remark about Green Berets.

At first they ignored the intrusion, but when it continued the two Special Forces sergeants turned and faced their tormentor only to discover there was more than one. While Hank Williams was crooning "Your Cheating Heart" on the jukebox, Cleat took a quick headcount in the dimly lit room and came up with six Marines sitting at a large table on the upper tier. At three o'clock a group of sailors were highly interested in what was about to take place.

"No use in hunting trouble 'Jarhead'. We're all on the same team over here." Cleat smiled his most winning smile.

"Who the hell are you calling 'Jarhead' you silly looking piss ant?" The Gunny sergeant was acting as the antagonist, and he looked mean and surly.

"Leave it be, Marine." Cleat was *way* past tired of the Gunny's bullshit.

Cleat and Coon turned back to the bar and found the once smiling barkeep extremely nervous over the exchange of words. Coon watched Cleat out of the corner of his eye, knowing full well a whole passel of trouble was brewing. Behind him the shuffling of boots and the scraping of chair legs confirmed his suspicions.

"Hell, there's only two of them boys. Let's go kick some sanctimonious ass."

"Better make that three, and if you want some sound advice you best be calling for reinforcements before you start something you ain't got a chance in hell finishing."

From out of the shadows a strongly built man dressed in civilian clothes appeared. There was something vaguely familiar about him, but there wasn't enough light to see any distinguishing features.

"Cleat Davis and John Truman, what brings a couple of Florida boys to this godforsaken country? What…you two don't recognize an old friend?"

"Holy shit, Cleat…its Harvey Blake!" Coon was dumbfounded.

"Well I'll be damned. Harv, what the hell are you doing over here?"

"I'll fill you in after we take care of some business." Blake faced the Marines with an evil grin. "It's been a long time since I've been to a party, gentlemen. I hope you outstanding Marines have your navy corpsman nearby, because your sure as hell gonna need him when this dance is over."

The Gunny eyed the man dressed in civilian clothes, and decided he had the earmark of an officer, not only that, he looked like a killer with an ax to grind. His two buddies didn't look like slouches either. "Hey, we were only kidding around, you know, service rivalry *and* all that shit. No harm, no foul. We lost a couple of buddies after spending ten days in the bush, and we're a little worse for wear." The gunnery sergeant croaked.

"Out-fucking-standing, let cooler heads prevail, we have enough problems in d'Nam as is. Belly-up to the bar, Marines, and let us *Snake Eaters* buy y'all a drink." Harvey motioned the Marines on down. "We'll swap war stories and determine who the *badest* liar in the valley."

As it turned out, Blake had flunked out of Notre Dam after his freshman year and joined the Army. Unlike Cleat and Coon, however, he chose OCS and received a commission as a second lieutenant. After going through Ranger School he went straight into the Special Forces. He was now a 1st Lieutenant serving as executive officer on an A- team located in the Delta. Harvey had less than three months to go on his tour of duty, and a little less than a year before his enlistment was fulfilled. The three of them spent the rest of the night talking of home, the championship game, and their plans on going back to college. Around 2300 hours they called it an evening and promised to stay in touch once they were settled in.

During three days of indoctrination Cleat and Coon learned more than they really thought was possible after all of their prior training. Overall they were impressed with their instructors' knowledge of Vietnam, and the insurgents they would be dealing with. At 0830 on the morning of their fourth day they were flying in a Huey thirty five hundred feet above the hot, suffocating heat pervading the air at ground level. The two hour flight to their 'A' camp deep in the central highlands was exhilarating. The steady whomp-whomping of the rotors and the cool crisp air was refreshing and the scenery below was breathtaking. It was hard to believe there were men waging war in such a beautiful land. In the distance they could see a humongous waterfall cascading off of a mountain surrounded by fluffy clouds. Before long, the steady drumming and vibration of the craft lulled them into a light slumber. Less than an hour into their flight the crew chief nudged them awake and yelled they were diverting to a patrol on the run and for them to lock and load.

"How far out?" Cleat yelled above the noise. The pounding in Cleat's chest sounded louder than the whirling rotors and wind rushing through the open doors. He watched as the gunner opened and closed his hand twice indicating ten minutes.

Coon gulped, this was the real deal. No more *training* exercises. Leaning into Cleat's shoulder he hollered into his ear. "No John Wayne bullshit, okay?"

Cleat looked into his friend's eyes and smiled, "John who?"

"Come on Cleat, I mean it man. Let's go by procedure."

"Don't worry Coon, just stick close to me."

"Like butt-ugly to your asshole."

The adrenaline pumping through Cleat's body was like a million needles pricking his skin. *Holy shit, is this what it's like?* All through training he never once felt the rush he was experiencing now. This was it. In the next few minutes they would be face to face with death. The thought was bothersome, but not overwhelming. What bothered him most was being killed before ever having the chance to prove his worth. After going through every *elite* infantry school the Army had to offer *and* honed to become the best, it was unconscionable to believe it could all be for naught.

A sudden banking of the Huey startled them both as it dove nose-down toward the PZ. Coon's racing heart leapt to his throat and Cleat's knuckles turned bone-white as he gripped his M16 even tighter. Below them operatic clashes of violence were quickly metamorphosing into a violent fight for survival. A dozen or so of the enemy were less than fifty meters behind the beleaguered patrol and they were closing fast. Cleat prayed there was enough time to rescue the men before they were overtaken.

Cleat could see what appeared to be four Americans crashing through the waist high elephant grass. A soldier was half carrying and dragging a wounded comrade while the remaining two provided a meager rearguard action. Just when Cleat thought there was a glimmer of hope he saw another American fall. The soldier fought to regain his footing, but fell again. His buddy reached down, threw a shoulder underneath his arm and helped him to his feet. They were able to struggle forward a few meters before being knocked to the ground. The patrol was in dire straights, the enemy held the upper hand in mobility *and* firepower.

As the chopper made its final approach an RPG sailed across its stern, undeterred the pilot continued his daring maneuver while deadly steel perforated the chopper's thin skin. Miraculously the formidable Huey flew straight into the hailstorm retaliating with its own deadly arsenal.

The door gunner was hanging precariously out of the doorway strapped to his safety harness engaging the enemy with long bursts from his M-60. As the craft yawned to its right and dove for the small PZ the crew chief began signaling for Cleat and Coon to get ready.

When the chopper reached near ground level it flared its nose and came to a hover on a cushion of air sixty meters from the running patrol. Cleat and Coon jumped the remaining three feet into the flattened grass waving and shouting above the noise for the soldiers to hurry.

Everything seemed to be moving in slow motion as the battlegrounds ferocity swirled around him. His feet felt as if they were laden in cement. A millisecond later the wailing chaos transformed into clarity so shocking it almost spooked him. He became astutely aware of his surroundings *and* was cognizant of what needed to be done. A calming effect embraced his mind and body. This very place was a defining moment in his life *and* he knew it. As he was yelling encouragement to the running patrol the incessant hammering of the crew chief's machinegun fell silent. He whirled toward the open doorway and was about to scream for more firepower when he saw two of the enemy clad in black pajamas charging through waist-high grass. They were fifteen meters to his left firing their automatic AK-47's at point blank range. Cleat quickly leveled his M-16 and let loose a long sustained burst. He watched in fascination as the bodies twisted and fell out of sight.

"Cleat, they're in trouble." Coon yelled above the turmoil.

"Where!" Cleat tore his eyes from where the VC had fallen and looked across the sea of mustard-yellow.

"They're forty meters to our front and they're fagged-out." The steady downdraft from the Huey's blades was flattening a ten meter circle of grass underneath its shadow; Cleat stood just outside its circumference in an endless field of grass. The yellow-green blades swayed in the artificial breeze concealing everything beneath it.

"Goddammit, I can't see a fucking thing." Cleat squinted towards Coon.

Several AK-47 rounds snapped by Coon's ear causing him to crouch even lower. "They're on our November-echo and, they're hunkered down in the grass."

The patrol wasn't very far from where he and Coon stood, and *neither* was the enemy. When Cleat turned back to the chopper he was greeted with the lifeless form of the crew chief hanging from his straps. The door gunner on the opposite side was too preoccupied with his own troubles to realize his friend was dead. Cleat understood what that meant. The enemy was trying to outflank them. Out of the corner of his eye he caught the terrified look of the pilot. He was drenched in a cold sweat and rightfully so, the Plexiglas in front of him had been shattered in several places. The driver's misgivings were prevalent and near panic. If he and Coon didn't get the situation under control in the next few seconds they were going to be left behind.

"Cleat grabbed his friend by the collar and pulled him close. "Jump on the chopper and get that *sixty* back in action. Lay down a suppressing fire while I bring them in."

"You got it." Coon threw his M-16 on the chopper and hopped onboard.

"Don't let them leave without us." Cleat hollered over his shoulder.

A thumbs-up was Coon's only answer. Cocking the machinegun he let loose a burst of 7.62 steel jacketed rounds in the general direction of the enemy.

As an afterthought he retrieved the crew chiefs headset and slipped it on and was instantly in communication with the pilot and copilot.

Coon keyed the mike, "he's like fucking John Wayne…he'll bring 'em in, so hang tough and don't leave without 'em."

"We ain't got long, but we'll give you all we got *and* some." The pilot's voice was shaky, but full of resolve. "We've got gunships on the way…they're two mikes out. Just keep the gooks off our ass until then."

Thank God. Coon thought, as he opened up on a dark image slithering through the grass twenty meters to his immediate front. He gave the still form and extra burst just to make sure the fucker was dead. *Come-on Cleat get your ass back here. We ain't got a whole lot 'a time.*

Cleat ran in a crouch straight to where he hoped the patrol was located. He covered the forty meters in less than five seconds. Bullets were screaming overhead and snipping at the grass when he accidentally stumbled onto the huddled men.

"Give me an abbreviated SITREP." His question was addressed to the nearest soldier.

"I'm okay but we have one dead two wounded."

"Are the wounded ambulatory?" Cleat didn't bother to look. He was more concerned with the enemy.

"Jenkins is hit in the shoulder, but he can still hump. Wallace is gut shot and has a busted leg. Washington's dead."

"Do you and the wounded still have your weapons?"

"Fuck yeah. We're hard-charging Rangers…not a bunch of fucking legs."

Cleat faced the man he'd been speaking to and was surprised to see how young he appeared. Except for his dull hardened eyes he barely looked out of his teens. "Okay, which one of you is Jenkins?" An even younger looking soldier raised a bloody hand.

"That'd be me."

"Jenkins I want you to lead the way. The chopper is forty meters to our November-Whiskey. Prepare to move out." When Jenkins took off Cleat asked the unwounded soldier his name.

"Craven."

"Craven I want you to help Washington and I'll bring Wallace in. That's the plan. Let's move out."

Cleat placed Washington over Craven's shoulder and headed him towards the chopper and safety.

"Wallace, this might hurt some, but we got to get you to the chopper ASAP."

"Fuck the hurt; just get my sorry ass on that chopper."

Cleat hoisted Wallace in a fireman's carry and made for the chopper. As the enemy fire increased to a deafening roar two UH-1 gunships suddenly appeared over the PZ. They made several strafing runs with miniguns and rockets spitting death from above. There was never a more beautiful sight.

When he reached the craft there was scantly enough time for him to lift Wallace into awaiting hands and climb onboard. No sooner had his ass hit the deck the chopper snapped forward skimming across the grass. Within seconds they were cruising at 180 knots three thousand feet above the tropical rain forest. Every living soul on the chopper was in a similar state of shock, moments before all seemed lost and now they were relatively safe. It was a moment in time when sanity replaced the madness of combat and Cleat was glad that he was able to overcome the gut wrenching fear that had threaten to paralyze him.

Cleat stared at his shaking hands. Was it nerves or adrenalin? He didn't know or care, but he didn't want anyone else to see them. Hiding them under his arms he leaned forward and tried to digest what had happened. His *cherry* was busted sooner than expected and he had done his job without coming unglued. His doubts of how he would react under fire were no more, at least that questioned had been answered. He had preformed in an alien environment as if he were an experienced combat veteran and his friend had done likewise.

He'd killed two men and felt no revulsion in doing so. Did that make him a cold sadistic killer, or did it happen so fast the reality of his deed hadn't set in? He didn't know, and right now he didn't really give a shit one way or the other. He was just glad that he and Coon were still alive and they'd preformed heroically under extreme duress. Heroically…should he consider himself a hero? As a kid he'd always dreamed of becoming one, one that led the charge and saved the day, but those were childish dreams manifested by youthful imaginations. He was often considered a hero by others, but that was on the field of athletics. Something told Cleat heroes in Vietnam weren't long for this world.

Closing his eyes he rested his head against the vibrating bulkhead and drifted into a dream world of chaotic noise and confusion. Vivid snapshots of their harrowing experience were racing through his mind when something tugged at his sleeve.

"Thanks Sarge. If not for you we'd be cold-assed, dead motherfuckers."

Cleat tried to remember the Ranger's name, but couldn't place it at the moment. "No sweat Ranger, but we all had a hand in it, especially the pilots. It took brass balls to sit in the cockpit while all hell was busting loose."

"Yeah, I suppose so, and we're grateful, but it took a lot of guts for you to bring us in. We owe you one."

"You'd of done the same for us."

"I'd like to think so, but you never know until your shits in the wringer. By the way what's your name and where're you from?"

"Cleat…Cleat Davis, from Lakewood, Florida."

"Damn glad to meet'cha Cleat. I'm Joe Craven from Evansville, Indiana." Joe held his hand out.

"Same here Joe." Cleat was caught off guard when Joe's hand clasped his forearm.

"That's the way Rangers shake hands over here Cleat."

Cleat's grin was infectious. "Evansville is a nice town. When I was with the 101st at Fort Campbell my buddy and I," Cleat nodded at Coon, "went to their annual jazz festival."

Craven laughed, "Man that sure brings back memories. In 91 days I'll be heading back home, and I can hardly wait. How long do you have left in-country?"

Cleat smiled, "Oh I'd say about 361 days give or take a few."

"Shit! You mean to tell me you guys just got here?"

"I'm afraid so." Cleat laughed at Joe's incredulous expression. "And if this is anything like what the next twelve months are gonna be like then I'm ready to take the next flight home."

Joe joined in Cleat's nervous laughter. "Join the Army and travel *free* to exciting and exotic lands." Joe pondered a moment before continuing. "In all seriousness Cleat, the Rangers and Green Beanies see the worst of the worst. Be sure and keep your powder dry and your head down because Uncle Ho's boys are ass-kickers and widow-makers. They can fuck-up your world in a heartbeat. Of the original one hundred and thirty seven men that came over here with Charlie Company, 75th Ranger Regiment there ain't but a few of us left to talk the talk and walk the walk."

"I'll keep that in mind Joe, and thanks for painting such a pretty picture. It warmed the cockles of my heart."

"I ain't so sure what the fuck a *cockle* is but, 'Brother Charles' will light your ass up when you least expect it." Joe leaned back, "Cleat if you ever run into trouble call on Charlie Company 75th Rangers and we'll come a' running."

"Thanks Joe, if the time comes I'll be sure and hold you to that."

"You've got it brother." Joe settled into a more comfortable position and closed his eyes thus signaling the end of their brief conversation.

Cleat knew the Grim Reaper had been canvassing the PZ in earnest, and this time he and Coon escaped his clutches. If there was a next time, and he was sure there would be, would they be so fortunate?

The open doorways and high elevation brought fresh clean air howling through the cabin. The sweat once running profusely between their shoulder blades, down their faces, and saturating their fatigues became cool areas of discomfort. With the passing of forty minutes and a few stolen moments of shut-eye the banged up Huey landed at the Army Ranger Camp. Within seconds a crowd of backslappers and well-wishers appeared. Coon and Cleat stood tall amongst the congratulatory Rangers.

The pilots climbed out of their jockey seats amidst a downdraft of billowing dust particles and maneuvered through the assembly until they reached Cleat. The pilot, a CW4, slapped him on the shoulder and grinned.

"You did one hell of a thing Sergeant. You can ride with me anytime and, by the way, tell your buddy I said John Wayne ain't got shit on you."

The peter-pilot shook his head in wonderment, "Man I don't think I could 'a done what you did. That was just plain fucking crazy."

Cleat looked at the copilot in disbelief, "I guess with all of those bullets hitting your chopper you thought you were safer than a bug in a rug behind that fucking Plexiglas. Hell, at least I had some grass to hide behind."

"Oh yeah, you're right." The copilot ruffled the floppy hat on top of Cleat's head, "I forgot how much those blades of grass were going to protect your skinny ass. Pardon the fuck out 'a me."

CW4 Bill Priestly shook hands with Cleat and Coon, "You boys take it easy tonight. Ol' Betsy done us good, but the ol' girl is shot to hell and back. A replacement will be flying in early tomorrow morning. We should be ready to depart by 0900."

Before the older man could leave, Cleat caught him by the sleeve of his flight suit, "I'm sorry about your door gunner, he did a hell of a job pinning the VC down. If it hadn't of been for his suppressing fire none of us would've made it."

"Yeah, he was a good man and we're gonna miss him."

"Yes sir, and thanks again for getting us the hell out a there."

"That's why they pay us the big bucks son; flight pay is what it's all about…that and three squares a day."

Cleat started to reply, but Coon jerked him backwards and hollered is his ear.

"Hey Cleat, they're talking about free beer and whores. These are my kind of people brother." Coon was grinning from ear-to-ear.

As the celebration was breaking up on the helipad an ambulance pulled next to the chopper and loaded Wallace and Jenkins onto stretchers and rushed them to the hospital with sirens blaring. Soon after a second ambulance arrived and carried Washington and the crew chief away. No lights, no sirens…the dead were in no hurry.

That night at the NCO Club, Cleat and Coon were privy to all the Rangers had to offer and then some. Cleat had never seen such a hard-drinking bunch of men, and most of them didn't stop until they dropped. As promised, dozens of girls were present and Coon hooked up with two lovely ladies right out of the chute. During the waning hours of night, or was it morning, a beautiful Eurasian led a slightly drunken Cleat down the wayward path of sexual deprivation. By late morning the two Green Berets were at the chopper pad sitting on sandbags paying dearly for their indiscretions.

A disgruntled Coon muttered, "That's the army for you…hurry up and wait. Where is that fucker anyway? We were supposed to be out'a here by 0900."

Cleat rubbed his throbbing temples and choked back the burning bile threatening to spew from his mouth. He started to answer his friend's whining question, but reasoned it wasn't worth the effort.

"Cleat, I have a question. Do you feel as bad as you look?"

"Worse." Unfortunately he was being truthful. His head was about to explode, his eyes felt like somebody ran sandpaper over them. Not only was he fighting nausea, somehow during his romp in the sack with *what's her name* he must've contorted his back in some god awful configuration. The end results were: he'd either twisted something out of kilter *or* pulled a muscle because it was killing him.

"Same here, but if I had last night to do over again I wouldn't change a fucking thing. Christ almighty those girls couldn't get enough of me."

"Coon, do me favor. If I ever try attempting whatever it was I did last night just save me the pain and shoot my ass."

Craven approached his new friends with a radiant smile on his face. "You two look like the walking dead. I thought you Special Forces dudes were mean motherfuckers and bad go-getters."

"Then you've been brainwashed just like us." Cleat tried to force a smile but it hurt too much.

"Here, take a couple of these, they'll make you feel better." Craven opened the palm of his hand and offered them four little pills.

"What are those?" Coon asked.

"I don't know but they work like a champ."

As bad as he felt Cleat was tempted, but neither of them had ever done drugs before and he wasn't planning on starting now, no matter how terrible he felt. "Thanks Joe, but drugs aren't our thing."

"Shit man, I'm not offering you drugs. The medic gave them to me when I told him how hung over you boys were. I promise this shit is army issue."

Coon held out an eager hand. "Fuck it man. I don't give a shit what it is if it'll make me feel better. I've never felt so bad in my entire life; if I'm lying I'm dying. I need a fucking miracle to get me over last night."

"You two and half the fucking company is out of sorts." Joe laughed as he dropped the pills in their outstretched hands. I heard from CQ it will be about another twenty minutes before your chopper arrives. Let's go over and wash these little beauties down with a couple of beers."

"Hot damn, what does it take to volunteer for this outfit?" Coon reached down to help Cleat to his feet.

"Not much buddy. The number one requirement is to have a mental lapse when they ask for volunteers. After that you have to fail the sanity test." Joe was still laughing at his joke when they entered the club.

Cleat paused, "How come I've never heard of the 75th Ranger Regiment. Both Coon and I went to Ranger School and nobody ever mention a regiment made entirely of Rangers."

"It's a concept based on the accomplishments of Rangers during WW II and Korea. We're an advance party. They wanted to get the best Company over to Vietnam ASAP and start kicking ass. They figured it'd be good to have a real fighting force over here since the Green Berets mostly sit around their camps and baby-sit. The higher-ups want an elite outfit like us to show the Gooks we're the badest motherfuckers in the jungle."

Cleat laughed and was astutely reminded of the pounding in his head. "I hope your elocutionary description of our primary mission is as easy as you orate, but somehow I believe it's not going to be as placid as you describe."

"Damn Cleat, you're talking way over my head and most everybody else's I know. This ain't college brother; this is one badass war zone. If you want to communicate with the men my best advice is to talk down to their level. I ain't disrespecting you none, an education is a fine thing, but shit man, you gotta get real. The grunts are gonna think you're speaking a foreign language and not understand half the words that come out of your mouth. Only officers talk like that and us grunts don't pay much attention to them unless they wallow in the mud with us."

"You're right Joe, but it's hard to quit when it's been drilled into you since birth. I'll take your sound advice and watch how I phrase my words."

At 1220 hours the replacement chopper arrived while Cleat and Coon were eating chow with Joe and a handful of his close friends. The usual bull-shit flew around the table with a couple of bawdy jokes thrown in to keep the conversation less than civil. Once they were through it was time to say their goodbyes. After settling into the ill comfort of the Huey's stark interior it wasn't long before they were fast asleep. An hour later the chopper approached the A-camp they would be calling home for the next several months.

It was a primitive encampment built roughly in the shape of a triangle, and it was surrounded with concertina wire fifty meters deep. The jungle was cleared around the camp for at least two hundred meters, and three bulldozers were hard at work clearing even more vegetation. A sheer cliff dropping several hundred feet to a rocky gorge protected the southwest corner of the camp.

As the Huey made its final approach to the landing pad dozens of men were bending over holding on to their soft covers trying to protect themselves from the swirling sand. The large welcoming committee was more than Cleat and Coon expected.

Shouldering their B-4 bags stuffed with everything but the kitchen sink they jumped off the chopper and were unceremoniously shoved aside while a line was quickly formed to offload much-needed supplies. After recovering from their soaring spirits being deflated by the naiveté of their own self-importance, Cleat and Coon joined the ragtag labor force of Americans and Montagnards.

When the last crate reached the end of the line a boyish looking soldier, shirtless and dressed in cut-off jungle fatigues approached them with a friendly smile. With each step a cloud of dry powdery dust exploded around his primitive looking pair of sandals made out of what looked tire treads.

"Hi, I'm Lieutenant Nicolas Gregorio, XO of this paradise. I take it you two are Davis and Truman, man are we glad to see you turtles." The lieutenant stepped between the two replacements and placed his hands on their shoulders. "Come with me, and I'll introduce you to the rest of the team."

"We're glad to be here Lieutenant." Cleat was slightly uncomfortable with the young lieutenant's familiarity.

"We'll see about that Sergeant Davis. In a couple of weeks I'll check back and see how happy you truly are. Oh, by the way, those Rangers you pulled out of the craper yesterday put both of you in for the Silver Star. I've never heard of anybody winning a medal that's been in-country less than a week, but the unexpected happens over here all the time."

"We just did what we've been trained to do Lieutenant." Cleat was thrilled and humbled that the Rangers thought their deed was worthy of a medal.

"I wouldn't get my hopes all bent outta shape on the Silver Star, it'll probably be downgraded to a Bronze Star with a "V" device for Valor. Now, that's not to say what you did doesn't warrant a Silver Star, but the higher-ups don't much care for us elitist. If you men are looking for medals the SF is the wrong outfit."

"No sir, we're here to make a difference." Cleat wasn't sure whether or not he was going to like the lieutenant. Something about him was grating.

"How about you Sergeant Truman, your name doesn't fit. You look Italian to me. Do you have relatives in the old country?"

"I'm not real sure of my heritage, but I don't think so. My dad claims we have some Native American blood running through out veins"

"Dammit, that's the problem with the Forces...there ain't enough Italians among us. Not to worry, I hear that both of you speak French and Spanish. Spanish ain't gonna help much in d'Nam, but French sure as hell will. A lot of the gooks speak French over here and that's a good thing."

"Uh, LT...why'd you call us turtles?" Coon asked quizzically.

"That's what we call all replacements...they're damn slow in getting here."

"Gotcha'." Coon liked the young lieutenant's personality. He wasn't like any officer he'd ever met, and he defiantly like his mode of dress.

CHAPTER 15

It was hard to believe they'd been in camp for three months, but on the other hand there were times when it seemed like a lifetime. Upon their arrival they were informed as to what had happened to the original team members they were replacing. It turned out they were wounded by harassing mortar fire from the local VC, and sent to the hospital at Camp Drake, Japan for further recovery. More than likely their next stop would be the good ol' USA. Their injuries weren't life threatening, and it was merely by happenstance they were wounded at all. As luck would have it the two men just happened to be in the wrong place at the wrong time. The indiscriminate shelling of the fledgling camp began with the first shovel of sod and it continued at least twice a week since then. In retrospect the A-Team was fortunate not to have suffered numerous casualties over the past ten months.

The primary mission of camp A-432 was that of force-multipliers and intelligence gathering from the infiltration routes branching off the Ho Chi Min Trail. Patrols were sent out twice daily at different times to prevent any predictability in their movements. The patrols rarely lasted more than two days, and more often than not provided very little intelligence. Occasionally they got lucky by killing, or capturing a few VC in preset ambushes, but they were never able to bag any NVA. Intelligence claimed regulars were in the AO, and from time to time they would find evidence they were about, but no visuals. The camp's main battle force was comprised of Montagnards from the Rhade tribe. They were fierce, dedicated warriors who not only hated the North Vietnamese, but all Vietnamese in general. In most cases their loyalties to the Special Forces were irrefutable.

"What do you think Cleat?" Coon sat on his bunk reassembling his M-16.

"About what?"

"Bong Thuot."

"I don't know anymore than you. If I recall, you were sitting next to me at the briefing."

Coon sighed in disgust. "Dammit Cleat, you know what I mean. What's your gut feeling?"

"I don't have one, but apparently you do so spit it out."

"Well for one thing it's not in our AO, and for another, no ones reconnoitered the area in over three years. We're walking into this fucking place blind as bats, *and* to make things even *worse* we have to call on the fucking *Marines* to bail our ass out of the wringer if we run into trouble."

"Marines are good people, Coon."

"Maybe so, but they're not our people." Before laying his weapon on the bed he replaced the magazine and pulled the slide back to chamber a round, his final step was to make sure the rifle's safety was on. Coon didn't like counting on *anybody* that wasn't directly connected to the Special Forces, especially since their last mission. The CIA ran that one and as the Aussies would say: *it was bloody bonkers from the begin mate.*

"I'm gonna take some downtime and write home, and I suggest you do the same." Grabbing some stationary Cleat began with: *Dear Mandy,* and that's as far as he got. Cleat had written Mandy more than a dozen times and she hadn't answered one of them. He crumpled the paper and pulled out another one.

Dear Family,

As usual the weather is lousy and Coon and I miss y'all terribly, especially your home cooking...

When Air America's black unmarked helicopter dropped the team close to the Laotian border they disembarked with sterile clothes and weapons. Both Cleat and Coon were carrying AK-47's and their tribesmen were equipped with MAT-49 French sub machineguns. Once their team of four loin-clothed Montagnards unlawfully crossed the border into Laos the reconnaissance mission began to quickly unravel. The CIA officer in charge of their infiltration arbitrarily *changed* the whole ballgame. Now, the once *simple* but dangerous recon had turned into a complicated *snatch and grab.* Not only that, they were ten klicks away from where they needed to be to carry out the change in plans.

Originally the mission was to last three days and two nights, but it turned into seven days and six nights of hell. It took them two days of hard travel through rice paddies and patches of jungle to reach the new location. Their primary target was a political officer who was traveling with a contingent of four to six guards. Supposedly he was a high ranking officer in the NVA and was extremely knowledgeable of the branches leading off the Ho Chi Minh Trail into Vietnam. Intelligence had him arriving at the small fishing village of Muang Sam on the 6th. Cleat's patrol was in position the night before.

The two friends were awake most of the night trying to figure the best way to accomplish their mission, but they were unable to come up with a set plan except to lay in wait and hope for luck. Six men attempting to ambush a likely number was not a good idea. Too many things could go wrong, and often times that was exactly what happened when you pressed the envelope. An advantage of two to one was minimally acceptable, three to one was optimal.

They both agreed it was best to divide the team in two. Coon was on the opposite side of the path with two of the scantly clad Montagnards and Cleat lay concealed on his side with the others. Buon, the tribal chief's nephew was on his right.

"We catch...you wait they come." Buon grinned at Cleat.

"Let's hope your right Buon." The small fifteen year old kid was all fight. It's what he lived for, and Cleat was glad Buon was with him.

From 0700 till 1430 the trail was sparsely used. A handful of farmers, villagers, and children passed, but nothing that could be misconstrued as the enemy. At 1752 it became deadly serious. Thirty meters from where they lay in wait, five men wearing NVA uniforms came into view. Cleat could tell by the officer's tab he was a full colonel. The four man security force traveling with him ranked from private to sergeant. Cleat caught Coon's attention to make sure he was aware of the approaching enemy, he was. Cleat held his hands in front of his face with opposing palms facing each other and interlaced his fingers twice in a rapid motion. Coon nodded that he understood. Cleat whispered to Buon in broken English what his plans were and asked him to relay the information to the young boy lying next to him, who happened to be Buon's cousin.

When the enemy came abreast of their hiding place, Cleat, Coon, and the Montagnards broke from cover and converged on the startled enemy. No shots were fired and no resistance was given. Coon motioned with his rifle for the colonel to step away from his men.

Cleat grabbed the nervous colonel and escorted him further down the trail to ensure privacy. He spoke softly in French telling his prisoner that he need not be afraid and if he cooperated no harm would come to him.

While he was busy with his interrogation the Rhades' huddled the rest of the captives' and tied their hands behind their backs. When the deed was done they shoved them to the ground with more force than necessary. Before Cleat and Coon realized what was happening the natives pounced on the frightened prisoners and slit their throats *and* whacked-off their ears.

Less than three words of condemnation escaped from Cleat's mouth when the trail was filled with bullets zinging through the air. Multiple wet smacking sounds toppled two of the Montagnards before anyone could react to the hostile fire. With Coon's AK-47 hammering in his ear Cleat got a glimpse of the attacker and the first thing he noticed was the Chinese radio he was carrying. The last he saw of the NVA straggler was a shade of khaki disappearing around a bend in the trail. Cleat new they were in serious trouble. If the radio operator hadn't communicated with his superiors beforehand he was surely going to do so. It was only a matter of time before their AO would be crawling with hunter-killer teams seeking retribution.

It was imperative for the team to be extracted ASAP *and* as far as Cleat knew the *nearest* PZ was over ten klicks away. Haste was the number one priority and their only shield would be darkness. Cleat glanced at his Rolex…it wouldn't be completely dark for another hour. He had Coon get on the horn and call in a SITREP to inform the case handler of their plight *and* ask if there was a closer PZ…there wasn't. Thirty minutes later they ran into trouble crossing one of a dozen dikes' separating a patchwork of rice paddies. A group of ragtag Pathet Lao opened up on them from a stand of bamboo on the far side. Buon's thirteen year old cousin crumpled to the ground without a whimper. His small body slid down the mud slope into the murky waters of a bacterial infested paddy.

Advancing into the withering firepower was suicidal, thus leaving them no other option, but to retrace their steps *and* to do so post haste. Being compromised was a problem. It wouldn't take the enemy long to figure out *who* they were and *where* they were headed. PZ Annabelle was no longer attainable, if they were to reach the border they had to travel eastwardly. With the NVA Colonel in tow they reached the other side without further contact and sought cover behind a tool shed and tried gathering their thoughts. Cleat's brow furrowed as he studied the dark silhouette of a mountain looming in the distance.

It was northeast of where they stood and it silently called to him.

Eight and a half hours later and cloaked in darkness they lay resting in the fringes of a heavily vegetated jungle filled with rocks and boulders. A call sign from Coon to the case officer went unanswered. Over the next four hours he tried again and again and was rewarded with the same results, dead silence, except for squelch. Half way up the torturous mountain they picked out an NDP, ate their last ration of food and settled in for the night. The following day at 1738 hours they lastly attained the summit. Coon immediately tried calling base on the weakened PRC-25 and to his surprise someone answered the call sign.

Cleat could tell that Coon was having grave difficulty talking to whoever was on the other end. "Here, give me the damn thing."

"Be my guest but don't get your hopes up."

Cleat put the handset to his ear, "Salamander this is Crazy Horse actual over."

"Roger Crazy Horse…Salamander here…over."

"We have one Papa-Oscar-Whiskey…one indig left, and my Tonto…we need Black Beauty on the morn…over."

"Crazy Horse what's your local…over."

"November Echo on top of "Old Smokey" and there's plenty of room for extraction." Cleat hoped that the man understood his cryptic analogy.

"Read you loud and clear but no can do on Black Beauty…"

"Salamander say again." Cleat couldn't believe his ears.

"You must cross the yellow brick road to ride Black Beauty…over.

Cleat knew the man was referring to the border. "Salamander this is Crazy Horse…you're talking about a four-bagger…over."

"Roger the reference, but it's the best we can do Crazy Horse…over."

"Salamander…we're out of Wheaties and low on juice…Alexander Bell won't last another day."

"Sorry…we've all got problems…Salamander over and out."

"I'm looking forward to a face to face Salamander…Crazy Horse actual over and out." Seething with anger Cleat handed the receiver back to Coon.

"They're bailing on us aren't they?"

"Yep."

"Why?"

"Your guess is as good as mine, but I aim to find out."

After four days of torturous humping over unbelievable terrain they managed to cross the border into Vietnam. Descending the mountain had been a bitch, but luck was on their six *and* God was walking point. Their bodies were depleted of energy and they were bone tired. They were fortunate enough to ford several streams so water hadn't been a problem, but food turned out to be a real motherfucker *and* an ass-kicker. Their stomachs were shrunken and tender to the touch.

They lay resting in a patch of jungle bordering a rice paddy and lethargy was threatening to envelope their minds. Cleat was aware of hallucinating twice before, at least he thought it was only twice. Hell he might be hallucinating now. They needed food and they needed it now. They hadn't been in communications with anybody since their last night on the mountain. The spare battery for the PRC-25 had run its course and the radio was nothing but dead weight. Cleat suggested for Coon to destroy it and throw the damn thing away, to which his friend willingly complied.

"Sergeant...Sergeant, I hear plane." Buon stood over his sergeant gently slapping him in the face.

Cleat could hear Mandy calling for him. He wasn't sure why she was addressing him by rank instead of using his name, but it didn't matter. Most importantly she was here and she wanted him. Forcing his eyes open he was surprised to see her hovering over him with barely any clothes on.

"Mandy. My God Mandy it's been so...so long."

Buon was confused by his leader's words, but the sound of the plane was more important than trying to interrupt his meaning. "Sergeant I hear plane...come quick. You me go see."

"Wh...what?" Cleat was thoroughly befuddled.

"Plane...we go now."

His mind wavered and then focused to the reality of where he was. "Where?"

"Quick...come...we go." Buon helped Cleat to his feet and all but dragged him into the open.

A single engine spotter plane commonly referred to as a *Bird Dog* was flying low over the paddy. Cleat fumbled in his pocket and pulled out a signal mirror reinforced with green tape and flashed an S.O.S. at the plane. It took three tries before the plane acknowledged his signal. Rushing back to the jungle with newfound enthusiasm he woke Coon and revived the Colonel. It took less than an hour for the CIA's black helicopter to arrive on the scene and pick them up. Forty-five minutes later they were landing at their original disembarkation sight. A crowd of South Vietnamese officers of varying rank were gathered around the CIA OIC, Thomas Pearlman. Two additional Caucasians were dressed identically as Pearlman in light khaki bush jackets and matching pants. Shoulder holsters crisscrossed their chest. They seemed anxious for their prize catch to be off-loaded. Unfortunately for Pearlman, Cleat was the first to jump off of the Huey.

Pearlman extended his hand, "Damn fine job ol' chum."

Cleat knocked him on his ass with a straight right that landed dead center between the agent's eyes. Cleat straddled Pearlman and grabbed his chickenshit safari jacket around the lapels and yanked his befuddled, semiconscious face within inches of his own. Cleat snarled through clinched teeth, "If I ever hear of you leaving men behind again I will hunt you down *and* rip your heart out. Remember my words asshole." With that said Cleat shoved the man back to the tarmac and stood surveying his surroundings.

"We got your back Cleat."

Cleat acknowledged his friend and Buon holding their sub machineguns gut-level at Pearlman's entourage. "Let's go home Coon."

"Wait a damn minute asshole." Pearlman scrambled to his feet trying to save face. "It wasn't like that at all *and* who in the hell do you think…" Thomas Pearlman almost choked on his own words when Sergeant Davis whirled around and pointed the AK-47 a foot from his pounding chest. The loaded weapon was scary, but the cold blue eyes of the sergeant had a deathly chilling effect. They were the eyes of death and it frightened him to the core. His skin tingled and his insides were in turmoil. He couldn't tear his eyes from the sergeant's icy stare. It wasn't like he hadn't experience danger in the past, after all he was on his second tour, but this was something far different. The darkest of thoughts encompassed his very being. Somehow he knew beyond a shadow of doubt if another word escaped from his trembling lips they would be his last.

"Come on Cleat, he ain't worth it man."

Karl Offenhimer, the big burley thirty-nine year old master sergeant, from Burlington, Minnesota reluctantly proceeded to the team house in search of Cleat and Coon. In the dank confines of the less than pleasant smelling hootch he found them playing a low stakes game of hearts with Torres and Wilson. "Da mission's been scrubbed men. The Higher-ups want da Rangers to handle it. Dey feel da Rangers are better equipped." Karl's English was getting better but there was no disguising his Germanic heritage.

"Well kiss my fucking ass Karl. I thought we were the best of the best." Coon threw his cards down, "Goddammit, I was raring to go and then you come in spouting a bunch of bullshit. I bet some fucking leg had a hand in making that misguided assumption."

"Ya know what Coon, sometimes I tink you are crazier din dat mad hatter." Offenhimer laughed as he shook his head.

"You big fucking Kraut, you don't even know what the fuck a mad hatter is."

"Dat might be da case but you are *still* fuckin' crazy."

"Shit Coon, all you've been doing since the word came down about this mission is bitch like a whore crying to her pimp. Sit your ass down and finish playing cards." TJ Wilson teased.

"Yeah Coon, you're losing again *and* you owe everybody at the table. Your ass ain't vamoosing nowhere gringo." Torres shook an accusatory finger at Coon.

Offenhimer placed a fatherly hand on Cleat's shoulder. "Cleat, I've got some bad news for you and Truman, your friend Blake was badly wounded when his chopper went down a couple of days ago…He's in da hospital asking for y'all. I've arranged a hop with a re-supply bird in thirty minutes."

The chopper had to make two supply stops along the way, and it was an agonizing three hours before they finally landed at China Beach. Upon arriving at the hospital they were fortunate enough to see the doctor and learn the extent of their friend's injuries. Thirty minutes later they were still sitting in the doctors vacant office too stunned to move.

"Fuck, this shit can't be happening." Coon blurted rupturing the morbid silence.

Coon's sudden outburst awakened Cleat from a remorseful state of mind,

"Well it did and prolonging the inevitable isn't gonna make it any easier. Let's get this over with." His words sounded angry and callous, but that was not his intent.

Even though Cleat and Coon were informed of their friend's injuries they weren't prepared to see Blake lying in a fitful slumber. Hanging overhead from a stainless steel pole were several bottles of clear liquid with tubes running into his body. A respirator was plugged into the wall with a tube leading to his throat where they'd preformed an emergency tracheotomy. The noise of the machine was dolefully depressing. The white linen sheets covering his ravaged body lay flat on the mattress below his knees. Cleat struggled to hold the scream of anguish threatening to leap from his throat…Coon uttered an oath under his breath and choked back a sob.

Cleat stepped quietly to Blake's bedside and plucked a tissue from a half-empty box of Kleenex. He folded the tissue in half and gently wiped the perspiration from his friend's forehead. When the young First Lieutenant's eyes fluttered open, they were glazed from drugs. "Hey Blake, it's me Cleat…I brought John with me as soon as we heard you were wounded."

Blake weakly clasped Cleat's outstretched hand. "My legs are gone," was all he was able to rasp before he began to cry. Cleat leaned over, cradling Blake in his arms and unashamedly cried with him.

Coon turned his back unable to watch. Rubbing the tears from his eyes he wondered if it was worth the sacrifice. The futility of it all seemed senseless. Brave young men were dying and being horridly wounded in a country none of them had ever heard of four years ago. How many more lives would be maimed or lost before it would end?

It took awhile for Harv to regain his composure and Coon saw Cleat struggling with his own. Coon couldn't deal with the emotional scene. It made him extremely uncomfortable. Even though the Davis's had taught him love and compassion over the past ten years he was still reluctant to let anyone else get too close. Unintentionally, and unknowingly, his dad was responsible for the invisible barrier, and on most occasions it was impenetrable. Only a trusted few were privy to his inner sanctum…Harv was one of those.

The summer following their senior year Harv was a constant presence at the beach house. While the three of them played, partied, and worked out together they became close friends who willing shared their dreams, wants, and desires. In the beginning Coon was upset when Cleat invited Harv to participate in their last summer before becoming young adults, but in a matter of days Harv's infectious personality won him over. It was a summer filled with cherished memories and now his friend was a mangled and emotional crippled. Coon was at a loss for words, and there was nothing he could do or say to make Harv feel better.

"What am I going to do Cleat. My life is over." Harv's words were inundated with fear.

"Don't talk crazy Harv. You've got your whole life ahead of you." Cleat reached out and held his friend's hand

"Yeah, as a fucking cripple. Is that how'd you...you'd like to live your life Cleat?"

"Nobody wants to experience a tragedy. Everybody wants to be strong and healthy, but people catch debilitating diseases everyday, and others survive crippling accidents but they go on to live happy successful lives. There are plenty of..."

"Thanks for the pep talk Cleat, but this is me you're talking to. My fucking legs are gone man. My life will be regulated to a wheelchair and wheelchairs can't do what I want to do. I want to fucking run for touchdowns and ride a bicycle, dance with my girl and go swimming. Hell I can't even drive a fucking car, and I'm sure as hell not gonna cruise around the drive-in hangout sitting in a chair with oversized wheels."

Cleat laughed at Harv's joke and started to sit at the foot of the bed but thought better of it.

"Go ahead and have a seat. There's plenty of room."

He didn't know whether to laugh or cry over Harv's morbid quip at humor, so he did neither. "Harv I've never known you to be a quitter, so why start now."

"Yeah, well I used to have two legs, but I left them out there in the fucking bush. I could say walk in my boots for a day, but I don't have any, nor will I ever need any."

"You still have a functional brain and a sense of humor, albeit blacker than a Bourbon Street whore's." Cleat lit a Salem and took a deep breath before slowly letting it filter between his lips. "You want a drag."

"No thanks, I never acquired the habit."

"Me neither, not until I joined the Army. Remember in basic when they used to say: "take ten, and smoke 'em if you got 'em." I never figured out what to do." Cleat waved his cigarette, "This is the end result." Cleat decided to accept Harv's previous offer and sat on the bed.

"I'm glad you and Coon could drop by. They're sending me to Japan in a couple of days for more surgery and then back to the States for rehab."

Coon stepped forward and placed a hesitant hand on Harv's shoulder. "I'm gonna see if I can find a Coke. Do y'all want one?"

"Yeah I'll take one, how about you Harv?"

"I can't. They're checking my fluid intake, but thanks anyway." Harv forced a smile, "God it's good to see y'all again, I just wish to hell it wasn't under these circumstances."

"I'll be back in a few." Coon was glad for the opportunity to leave. He needed a break. It was tearing him up inside to see Blake in his condition. The revelation that the same horror could happen to him and Cleat was disconcerting.

Coon stopped a medical orderly and asked for directions to the mess hall. After making two left turns his pace quickened when the aroma of food filtered down the hallway. When he pushed through the double doors he was surprised to see the mess hall was almost empty. Walking up to the serving line he stood behind two enlisted men dressed in hospital garb.

The taller of the two was complaining in a loud obnoxious voice about how busy they'd been over the past couple of days. "Christ, if you ask me, anybody dumb enough to volunteer for the airborne infantry deserves what he gets. What do you think their average IQ is...around 70? How pathetic is that?"

"Come on Clifford, don't be an asshole all your life. The 101st at Camp Eagle has been hit hard this week. They have families back home that are going to be devastated when they learn what happened to their love ones. Those boys are no different than the rest of us. They want to live and go back home in one piece and get on with their lives. Just because you were a premed student at Penn State doesn't make you better than they are.

"Donnie, fuck you and your sanctimonious ass, if my draft board would've accepted my claim as a conscientious objector I wouldn't even be in this fucked up war. Hell, I'd be protesting with the rest of the people who have enough sense to realize this fucking war is bullshit."

Coon was doing all he could to hold his temper in check, but inwardly he was about to explode. After waiting patiently for the two men to fill their trays they came to the end of the line where the desert section was displayed. There was a solitary piece of apple pie sandwiched between several slices of cherry. Apple pie was Coon's favorite of favorites, and when the whiner's bony hand reached for the last of the apple pie Coon grabbed his arm and squeezed.

"The apple pie is mine scum bag." Coon's grip tightened.

Clifford winched from the excruciating pain and turned to face his tormentor. What he saw made his Adams apple bobble. He found himself looking into brown pools of death. The soldier dressed in tiger fatigues emitted an aura of danger so prevalent it made Clifford's scrotum twitch. Incredulously, his mind raced with articulate, witty things he might say to challenge the acerbity of the man standing before him. That brief moment of insanity passed and better judgment won the day.

Clifford smiled, "Sure, be my guest…I like cherry just fine."

Coon handled the succulent prize and cold glass of milk like it was the Holy Grail. He moved to a table in the far corner and sat for a few minutes staring at the delicacies. It had been a long time. The crust wasn't as flakey as Grandma Marie's or Mama June's but it was a spectacular reminder of home. Coon hoarded over the delicacy as if he were a wild animal protecting a fresh kill. Fifteen minutes later a loud belch signified his approval, but coming to grips with an empty plate *and* the last drop of milk was another matter. He remembered someone saying: all good things must come to an end, whoever said that knew what the hell they were talking about. Reluctantly he pushed his chair away from the table and left the mess hall.

With two cokes in hand Coon made a sharp turn at the end of the hallway and almost ran headlong into Cleat.

"Blake's asleep. Let's leave this place." The whites of Cleat's eyes were streaked like a Rand McNally roadmap.

"Where do you want to go?"

"I might regret this later, but I'm willing to go wherever you feel like going."

"Here drink this." Coon handed Cleat the soft drink. "This might be the last nonalcoholic beverage you're gonna have in awhile."

After their merciful visit to the hospital they went to the nearest club and got hammered, *and* laid. The next morning they awoke in a downtown hotel with tremendous hangovers, and fiery, upset stomachs. Coon languished in a hot tub while Cleat attempted to shave without slicing his throat. They made a brief stop at the hospital to say their goodbyes and by 1140 they were at twenty-two hundred feet heading north with heavy hearts. Tomorrow would begin anew…searching for the elusive enemy.

The following morning Captain Brenner requested their presence in the team room, whereupon he informed them of Lieutenant Blake's death. Their friend had died alone, in the middle of the night from a blood clot. News of Blake's death was heart wrenching and it was the first time they had to deal with loosing a friend in Vietnam…it wouldn't be their last.

Although their friends death was tragic, both Cleat and Coon silently thought it was best that Blake died in his sleep. Harv didn't want to live as a cripple and neither did either of them. Everyday brought the possibility of death and everyone on the team knew their luck couldn't possibly hold out. Two many camps were being hit and too many Special Forces men were dying.

The camps fears were reinforced when twenty-four-year-old Staff Sergeant Timothy J. Wilson's lifeless body was brought through the gate on a makeshift stretcher. He had triggered a booby trap that severed his right arm *and* right leg, the communications sergeant died so quickly there wasn't enough time to call for a Dust-Off. The young sergeant from Morgantown, Pennsylvania had twenty-one days left on his tour of duty.

After Coon labeled Wilson "TJ" everyone called him that, and you could tell by his swagger he liked his nickname. Every time he talked of home and family you could hear the excitement in his voice. He was a good man, and one of two blacks on the team. TJ's good-natured personality and outrageous pranks were going to be sorely missed. His wife and two preschool children would miss him even more. Mrs. Tonya Wilson would receive notice of his death the day before their sixth wedding anniversary *and* a day before his eldest son's birthday.

Two weeks after Wilson's body was shipped stateside, Cleat and Coon led a five-day heavy patrol consisting of twenty tribesmen into the northwest section of their AO. Their mission was to recon a village being terrorized by the VC. On the second day they ran into trouble when the point guard crested a rise, and ran head-on into a reinforced company of NVA.

The enemy's initial onslaught of firepower was devastating. Four Montagnards from the scout element were killed outright and two were wounded, one of them seriously. The patrol quickly consolidated and returned fire. Although his patrol had temporarily slowed the enemy's advance with a withering volume of firepower, it was only a matter of time before the NVA realized they far outnumbered the beleaguered patrol. Cleat figured he had less than five minutes before the enemy would send out flankers and cut-off any chance of escape.

"Coon, I want you to stick with me. Buon pick eight of you best and have the rest carry the wounded to Dragonfly. Tell them to set up a defensive position."

"Yes sergeant."

"Coon, get on the horn and call it in."

While Coon was busy on the radio requesting gunships and an immediate extraction, Cleat helped two of the warriors hastily set out several Claymores to cover their retreat. The team needed to delay the enemy as long as possible. If they were extremely lucky it would be enough to slow the enemy's pursuit. Thankfully PZ Dragonfly was all-downhill from where they stood and only two klicks away.

As they hurriedly camouflaged several booby-traps Cleat's fear of a flanking attack came to fruition. A hail of automatic fire from an AK-47 zinged by his left ear and smacked into flesh. The Montagnard next to him slumped over with a neat round hole in the center of his naked chest. Six kaki-clad NVA converged on them with their assault rifles spewing rounds on both sides of the trail. Two more of his warriors were killed before the NVA was eliminated as a threat. The NVA seemed to be everywhere at once and the sound of warfare filled the air with screams, shouts, rifle fire, and explosions. It was beyond deafening.

Cleat shot another NVA when he charged through the bushes less than ten meters away. A half a dozen more were circling on his three o'clock when Buon and two of his tribesmen cut them down with automatic fire. The native squatting next to Buon suddenly collapsed. At present half of his patrol had been killed or wounded, if the attrition rate continued at this pace none of them would make it to the PZ.

Coon had dropped the handset of the PRC-25 and was firing well placed shots at a group hidden over the rise. Time was running out. They couldn't hold them off much longer. "Cleat they're massing to our front for an assault."

Cleat slipped the M-79 and ammo pouch off of the dead native lying at his feet and yelled, "Here, take this, you're better with it than I am."

Coon grabbed the weapon and loaded an HE round. Without using the sights he fired, reloaded and fired again. The canisters of high explosives landed just beyond the rise right where he intended.

Cleat pulled Coon close, "We need air support…Tell TOC whatever they can find, but we need it NOW!" Cleat took inventory of the able bodied men left. "We have to leave the dead…everybody else help with the wounded." He noticed the tribesmen reluctant expressions, but it was the only thing that made any sense if they were going to survive.

"Buon, tell your men we'll retrieve the bodies later."

"Yes Sergeant."

The rear guard had covered approximately two hundred meters when they heard the distant muffled explosions. If possible, his men quickened their pace. Within minutes of the Claymore's detonation, low-flying jets screamed overhead skimming the tree tops. Coon switched to tac-air and was in immediate contact with the jet-jockeys, seconds later you could hear their ordinance bombarding the trail behind them.

For the next hour and a half there was no further confrontation with the enemy. Cleat doubted his patrol was still being pursued, because of the air support covering their withdrawal. His next worry was whether or not the enemy had set-up a blocking force at PZ Dragonfly.

As they neared the PZ their ebullience heightened when they heard the extraction choppers circling above the trees. Through a small opening in the overhang Cleat surveyed the burned grass and blistered stumps that once was a flourishing meadow, all that was left was a scarred landscape barren of any living foliage for hundreds of meters. Somehow, against all odds they'd made it to the PZ. They were lucky, and he knew it. A C&C chopper was flying high above the PZ while three dust-offs were circling overhead with four gunships riding shotgun.

"Okay, the wounded board first. Coon let 'em know we're northeast of station and anything to our rear is a free fire zone. You and I will hold position until everyone's safely onboard. I'll pull security while you call it in." Cleat crawled to a large boulder next to a scraggly tree of unknown origin. He settled in and listened to the jungle for any telltale signs of the approaching enemy.

The lead dust-off peeled out of the sky and headed for the center of the PZ seventy-five meters from where the patrol lay hidden in the jungle. Cleat signaled for the Montagnards to move out.

"Me and Duen stay with you." Buon tugged at the sleeve of Cleat's fatigue shirt.

"No...go with your people. We will be okay. Go now!" Cleat ordered pointing in the direction of the hovering craft.

"Okay."

Cleat and Coon stayed behind while the rest of the men carried the wounded to the waiting chopper. He was relieved to see the bird take off with everybody safely onboard, all except for two men kneeling in the middle of the PZ with their rifles ready. The second Dust-Off landed beside them...the third chopper wouldn't be needed.

"Hey squirt, you still think you're faster than me?"

"You bet your ass, even with this forty-pound piece of shit on my back." Coon's grin was wider than Cleat's

"Loser buys the beer, brother."

"You're on, slowpoke."

Cleat and Coon burst from the jungles cover at breakneck speed...the first ten yards Coon was slightly ahead, but Cleat was slowly gaining on him as he thrust his longs legs forward, easily out striding his best friend. When he saw Coon stumble, a grin slid across his face as he passed him by. He could already taste the cold beer from the newly acquired refrigerator Torres scrounged from the CB's. The door gunner was forty meters away manning the M-60 spraying hot lead into the jungle. Buon and Duen added their suppressing fire as they stood outside the Huey.

As Cleat drew closer he noticed the crew chief waving frantically. When he came to a stop near the Huey's door he turned to gloat over his victory and was surprised not to see Coon a few steps behind him. All that met his eyes was a barren landscape. It was then he heard the door gunner screaming.

"Your buddy went down fifty meters back."

"Coon...he hurt." Buon grabbed Cleat's arm and pointed to a splintered trunk.

Cleat spotted his friend lying face down in the burned out grass. Bullets began to ping and pluck at the choppers light armor. Cleat yelled at the crew chief he was going after Coon and for the chopper to wait until he got back.

"Man…you're fuckin' crazy? You ain't got a chance in hell of…" He opened up with a long burst from his M-60. "Shit…you see all that incoming? There must be more than a hundred of them fuckers back there. Ain't no way you gonna make it, dude…you'll be throwing your life away."

"I'll make it if you'll get those gunships to give me some cover, that's all I ask man…do what you can."

Without waiting for confirmation, Cleat threw his weapon and ruck on the chopper and took off at a dead run. The sound of angry hornets buzzed by his head and nipped at his fatigues as he willed his feet for speed. His determination might've dampened if he would've taken his eyes off of the stump where Coon lay and looked in the direction of the jungle where hundreds of green tracers were flying his way. Never once did he waver from trying to reach his friend. A bullet burned his right cheek to the bone as it sizzled by. A solid blow with the force of a mule's kick slammed into his left shoulder and knocked him down twenty meters short of his objective.

He was unaware of the support fire coming from his rear and overhead. Nothing hindered his thoughts from reaching his objective. Scrambling to his feet he was up and running again, but his boots felt like they were made of lead. A bullet tore the soft cover from his head taking with it a piece of his scalp… two rounds struck the ground in front of him sending shrapnel deep into his right thigh. Five meters from his objective a sledgehammer belted him in his right upper chest just below the collarbone. He managed to stagger forward the few remaining feet before falling at Coon's side.

Ignoring the pain, he lay gasping for breath. Sweat burned his eyes, and his tongue was so thick he couldn't swallow. As he lay praying for strength a ricochet tore into the meaty part of his left arm, lodging next to the bone. The loudness of a jet flying close cover startled him, a heartbeat later the hair on his arms were singed from the scorching heat of napalm. Cleat knew the enemy would recover in a matter of seconds. It was now or never. Throwing Coon over his shoulder in a classic fireman's carry, he lunged to his feet. His first few steps were awkward, but tilting forward under the additional weight he was able to adjust and find a semblance of rhythm as he rushed to the center of Dragonfly.

Something slugged him hard on his lower back, propelling him clumsily toward his goal. "Jesus Christ, where in the fuck are all these guys coming from?" Cleat's mind reverted back to 'The Game'. He had a second chance…this time he knew he could score. A voice shouted in his head, "You can do this…you can do this."

A defender tried to tackle him, but he shrugged it off and ran even harder …another would-be tackler snatched at his right leg, throwing him off balance…the goal line was so close, this time he would not be denied. Standing in the end zone he could see his teammates cheering him on.

The last thing he could remember after crossing the goal was falling into the arms of his shouting teammates. He was gasping for breath when they grabbed him under the arms and lifted him up. Their faces were different, and the uniforms weren't the traditional orange and black of LHS, but he didn't care, most importantly he was given a *second* chance, and this time he *won* the game. He just couldn't figure out why he carried the football on top of his shoulders the whole way, *and* why in the hell did it weigh so much?

CHAPTER 16

Cleat's head felt puffy and swollen and for some unknown reason a bass drum was hammering inside his skull. Never in his life had he experienced such excruciating pain. His first try at opening his eyelids failed. When he tried lifting his left hand to rid the dried crust forcing them shut a jolt of pain shot through him so painful his eyes popped wide-open. "Ahhh, Christ almighty…fuck me that hurt." Cleat looked around at the strange surroundings trying to figure out where he was. For the life of him he couldn't remember anything that happened after their initial contact with the NVA.

Next to his bed was a bottle of clear liquid hanging from a stainless steel pole with a tube leading into his right arm. The picture of Blake lying in the same kind of bed flashed through his mind, and with great effort he lifted his head to see if his legs were there, thank God they were.

"About fucking time you woke up. I've been lying here all morning waiting to say thanks for saving my life." Coon was sitting in the next bed over with a bandage wrapped tightly around his head

"What the fuck happened and where the hell are we?"

"All I can tell you is what I've been told. I was clipped in the head at Dragonfly and knocked unconscious, that's when you turned into John-fucking-Wayne and made like the 7th fucking cavalry. The story is: you're a genuine hero of Herculean fame. By the way asshole, you received six wounds playing Audie-fucking-Murphy, thankfully most of them were minor. I also hear we're getting the Purple Heart and some other trinkets."

"Where was I hit?"

"Where weren't you hit is more like it. You were hit in the head, shoulder, legs, back, arm, and chest. I think that about covers it, although I might've left one or two spots out here and there."

"That must be why I hurt all over." Cleat grimaced when he tried shifting his body to a more comfortable position.

"Perry Mason would be proud of that deduction."

Coon was awarded the Bronze Star and Purple Heart at a small ceremony before being released back to duty two weeks later. Before returning to Camp A-432 Coon visited Cleat in the hospital. He wasn't anxious to leave his friend, but he couldn't stay either.

"Hey ol' buddy, you gonna lay in the sack all day?"

"Screw you and the horse you rode in on. They won't let my grungy-ass outa here. I've begged, pleaded and threatened their sorry asses, but to no avail."

Coon laughed, "Believe when I say this, they want your sorry ass outa here more than you want to leave. You've been nothing but trouble to these fine folks. They wait on you night and day while you lay on clean sheets and give them hell every waking moment"

"Come on Coon, I'm not that bad. See if you can pull some strings and get me outa here. I swear I can't take this shit much longer."

Coon ran a rough hand over the top of Cleat's short cropped hair, "I'll do what I can, but no promises." Coon looked at his watch, "I have to go brother …that chopper ain't gonna wait on my ass. I'll see you soon. Do what the doctors and nurses tell you and you'll be back at camp in no time."

After Coon's departure the days seemed to never end, Cleat's was miserable without his friend. It was the longest they had ever been apart, except for when he ran off to Miami and MOS training. A constant stream of orderlies, nurses, and doctors visited his bedside asking inane questions, while probing his body and dressing his wounds. He pestered anybody, and everybody that would listen for his immediate release. He demanded to be returned to his team. Even though the staff was sympathetic and marveled over how quickly Cleat was recovering, they still insisted he wasn't ready for active duty. The most serious wound was in his chest below the collarbone, it was a through-and-through, and left an ugly exit hole in his back the size of a golf ball.

After several more weeks of taking antibiotics and wallowing in his mundane recovery, the staff of well-wishers notified him that his status was being upgraded to light duty and he would be released the following Monday. On Friday morning shortly before chow he was placed in a wheelchair and rolled into a large room where eleven other wounded were gathered.

The men were a mixed bag of individuals representing all branches of the Armed Forces in Vietnam, there was even a representative signifying the Coast Guard's presence. The wounded men found themselves center stage in an awards ceremony. Cleat was awarded the Purple Heart, Silver Star, and the Combat Infantryman's Badge. His was the second highest award issued. A young Marine Lance Corporal missing half of his face received the Navy Cross. Nine days after the awards ceremony he was discharged from the hospital and classified as *light duty*. His orders hastened his return to Camp A-432 with the medical personnel's blessings.

Six weeks had gone by since his release from the hospital, and his counterparts at A-432 were still treating him like an invalid. He was damn sick of it and vehemently let everyone know about his castigation over the matter. As far as he was concerned enough was enough or he was going to lose his sanity hanging around camp doing menial chores. Coon tried to boost his spirits, but nothing would change his attitude until he was back in the field doing the job he was trained to do.

"Hey Cleat, Cap wants to see you and Coon Dog in the Com-Shack ASAP."

"Thanks Kelly, I'll roust Coon, and we'll be there post-haste."

The Com-Shack was one third underground and heavily sandbagged on the sides and top. Every six feet small gun ports were installed for the camps defense. The bunker could withstand most anything the enemy could throw at them. The interior walls were wood planked and the floor was made from double sheeted ¾ inch plywood sealed and painted a dark green. The CB's took great pride in their work and went overboard in constructing the facility. A liberated generator was ventilated through the roof and provided sparse lighting twenty-four hours a day. The inside was large enough to accommodate not only the radios it was designed for, but it also provided a large enough space in the rear for Doc Leftwitch to set up a emergency operating table if the camp came under attack. The team medic nicknamed the structure *The Alamo*. Leftwitch couldn't have chosen a more appropriate name, for it was here they would make their *last stand* if the camp were ever overrun.

"Everybody tells me you're raring to go, Cleat." Captain Brenner met them as they were coming down the sandbag steps.

"I'm chomping at the bit sir." Cleat grinned at the captain, who looked less like a warrior than *Mister McGoo*. He was short, balding, and extremely thin, but he was one of the toughest men Cleat had ever met. Brenner looked ten years older than his thirty-two years, but he could outmatch you in any mental or physical task if challenged. He was a hardcore maverick who made it through the ranks from private to captain, and what endeared him most among his men was the utter contempt he held for the top brass, and their bullshit.

"I want you and Truman to assist Jake on a recon patrol before first light. Torres and Kelly will be taking another patrol out at the same time. I know its Tet, and there's supposed to be a ceasefire, but we've acquired some local Intel from the 'little people' informing us there's been a lot of movement in our AO. Not only that, aerial recon developed photos confirming said information. Those fuckers are up to something, and by all that's holy I want to know what the hell it is before somebody gets waxed."

Brenner clasped his hands behind his back and began pacing. "I'm counting on you men to get the job done. You'll find Jake and the others over at the team hootch going over the mission."

"Yes sir and thank you sir." Cleat wanted to hug the officer for setting him free. Once outside Cleat couldn't contain his eagerness, or the smile spread across his face

"Talk about a possum eating grin."

"Kiss my ass Coon. You don't know what it's been like laying around day and night doing nothing but eating and sleeping."

"Fuck me, I should be so lucky. It sounds like pure fucking torture to me."

"Hell, it's gonna be good to leave the gate again, I just hate like hell your little scrawny ass is tagging along." Cleat smiled at his friend.

"Hey, somebody's got to look after your accident prone ass. You're too fucking stupid to stay out of harms way."

When they walked from the sunlight into the dimly lit team house they were momentarily blinded.

"Hey Cleat, I hear the Ol' Man's sending you out with us. It's about time you started earning your keep."

Cleat's eyes still hadn't adjusted completely but he easily recognized the voice of Kaminski. Staff Sergeant John H. Kaminski was Wilson's replacement and he bonded well with his counterparts. He was a big strong farm boy from a small farming town in Minnesota with a heavy German population. Kaminski and Offenhimer became friends instantly. Their ages were more than a decade apart but otherwise they were two peas in a pod.

Kaminski, Offenhimer, Kelly, and Jakubec were sitting around a makeshift table playing poker. Torres was sitting in a chair reading a novel and Ramirez was busy writing a letter home.

"Hey Cleat, are you sure that you're up for the patrol?" Sergeant First Class Kelly asked good-naturedly.

"Man, I tell 'ya what Kelly I've *been* up for it."

Kelly threw a blue chip into the pot, "It'll cost you five more."

Kaminski threw his hand in. "I'm out."

Offenhimer followed suit.

"Shit!" Jakubec griped. "How many cards did you draw?"

"Ask the dealer." Kelly smiled at his best friend on the team. Their wives were sisters back at Fort Bragg.

"For Christ sakes you're the fucking dealer." Ron was fuming.

"I already said how many I was taking before I drew my cards."

"Well how many was it?"

"I already said."

"Goddammit Bryant! Offenhimer tell him that shit ain't right."

"I folded, I got no say." Karl shoved away from the table and stretched his beefy arms.

"Fuck it, I call." Ron tossed a blue chip in the middle of the pile. "What'ya got?"

"I stood pat with a nine high straight."

"Dammit. You mean to tell me you didn't draw any fucking cards?"

Bryant laughed, "Sure do."

"You're a fucking asshole Bryant."

"Thanks brother-in-law. I need the money to buy a present for Bryant junior when I get home."

"Home sweet home, in twenty-seven days we'll all be heading home." Ron yelled, and then looked around the room. "Well *almost* all of us."

"We're gonna miss y'all." Cleat slapped his teammate on the back. "When are the replacements due in?"

"Da A-Detachment is due in two weeks." Offenhimer frowned.

"They're sending a whole team?" Cleat was surprised.

"Ya, one whole team dey sending."

"What the hell is going to happen to us?" Coon asked.

"Don't know fa 'sure, but Captain Brenner or Lieutenant Gregorio would know."

Kelly tried to laugh it off but failed when he told Cleat they would probably fall into the replacement category again.

At 0430 the two teams, with a complement of four 'native' tribesmen each, moved through the gate in total darkness. Cleat and Coon were attached to Jakubec's patrol and were assigned the Western part of the camps AO. Torres and Kelly were going to be covering the NW quadrant. They had enough rations for five days and they all hoped it wouldn't take that long. Five days in the bush could turn into an eternity. Within moments of leaving the protective confines of camp all hell broke loose.

It began when four large artillery rounds landed in the center of camp briefly flashing night into day. Milliseconds later heavy and light mortar shells blanketed the compound and every main structure above ground. RPGs soared through the air crashing into bunkers. Suddenly the west gate exploded, and a section of the wall collapsed inward. Huge blasts were erupting in the wire creating gaps where scores of the enemy were pouring through. They looked like angry black ants disturbed from their nest.

Both patrols were caught in the open, chaos swirled around them as the sound of small arms added to the crescendo. Sergeant Jakubec grabbed Cleat by the arm, his mouth opened to shout a command, but an utterance never came forth. Ronald Jakubec from Ashville, North Carolina slumped slowly to his knees, and fell over backward, shot through the heart. His wife of twelve years, Carrie Ann, and his two boys, Ronald Jr. age ten, and his youngest son, Donald, age eight would learn of his death in seven days time. Their lives would never be the same without their champion.

AK-47's and RPD's were firing on full-automatic sending long bursts of deadly steel twanging through the wire. Clods of dirt flung in the air on either side of Cleat and Coon. The noise was unbelievable.

"Back inside…let's go…move it." Cleat screamed, but wasn't sure if anyone heard him. It didn't matter…it was time to act, or die where they lay.

Cleat rushed the gate ignoring the Vietnamese voices screaming behind him. Kneeling beside the gatepost he opened up with his M-16, laying down as much covering fire as he could. Coon slid next to him, and added his suppressing fire. Cleat mentally counted each man as they passed through the gate. As yet, only a few of the Yards had scrambled inside. Torres was the first American; he came scrambling in on all fours, weaponless. Cleat grabbed him by his shirt and hollered, "Where's Kelly?"

"I'm hit, man…Kelly's dead!" Torres screamed…his eyes were wild and crazy.

Cleat yelled, "Coon…check Torres out."

Coon scooted close to the wounded man and began searching for entry wounds "Here, let me take a look. Where're you hit?"

Torres held up a trembling right hand exhibiting a thumb and first two fingers missing, what was left of his hand didn't look much better. "I'm fucking hit in the ass, too."

"Can you walk?" One look told him Torres was going to lose the rest of his hand, short of a miracle.

"If I can't I'll fucking crawl my…" Torres' body jerked from a round boring into the center of his back…he looked into Coon's eyes. "Shit…I'm dead." Without another word Torres crumpled to the ground. His promiscuous wife in El Paso wouldn't miss him, months earlier she'd filed for divorce. When learning of his fate she *anxiously* counted the days for her dead husband's insurance check to arrive.

"Coon, help me close the gate…nobody else is coming in…they're all dead."

Running inside their camp, the scene was worse than Cleat had imagined. Thunderous explosions continued to fall and this time they were from much heavier weapons. The blasts created huge geysers of bright red-orange and its center flung hot jagged shrapnel in a deadly 360. It was turning their camp into a fiery inferno. A shell landed too close for comfort and the shockwaves knocked both of them off their feet.

Cleat quickly scrambling to his knees and suddenly realized most of the bunkers armed with M-60's were either destroyed or out of action. And worse yet, the four fifty-caliber machine guns placed on the corner walls were noticeably silent. This was serious, somehow they had to create more firepower, or all was lost. The shelling seemed to increase as they leapt into the sandbagged defensive fortification of the 81mm's.

Lieutenant Gregorio, Offenhimer and several Montagnards were putting out rounds at a feverous rate. Twenty meters from their position the mortar pit holding the 60mm tubes was a smoldering pile of rubble, three bodies were strewn like rag dolls outside the hole. Without question, one of them was a fellow team member.

Lieutenant Gregorio saw Cleat staring at the body. "It's Ramirez!" Gregorio hollered above the noise.

The 60mm mortar had been scratched from the U.S. Army's TO&E (Table of Organization and Equipment) several years ago, but somehow Ramirez managed to acquire the small mortar from one of his friends in Na Trang. It was his pride and joy.

Cleat nodded. "Jakubec, Torres, and Kelly are dead…we got caught outside the gate when the shit hit the fan. What can we do to help?"

"You can round up some Yards, and bring us some more ammo…we're running low, and while you're at it, find some goddamn water to pour on the tubes before they fucking melt."

Most of the lieutenant's words were muffled by thunderous explosions, but over the excruciating noise and reading the lieutenant's lips Cleat understood what needed to be done. He grabbed Coon and ran in the direction of the ammo dump, hoping to find some help along the way to carry the heavy crates of ammo. Thankfully they found enough men to complete their mission. Carrying as much ammo as they could, and a *jerry* can of water, the small band of men returned to the mortar pit.

"Thank God…we were down to our last two rounds." Gregorio was appreciative. "Take some men and get those fifties back in action, or we're going to be in a world of hurt." The lieutenant opened the can of water and began cooling the tubes.

"Where is Kaminski?" Cleat hollered.

"He's manning the fifty on the northwest corner." Gregorio hollered.

No sooner had the Lieutenant's words left his mouth, two rounds from an enemy 57mm recoilless rifle slammed into the northwest corner. The block-house housing the fifty shuddered and crumbled to the ground burying its valiant defenders.

"Jesus Christ! How'd they get all of this shit here without us knowing?" Cleat's question went unanswered as another salvo of artillery landed.

A flare ship arrived overhead and dropped its parachute flares over the camp. There artificial light cast ghostly shadows across the area making every-thing seem surreal. Men were darting to and fro with enemy and friendly alike firing indiscriminately at anything that resembled a threat.

Cleat peaked over the sandbags and saw the defenders red tracers lashing across the open ground crisscrossing with the enemies green tracers. The green far outnumbered the red. Bullets were tearing through the air amongst ear-shattering rings of explosions. The dead and dying scattered about looked like small discarded bundles of clothing. Cleat shook his head to clear his senses and wondered what size of force the enemy had thrown at them. It was cer-tainly larger than anyone ever anticipated. It put into question the team's intel-ligence gathering capabilities.

"Coon you're on me…we gotta get those fifties working."

"Fuck it man…I'm ready when you are."

Cleat ordered the Montagnards to follow them to the east wall, where two of the four fifty caliber machine guns were located. Things were running amuck, the west wall was breached from the onset, and at least a third of the Americans were KIA. Bodies of friendly and that of the enemy were laying everywhere you looked. Mayhem was a mild description for what was going on inside the besieged camp. The tribesmen were doing one hell of a job amidst the turmoil, it wasn't just a battle for them…it was a fight for survival. Most of them had families living inside the camp. Cleat prayed help would be coming soon, if it didn't, he couldn't see the camp holding out another hour, and even that was a stretch.

The first machine gun emplacement they went to had been disabled either by a direct hit from a communist 122mm mortar round, or from an artillery shell. There was too much damage for it to have been anything else. Sprawled around the jumbled mess were the dead bodies of the crew members, they were mangled beyond recognition. Fortunately, the second fifty was in perfect work-ing order and loaded with a fresh belt. Unfortunately, the men manning the position were dead from small arms fire. Cleat shuddered to think of the damage the enemy could've done if they had taken the time to turn the weapon loose inside the camp.

"Coon, you feed me...the rest of you spread out and provide security." He mostly spoke in French, and used hand signals giving his orders, although he was beginning to grasp some of their singsong language, now wasn't the time.

The enemy was still pouring through the wire when Cleat opened up with the fifty, saturating the area with large caliber rounds that cut a deadly swathe through the human wave. The formidable weapon blew limbs from bodies and exploding heads like ripe melons. If you were hit by a fifty caliber round there was no such thing as receiving a superficial wound, most often it was catastrophic in nature. The heavy caliber machinegun's devastating effect amongst the attacking NVA was short lived, hell came calling when a B-40 rocket roared over their redoubt barely missing its target. The errant missile was quickly followed by a RPG that exploded beneath their protective wall with enough force to collapse a majority of the sandbags protecting them. Rifle fire and automatic weapons zeroed in on their position and started taking a deadly toll. Three of his Yards tumbled from the wall, within seconds two others were badly wounded. Their defensive fortification became a focal point rendering it untenable.

"We gotta get the fuck outta here Coon." He ordered two natives who weren't wounded to breakdown the fifty. He gestured for another to grab the ammo cans. "We're heading for the Com-Shack. Coon, bring the spare barrel with you."

Cleat led the survivors across the open ground, dodging, ducking, and scrambling for cover as enemy weapons continued to assail the camp. Suddenly he was knocked off his feet when an enormous explosion sent a hail of shrapnel and dirt screaming through the night. On his hands and knees surrounded by a dust cloud, he coughed up a mouthful of blood, his ears were ringing, and he felt sick to his stomach. A sharp pain in his side rudely let him know he'd taken a hit, shaking his head to clear his blurred vision he ascertained his wound wasn't serious since all of his extremities were working just fine. Through the smoke he recognized a friendly face staring at him.

"You okay, Cleat?"

"Yeah, how about you?"

"Took some shit in my left shoulder, but I'm okay."

Cleat looked for the rest of his contingent…of the eight Montagnards following him two were dead and one had a nasty gash in his forearm. "What the shit was that?"

Coon nodded toward the 81mm pit. Cleat stood on unsteady legs and followed his friend's nod, there was nothing left, you couldn't even tell it was ever there, all that remained was a big hole in the ground.

Cleat pulled one of the Montagnards close. "Tell your chief the camp is lost…gather his people and exit the south gate…tell him help is on the way. Now go." Cleat gave the boy a gentle shove. "Coon, find as many M-79's and ammo you can carry, then meet me on top of the Com-Shack…bring some help while you're at it." Facing the five remaining warriors, he motioned for them to follow him.

Around the Com-Shack a dozen or so tribesmen were embedded in sandbagged positions, nervously waiting for the enemy. Fortunately, the North Vietnamese hadn't penetrated this far, but with most of the friendlies pulling out it wouldn't be long before they'd be swarming all over the place. He prayed for enough time to initiate his plan of action.

He pointed to the sandbagged roof of the Com-Shack and told his followers to climb on top and build a defensive position four sandbags deep and chest high. He selected six others to help, the rest he formed into a human chain passing sandbags to the bulwark on top.

Cleat paused at the entrance to the Com-Shack and hollered, "Its Davis…I'm coming in." Taking the steps two at a time, he entered the communications room and found SFC Hollister busy on the radios. Two Montagnards sat beside him yammering frantically on their own radios, while three others held their weapons ready, guarding the only entrance. Cleat searched the room for Captain Brenner, when he didn't see him he asked Hollister where the captain was, without missing a beat Hollister jerked his thumb to the back of the room where Doc had set up his emergency treatment area.

He found Doc hovering over a table with two of his Yard assistants. "Doc, have you seen the Captain?" A dozen wounded were lined up against the wall waiting their turn.

"Yeah…I'm trying to save his life as we speak."

Cleat moved closer for a better look. The Captain was ashen, his left side was split wide open exposing shattered ribs, and there was a wound starting below his ear that wrapped jaggedly around his neck. A bluish colored artery was clamped off with two different size clamps, and where his left eye should've been was an empty socket filled with blood. Cleat's stomach did a flip. "Jesus...is he going to make it?"

"The question is...are *any* of us going to make it."

"I gotta admit Doc, it doesn't look good. Coon and I are all that's left of the team besides you and Hollister. I ordered the Yards to leave camp by way of the south gate. We're building a fighting position on top of the Com-Shack, but it's only going to buy us a little time, if help doesn't arrive most rickety-tic, we ain't gonna need any."

"As you can see I've got my hands full...you're in command now, so it's your call."

Cleat's knees weakened when Doc's words registered, life and death depended on him making the right decision, how in the hell was he supposed to know what to do? He looked around for a place to spit and spotted a bucket near the operating table. It was being used to catch the drainage of blood, he added to the half-full container.

"Where's that blood coming from you spit out?" Doc asked.

"I don't know."

"Here, let me take a look." Doc looked at Cleat's blood-smeared mouth and frowned, lifting Cleat's shirt he inspected the front and found nothing but scrapes and bruises. Turning Cleat around he discovered a nasty looking hole just below his ribcage. "Are you finding it difficult to breathe?"

"Yeah...a little I guess."

"Uh huh, go ahead and take your shirt off." Doc dug into his medical bag until he found what he was looking for. "This is only temporary, but it should help with your discomfort, you probably have a punctured lung, if its gets any worse come see me." Doc finished taping his back. "See the nurse at the front desk and she'll make you a follow-up appointment for next week."

"You're a real fucking comedian, Doc, which must be the reason you and Coon get along so well!"

"Is he doing all right?" Doc was replacing a bottle of glucose hanging beside the captain.

"He's doing fine, Doc, he's above us building our last ditch stand...I'll get us through this Doc, don't worry."

"There's no doubt Cleat, no doubt whatsoever. Now get your ass outta here and let me earn my keep."

Cleat stopped by the bank of radios and marveled over the calmness in Hollister's voice. When there was a break he placed his hand on the communication sergeant's shoulder, "We might be able to hold them off for thirty minutes, but that's about it. Try and get us some help before it's too late."

"Cleat, everybody in d'Nam knows we're being hit hard. I'm linked up with the Air Force, Firebase Henry, C and C Central, the Cav, and anyone else you can think of. Every damn city *and* major installation in South Vietnam is under attack. I'm doing all I can."

"I know you are, but our situation is not only desperate, it's fucking hopeless. I want you to radio *Broken Arrow*...let 'em know all friendlies will be inside the communications bunker by..." Cleat removed the olive-drab tape from his watch and checked the aluminous dial for the time...it was only 0458 hours. Jesus...less than thirty minutes had passed since the attack began. How could that be? It seemed more like hours. "Have them on station ASAP. We can't holdout very long. Its 0500 now, we'll be lucky if we can make till 0530. Remind them we'll be inside the Communications bunker. When the time comes I'll get everyone safely inside. While I'm topside have everybody that can fire a weapon man the firing ports. We're going to need all the help we can muster." Cleat took a painful breath, "I'm going up top and buy us some time...when it gets too hot we're coming in so don't get trigger happy."

"Good luck, Cleat."

"Thanks, we're all going to need it."

Coon was huddled with seventeen Yards preparing for the coming attack. He was glad to see Cleat

"Christ, I thought you'd never get here. I was afraid you were going to miss all the fun."

Cleat knelt beside his friend, "How's your shoulder?"

"Not well enough to handle the fifty, I think whatever hit me dislocated the damn thing."

"How many M-79's did you round up?"

"Enough to go around twice over, and we gathered more than a hundred rounds of HE, a few smokers and some flechette rounds. We also have four M-60's, the fifty and plenty of ammo. We're loaded for bear if they don't drop something on top of us."

"Can you feed the fifty?"

"Yeah, no problem."

All of a sudden a tremendous volley of incoming fire pelted their position relentlessly for a full minute. All nineteen men stayed well below the four-foot thick walls and retaliated with M-79's, firing lethal high explosive projectiles in every direction. A rain of death fell on the enemy below. When there was a lull Cleat scrambled to the fifty-caliber machinegun just in time to catch a dozen of the enemy creeping around what was left of the team hootch. Holding onto both handles he opened fired; they never had a chance. The large caliber rounds ripped into their bodies tearing flesh from bones and turning bone to splinters. Another group of six charged the Com-Shack and was cut down by two of the M-60's manned by the Yards. He knew the rest of his men were engaged by the sound of their automatic fire answering the enemies. Cleat looked at his watch for the third time in as many minutes; it was only 0510. Why was it when you wanted time to fly it invariably crawled at a snails pace?

It was good they were holding their own, but the enemy knew where they were, and the next time they would use more caution. No sooner had those thoughts entered Cleat's mind than an RPG crashed below them, and was quickly followed by another that shook the foundation. It was getting light enough to see the camp, and everywhere you looked there were dead bodies, no longer could the night conceal the scope of horror inflicted on humanity. The enemies' dead were mixed with friendlies as they lay amid the smoldering ruins. Scattered about were smaller cadavers of women and infant children that were caught in the hellfire. The macabre scene instilled an unforgettable sadness mixed with anger.

The lull once enveloping camp A-432 erupted in a crescendo of explosions. Mortar rounds fell in clusters around their precarious position; it was time to go inside. The defenders had no protective defense against aerial bombardment.

"Coon, in fifteen seconds have everybody fire as many HE's as they can, and then fire the smoke canisters…I want all of you inside in thirty seconds."

"What about you?"

"Goddammit do like I say."

"I ain't going anywhere until you tell me what you're gonna do."

"I'm staying up here on the fifty till everyone's inside."

"Fuck it, then I'm gonna stay too."

"Dammit, Coon, don't argue with me, get these men off the roof."

Coon crawled to the men squatting beneath the wall of sandbags and explained to them what was going on. They loaded the M-79's and fired shot after shot without exposing themselves, or bothering to take aim. The last ten rounds were smoke and engulfed the whole area in a multitude of clouded colors. Coon quickly hurried the Yards off the embattled roof, satisfied they were clear he yanked a belted M-60 off the floor and rejoined his friend. "REMEMBER THE FUCKING ALAMO YOU FUCKING SLOPES!"

Cleat wasn't surprised when his hardheaded friend leaned against the wall firing the *Hog* with his good right arm. He started to chew his ass out, but he spotted a large group of infantry advancing through a mass of dissipating smoke. Most of them were wearing the light colored uniforms of the NVA. He still wondered how in the hell Intelligence failed to miss the massing of NVA in their AO.

"Fuck man...where'd they all come from? You believe this shit? They must've hit us with a reinforced battalion." Coon struggled to be heard over the incredible clamor of combat.

"Who knows and who the hell cares." Cleat screamed. "This is bad shit brother. We got no place to go until help gets here."

"Well they sure as hell better hurry up, because we're gonna need'em sooner than later." Coon braced the barrel of his M-60 on a chewed up sandbag and leveled his weapon at the advancing enemy forming to their front. He pulled the trigger and didn't let up until the belt ran dry.

CHAPTER 17

"**G**ET DOWN!" Cleat yelled. He sat straight up in bed, with his eyes ablaze.

"Looks kinda familiar, don't it? This must be what the French mean by déjà vu. Hell, they even got us in the same fucking ward if you can believe that shit."

"How'd we get here?" Cleat's head was spinning.

"I don't suppose you'd believe I carried you over my shoulders out of harm's way while dodging enemy bullets. That would kinda make us even, wouldn't it?"

"My head hurts too much to listen to your line of horseshit. What about Doc and Hollister?"

"They made it out just fine...not even a fucking scratch. They flew Captain Brenner to Japan a few days ago...its kind of iffy with the Captain."

"What happened to us?"

"Well, let's start off with you being John-fucking-Wayne all over again. You know somebody could get themselves seriously hurt hanging around you."

"Dammit to hell, just cut to the chase and tell me what the hell happened."

"You're no fun at all..."

"Christ, I haven't the strength." Cleat threw his arms up, and fell back on his pillows. He knew that he'd made a mistake when the white-hot searing pain discharged in his brain. He wished now he hadn't acted so melodramatic.

Coon grinned at Cleat, "Serves you right butthead. Okay, okay...the best I can remember is a grenade sailed in from nowhere and you shoved me down. The Goddamn thing went off catching a good part of your ass, and another piece clipped you in the chin, knocking you out. Me, I got hit in the good arm and my good leg. After the smoke and dust cleared I hauled you off the roof and dragged you inside the Com-Shack just before the whole freaking Air Force showed up and dumped everything but the kitchen sink on our camp. What gripes me the most is those fuckin' Hollywood Marines came in and rescued our ass and shipped us to Da Nang. Now that's something I'll never tell my grandkids about. Oh, one other thing…a piece of shrapnel partially bruised your right lung, but you're okay now."

"Thanks, Coon…I wouldn't have expected any less from my brother." Cleat closed his eyes and drifted off to sleep before he heard his friend's reply.

"I love you too man, you're the best brother anyone could ever have."

By their fifth week in the hospital things were shaping up. They'd been ambulatory for a full week, and for the coming weekend they'd been issued overnight passes. Late Thursday they received almost identical letters from the family except for a portion of the content. Coon received a letter from Anne telling him how sorry she was, but she wouldn't be able to write anymore, or even see him when he returned home. She had fallen in love with a graduate student involved in the underground movement protesting the war. Coon acted as if it were no big deal because he was never really serious over Anne, but deep down Cleat knew it hurt. At the very least she was someone back home he could write to besides family.

Coon hoped one of Cleat's letters was from Mandy, and was disappointed when he learned it was from Sissy. He didn't understand why Mandy didn't write Cleat. If she wasn't going to answer his letters then why in hell did she come over to the house before they left? Shit, women, who in hell could figure them out?

Cleat's letters gave him a tinge of homesickness, but that was to be expected. Sissy's letter was particularly humorous, and filled with gossip. Not surprisingly, there was a lot going on in the small southern town of Lakewood. He got a kick out of her descriptive penmanship, even though it was mostly about her friends. He was glad that she included the news of Bo Collier entering Harvard Medical School in the spring. She also mentioned that Audrey was married last month to a New York lawyer several years her senior.

The more he read the better he felt, as some of her paragraphs were downright hilarious, it was hard to imagine his little sister with pigtails was growing up. He kept a smile on his face until the last two passages, when she informed him Gene Reese had been killed in an automobile wreck with two other boys on their way home from Troy, Alabama. He'd won the starting quarterback position at Troy State midway through his freshman season. Cleat felt particularly bad since his last thoughts of Gene were on the negative side. The next paragraph was a real downer; it started with an apology, and ended with the gruesome fact that Mister Truman was burned to death when his house went up in flames Saturday a week ago. She thought it would be best if Cleat was the one to tell Coon.

He knew when Coon joined the Army he'd listed the Davis's as his next of kin, if he'd listed his dad as his only next of kin the Army would've notified him of his father's demise. Now it was Cleat's responsibility to tell his best friend the horrific news. He struggled for hours trying to figure out the best way to let Coon know, but in the end he realized there was no best way to tell a friend his father had burned to death.

"Hey Coon, let's take a walk, and work out the kinks…I want to be in shape for this weekend."

"Sounds like a winner to me, but I'll tell you what good buddy, it ain't gonna take much effort on my part to lie between a girl's legs and smell her sweet breath."

"Does your mind ever drift far from the female persuasion?"

"I can't help it if I'm a hardcore all American male."

They'd been walking for fifteen minutes talking about being short timers and going home when Cleat recommended sitting underneath a large shade tree where a white wooden bench nestled against its thick trunk.

"Man, all I need right now is a cold beer." Coon smacked his lips. "One so fucking cold it'd hurt your throat going down. You know, like the ones we used to drink at the beach after they'd been chilling in a cooler for about four hours."

Cleat smiled a crooked smile, "At least there are some pure thoughts in that oversexed brain of yours."

"Shit…I thought the beach, cold beer and pretty girls went together without saying."

"Coon, uh…I got some bad news from home."

"What kind of bad news? Nobody wrote to me about any bad news."

"The letter I got from Sissy mentioned it. Coon, I wish there was a better way to let you know but I…"

"Fuck man, spit it out."

Cleat put his hand on Coon's shoulder and gave it a squeeze, "Your father died last week…they buried him on Saturday." Cleat felt his friend's body tense ever so briefly.

"Fuck…he's better off dead. He was living a miserable life, and didn't give a shit about anybody, or anything except alcohol. I'm sure the good citizens of Lakewood didn't shed any tears, nor will they miss his sorry ass."

"Coon, he was your father, and he loved you very much, he…"

"Bullshit!" Coon leaped from the bench, pointing his finger at Cleat. "What the fuck do you know? My old man didn't love me…he was incapable of love. That fucker treated me like shit, and what's crazy, I kept going back time after time for more of the same fucking abuse trying to prove I was worthy of his love. How sick was that? Until I moved in with your family I had no concept of family life. I was lost in a world of neglect and hunger. My world was dark…I was a skinny little snot-nosed kid who never knew if his real dad was going to walk through the door, or some mean scary son-of-a-bitch that would knock me around the house. At night I would take a flashlight I stole from Sears, and hide in my closet under a pile of dirty clothes hoping he wouldn't find me. There were times I'd get so frightened hearing him move around in the dark calling my name I'd pee in my pants."

Using the palms of his hands Coon brushed away the tears. "Without you and your family there's no telling what would've happened to me. I'll never be able to repay the love and kindness y'all so graciously shared with me. Your family is special Cleat, more special than you'll ever realize. It takes someone like me who's never been able to take love for granted to understand how special they really are. I've been treated like a brother, a son, and a grandson, but most importantly I've been treated with love. There was something missing in my life until I met you, the day you called me your friend was a new beginning for me, after that my life changed drastically. My God Cleat, if you only knew how influential your mom and dad have been in my life, even Mama Marie, Randy, and Sissy has been instrumental in my growth as a human being."

Cleat started to interrupt, but he knew his friend was suffering inside and decided to let him finish what he had to say.

Coon sat down on the bench, clasped hands and stared at the sidewalk. After a few minutes of silence he leaned forward and rested his elbows on his knees. "The holiday seasons were always the best of times, not because school was out, it was the smells coming from the kitchen with Mama June, and Mama Marie cooking and baking. Their laughter warmed my heart. I used to listen to their stories about growing up during the depression when they had to scrimp, and scrape just to make ends meet. They spoke of times when the family held together during WW II, and contributed to the war effort by collecting pots and pans, and anything else that could help win the war.

Sitting at the table during Christmas Eve dinner was worth more to me than any presents under the tree. Just to feel the love and warmth in the room, and know somehow, someway I was part of a real family. My past life, although painful, is just a distant memory, and my father's death is no more tragic to me than a stranger's."

"Are you finished?"

"Yeah…for now anyway."

"You're wrong about your dad, I saw him before we joined the Army, as a matter of fact he's the one that suggested I join the Army, and straighten out my life. Did you know he never missed a football game you ever played in? He went to all of them and stayed hidden in the crowd so he wouldn't embarrass you in front of your friends. Your father kept every newspaper clipping that ever mentioned your name. He was proud of his son, but he knew you wouldn't stand a chance in hell staying with him. The demons had your father Coon, and they wouldn't let him go. He knew you'd go down with him if he didn't set you free. Your father wanted you to have a chance in this world so badly he was willing to extinguish a son's love for his father in order to do so. Never forget Coon, he loved you more than life itself."

By the time Cleat was through, Coon couldn't control the flow of tears. "How did he die?"

Cleat gulped, he'd hoped beyond hope that the question wouldn't arise. "He was asleep when the house burned to the ground."

"Oh God…noooo!" Coon fell to his knees covering his face. His body shook with sobs of anguish. No matter how hard he tried, never once had he ever stopped loving his father. The little boy inside couldn't help but remember all the good times they'd shared together as father and son before he became lost in the crippling fog of alcohol.

Cleat knelt beside Coon and wrapped him in his arms. "I'm sorry Coon. I wish I could make the suffering go away."

Passersby's raised quizzical eyebrows at the two Special Forces men kneeling in a loving embrace.

Sergeant Major Klaus was the highest ranking NCO with Special Forces, Fifth Group. His duty station was Headquarters Company, Na Trang. He was big, gruff, and demanding, but was loved and respected by everyone. Although Special Ops was his primary concern, he drew great pleasure making life more durable for his troops. He beamed with pride over his latest effort. He'd been adamant over Sergeant Davis and Sergeant Truman staying at the SF safe house for as long as necessary to recover from their ordeal. Out of the goodness of his heart he handpicked two of his most beautiful Eurasian girls to keep them company. Klaus was well-known for having some of the finest, most desirable female host in all of Vietnam. Usually he called on them to accommodate and *entertain* special guests such as visiting generals and politicians. After what his sergeants had been through, he felt they deserved the best, and that's what he sent them…the very best.

When he finished making the call an envious smile spread across his Slavic features, he knew they were in for one hell of goodtime. He'd give them a few days before informing them of their awards for valor. Davis was being awarded the Distinguished Service Cross for his actions during the defense of Camp A-432, and Truman was receiving the Silver Star. Good publicity in Vietnam was a rare thing and he was going to make sure their heroics were well documented and damn-well made National headlines.

"You likie Susie, me likie you. You bang-bang Susie longtime…you berry *big* down there, but Susie likie *too* much." Susie snuggled next to Cleat, purring in his ear.

"Yeah, I like Susie very much too." Cleat stretched the full length of his body on the clean sheets. This was their second night in 5th Group's French villa they leased as a safe house.

The safe house was like a castle compared to what they were use to. As you entered the grand foyer a richly burnished boiserie took your breath away, along its walls were oil paintings of mid-ninetieth century Vietnam when it was a French colony. On either side of the open archway leading to the main rooms were life-size statues of Vietnamese maidens carrying urns. The warm terra-cotta tile covering the entire expanse was inviting and pleasantly appealing to the senses. Once through the archway a lavishly furnished living room was on the right and an elegant dinning room with all its splendor was to the left. These rooms were purposely furnished to impress any of the world's top dignitaries. A recently remodeled kitchen proudly brandished the most modern of appliances.

Most of the men spent their downtime in the rear of the house where a pool table was place center stage of a huge game room. Harden men laughed, drank beer, shot pool, threw darts, and played pinball on one of the four pinball machines. At night the more ambitious and adventurous would play high stakes poker on an antique gaming table. Another large room doubled as a movie and TV room. Adjacent to the theater was a wet bar that was fully stocked with enough variances of alcohol to suit the taste of grunts, blue collar workers, corporate executives, and visiting kings. Beveled French doors led outdoors to a stone-laid patio that wound its way to an Olympic size swimming pool. One the far side of the pool stood a row of cabañas and behind them, almost hidden from the main house was a guesthouse. Three fulltime gardeners kept the grounds in botanical splendor.

A winding staircase led to the second landing where six grandiose bedrooms with adjacent bathrooms housed the tired and weary. Each bedroom exhibited a fireplace and private balcony overlooking the gardens. The upstairs also promulgated a decadent hot communal bath laden with inlayed marble and exotic statues. In the corner was a steam room with weathered seats to open your pours and clear your sinuses. The villa was manned by eight servants, while three of the staff lived in the villa year-round at everyone's beck and call, no matter the time of day or night.

A knock on Cleat's door interrupted Susie's zest for sex. He never thought he would ever be relieved to miss an opportunity to make love to a beautiful woman, but he was wrong. The past forty-eight hours had been a marathon of sexual pleasures beyond belief, and he was worn out. He'd only had sex a couple of times since his arrival in Vietnam, and they were kinda depressing under primitive conditions and more than forgettable.

"Come in." Cleat pushed Susie's prowling hand away from under the covers.

Coon walked in with a white towel wrapped around his waist exposing the ugly healing scars on his bare chest. His girl Kay wore a floral robe of many colors, and she was almost as beautiful as Susie. He and Coon got into a heated argument after downing too many beers over which one of the girls was the prettiest.

"Let's take a hot bath, brother. I got an ice cold bottle of Duck, and Kay has the wine glasses and cheese."

"Sounds good to me, give us a minute and we'll be right there."

When Cleat and Susie walked into the tiled room wearing identical terrycloth robes they weren't surprised to see Coon and Kay already in the steaming hot tub playing touchy-feely. Susie grabbed his hand and led him to the open shower to wash before joining the others. Cleat hung his robe on a bronze hook next to the door.

Kay squealed from the hot tub, "Ooooweee, Susie say all time you berry-berry *big*...I nevuh see so *big* before." Kay punched Coon in the ribs. "How come you no *big* like your friend?"

"Hey, I'll switch if you want to, I wouldn't mind a taste of Miss Susie Q."

"No, no trade...you good lover...you makie Kay scream *too* much."

After an erotic shower of washing each other with sensual soapy hands, Cleat's manhood blossomed into a full-blown erection.

"Ohhhhh, Coon, lookie-lookie at your friend, he grow too much too big."

"Dammit Kay, would you take you eyes off of his pecker and pay attention to mine."

Susie, giggled shyly, and held Cleat's hand as they stepped into the pool of hot steaming water.

"Christ, almighty Coon, what's the temperature of this water...we're going to cook our balls if we're not careful."

"Shut the fuck up, and have some wine and cheese, you're in fuckin' heaven and don't even know it." Coon passed him a wine glass brimming at the top.

After an hour of slow cooking and a half a bottle of wine, Cleat found enough courage to tell Coon what he'd been thinking about for the past week. "Coon, I...Uh, I got uhh...something to tell you, but first you have to promise me you won't get mad."

"Oh shit, what's up now? When you start uhhing there's some bad shit coming down."

"Well, you know our tour is up in a couple of weeks and..."

"Shit, you don't need to tell me. I can give you the days, hours, and the fucking minutes we have left over here."

"Coon, you're not going to like this, but I've...uh, decided to extend my tour, and volunteer for the Rangers."

"What...are you fucking crazy...we're going home for Christ's sake. Have you gone loco?"

"No, just hear me out. I want to make a difference. All we've accomplished so far is losing most of our teammates. I'm tired of taking it on the chin. Do you remember Craven and those others Rangers we met?"

"Yeah, they were in a world of shit, but what the hell does that have to do with anything?

Their mission is to find the enemy by using small units called long-range-reconnaissance-patrols and the anachronism for these teams is *Lurps*. When they locate the enemy they have the capabilities of bringing hell on earth right on their doorstep. If we're to win this war then we have to take it to them. We can't sit around in defensive positions, and wait for them to come to us. If we continue that strategy we'll be doing what the French did, and *they* fucking lost their war and by God I want to win ours. I want you to go home and go back to college. I don't have anything waiting for me back there. I belong here doing the job I was trained for."

"You're fucking insane...you know that, don't you?"

"Maybe I am, I don't know, but my mind's made up."

"Goddammit to hell Cleat, have you thought this through? This war is for shit! Half the time our hands are tied while we're trying to fight the damn thing. Politics are running this 'clusterfuck' and those assholes haven't a fucking clue to what's going on over here. Vietnam has turned from bad to worse since we got here, and the way I see it, the worse is yet to come. For Christ sakes Cleat, we have family back home and they want us back there safe and sound. We've made it man...yeah we've been wounded and suffered a few cuts and bruises, but we're whole man. Christ...how far do you want to push our luck, besides that, what about you and Mandy? If you spend another year over here you might lose her forever."

"You know as well as I do she hasn't answered any of my letters. I can't go the rest of my life trying to convince her differently. I love her, but somehow that doesn't seem to be enough" The thought of extending his tour and going two years without seeing Mandy was painful, but a force more compelling told him he was making the right decision.

"That doesn't mean she doesn't love you. What the fuck's in a letter anyway?"

"I've given this a great deal of thought, so there's no sense in you trying to talk me out of it." Cleat wiped the beaded perspiration from his forehead with an open hand. "I have some unfinished business over here Coon and I'm not leaving until it's done."

Coon gave his friend an incredulous look, "Now what in the fuck does that mean."

"There's a lot left undone and I can be of help. We've lost a lot of friends and I feel like we owe them."

"That's a crock of shit Cleat, and you know it. Every single one of our buddies would tell us to pack our fuckin' rucks and get the hell out of Dodge. If you stayed and were personally responsible for killing ten thousand of the 'little fuckers' it wouldn't make a goddamn bit of difference. You're only one man Cleat. You're not going to change the course of history. There's only so much you can do. Dammit man, we've both done enough, let's go home."

"No matter what you say Coon...I'm staying. I have this feeling it's the right thing to do."

"Oh fuck me. There you go with those fuckin' feelings again. I guess you're hearing voices too. Well fuck it then, I'm extending too. I go where you go. I ain't going to quit in the middle of the game and go home. Fuck it...I'm staying too man"

"No goddammit! You're going home and getting the hell out of this place. I don't want you over here on my conscience. If something happened to you it would be my fault."

"Tough shit brother, but if you think I'm going to leave you over here with nobody watching your six, then you got another think coming."

"Listen to reason Coon!" Cleat shouted. "Dammit, you've got everything going for you. When you get home your ass is gonna' enroll in college and make something out of your life. For now...mine is over here. It's where I belong."

"Then so is mine." Coon lunged for Cleat and dunked his head under the water.

Susie and Kay huddled on the other side of the tub wrapped in each others arms. They weren't sure if all the yelling and physicality was a prelude to a fight or merely an argument between friends.

Cleat regained the surface spitting and sputtering with arms flailing gasping for breath, before he was able to fully recover Coon yanked him by the ears and smiled. "Get one thing straight ol' buddy, where you go, I go. We came over here together and by God we're going home together."

"I love you brother." Cleat placed an arm over Coon's shoulder.

"Yeah, me too, but if you're looking for a big fat slobbering kiss then you're crazier than hell."

Cleat placed his hands on either side of Coon's cheeks and planted a kiss on the middle of his forehead.

"You fuckin' homo, I ought to…" Coon barely got those words out before he found himself submerged. When he was able to come up for air there was a big smile spread across his face. "Airborne all-the-way."

Susie and Kay scurried over to their partners. Whatever it was they were arguing about had passed.

Susie stroked Cleat's wet hair and giggled, "No more fight…you-me go makie beaucoup boom-boom." Susie dipped her hand under the water searching for Cleat's privates, when she found them she cooed, "We go room now…Susie love you longtime."

Coon drew Kay's inviting body to his and gave her a French-kiss, "You-me same-same. We go bedroom and boom-boom longtime…okay." Coon lifted the petite Kay into his arms and stepped from the hot tub and winked at Cleat. "It's the two of us brother, Rangers lead the way. We're motivated, dedicated, and lethal and right now I'm going upstairs to continue the mission."

Cleat grinned, "Airborne all the way." When all he could see of Coon was his backside a deep furrow formed on his brow. He knew extending his tour was going to put both of their lives at risk. He wasn't totally sure why he felt obligated to do so, but he did and that was enough for him. Fate would decide if he had made the right decision, that and a whole lot of luck. What the hell…time would tell all.

It was on the far-side of midnight before the sounds of Coon's lovemaking in the next room finally subsided. Cleat lay awake as beautiful, sweet Susie's breath blew softly on his neck. Cleat tried to sleep, but his mind was filled with self-doubt. Had he made the right decision to extend his tour? Would he be able to accept the consequences no matter what? He was angry at Coon for being so pigheaded and yet he was glad that his friend was staying with him. Was that selfish, probably so, but he knew if it was Coon who had made the decision to extend, he would have extended too…no matter what.

Cleat gently lifted Susie's arm from across his bare chest and rolled silently out of bed. In the cloak of darkness he maneuvered downstairs to the far corner of the sitting room where an antique secretary was located. Switching on a baroque floor lamp left of the desk he slumped in a cushioned swivel chair and sighed. Pausing briefly, he closed the dark wooden shutters covering the beveled pane windows and picked up a ball point pen. Placing a single sheet of beige stationary in front of him he let out another deep sigh before gathering his thoughts. His family needed to know, but where was he to begin *and* how was he going to explain his decision when even *he* didn't understand the reason why. After dozens of failed attempts he became frustrated. The wastebasket full of wadded paper with a like amount scattered on the floor was testimonial to his inner struggle.

It was the hardest letter he had ever tried to write. It was just before sunrise when Cleat laid the pen down and returned to his bedroom. He knew his family would not understand his rational and he saw no point in trying to explain the unexplainable. Something beyond his understanding was compelling him to stay. Coon was going to be a burden of responsibility and if anything happened to his friend he would never be able to justify the extension. Finally, exhausted and spent, blessed sleep came.

In the study downstairs the beginning of an Asian dawn cast soft golden shafts of sunlight through slatted shutters, highlighting a sealed envelope ready to be mailed.

Advanced Preview of

SONS OF
OUR FATHERS

Book Two of "THE FINAL FAREWELL"

CHAPTER 1

The tangle of vines blocking Cleat's progress was more of a nuisance than a formidable obstacle. As he squatted next to a large tree trunk clothed in vines his eyes carefully followed the interwoven cords twisting their way across his path, crisscrossing back and forth, continually spiraling upward until lost in the overgrowth of leaf-laden branches. Two massive trees were conjoined by nature's twine in a lifetime of struggle for their rightful space in the jungle infested mountain. It was ironic that the habitat they fought so desperately to survive in also threatened to strangle their very existence.

Slipping under the entanglement he crept closer to the jungle's edge, silently maneuvering through the thickening vegetation until he could go no further without risking exposure. He could hear a faint muttering of voices and the familiar sounds of men breaking camp. Cleat eased to the ground, knowing his position was danger close. Using extreme prejudice, he removed the fiddlehead fern clear of his vision, and crept closer to the NVA's encampment. He was overtly cautious not to make any sudden movement or noise that would give his location away.

Attention to detail took precedence; detection would probably result in his immediate death, and circumvent the survival of his team. You never knew what might alert the enemy of your presence, and most often it was through no fault of your own. A monkey or fowl could screech for no apparent reason, or a wild animal could snort while burrowing for food. Of course there was always Mother Nature herself to contend with, a rotted tree limb might fall and land in a morass of foliage, or a weakened branch could decide at the most inopportune moment to detach from its life-giver and splash into a body of water. You had no party in making these obtrusive sounds, nor did you have any control in circumventing the results, but to an inquisitive enemy any noise not pursuant to their surroundings would warrant an immediate investigation.

Disturbing the overhead fern initiated a tiered release of goblets of morning dew that quickly gained momentum cascading from leaf to leaf until it gathered at Cleat's booted feet. The incessant thirst of the jungles floor quickly drank its fill. To Cleat, the audible splashing of water sounded as loud as a toilet being flushed inside a tiled bathroom. When your mind prayed for silence any noise seemed to amplify a hundred times over.

Cleat was anxious to put faces and numbers on the muffled voices carrying across the small tributary. He'd hoped by moving the ferns it would've offered an unobstructed view, but was disappointed. The dawn's thick rolling fog blanketed the ground with a gray-white shroud, making visibility highly unlikely for several hours. It would take time for the sun to evaporate the low-lying veil and, time was what he didn't have. By the sound of the voices to his forefront he could tell they were very close. He cursed silently under his breath. He was hoping to at least formulate an idea how many Vietnamese were tracking them, as for now there was no way to approximate an intelligent guess, but one thing he knew for sure: his team was dealing with a determined group.

As it was, visibility was less than twenty per cent, and it wasn't going to get any better before the enemy left their campsite. Hearing the enemy gathering their gear made his decision even easier, the tracking force would soon be on the move. His team had to hat-up, and put as much distance between themselves and the enemy as humanly possible. It wouldn't be prudent to have the NVA hot on the trail when they reached their pick-up point.

As Cleat stood perfectly still, he watched a small-winged insect with transparent wings struggle valiantly through rivulets of sweat as it ferried its way down Cleat bare forearm. Its future was in doubt until it reached a dry spot on his wristband. The bug seemed to take a breather after going through such a harrowing ordeal. Obviously shaken from its near death experience, it stood on trembling hind legs, frantically fluttering its wings until they air dried. At last, satisfied it was once again capable of fight; it quickly flew deeper into the ominous jungle.

The smell of rotting decomposition was pungent and the dense foliage enveloping his hiding place was damp as was the vegetation surrounding him. It was impossible to stay dry in the field. You were either wet with your own sweat, or close to drowning during the monsoon season. Once the acceptance of being constantly wet was achieved it was one less thing to worry about in d'Nam.

Ignoring the droplet of sweat dangling from his nose he slowly eased the fern back to its original position. There was no sense in wasting time for they had to distance themselves from the trackers.

It was unbearably hot under the jungles double and triple canopy and he was troubled how near exhaustion he was. The suffocating humidity was like a pressure cooker. He knew the team was as tired and exasperated as he was. They had been running almost nonstop since yesterday's insertion and it was due to a serious lack of military intelligence…they didn't know how many were on their trail, or which way the enemy was headed. Hell, they didn't even know if it was the only group searching for them, and he hoped to never find out. If his team was lucky enough to evade the NVA hunter-killer team, he figured it would be late tomorrow morning before they could make it to the PZ. Once onboard the Huey they would be back at camp by mid-afternoon, that is, if their luck held out and that was a big *if*.

Cleat rejoined his team secluded in the jungle and grimaced when he saw their beleaguered faces. He looked into the eyes of Coon, his childhood friend, who was lying a few feet away. John Truman was Coon's given name and, they had been together since they were eight years old. Coon came from a broken home and was raised by an alcoholic father until he was ten years old. After Mister Truman became surly, mean and unable to care for his son the Davis's brought him into their home to raise as one of theirs. His nickname came about when Cleat's father laughingly teased John for getting so excited during hunting season. His father swore that John became more rambunctious than his old coon dogs, and there the legend of "Coon Dog" began; later on, his name was shortened to just plain ol' "Coon".

"What the fuck's up?" Coon whispered.

Cleat shrugged his shoulders, "They're on the move, but I couldn't see a goddamn thing buddy, the fog's too damn thick." Rivers of sweat had washed most of the greasepaint from his friends face masking it with blended hues of green, black, and brown. *Christ, he's one scary looking fucker.*

"Jesus Christ, it'll be another hour before the sun burns this shit off. Goddammit, my damn legs are starting to fuckin' cramp and, I'm fucking covered with leaches." Coon detested the slimy little bloodsuckers. They could penetrate through anything no matter how many precautionary actions you took.

Cleat smiled before puckering his lips, and mimicking a kiss, which Coon promptly answered by flipping him the finger and mouthing, *fuck you.*

A sudden rustling of clothing and equipment brought Cleat back to his immediate front. Squinting through the dense brush, he caught a glimpse of shadowy images resembling ghosts fading into the mist. Shit, they were moving southwest, and that wasn't good. His mind replayed the surreal scene, how utterly absurd it was, here they were thousands of miles from home in the middle of a jungle, cut off from the rest of the world while insidious men were hunting them down with the sole, malicious intent of eliminating them from the living. No longer was it the exciting neighborhood game of war they played as children, serious dedicated men were on their trail, committed to finding his patrol, and killing them without any show of remorse.

Yesterday mornings insertion had been almost thirty-nine hours ago and the grueling pace forced on them was taxing to put it mildly. When they jumped off the chopper after first light it became apparent within fifteen minutes they were in serious trouble when a trail-spotter fired a few harassing rounds in their direction before swiftly disappearing into the jungle. Cleat's team immediately began to escape and evade, knowing there was very little time if they were going to have any chance at all of escaping the enemy's grasp. An hour later they heard the trackers on the move, and to everyone's chagrin they were using dogs. Just before dusk the team collapsed off the side of the trail thoroughly exhausted. They were completely spent, and lay where they fell.

Whoever said "time flies" never had the pleasure of being hunted by an NVA Hunter-Killer team deep in the jungles of South Vietnam. It seemed like they had been running forever, stopping only briefly to look at the map and shoot an azimuth to their alternate PZ. Periodically Cleat had been sprinkling CS powder on the trail to keep the dogs off their scent. Amazingly, this seemed to be working, because it had been awhile since they had heard any sound from the canines.

After quenching his thirst, it wasn't long before the team was looking at Cleat for leadership. He was astutely aware of their stares…he could smell the fear-based sweat emitting from their overworked bodies. This was the part he hated the most, the balance of life and death being determined by his decisions. He'd lived most of his life either being the decision maker, or looked upon as a leader, but now the choices he made were considerably more important than the ones he'd made as an athlete. A wrong move in the jungles of Vietnam could result in much dire consequences than those on the field of athletics.

"What do you think, Sarge? It looks pretty bad, doesn't it?" Sally asked.

Cleat glanced over at the new team member lying against a fallen log caught in a tangle of vines. Specialist Enrique Salvador Garcia's handsome features were disturbing and it made Cleat wonder whether or not he would be able to hack-it in the bush. Traversing the jungle-invested mountains was a dangerous tough go, and it took a lot of endurance to maneuver under such adverse conditions. Another factor that bothered Cleat was the kid's frailness; there was hardly any meat on his bones.

Coon nicknamed the young Cuban American "Sally" the first day he joined the team. Coon felt it was his responsibility alone to endear each man in the company with nicknames, believing it would draw the men closer together. Strangely enough, the crazy idea seemed to work. Cleat noticed that Sally's grimy hands were shaking uncontrollably as he tried to screw the cap back on his canteen...the kid's glasses were so fogged-up it was impossible to see his eyes.

He was worried about the new kid, it was his first combat action, and they knew very little about him other than he wore the Ranger tab and was a certified RTO. Salvador had been a new replacement who was arbitrarily place on his team two days before the mission. He was replacing Richard "Hard Rock" Harden, who was gut-shot on their last mission and out of the war recuperating in Japan. Right now Salvador was an anomaly, but being the RTO he was an intricate part of the team, he was their lifeline.

"Yeah, it looks bad, but the team's been in worse shit before and I've always gotten us out, so don't get your ass in an uproar just yet." He could tell the kid was nervous, but he had no time to baby-sit. That was the very reason he'd argued with Top Braxton against taking him along. He strongly believed that each "cherry" should spend several days having their skills tested before being sent into the bush.

"Coon, check our six and get back here ASAP. Cowboy, go check our twelve o'clock and hold up 'til I send for you." Cleat smiled, watching the little Yard scampering off, no questions asked, and ready to please. He was lucky to have the chief's son as his team scout, and he was absolutely amazed how his smaller counterparts handled themselves. They never seemed to tire and they adapted to every situation, no matter how diverse. Cleat knew there were many reasons for him to feel extremely grateful to have such reliable men under his command, and it was a relief never having to question their loyalty or friendship. Some of the other Ranger Companies weren't as fortunate as Bravo Company.

Within a few minutes Coon was back at his side. "Nothing I could see, smell, or hear, Boss. If they're out there then they're being *damn* sneaky about it." Coon raised his forearm to wipe some of the sweat rolling down his bronzed face. The Asian sun had added several shades to his olive complexion. His appearance, along with the multi-colors of grease paint mingled with sweat and jungle crud, was really quite frightful.

"Cleat, you know it's going to get dark most rickety-tic under this fucking canopy, and it'll be a real bitch trying to find a place to hunker down, not only that, we're just plain bone-tired. There's not much left in the tank, brother."

"Well one thing for sure, if you're tired then the rest of us must be beat, because you can hang with the 'Yards' better than anyone I know." Cleat slowly stood up, arching his back and stretching his arms high overhead, trying to release the pent-up tension that'd been building since they were compromised. "I'll go up the trail and let Cowboy and Tuey know what's up."

Coon laughed. "You be careful and don't get your ass lit up, you know how trigger-happy they get when they haven't fired their weapons in a long time." He smiled as he watched his friend walk up the trail in search of Cowboy, and his first cousin, Tuey. *God*, he thought, *what did I ever do to deserve such a friend?*

"Dear Lord," Coon prayed aloud, "please see us through this mess and get us the hell back home in one piece."

Darkness fell as quickly as if someone had turned off a light switch. The sounds of the night were so different than that of the day. The smaller creatures that thrived in daylight had already found safe havens to settle in before dusk fell, hoping they would be fortunate enough to live for another passing of dawn. Monkeys and other inhabitants of the jungle quietly bedded down, sleeping lightly for fear of the predators that used the veil of darkness to hunt for food. The team looked for just such a place to protect them until the light of dawn rekindled the deadly game of survival and endurance.

Cleat retraced his footsteps, slowly lifting one foot in front of the other, toes down, sliding underneath the vegetation before putting the heel down just as he was taught in Jungle Warfare School. It was the same technique that deer and other animals of the wild used when they were moving through the wilderness. He spotted Coon, who was barely distinguishable in the blackness. His childhood friend was lying with his back against the base of a large tree, and his tired legs were stretched out in front of him spread-eagled. Coon's boonie hat was pulled forward over his eyes.

"Man, I sure hope you found something real close, because I'm absolutely fucking beat, and I personally don't give a shit what the little people say, because I know they've had it to," Coon muttered.

Cleat rubbed the top of Coon's head and chuckled. "Come on partner, you got a couple of more klicks in you. We're only talking a short walk up the trail my man, it's like a walk in the moonlight without the moon. You'll just love the little cubbyhole we found." Cleat squatted beside the one true friend he'd always been able to count on for as far back as he could remember.

"Don't yank my chain. I'm serious Cleat, tired ain't the right word for how I feel right now. I know there's a better word somewhere in the English language, but I'm just too damn worn-out to try and think of it."

"Okay buddy, I read you five-by-five. You go with Sally and Tuey, Cowboy is already at the laager waiting for y'all. Get everybody settled in and I'll cover our six."

"You got it, Boss. Airborne all the way."

Cleat smiled as he watched Coon fade into the darkness. *Well,* he prayed in kind, *it's going to be a long, hellish night, so please dear God in heaven, help us through it one more time…I can't do it all by myself, I'm as tired as the rest of them.*

Closely scrutinizing the area for anything left behind that would alert the enemy of their presence was more precautionary than anything else, because his team was too well trained to make such a rookie mistake. Never the less Salvador was new to the field and Cleat had learned the hard way to never take anything for granted when lives depended on every decision you made, you weren't often given a second chance. Careless people mostly ended up in body bags, it was difficult enough to stay alive when you did everything right.

Inspecting the surrounding area he made sure it met his satisfaction before leaving to join his team. He was pleased with the thicket of scrub and stand of bamboo Cowboy had found to hunker down for the night, it should make a good place for them to rest until dawn. There were a few drawbacks, such as proper fields of fire and an easy escape route, but for now the pros far outweighed the cons and, besides, he'd heard somebody say beggars shouldn't be choosers.

One thing he definitely liked about the hideout was it provided enough natural security to prevent the enemy from sneaking up on them without being heard well in advance. The enemy was good, but not that good and, besides, Cleat would put his 'Yards' up against anyone, past, present, or future. They were the best of the best, and not only did he know it, the bad guys knew it too. No matter who was following them he felt sure his team would be safe tonight. Contrary to most beliefs, the enemy did not own the night. They might have at one time, but the Rangers and their scouts had taken it back. He'd heard the enemy feared the Rangers more than anyone else and they called them "ghosts with green faces."

By the time Cleat reached the point where he thought the team should be it was so dark he was having difficulty *seeing* the trail, much less staying on it. "Shit," he uttered softly as he stumbled on a root.

"Well, fuck me, I just lost five bucks to Cowboy," Coon whispered from the darkness in a gravely voice.

Cleat's heart leapt to his throat. "Jesus Christ!" Cleat grumbled through clenched teeth. "Have you fucking lost your mind? You scared the living shit out of me. Dammit man, *don't* do that shit. Christ almighty this ain't the time or place for that kind'a horseshit,"

"I'm sorry Cleat, but dammit, I bet Cowboy it was an elephant making all the racket and he said it was you, and that, my friend, cost me five bucks American."

Cleat peered into the darkness trying to make out his friend's features, but there was no way he could distinguish anything around him. Hell, he could barely see his hand in front of his face. "You little fucking turd, I suppose you think that's funny?"

"Nope, what's funny is you standing in the middle of the trail not knowing where the fuck to go, or what to do. Just move your ass a couple of meters to the right and I'll reach out and grab you by the hand and lead you into our quaint little domicile."

The two friends stepped into the thicket together and were completely engulfed in pitch-black, where absolutely nothing was visible. It was as if they'd been blinded by the night.

Cleat felt something tug on his pant leg. "Sergeant, you sit by Cowboy. Me make number one place for you...you stay by me, okay...Cowboy do good my Sergeant. You sleep first, safe by me...no bad ting happen now...spirits are with us. They old and wise...spirits watch over us 'til sun come up...then they no more...go back to spirit world...you lie down sleep. It be a-okay."

"Okay, my friend, I'll do as you say. Cowboy you are always looking out for us, and it is an honor to call you my friend. You will always be respected by us as a great warrior and leader of his people." Sitting down beside Cowboy he put his arm around the little warrior's shoulder, and gave him a hug outwardly expressing the great affection he held for the boy.

The night went without incident. The dawn slowly beat through the jungle's canopy as morning rays shimmered through the trees spotlighting the moist compost of the jungle's floor. As the rising sun cast a dim light on their surroundings, one could see small creatures beginning to stir, getting ready to start another day toiling for food with the constant threat of survival threatening every move they made. The odds would be against them, but they wouldn't understand that concept, they'd just go about their business as pragmatists, paying no mind to what the new dawn might bring.

Cleat pondered the moment as he watched a beetle with long legs come out from underneath a pile of leaves he'd used as a haven during the night. It paused momentarily before preceding a few inches until it encountered a large red ant impeding his progress. They both stood still, contemplating their next move, with instincts created from millions of years of surviving the passage of time, they knew their next move could prove to be critical. They were like two miniature gladiators in an old Roman coliseum when one false step could be their undoing. After what seemed an eternity to Cleat the beetle finally made a life and death decision, even though it was much larger than the solitary ant, it really wasn't looking for an altercation. Backing up slowly, it made an ill-fated miscalculation in its adversary's intentions when it turned its back exposing itself to a surprise attack from the rear. When the beetle was most vulnerable the ant darted in, clamping its pinchers onto one of the beetle's hind legs. The beetle tried turning to defend itself, but with the ant holding on it was difficult for him to maneuver, unfortunately for the beetle it stumbled in its effort to break free and flipped on its side.

Suddenly, from out of nowhere, dozens of ants scurried to assist their comrade. In just a short while it was all over. Cleat marveled over what he'd witnessed on the jungle floor...was this a well-planed ambush, or a circumstance in the survival of the fittest? If it was an ambush he was wholly impressed with the precise way it was carried out. The timing was impeccable, and the chance of the solitary ant exposing his comrades to danger was minimal. Precisely what a good leader was expected to do. To plan, execute, and complete the mission with the least amount of exposure to casualties. Cleat thought if ever a medal was more deserving, he didn't know of one.

Feeling movement to his right, Cleat turned to see Tuey sitting up and rubbing the sleep from his eyes. Grumbling, the smallish young man stood stretching his arms overhead and muttered something to Cowboy, who offered his own guttural reply in return. Tuey nodded, grabbed his equipment, and slipped his harness on. He moved cautiously to the edge of the bush where, just beyond, was the trail they had previously left the night before. Cleat watched the little warrior's shoulders heave as he took in a deep breath before stepping out onto the path. As he turned to face the team, automatic fire ripped through the air. Cleat watched in shock as Tuey was hit numerous times in the chest and head; the back of his head disappeared in bloody chunks of matted hair and skull as he crumpled lifeless to the jungle trail, at fifteen-years-old he'd drawn his last breath. All that was visible from where Tuey once stood was a pink, gritty mist blending with an early morning fog.

The team quickly reacted without any verbal orders as the enemies' bullets flew savagely through the air clipping limbs, twigs, leaves, and anything else that got in the way. The enemy was firing indiscriminately, not knowing the team's exact location. Cleat's men reacted by scrambling down the incline frantically scurrying on their hands and knees grabbing equipment along the way. Their utmost concern was surviving the withering fuselage of firepower.

The volume was steadily increasing as more of the enemy brought their weapons to bear. The team knew they had to move as quickly as possible, if they were to survive the onslaught. Leaving Tuey behind was unsettling, but in reality there wasn't any choice if the living were to survive. The immediate goal was to put as much distance from their NDP (night defensive position) and the enemy in as short an amount of time as possible. The enemy didn't know exactly where they were or where they were headed, but they damn well knew they were close. Cleat had to move the team and do it with as much noise discipline as possible under the circumstances.

"Cowboy, take point and head southeast paralleling the trail. Coon, you got drag." Cleat turned and looked into Sally's eyes. "Look, I know you're a little green, but we're going to get out of this 'clusterfuck'. You just stick with me and keep your wits about you. I want you to keep your eyes peeled to our left flank, and fire only at a visual target. The only way we're going to make it out of here is by not getting compromised again. We're going to move-out, so remember you got our left…I got our right, Coon's got drag, and Cowboy's on point."

Cleat looked into Sally's eyes and didn't like what he saw. "God dammit," Cleat whispered. "Are you fucking hearing me?" Cleat reached over, grabbing Sally by his shirtfront and pulled him close enough to smell his stale morning breath. "Come on, Sally, get with the program; we ain't got time for this shit."

"Okay Sarge, I got it. I'm all right. I uh-uh, I was just thinking ab…ab…about Tuey, it went so fa…fast. He was there and th…th…then he was gone." With trembling hands, Salvador straightened the black-framed glasses that were askew on the bridge of his nose.

"Sally, pull it together man, I can't say it gets any better, or that you'll get used to it, because you don't…not ever. You just have to do your job the best you can, because everyone depends on each other doing just that. Hang tough, the rest of the shit don't mean nothin'. Can I count on you?"

"Yeah Sarge, I'm okay," Sally replied with false bravado.

The sounds of automatic fire erupted to their northeast. Cleat knew it was merely a probe trying to draw return fire so they could locate the team's position. That was encouraging, because it meant they hadn't found their trail yet, but he knew they would find it soon enough, so time was extremely critical.

"Coon, you and Cowboy put some Claymores out, and we'll see if we can't slow these little fuckers down when they discover our trail. Sally and I will pull security. All right, let's do it!"

He watched his two teammates trot down the trail they'd broken through earlier, once the deadly Claymores were in place they would do a great deal of damage if the enemy triggered them. A deadly swath of steel balls would cut through their ranks creating human carnage beyond belief. He vividly remembered the scene from his first ambush almost a year ago, the bloody gore, and especially the stench of feces made him throw up. Some of the bodies were so mangled it was hard to tell if they were human. There were pieces of meat strewn helter-skelter, hanging from trees and bushes, and the awful smell of cordite mingled with the metallic fragrance of blood lingering in the air was overpowering. The ones that weren't killed were instantly traumatized from missing limbs, or they lay groaning in agony trying desperately to stave off death from mortal wounds. Some of the wounded tried holding their intestines in with quivering hands, while others just lay on the ground whimpering, knowing full well they were going to die.

During the ambush one of Cleat and Coon's teammates caught a stray round high in the middle of his chest. Gunter Shultz died quietly in Coon's arms, asking them to tell his wife, Greta, and the kids that he loved them. He was a thirty-three-year-old Korean War veteran with fifteen years of service. Cleat still had dreams of seeing "Big Dutch" die quietly in Coon's lap. It was strange that the sheer horror of his first ambush was by far the most prevalent in his frequent nightmares. He wasn't sure why, because he'd certainly seen worse since. He'd lost friends and team members in the past, but his dreams relived the death of "Dutch" and the enemy dead from his very first bloodletting with the Special Forces.

A droplet of sweat trickling into the corner of his right eye brought him back to the present. Wiping the stinging sweat with the heel of his palm, he cursed himself for lapsing like some dumb-ass cherry.

Damn, he thought, *I can't let my mind drift like that...too many lives are depending on me to stay alert. That was a fucking "cherry" thing to do.* He promised not to let it happen again, there was too much at stake to be drifting in and out of the present. He was a team leader for Christ's sake, he damn well knew better. He felt Coon and Cowboy crawl up beside him.

"Hey old buddy, Cowboy and I got the job done. Those fuckers are going to run into a world of hurt if they try and follow us boonie rats."

"Yes my Sergeant, Coon right. We fix many ways they meet ancestors. It make plenty bad time for NVA...numba fuckin ten." Cowboy grinned.

"Yeah Cleat, we put one at ground level facing down trail, the second one we wrapped securely in a tree about four feet off the ground facing front, and then we put the last one behind the fuckers so when they blow, if everything works like it should, they'll be getting it from the front, top, and the ass-end. Shit, that ain't even counting the grenades I straightened the pins on, when those babies work loose, 'BOOM'. Whoever's left from the initial blast will have their day *really* fucked up." Coon beamed with excitement.

"Many boom-booms, they fuck up bad." Cowboy added with his hands gesturing wildly.

Cleat looked at the two grinning buffoons. He couldn't believe it; if he didn't know better, they looked like they were having fun. "Okay you fucking grunts…the good times are over. We're going to have to hump out of here and believe me when I say it's not going to be a walk in the park. Cowboy, you take point. Coon, you got drag, I'll take slack…Sally, stay close to me with the radio. I want a commo check before we take off. While I'm doing that, I want some security out and I mean right now."

"Damn, Cleat, take it easy man, we know what we're doing. We ain't fucking cherries."

"I know that Coon, just fucking do it without any lip, okay?"

"Sure, Cleat. You got it brother. Hey Cowboy, let's do like the man says, we've got our orders." He turned to Cleat and gave him a wink, punctuating it with a thumbs-up.

"Give me the handset, Sally." Stepping closer, Sally quickly did as he was told. Cleat noticed Sally's hands were still shaking, and his darting eyes all but validated what the RTO was going through. Cleat put his hand on Sally's shoulder. "It's going to be all right, kid. We're getting out of this mess, and by tomorrow we'll be laughing about this boondoggle over a few beers. Hell man, I'll even buy the first round. Just hang in there buddy, before you know it we'll be on a chopper, and this shit will be nothing but ancient history. It'll make a war story to tell the rest of the guys when we get back." He gave the RTO a reassuring squeeze on the shoulder before releasing him. Cleat brought the black handset to his mouth.

"Bambi…This is Tracker One. Over.

"This is Bambi, Tracker One…give me a sit rep…over."

"The shit's hit the fan…we got one local KIA, and the banditos are hot on our ass…we need the closest Papa Zulu ASAP…over."

"Roger that…look on your map and tell me if PZ Lollipop looks good?"

Cleat pulled out his map thankful it was an American map instead of one of those fucked up French ones. The fucking French were the only people he knew of that used Paris as the point of origin instead of London…if two people weren't using the same kind of map things could get fucked up in a hurry.

"Bambi… this is Tracker One…Lollipop's a no go…too far and the terrain is not conducive to our location…we need to head for PZ Whiskey…Our ETA should be 1400 to 1430…have the slicks and guns ready in case we need help…Over"

"Copy that loud and clear. PZ Whiskey…1400 to 1430. The Lone Ranger and Tonto will be waiting with guns galore. Good luck…over and out."

"Copy that five by five. See you then…over." Cleat handed the handset back to Salvador.

Cleat snapped his fingers to bring the team in. When they were all present he knelt down and removed his boonie hat. Using his forearm to wipe the sweat from his brow he gave his men a stern look. "This is what we're facing: PZ Whiskey is where we're headed, and we have to rendezvous with the chopper no later than 1430 hours. Whiskey's right here on the map," Cleat pointed at the location with a twig. "It's not too far and the lay of the land isn't too bad. When we move out I want you alert, using as much noise discipline as possible, but our primary concern is speed. If we make contact, we break it off and bug the hell out of there. If we're compromised noise won't make a damn bit of difference so forget about it until we're clear of pursuit. That's it, Rangers. It's about three hours to Whiskey, which gives us an hour's cushion, so time-wise I think we're okay."

With the most encouraging smile he could muster, Cleat looked into each face, "If anybody has anything to add now's the time to ask." After no response, Cleat stood, "All right, let's do it. We got cold beer waiting for us, and the first ones are on me."

Forty-five minutes later a thunderous chorus of "KABOOMS" resounded through the jungle and was followed closely by several muffled explosions, notifying them the ambush had been successful.

Coon came running up the trail. "By God, it sounds like we got some Cleat. Whoopee, I bet that put a real hurt on 'em. I bet those little fuckers will move a lot slower now. Shit, they'll be tiptoeing if there's anybody left to move at all. That'll teach 'em to fuck with the ol' Coon Dog and Cowboy."

Cleat grinned at his friend. "You done good Coon, but we're not out of the wringer yet. We're moving pretty good, and you're right, that should slow 'em down, but there might be more patrols looking for us than the one that's been on our ass, so let's stay alert and keep moving, we don't want any surprises coming our way."

Fortunately, the team's torturous trek to PZ Whiskey went without further incident. However as they approached the PZ, they still used caution. They knew one of the most dangerous times of any mission was when it was almost over. Sergeant Ice from jump school always said, "It ain't over till the fat lady sings." Those were words to live by, especially if you wanted to live a long, healthy life. The Nam was not a place to relax and let your guard down, you never knew when ol' "Murphy" would raise his ugly head and fuck up your world. Cleat rolled to his side, and motioned for the handset.

"Sally, get me Bambi."

"You got it, Sarge." Salvador crawled beside Cleat.

Cleat noticed that the specialist looked a hell of lot better than he did several hours ago. He knew the kid had a rough go, especially the way the mission started.

"Coon, you and Cowboy check out our rear…I'm going to bring the chopper in."

"Roger that, Sarge. Come on Cowboy, let's go check it out." Coon gestured for Cowboy to follow him, pausing he turned toward Cleat and offered, "Hey, you ain't gonna leave us the fuck out here, are 'ya? I mean, you did say you were buying the beer, and I know how fucking cheap you are."

Cleat threw a stick at Coon. "Would you get the fuck out of here and do what I tell you to do? Besides, if I was you I wouldn't be giving me any bright ideas."

Coon smiled, giving him a thumbs-up before slipping into the underbrush.

"Bambi, this is Tracker One…we're at third base waiting for the steal sign. We'll pop smoke as soon as you're on station…over."

"I read you five-by-five, Tracker One…we're on your November Echo…home plate's in sight…pop smoke now…our slick will be over you in one mike…guns are riding herd…over."

"Bambi, this is Tracker One…smoke's out…I say again, smoke is out…over."

"I see beautiful lavender blue, Tracker One."

"That's a roger on our smoke…over."

"We'll be there before you can say dilly-dilly…over."

"That's a copy and, by the way dilly-dilly, it's damn good to see ya." Cleat could hear the Huey's beautiful whop-whop-whopping of the rotors that every

GI loved, it always meant some form of relief, either extraction, fire support, or re-supply. Cleat couldn't think of a sweeter sound than what he was hearing right now. He turned to his rear to recall his security team, but before he was able to give the signal they were already halfway there. At first it worried him, thinking they were being pursued, but when he saw the smiles on their faces he instantly realized they'd heard the choppers too. "All right, let's move out. Let's do it the right way, y'all know the drill."

Ten minutes later the newest of the Bell model 205A1 UH-1H helicopters fitted with a more powerful Lycoming 1400 shp turbo shafted engine was cruising along at 110 knots 3500 feet above the treetops. The team of Rangers rested against the bulkhead absently staring out the open cargo doors watching the landscape whiz by at a rapid clip. A wonderful euphoric feeling of relief filled them with exuberance as they enjoyed the fresh, chilly wind whipping through the cabin. It flapped at their loose fitting clothing and cooled their worn-out, over heated bodies. All of their machismo and bravado was back as they languished in the relative comfort. Considering where they'd been only moments ago, life was pretty damn good. Once again they'd danced with the Grim Reaper, and escaped his greedy clutches.

Although the men were filled with relief that their ordeal was over, Cleat knew his men were struggling with the same emotions troubling him. They were safely onboard the Huey heading back to base, but one of their teammates was left behind on the jungle floor. Dealing with Tuey's death was going to be extremely difficult, especially for him and Coon, not only were they forced to leave his body behind, but Tuey had been part of the team ever since the two of them first arrived. They would miss Tuey. He was a friend and a valuable member of the team; it would also be a staunch reminder of how precarious life could be. Even though they had done everything right it didn't make a damn bit of difference to Tuey, for he was with his ancestors now. It would gnaw at Cleat that he had somehow, someway, let the boy down.

The rest of the team was just plain lucky. Soon the reality would set in that it could've just as easily been any one of them lying out there in the jungle, Tuey just happened to be the first one awake enough to check the trail.

They all knew death could happen at any time, but they also held on to that ray of hope that it would be the other guy and not them, at least most of 'em did, but not Cleat. He'd accepted the fact that he was more than likely not going to survive his tour extension, once he was able to come to terms with death, it numbed his fear of dying, he just hoped when his time came it would be swift.

Death could tap you on the shoulder at any moment, laying claim to whosoever it desired. He had seen enough death to last a lifetime. Friends were the worst to lose. It was harder to take when you lost someone close, that's why Cleat was hesitant in making new ones. Most of the old vets like he and Coon were long gone, and the ones who remained were pretty much short timers. His main concern was his team, and that was more than enough for him.

Today he lost one—and another piece of himself. He would shoulder the responsibility and carry on, but the guilt over Tuey's death would remain for a lifetime. The little warrior's smiling face would always be implanted in his memory. It was still hard to accept he was gone, and to make things worse they weren't able to bring the body out. Cleat made a mental note to apologize to Cowboy, because he knew how important it was for the family to have a proper burial for their loved ones. Maybe they could try and retrieve the body at a later date. He would run it by the major, that's the least he could do.

Twenty-four minutes later the Huey's tail flared upward before putting them safely on the landing pad. The men hopped out of the bird and were immediately surrounded by a jubilant crowd of well-wishers before the chopper even had a chance to shut down. The back slapping and ribbing went on for several minutes until First Sergeant Braxton's baritone voice broke through the crowd.

"All right you hard-chargers, let's break up this tea-party, or I'll find something for you slackers to do that would be more beneficial to Bravo Company. This is a Ranger company, not a piss-ant Boy Scout troop. Now let's *move it* out in a military fashion...on the double." The Sergeant's presence motivated the troopers to disperse with extreme haste.

"Hey Top, it's good to see you, too." Cleat smiled at the small, black First Sergeant.

"You sure gave us a scare, son. I'm sorry about y'all losing Tuey; he was a dang good trooper." Top Sergeant Braxton put his arm around Cleat's broad shoulders, pausing a moment before turning to the rest of the team. "You men did a heck of a job, now y'all go on and get cleaned up. Compliments of your ol' sweetheart of a Top Sergeant, I made sure "Cookie" spread out some sandwiches and cold beer over at the dinning hall." Sergeant Braxton's chest swelled when he took in their appreciative looks. Grabbing Cleat by the arm he escorted him to the headquarters hootch. "Son, was it as bad as I think it was out there?"

"Yeah, it was pretty hairy and about as bad as it gets. Anytime you lose somebody it's bad…real bad."

Braxton knew what the kid was thinking, and what he was feeling. It wasn't too long ago he'd been in the same position many times over. It was something you never got used to, but the good ones learned to adjust by remembering only the good times. Even so, losing a friend or a team member remained in your subconscious and slowly ate at your innards. The feelings of self-doubt would stay with you forever. While operating in a combat zone you needed to face the reality of death walking in your footsteps. He just hoped Cleat would be able to endure all the horror he'd seen, and the horror that was sure to come. It was their job description, and in all wars it was always up to young men to see it through.

When he served in Korea, thousands of Americans died for political reasons only the politicians understood. This was the same type of war, only the landscape was different, but the politics were mirrored copies of one another. As the war grew in its intensity more and more politicians became involved, and their involvement usually meant more restraints on the military. He knew what the problem was, and every solider worth his salt did. It was the politicos back in Washington holding the real power and, "Collateral damage" was the buzzword. Unfortunately, in military terms that meant more American boys were going to die for no good reason whatsoever.

In WW II, nobody worried about collateral damage, if civilians got in the way it was just too darn bad, we just wanted to kill the enemy and end the war as quickly as possible. We leveled cities and towns in Germany killing hundreds and thousands of civilians. When we dropped the atomic bomb on Nagasaki and Hiroshima we didn't worry how many civilians we killed. We wanted to save American lives no matter what and, besides, whom did the politicians think drove the military machine? Civilians were the ones who feed the troops and manufacture the war material.

Korea was where he first heard the phrase "collateral damage" and if he could find the politician, or whichever fool came up with it, he would make sure they died a slow, painful death. And here we are fifteen years later repeating mistakes we made back then. The Washington bureaucrats were allowing the enemy sanctuaries, and "collateral damage" was overseeing their judgment to a point where it was costing servicemen their lives. How gall-darn stupid can you get? Allowing the enemy to cross the boarders of Cambodia and Laos and cause great bodily harm, destruction, mayhem, and chaos, and then run back across the border to a safe-haven without fear of reprisals. The concept made absolutely no frigging sense.

Streater Fenton
August, 1961